WHAT
SHE
SAID

Harper Grant Mystery Series:

A Witchy Business

A Witchy Mystery

A Witchy Christmas

A Witchy Valentine

Harper Grant and the Poisoned Pumpkin Pie

WHAT SHE SAID

DETECTIVE KAREN HART SERIES

D.S. BUTLER

THOMAS & MERCER

Published by Thomas & Mercer, Seattle

www.apub.com

Amazon, the Amazon logo, and Thomas & Mercer are trademarks of Amazon.com, Inc., or its affiliates.

ISBN-13: 9781542036252
ISBN-10: 1542036259

Cover design by @blacksheep-uk.com

Printed in the United States of America

For my mum and dad,
the best parents a person could hope for.

PROLOGUE

Molly McCarthy sat her doll next to Teddy on the floor. It was almost her birthday. One more sleep and she would be five.

'I'll have a birthday party,' she told the toys. 'And there'll be cupcakes and presents.'

Teddy gazed at her with shiny brown eyes. He looked sad.

'You'll still be my favourite,' she told him, patting his furry head.

Molly didn't want any more stuffed toys or dolls. She wanted a big girl's present – a bike. A brand-new, shiny, extra-fast bike.

She'd asked Father Christmas for one – even written him a letter and sent it to the North Pole – but her mum said Father Christmas thought she was too little for a grown-up bike and she would have to make do with her tricycle.

But now she was going to be five, and that was old enough for a big girl's bike.

'I'm bigger now, aren't I, Teddy?' She leaned over and pushed the stuffed toy's head to make it appear as though the bear was nodding.

She was supposed to be getting dressed, but she was still wearing her daisy-patterned nightdress.

Her mother was moving about downstairs in the kitchen. Soon she would call Molly for breakfast. Then she would tell Molly off for not being dressed, as she did every morning.

Her mother had tried to lay Molly's clothes out the night before, to save time in the morning. But Molly didn't like that. She liked to choose her own outfits, even if they were mismatched. And sometimes she liked to wear a pink princess skirt with netting, together with a pair of purple and yellow striped tights. Her mother would sigh, but her father would laugh and say Molly had her own style.

'What colour do you think my bike will be, Ted?' Molly asked, sitting down beside the bear on her soft grey bedroom carpet. 'I hope it's purple.'

Purple was Molly's favourite colour. It used to be pink. But purple was more grown-up.

'Molly!' Her mother's voice carried up the stairs. 'Are you dressed?'

Molly didn't reply, because she wasn't dressed, so she couldn't say yes – because that would be a lie, and lies were bad. She wasn't supposed to tell lies. She'd got into trouble last week for lying, although Molly didn't think she'd done anything wrong. She'd just been telling a story.

Molly had been having a picnic with Teddy in the garden, when Mrs Green, their elderly next-door neighbour, had come over to the fence to say hello. Molly told the woman she'd seen Tiddles, Mrs Green's marmalade cat, and Mrs Green said Tiddles was probably out having an adventure. Molly had agreed, and said she'd seen the cat grow fairy wings and fly off over the rooftops.

She'd looked so happy at the thought of her cat soaring through the sky on an adventure that Molly had continued her story, adding more details. By the time she'd finished, Mrs Green had been

2

laughing so hard she had tears rolling down her cheeks. Grown-ups were strange.

Molly stood up and opened the top drawer of her dresser, pulling out some underwear and a pair of white and yellow ankle socks. She put on her underwear then split the socks apart and sat down on the floor and wiggled her toes. She didn't like socks. She tugged the first one on and looked at her feet, wiggled her toes again, then lifted her nightshirt over her head and tugged open a second drawer. She was going to the big school today – visiting, getting ready for when it would be her time to go to the big school all day, not nursery with all the babies like she did at the moment.

She selected a green T-shirt and a pink pair of dungarees. The T-shirt went on all right, but the dungarees were more difficult, and she gave up, leaving them in a heap on the floor.

'Molly, where are you?' her mother called. 'Your breakfast is ready. It'll get soggy, and you'll still have to eat it!'

Molly knew that wasn't true. Her mother never added the milk until Molly got down to the kitchen, because she knew Molly wouldn't eat the cereal if it was soggy. Her dad said they were both as stubborn as each other.

Molly picked up a bobble from the floor. She couldn't do her own hair yet. That was too tricky, so she'd have to let her mother help her.

She left the dungarees on the floor and went downstairs in her T-shirt, knickers and one sock, humming 'Humpty Dumpty'.

Rather than go straight to the kitchen, Molly walked into the lounge and wandered over to the window. Sometimes she saw Geri go past on her bike in the mornings.

Geri worked in the corner shop at the weekends and sometimes gave Molly free sweets. Geri went to university and was very clever. Her mother said that's where Molly would go when she was older, to make them all proud, because no one else in the family had gone

3

to university yet. Molly wasn't quite sure what university was, but it sounded important, and if Geri went there, then Molly thought it had to be an exciting place.

She climbed on to the leather sofa, rested her arms on top of the cushions and looked out of the window. It was a grey day and big splotches of rain hit the glass. Molly liked the rain. She liked wearing her wellington boots and jumping in the puddles, but her mother didn't like the rain. She'd look out of the front door and tut, and then she'd spend five minutes looking for her umbrella, then blame Molly because they weren't ready on time.

There was a white van parked on the other side of the road. It looked like her dad's, but it didn't have writing on the side. And besides, her dad always left very early for work, before Molly got up. The van wasn't very interesting, so Molly craned her neck, looking down the road to see if Geri would appear. Geri's bike was blue and very fast.

There was no sign of her. Molly sat on the arm of the sofa, looking down at her feet. One had a sock, the other was bare. She wondered where the other sock had gone.

'Molly,' her mother said, appearing in the doorway, 'why aren't you dressed?'

'I am,' Molly said. 'Nearly dressed.' She started to explain about the dungarees, but her mother waved her words away.

'If you want to choose your own clothes, Molly, you can't keep coming downstairs half-dressed. You need to get dressed properly.'

Molly said, 'Dungarees—' but her mother had already left the room and was stomping up the stairs.

Molly was expected to follow, find her other sock and let her mother help her with the dungarees. But just then she saw a movement. Someone was coming down the road towards the house. She moved forward, leaning on the windowsill, but it wasn't Geri.

4

Another woman, older than Geri, was walking quickly along the pavement holding an umbrella. Molly sighed when she heard her mother call her from upstairs. She was about to turn away and do what she was told when suddenly the white van's back doors flew open. A man appeared and grabbed the woman with the umbrella. He shoved her into the back of the van before slamming the doors.

Molly stared. She hadn't seen anything like that happen before, and it made her feel bad. Her stomach hurt.

The van's engine roared to life like an angry animal.

The white van pulled away, driving off quickly.

'Molly!' her mother shouted.

Molly slid off the sofa and hurried upstairs.

CHAPTER ONE

The previous evening

'What did you think?' DC Sophie Jones asked, raising her voice above the sound of applause.

The main lights in the lecture theatre were switched back on, causing DS Karen Hart to blink at the sudden brightness. 'I enjoyed it.'

And she really had. She'd been expecting the evening to drag and had only agreed to attend because it was important to Sophie.

Sophie was fascinated by Dr Michaels, a self-proclaimed serial killer expert based in Virginia, USA. Karen had anticipated descriptions of sensationalised cases, exaggerating the doctor's starring role, but she'd been impressed by the careful presentation of evidence and the respectful way he spoke about the victims.

Dr Michaels handled his audience well. Charisma and a self-deprecating manner combined to make him a talented public speaker. Well-groomed, his light brown hair was threaded with blonde strands. Naturally sun-kissed, or created in a salon? The verdict was still out on that. His tan drew attention to his startlingly white teeth, noticeable every time he smiled – which was often.

Definitely a well-polished appearance, but Karen had still warmed to his presenting style, and after the first few minutes had forgotten his highlights and gleaming teeth, instead focusing on his slides.

As the applause died away, Sophie scrambled to her feet, grabbing her coat and bag. 'Quick!'

Karen raised an eyebrow. She was keen to get home. They were in King's Lynn, more than an hour's drive back to Lincoln. But she'd known Sophie would want to hang around for a while longer and soak up the atmosphere. Earlier, Sophie had confessed she hoped to get an opportunity to speak to the great man himself, so her apparent eagerness to get home was an unexpected surprise.

'It's all right,' Karen said. 'We've got another hour on the parking.'

'Yes, but we've got to be one of the first in line.'

'In line?' Karen asked. She didn't like the sound of that.

'Yes, I need to get my book signed.' Sophie reached inside her extra-large handbag and pulled out a hefty hardback copy of Dr Michaels's latest book.

Karen struggled to hide her disappointment. 'Oh, there's a signing afterwards, is there?'

There was a rush for the door. Sophie's face fell. 'Oh no, we're going to be at the back of the queue.'

Resigned to spending a little longer in King's Lynn, Karen scooped up her own coat and bag and followed Sophie as she made a beeline for the signing room. They left the small lecture theatre and walked out into the main atrium. Tables stacked with books surrounded them. Maybe staying a bit longer wouldn't be too bad after all, Karen thought, especially if that time could be spent looking through piles of books.

'I'll take a look around here,' Karen said. 'Come and find me when you're done.'

'Don't you want to get a book signed?'

'No, I'm fine.'

Sophie joined the end of the signing line, which already snaked out of the seminar room and partly around the atrium. Karen couldn't see Dr Michaels, but hoped he was already busy signing. She glanced at her watch. It looked like they'd be getting home later than expected. She pulled out her mobile phone and sent a quick text to Mike. She pictured him, wine glass in hand, Netflix on the TV, sitting on the sofa with Sandy curled contentedly at his feet.

Karen sighed and moved towards the first table of books.

Glasses filled with red and white wine sat on a long table to Karen's left, along with two large platters of cheese and smaller plates of crackers. Those who didn't join the end of the signing queue quickly surrounded the refreshments table, eager to partake in the free alcohol. Karen might have been tempted to join them if she didn't have to drive home.

The first table Karen came to was piled high with a variety of hardbacks with illustrated covers. They had titles like *Detectives vs Monsters* and *The Slasher Conspiracy*. All true crime, and on closer inspection, Karen realised they were all written by Dr Michaels.

'He's got a bit of a monopoly here,' Karen commented to a woman who'd stopped by the table and plucked a book off the top of a pile. The woman gave her a tight smile but didn't reply, and then hurried off to join the end of the signing line.

Karen selected a blue hardback, turned it over and inspected the blurb. 'Decade-old crime solved by a cat!' Karen read aloud and shook her head in disbelief. Was this true crime? It sounded more like fiction.

'That's an old one,' a low voice said.

Karen turned and saw a tall, well-built man with thick, wavy dark brown hair that fell over his eyes. He wore a zipped-up blue anorak and held an expensive-looking camera in one hand. He pushed his fringe from his eyes, and peered at Karen.

'Sorry?' Karen said.

'It's one of Dr Michaels's first books. Not one of his best, in my opinion.'

'Oh, I see,' Karen said, replacing the book on the stack. 'Thanks for the heads-up.'

'You're welcome,' he said. 'You should get his latest one. The cases are more interesting.' He raised the camera. 'Can you hold the book up?'

'Why?'

'I want to take your picture. I'm the book tour's official photographer. Nicholas Finney.' He smiled proudly.

'I didn't realise book tours had official photographers.'

'Sometimes they do.' He shrugged. 'This tour is quite a big deal. I'm hoping to get the local press interested. I'm writing the story too.'

'So you're freelance?'

'Yes. But two local papers are already keen. So how about it?' He held up the camera. 'A quick snap?'

Karen was conflicted. Working freelance could be a tough way to make a living, but she didn't want her picture published goodness knows where, holding up a book she hadn't even read.

'Sorry, Nicholas. I don't like having my photograph taken.'

'C'mon. Just one. Promise it won't hurt.'

'No thanks. Try someone else.'

His face fell, and he nodded and moved away.

Karen made her way to the next table. Again, all the books were by Dr Michaels. He was certainly industrious. How did he manage to fit police work around his writing? She picked up a book that had a selection of playing cards on the front. The cover looked more suited to an Agatha Christie novel, with a large magnifying glass artfully poking through the title.

Karen glanced over her shoulder towards the signing line. The photographer – Finney – now had plenty of willing subjects, who were proudly holding up their books as they waited to meet Dr Michaels. Sophie was no longer near the end of the queue. Though that wasn't because Dr Michaels was signing quickly, but just that even more people had joined the line. She sighed again and checked the time. She could always add some extra money to the parking app. She stifled a yawn and reached for another book, this time a bright-yellow paperback.

'I hope you didn't find this evening boring?'

Karen turned to see a tall young man – American, judging from his accent. He was dark-haired, brown-eyed and very slender, his form accentuated by his tight-fitting patterned shirt and pale skinny jeans. He stood with one hand on his hip, in a model-like pose. In his other hand he held a glass of white wine.

Karen had struggled to understand the current obsession with skinny jeans. She'd come to the conclusion that they flattered very few people. She'd resisted them for some time, before finally purchasing a pair at her sister's urging. She had to admit they were incredibly comfortable. It was all in the stretch – very forgiving material. But after a few hours' wear, they were getting baggy at the knees, and despite wearing a belt she felt as though she needed to hitch them up every few minutes. No – skinny jeans were not for her, but this man made them look high-fashion. He seemed more suited to a catwalk than a literary evening.

'No,' Karen said. 'It's just been a long day.'

'Law enforcement, aren't you?' he asked with a knowing smile.

Karen raised an eyebrow. 'Is it that obvious?'

He grinned. 'Yeah, pretty obvious. So, what did you think of the talk – honestly, I mean?'

'I thought it was very interesting. The methods Dr Michaels described were clever and insightful, but I'm very glad we don't have to deal with that type of thing very often here in the UK.'

'But you've had your fair share of serial killers over here,' he said.

Karen acknowledged that with a nod. She'd faced a number of dangerous criminals during her time on the force – some closer to home than she'd expected.

The man stuck out his hand. 'Zane Dwight,' he said. 'I'm Dr Michaels's assistant. In charge of public relations, bookings, and a hundred other things.'

'His assistant?' Karen smiled. 'And if I'd told you I hadn't enjoyed tonight's talk, would you have had me thrown out?'

Zane chuckled. 'No, but I probably wouldn't have given your feedback to Dr Michaels. He's quite sensitive.'

'Is he? I find that surprising, considering his job.'

'Believe me,' Zane said, 'for all his bluster, he's got a fragile ego!' Then he flushed and pressed a hand to his chest. 'Sorry, that wasn't very professional. I shouldn't have said that.'

'You're all right. I won't tell him,' Karen said.

'Have you followed his work for long?' Zane asked.

'No, but a colleague of mine, Sophie Jones, is probably Dr Michaels's biggest fan. She's in the signing queue at the moment.'

'Really?' Zane turned to look at the line of people waiting to get their books signed. 'Dr Michaels hasn't even started the signing yet. I'll tell you what – why don't you both come with me, and you can meet him before everyone else? Save all this waiting around. It's going to be at least an hour and a half otherwise. Trust me, I've been doing this for the last six weeks.'

'Six weeks?' Karen was impressed that a literary talk could demand that much attention from the public.

'Oh yes. There's an insatiable appetite for true crime in the UK. So, what do you think? Do you want to meet him?'

'Well, I don't want to put you out,' Karen said.

'Not at all. It'll be a distraction for him.'

'A distraction?' Karen said as they started walking towards the signing queue.

'Yeah, the signing's been delayed because he got a call from his ex-wife. Something to do with their kids.' He rolled his eyes, as though people having kids was a terrible inconvenience.

'Well, I wouldn't want to interrupt his phone call,' Karen said, hesitating.

'Oh, don't worry. You won't. He'll only be on the phone to her for five minutes, tops. That's all they can manage before everything breaks down into an out-and-out shouting match.' He checked the shiny, oversized watch on his wrist. 'He'll have finished the call and will have moved on to the ranting stage by now.' He stopped suddenly and pressed a hand to his chest again. 'Sorry, I'm not usually so indiscreet. It's been a long book tour.'

Zane was certainly not shy in sharing his opinions, seemingly blurting out the first thing that came into his mind. It wasn't the best attribute for an assistant in charge of PR, Karen thought. 'How long have you been working for Dr Michaels?'

'A couple of years. It's a fascinating job. Lots of responsibilities, more than you might think.' He nodded over Karen's shoulder, and she turned. 'See that woman over there, the one with the long, dark hair?'

'Yes,' Karen said. 'The one in the red coat?'

'Yes. She's definitely someone I'm keeping an eye on. She's attended the last three talks.'

'Really?'

He nodded. 'Some fans get obsessive, and it's my job to keep them away from Dr Michaels.' He turned back to Karen. 'That's not the only thing I do, of course. I have to handle his schedule, book venues and transport, work with the publisher's PR team, deal with his emails.' He waved a hand. 'See the man over there?'

He was gesturing to the photographer Karen had spoken with moments ago. 'Yes.'

'Well, I've organised it so he's covering the tour for free! He's a photographer but he's also had some articles published, and he's got contacts with the local press. So, thanks to me, the tour will get extra publicity.'

Zane looked extremely pleased with himself, but Karen couldn't help feeling sorry for the photographer, who had no guarantee he'd be reimbursed for his efforts. She couldn't imagine the local press would pay him a great deal for his work, even if they accepted an article for publication.

Zane took a sip of wine before continuing. 'I'm trusting you. If I give you and your friend a personal introduction to Dr Michaels, I'd better not find out that your colleague is one of these crazy fans.' He grinned.

Karen stifled a laugh. 'Well, she's not crazy, but she is a pretty big fan. She's watched every one of his YouTube lectures, and she quotes from his books all the time.' Although their cases were often different to those Michaels dealt with, Karen had to admit the information Sophie had gleaned from his books had sometimes been useful during investigations.

'How many times has she been to the talk?'

'Only once,' Karen said.

'All right then, I think she's safe. Now, which one is she?' he asked, scanning the queue.

'This one,' Karen said, reaching out and putting her hand on Sophie's arm. 'Sophie, come with me.'

'Oh, but I can't. I'll lose my spot.' She looked behind her. 'Look at all these people.'

'You won't. Just trust me,' Karen said.

Sophie reluctantly left the queue and followed Karen. 'Who's that?' she asked, nodding at the slender American man leading the way.

'Zane Dwight, Dr Michaels's assistant,' Karen said. 'He's going to take you to see Dr Michaels now.'

'He is?' Sophie's jaw dropped. 'Oh, that's amazing.' She raised her voice so Zane could hear her. 'Thank you so much.'

'Not a problem,' he said. 'Follow me.' He led them past the waiting line of people into the seminar room, where there was a bench with bottles of water and multiple pens set out ready for Dr Michaels.

They went through a door at the back of the room that led into a smaller area, which looked like it could be a staff room, with armchairs, coffee tables and a small kitchenette. Dr Michaels stood with his back to them, staring out of the window, muttering expletives.

Zane cleared his throat.

Dr Michaels turned. 'Ah, there you are. I wondered where you'd gone.' He held his mobile phone and shook it. 'She's driving me crazy, Zane,' he said.

'Ah, yes,' Zane said. 'Perhaps we'll talk about that later, but now I've got two people for you to meet.'

Karen thought she saw a slight flicker of irritation pass across Dr Michaels's features, before he arranged his face into a welcoming smile and apologised for swearing.

'I'm sorry. I just got off a rather tense phone call,' he explained. 'It's great to meet you both. Were you at the talk?'

'Yes, it was wonderful,' Sophie said. 'A highlight of my year. I absolutely loved it. Especially the way you handled the last case in Virginia. I found it very emotional.'

'Well, thank you very much,' he said. 'Would you like me to sign that?' He pointed to the book Sophie was clutching to her chest.

'Oh yes, please.' She held it out.

'They're in law enforcement,' Zane offered.

'Oh, really,' Dr Michaels said, replacing the cap on his pen after he'd signed the inside cover of the book. 'British police? Based in Norfolk?'

'No, Lincoln,' Karen said. 'Not too far from here.' She wasn't sure how familiar Dr Michaels was with the geography of the UK. 'About an hour and thirty minutes' drive.'

'Fascinating,' he said. 'I've always wanted to learn more about how the Brits operate. It's a very different police system.'

'No guns,' Zane said.

'We do have specialist firearms teams,' Karen clarified, 'but most officers don't carry guns.'

'Well, I'd be honoured to come and see how the Brits work if you could put up with me. Perhaps you could give me a tour of your station?' Dr Michaels said.

Karen thought Sophie might explode with excitement. 'Oh, that would be amazing. Absolutely awesome.'

Zane folded his arms over his chest and narrowed his eyes. He didn't seem keen on the idea.

'I'm not so sure,' Karen said. 'I think you might find it a bit boring. We don't have the sort of cases you're used to and—'

Sophie interrupted. 'Just two months ago we were on the trail of a serial killer and we both nearly lost our lives bringing the perpetrator to justice! We get our fair share of exciting cases.'

Both Zane and Dr Michaels looked impressed. Zane put a hand to his chest. 'Really?'

'Yes,' Sophie said. 'It was quite a big deal. It was in all the papers, and I had a concussion.'

'I hope you're doing okay now,' Dr Michaels said. 'It must have been an extremely traumatic experience.'

'It was, and admittedly it didn't turn out exactly the way I expected, but—'

It was Karen's turn to interrupt. 'I'm sure Dr Michaels needs to get on with his signing now. There's lots of people waiting.'

'Oh, yes. Sorry. I'm babbling.'

'Not at all,' Dr Michaels said. 'Zane, would you mind taking their details? I'll get on with the signing now, but I really would love to stop by and see how you guys operate . . . if you'll have me?'

'Oh, absolutely,' Sophie said.

Karen gave her a sideways glance. Michaels visiting the station would need to be cleared with the DCI.

As Dr Michaels walked out of the room, Sophie called after him. 'It was an honour to meet you!'

'If you give me your cards,' Zane said, 'I'll make sure Dr Michaels gets them. I know he said he'd like to come and see you at work . . .' He shrugged. 'But his schedule is packed at the moment, and it's unlikely he'll be able to get around to visiting you. It's nothing personal. He's a busy man.'

'But he seemed really enthusiastic,' Sophie said, looking crestfallen.

'Yes, and I know that he would love to come and see your quaint little English police station, and he *might* be able to squeeze it into his schedule, but he's crazy busy right now and doesn't get to do all the things he wants to. You shouldn't get your hopes up.'

'It's fine,' Karen said. 'We won't. Thanks very much, Zane, and thanks for letting us jump to the front of the queue to see Dr Michaels. We really appreciate it.'

'Yeah,' Sophie said, mustering up a smile. 'Thanks.'

As they headed back to the car, Sophie slowly regained some of her lost enthusiasm and she began to go back over the presentation. Karen didn't need a recap. Sophie could go on for hours once she'd warmed to her favourite topic – Dr Michaels – so Karen swiftly changed the subject.

'How are you and Harinder getting along? All good?'

Sophie gave a shy smile. She'd been on a few dates with Harinder, the station's resident tech genius, recently.

'Great. Things are going really well.'

Karen smiled. 'Good. I'm pleased for you.' She rummaged through her handbag, looking for her keys. It was nice to see Sophie enjoying herself after everything she'd been through. She deserved to be happy, and if listening to talks on serial killers was what made her happy, then Karen could put up with that. Tomorrow, Sophie would have a station full of victims she could lecture about Dr Michaels.

As her fingers closed around the car keys, Karen noticed a movement out of the corner of her eye. She turned, scanning the dark street.

It was late. There was no one in the street except the two of them, only Karen had been sure . . .

Sophie froze. 'What is it?'

'I thought I saw something back there.'

Sophie tugged her coat closed and shivered. 'I can't see anything.'

'No. Overactive imagination, I think.'

'That's not surprising. Considering.'

'True.'

They started walking again, and within two minutes were safely back in Karen's car.

They'd been on the road for less than five minutes when Sophie fell asleep. Karen hummed along to the radio. It looked like she wouldn't have to suffer a blow-by-blow repeat of Dr Michaels's talk after all.

CHAPTER TWO

The paperwork was never-ending. Karen shuffled the stack of papers in her out tray, wondering if she'd ever get on top of it.

But that was a pipe dream. No one ever got on top of paperwork, did they? Even Sophie, with her precise methods and love of admin, always had a backlog. It was the thing Karen liked least about police work: the mundane monotony of the form-filling and typing, and yet she had no choice because cases relied on it. Prosecutions could fall apart if paperwork wasn't thoroughly and precisely completed.

Sophie was enthusiastically giving DC Rick Cooper a beat-by-beat breakdown of Dr Michaels's talk from last night. She'd already told Farzana Shah all about it as soon as the unsuspecting detective constable had arrived for work, not even waiting until Farzana had taken her coat off. Sophie had less success with the canny DS Arnie Hodgson, who, as soon as Sophie mentioned the name Dr Michaels, had quickly made the excuse that he needed to nip to the canteen for a sausage roll, and hadn't been seen since.

Karen, although pleased Sophie was brighter now and seeming more like her old self, was glad someone else was getting the repeat lecture. There were only so many times she wanted to hear about the late-night stake-outs involved in catching the Washington Night Creeper.

She couldn't help noticing that there was something odd about the interaction between Sophie and Rick though. Sophie seemed her normal chatty self, sitting opposite Rick, methodically working her way through her checklist as she talked. Rick, on the other hand, looked like he was barely listening. He was staring blankly at the computer screen in front of him. That wasn't like Rick.

He'd usually be teasing Sophie by now, maybe performing some exaggerated yawns and rolling his eyes, but he was hardly reacting. A grunt and a nod now and then, and that was all.

Karen grabbed the empty coffee mug from her desk and walked over. 'Can I get either of you a coffee?' she offered.

They both looked up. 'I've still got one, thanks,' Sophie said, pointing at the half-full mug in front of her.

'No, I'm fine thanks, Sarge,' Rick said. He briefly glanced at Karen before his gaze returned to the rows of numbers on his computer screen.

'Everything all right, Rick?' she asked.

He looked up again. 'Oh, yeah. Just tired, you know.'

Rick lived with his mother, who was suffering from dementia. They had a carer for most of the day, but at night everything fell to Rick. Some nights were fine if she slept straight through, but others were difficult. If his mother woke and was distressed, that meant Rick didn't get much sleep, and then he still had to get up for work the next day.

It was an impossible situation, and Karen, not having been through it herself, didn't want to make matters worse by offering suggestions Rick had probably already thought of and tried.

'Well, if you need anything, you know where I am,' Karen said.

'Thanks, Sarge,' Rick said.

Karen had turned away, ready to head to the coffee machine, when a voice behind made her pause. 'Ah, DS Hart, just the person I was looking for.'

Karen turned slowly. 'DCI Churchill.'

She'd disliked him almost instantly, and hadn't trusted him one bit when he'd first transferred to Nettleham. As it turned out, most of Karen's fears had been misplaced.

But that didn't mean he wasn't annoying. Because he was. Very annoying. Despite that, everyone else seemed to be getting on with him now. Karen had been making an effort, but he didn't make it easy.

Arnie had tried to give Karen tips on handling Churchill, but there was something about the man that wound Karen up. Perhaps it was his impossibly polished appearance, pristine white shirts, the suits that always looked as though they'd been freshly pressed, and she'd never seen him with a single hair out of place, let alone with a stain on his tie, or his shirtsleeves rolled up.

'Sir,' Karen said, forcing a smile.

'My office,' he said.

So much for coffee, Karen thought, and put her mug back on her desk as she followed him out of the open-plan area.

Churchill's office was one floor up.

'Did you have a nice time last night?' he asked. The personal question caught Karen off guard.

'Last night?'

'Yes, you went to a talk. Dr Michaels, wasn't it?'

'Oh right, yes. How did you know about that?' she asked.

'DC Jones told me.'

Of course. Sophie would have told everybody by now.

'It was interesting,' Karen said. 'Better than I'd expected actually. He—'

Before Karen could continue, Churchill cut her off. 'I've heard about him. He was on the radio a while ago. I thought perhaps he might have been exaggerating some of the cases.'

Karen inexplicably felt the need to defend Dr Michaels, even though she'd shared the same impression of the doctor before she'd gone to his talk. But that was probably because she wanted to take the opposite stance to Churchill.

'He was great. It wasn't over-dramatised. It was all sensitively presented. He was very good.'

'Is he a real doctor?'

'He has a PhD in criminology.'

They'd reached his office, and Churchill pushed the door open. 'Take a seat,' he said.

Karen did so, then waited for Churchill to get comfortable on the other side of his desk.

'We've had a report of an abduction,' he said. 'An adult female. I'd like you and Morgan on the case.' He paused, as though he was waiting for Karen's input.

'Morgan—'

'Don't interrupt.'

Karen clenched her teeth.

He glanced at his computer screen and reeled off more details. 'No ID for the victim. All we know is it involved a white van on Royal Oak Lane.'

'Aubourn?' Karen said, making the mistake of thinking aloud.

Churchill glowered at the interruption.

Aubourn was a tiny place. A few residential streets, a Norman church and a pub.

Churchill remained stubbornly silent.

'Sorry,' Karen said. 'I was just surprised. Aubourn is a quiet village. Not somewhere you'd expect an abduction.'

'Abductions can happen anywhere,' Churchill snapped. 'As you should be aware, DS Hart.'

'Yes, of course.'

After a few silent seconds passed, Karen asked, 'Are there any more details?'

He used the trackpad on his desk to scroll through the information on his screen. 'Doesn't look like it.'

'Do we know when it happened?' Karen put her hands on the arms of the chair, ready to get moving. Why hadn't Churchill just told her all this downstairs, to save precious time?

'It happened this morning,' he said. 'About two hours ago.'

'Two hours,' Karen repeated. 'That's a long time.'

'Yes, it's a bit complicated,' Churchill said.

'Complicated how?'

'The only witness to this abduction is a four-year-old girl.'

'Was the abduction victim her mother? Family member?'

'No, she saw it from the window of her house – her living room, I think. Doesn't know who the woman is. And to further complicate things, her mother thinks she might have made it up. Apparently, she has an overactive imagination.'

'Right, but we can't rule it out until—'

'Exactly,' Churchill cut in. 'Which is what I want you and Morgan to do.'

He reeled off the address for Karen. 'Uniform are on the scene already, of course, and a door-to-door has been authorised, so with luck, they may come up with another witness by the time you get there.'

'Right,' Karen said, standing up. 'As I attempted to tell you, Morgan is out of the station this morning, on a course.'

'A course?'

'Yes, safety-in-the-workplace training.'

'Oh, yes.' Churchill waved a hand. 'He did mention that. Who do you want to take with you then?'

'Rick.'

'Very well, let me know how you get on,' Churchill said, turning away and beginning to tap on his keyboard.

Yes, Karen thought as she left his office. *Still very annoying.*

CHAPTER THREE

The living room at the McCarthy house was a fair size, but it felt small and claustrophobic due to the amount of furniture in the room and the knick-knacks that cluttered every surface.

There were cream wooden blocks printed with gold letters spelling out *family* and *love* on the mantelpiece over the gas fire. An oversized cream leather sofa sat in front of the window, with matching armchairs opposite. Cream was a brave choice with a child under five in the house.

Karen was perched on the sofa, eyeing what looked suspiciously like a mark made by an orange crayon, while the child played with a plastic truck on the floor. Karen had left Rick outside to get as much information as he could from the officers who'd been first on the scene. The child's mother sat opposite Karen on one of the armchairs.

Molly was a cute kid. A little small for her age, with big eyes and soft wispy hair. She was currently busy playing, but every so often, she shot a curious glance at Karen.

Whenever Karen saw children around Molly's age, it made her think of her own daughter, Tilly.

Molly was murmuring, lost in her own playtime world. She had a good imagination, another thing that reminded Karen of her own daughter. Occasionally, Karen used to stop by the door of the playroom and watch Tilly, marvelling at the endless games she came up with. Like Molly, Tilly had been an only child. Perhaps that was behind their active imaginations – keeping themselves entertained, as they had no brothers and sisters to play with.

Karen watched the child roll the truck along the carpet then stop to pick up two tiny dolls, asking them to pay a fare for a trip to the moon. She performed all the roles – the truck driver and the passengers. Changing her voice for each one.

Would she be as creative as she grew older? Perhaps a career as an actress or an author beckoned. She had so much potential. That thought gave Karen a pang of pain. Tilly would never have the chance to fulfil her own potential. She would stay five years old forever, locked in Karen's memories.

'I really don't know what to tell you,' Mrs McCarthy said, her hands fluttering up to her face and then back down to her lap. 'I'm sorry, but I think this is probably a waste of time. Molly makes things up. She has a tendency to invent things. She's a bit of a storyteller.'

'I'm not lying,' Molly said, looking up from her toy and frowning at her mother.

'I didn't say lying, darling. I said telling stories.' Mrs McCarthy shot Karen an apologetic look that seemed to say: *See what I'm dealing with?*

Karen had hoped to talk to the child without this kind of influence, but when talking with an almost-five-year-old, it was hardly fair to expect a parent not to interrupt. It wasn't always easy to get the truth from children. Maybe Molly was embellishing a bit. Or maybe she'd made up the whole thing because she didn't understand the consequences.

'Is it all right if I have a word with Molly?' Karen asked.

Molly's mother raised her eyebrows. 'Yes, I suppose so, as long as I can stay in the room.'

'Of course,' Karen said. She left her notebook on the arm of the sofa and sat on the carpet beside Molly.

'Can you tell me what you saw this morning?'

Molly seemed disinterested and kept her eyes on the bright-red truck. 'I'm not lying,' she muttered again.

'I'm sure you're not lying,' Karen said. 'That's why it's important you tell me what you saw.'

'Molly, sweetheart, you can't waste the police's time if it's just one of your stories,' Mrs McCarthy said.

'Don't worry about that,' Karen said. 'It's better to be safe than sorry. Now, Molly,' she said, turning her attention back to the child. 'This is a very nice truck. When did you get it?'

Molly shrugged. 'It's not a truck. It's a spaceship, and it's going to the moon.'

'Oh, I see. Did you get it for Christmas?'

The child shook her head.

'It was a hand-me-down from our neighbours across the road . . .' Mrs McCarthy trailed off. 'Sorry, I'll stop interrupting.'

'Can you tell me about the van you saw outside this morning?'

Molly looked up, scepticism written all over her young face. She stared directly at Karen for a moment before saying, 'It was white, like Daddy's.'

'Was it Daddy's van?'

'No, there was no writing on the side.'

'And where was the van? Can you point and show me?'

Molly stood up and climbed on to the sofa. Leaning against the back cushions, she pointed across the street. 'Over there.'

'So it was on the other side of the road?' Karen asked.

The child nodded.

It was some distance. The family lived in a small semi-detached house, but it had a large frontage with a long garden and driveway.

26

Factoring in the width of the road would mean Molly had been a good thirty feet away from the van.

'How long had the van been there, Molly?'

Molly shook her head. 'I don't know.'

'Can you tell me exactly what you saw? It could be very important.' Karen wished she'd been able to talk to the child before all this negativity about lying and storytelling had been brought into the equation.

The truth was young children did make stuff up, as Karen knew from experience. But she also knew if Molly was anything like Tilly, she might also be very sensitive to criticism. The situation needed to be handled with care. Too much encouragement from Karen could lead to Molly making things up for attention, but too little and the young girl could hide key details, fearing she wouldn't be believed.

'Are you a police lady?' Molly asked.

Karen nodded. 'Yes, that's right, I'm a detective.'

'You tell people off when they've been bad?'

'Yes, and we try to stop bad things happening.'

'You didn't stop the bad thing this morning.'

'No, and that's why I need your help. I need you to tell me what happened, so I can—'

'So you can catch the bad man?' Molly asked.

'Exactly. So what were you doing this morning just before you saw the van?'

'I was getting dressed,' Molly said. 'Then I came downstairs for breakfast and looked out of the window.'

'Yes, I called her down for breakfast. Whatever she saw must have been over in seconds,' Mrs McCarthy said, 'because I didn't see anything.'

Karen didn't respond, keeping her attention on Molly. If the child was telling the truth, she needed to know that someone was listening to her. 'When you looked out of the window, what did you see?'

'I saw the white van,' Molly said.

'Was anyone else around? Did you see any people out there?'

'No.'

'Any of your neighbours?'

Molly shook her head.

'She was probably looking out for Geri – one of our neighbours. She lives in a houseshare just up the road. She's lovely to Molly, and she has a bike that Molly is quite taken with. So she tries to look out for Geri when she leaves for university in the morning, don't you, sweetheart?'

Molly shrugged, clearly still put out at the fact her mother hadn't believed her.

'When you saw the van, were you on the sofa as you are now?'

Molly nodded.

'Can you tell me what happened next?'

'A lady came, and somebody grabbed her.'

'Can you tell me what she looked like?'

'She had an umbrella,' Molly said.

'What colour was the umbrella?'

'Not sure.' Molly bit her lip and rubbed her eyes. She looked upset, and worried because she couldn't remember the detail.

'It's okay, Molly. You're doing really well. It's hard to remember everything, isn't it?'

'Yes.'

'What was the lady wearing?'

'She had boots on.'

'Like wellington boots?' Mrs McCarthy asked.

Molly shook her head. 'No, like your black boots.'

'Oh, okay,' Mrs McCarthy said.

'Do you have the boots?' Karen asked, looking at Molly's mother. 'It would be really helpful if I could see them.'

'I'll get them after you've finished talking to Molly,' she said, clearly not wanting to leave her daughter alone to be questioned. A response that was understandable.

'And what happened to the lady, Molly? Did she get into the front of the van or the side of the van or the back of the van?'

'The doors opened at the back; a man pulled her in.'

'Did she try to get away or cry out?'

'Don't know,' Molly said, sliding down the sofa cushions and back on to the floor. Almost-five-year-olds didn't have the best attention spans, and Karen knew she was very close to losing Molly to the spaceship game again.

'Okay, Molly. I've only got a few more questions. After the lady was in the van, what happened to the man?'

Molly shrugged.

'Did you see the van leave?'

'Yes.'

'What way did it go?' Karen asked.

Molly turned back to the window and pointed to the left.

The traffic was one-way on this street, so the van would have had to go left. It was a small way to test if Molly's story was reliable.

'And what did you do after you saw the van leave?'

'I went upstairs to tell Mummy.'

'What time was that?' Karen directed the question to Molly's mother.

'It must have been about eight fifteen,' Mrs McCarthy replied.

Karen did her best to keep her expression unreadable. 'But you didn't call us until nearly two hours later. Why was that?'

The woman opened her mouth, but no sound came out at first. Then she shrugged and shifted her position in the armchair.

'Look, if I'd seen something suspicious, I would have called you straightaway, but I didn't.'

'Weren't you worried that Molly might be telling the truth, that she'd witnessed an abduction?'

'I just thought it was unlikely. Molly gets ideas in her head sometimes. Last week, she told our next-door neighbour their cat had learned to fly.' She lifted her hands, palms up. 'Clearly *that* didn't happen, and I thought this was just a story too, but then I spoke to my husband, and he thought I should call you, so I did. Did anyone else see anything?'

'I don't think so. We have officers doing door-to-door enquiries,' Karen said. 'Just to make sure.'

'Right. I'm sorry if I did the wrong thing. I just thought she was making it up. I still do, to be honest.'

'I'm not!' Molly said, picking up her truck and walking out of the room.

Mrs McCarthy put a hand on her forehead. 'She's not naughty. She's just an imaginative child. There is another reason I thought she was making it up, though.' Mrs McCarthy chewed her bottom lip and looked down at her hands before continuing. 'I've been watching that new soap, *Green Hills*, while Molly is on her iPad. It's on in the afternoons. Yesterday there was an abduction storyline. A woman was kidnapped.'

'Ah, I see. You think that influenced Molly?'

'It seems likely, doesn't it?'

'It's possible.'

'So now you understand why I didn't call the police straightaway.' Mrs McCarthy smiled. 'I didn't want to waste your time.'

Molly watching a daytime drama centring on a woman's abduction did add weight to the theory that the child's vivid imagination had led to an investigation into a non-existent crime. Karen hoped Mrs McCarthy was correct. The alternative was that a woman had

30

been snatched off the street in broad daylight and no one had reported her missing for hours.

'Molly's the apple of our eye, but we have had a few problems distinguishing between truth and lies recently. She's going through a stage. You know what it's like. Do you have children?'

Karen hesitated. She hated this question. She didn't reply for moment, then gave a small shake of her head, feeling treacherous as she did so.

'That's all the questions I have for Molly right now. Could I see your boots? The ones she mentioned?'

'Yes, of course.' Mrs McCarthy left the room and came back with a pair of low-heeled black ankle boots.

'I think we're done for now,' Karen said after examining the boots. 'Thanks for your help and letting me talk to Molly. We'll keep going with the door-to-door enquiries.'

'I'm really sorry we've wasted your time.'

'Calling us was the right thing to do.'

Mrs McCarthy sighed, tension leaving her like a deflated balloon. 'Oh, that's reassuring. I was worried we'd get a telling off for wasting police time. I rang Terry, my husband, at work, and he thought we should report it. Better safe than sorry. So I called.'

'I'm glad you did.'

Mrs McCarthy reached up to rub the back of her neck. 'You know, I was so certain that Molly had made it up before I called you. But now I'm thinking I should have called you earlier . . .'

Karen said nothing.

'I mean, if it does turn out to be an abduction. I didn't tell anyone for two hours . . .' She ran a hand through her hair and shot a guilty look towards the doorway. 'I couldn't live with myself if something—'

'Let's hope it doesn't come to that.' Karen followed Mrs McCarthy out of the living room but stopped in the hallway. Molly stood at the top of the stairs, clutching her red truck in one hand and a battered teddy bear in the other.

'Goodbye, Molly. Thank you for your help.'

The little girl's gaze locked with Karen's. 'I'm not telling fibs.'

Karen had spent her career dealing with cold hard facts and indisputable evidence, but had learned never to ignore her gut, and right now, it was telling her this little girl was telling the truth.

CHAPTER FOUR

The crime scene had been secured and the road closed, which made the quiet village even more peaceful than usual. The neat front gardens, attractive red-brick houses and smaller bungalows made the area appear pleasantly tranquil. There was no indication that a violent abduction had taken place recently. A few neighbours were in their front gardens, tending to plants – or, at least, pretending to – as they gawped wide-eyed at the SOCOs and uniformed officers.

A combination of blue-and-white tape and yellow hazard tape cordoned off the road. Members of the team wandered around covered up by white paper suits. A crime scene photographer crouched down to take a picture of a parked red Nissan Micra.

Karen looked up and down the road. There was no CCTV, but with luck one of the houses in the vicinity would have a private security system installed.

Karen scanned the area for Rick and saw him standing beside a black Volvo, talking to a tall, uniformed officer with steel-grey hair.

Most of the other cars in the area were parked on driveways. It was the type of village where neighbours would notice anything unusual going on, and wouldn't be reticent about telling the police what they'd seen. A few of the houses had neighbourhood-watch signs stuck to the windows and front doors. If Molly McCarthy was telling the truth, then surely someone else must have seen something.

It was a cold day, and despite the fact they were edging towards lunchtime, frost clung to the bare twigs and shrubs in the front gardens. Karen had been through this village on multiple occasions, usually in the summer, on the way to the garden centre, when the pretty gardens were packed full of brightly coloured bedding plants, the lawns were lush and green, and cheerful hanging baskets decorated the fronts of most of the houses.

She looked around, trying to find someone from the crime scene team she'd worked with before. It wasn't easy, as their paper suits had hoods which partly obscured their faces, but Karen didn't have to wait long before one of them walked towards her.

His face was a squashed red circle, contrasting against the bright-white suit. She didn't recognise him.

'And you are?' he enquired, tilting his head back and looking Karen up and down.

He made a movement as though to thrust his thumbs into his belt loops, perhaps forgetting he was wearing the white suit. His hands ended up fluttering at his sides before he folded his arms across his chest. His body language was stand-offish and a little arrogant.

She showed him her ID. 'Detective Sergeant Karen Hart.'

'Oh, your boss is over there.' He jerked his head in Rick's direction.

Karen resisted the urge to roll her eyes. The fact Rick was male obviously meant *he* would be the one in charge.

'What have you found?' she asked as he began to walk away.

He circled back and gave an impatient sigh. 'Nothing really. It's all a waste of time. Kid's a bit of a storyteller, by all accounts. Have you spoken to her?'

'I have, and until otherwise, we should still treat this as a potential abduction. Who's in charge of the scene?'

He bristled, squaring his shoulders, probably trying to look intimidating, but it was hard to do that dressed in a white paper suit that rustled with every movement.

'I am.'

Great. Most of the SOCOs Karen had dealt with in the past had been professional, courteous and, most importantly, excellent at their jobs. 'So, can you give me a quick report on what you've found so far, please?'

'Yes. It will be a very short report, though. As I said, we've not found much.'

'*Not found much* isn't very helpful. Can you provide more detail?'

He scowled. 'I doubt it's significant. There's a bit of mud near the gutter. Possible tyre tracks. Could be from any vehicle, though.' He pointed to an area on the other side of the road. Exactly where Molly had said the white van had parked.

'Have you taken photographs of the tyre tracks?'

He made an odd wheezing sound. 'We're not idiots!'

'Right,' Karen said slowly. 'Just checking. Is it all right if I take a look?'

'Knock yourself out.'

She slowly walked over to the small, numbered marker to look at the tracks. The dark, almost black, mud had only the faint imprint of a tyre. To the right of the tyre track was a drain. She crouched to take a closer look.

Standing up again, she crooked a finger, indicating the scenes of crime officer should join her.

Reluctantly, he walked over.

'What's your name?'

'Tim Farthing,' he said. 'I've just moved up here from London. It's been like a nice little holiday for me so far.'

'So pleased to hear that, Tim,' Karen said, her tone indicating otherwise. 'Perhaps you could talk me through how you've processed the scene. We like to be thorough up here.'

He inclined his head stiffly and then described what they'd found so far at the scene – which, true to his word, was not a lot.

Karen pulled a small torch from her pocket and shone it down the drain.

'Did you look down here?' she asked.

'I think that's overkill. Even the mother said the kid is away with the fairies. She's obviously seen something on TV and conjured up some fanciful scenario that—'

'I'm glad that's so obvious to you, Tim,' Karen said, not bothering to hide her sarcasm. 'What's this?' She nodded at the drain.

Something small and white showed up in the beam from the torch. Paper? It stood out amongst the grime and the soggy rotting leaves at the bottom of the drain.

He sighed. Then peered over Karen's shoulder.

'Bit of rubbish probably.' He shrugged.

He could be right. But it didn't look like it had been down there long. It was too bright, too clean. She angled the torch beam to look into the corners but couldn't see anything else.

'I think you'll have to take up the drain cover and have a proper look.'

Tim shook his head. 'No, there's nothing to suggest that—'

'Just to make it clear, I wasn't asking you. I'm telling you. I want whatever that is down there in an evidence bag.' She straightened and switched off the torch.

'Maybe I should have a word with your boss,' Tim said, eyes narrowing. He glanced past Karen at Rick, who was still talking to the uniformed officer.

Karen stared at him. 'Just do your job, Tim.' She slid the torch back into her pocket. 'I'm in charge. Report to me when you're done.'

She strode off, heading towards Rick. She had no idea why Tim Farthing had such an attitude problem. Perhaps she could have been more diplomatic, but nothing irritated her more than someone half-heartedly doing their job, especially in their line of work. It had come as a surprise too, as the other SOCOs were so diligent.

There was every chance that the object in the drain had nothing to do with the investigation, but they couldn't just ignore it because it was a bit chilly and they'd all like to get back to the station for a hot cup of tea.

She wondered how long Tim Farthing would stick around. She couldn't imagine he would fit in well with the other SOCOs on her patch, who she knew to be professional, and who would never shirk their responsibility on a case.

She stopped beside Rick, who introduced her to the uniformed officer. 'Sarge, this is Inspector Travis. He initiated the door-to-door search of this road. He's asked his team to request access to any private security footage.'

'Great,' Karen said. 'Anything so far?'

'Not yet.' Inspector Travis turned to look at Karen. He had a stern face, a deep groove between his eyebrows and no laughter lines near his eyes, indicating he spent more time frowning than smiling.

'Have you spoken to the little girl and her mother?' she asked the inspector.

'I have.'

'What was your impression?'

He hesitated. 'She's very young.'

'So you think it's down to an overactive imagination?'

'I think that's the most likely scenario, but I wouldn't like to make that call. I think we need to make sure.'

'I agree,' Karen said, looking back along the street. 'The traffic is on a one-way system. So the van would have come in from the right and stopped there.' She pointed at the spot where Tim Farthing was currently hunched over the drain. 'Then the woman was bundled into the van, and it carried on up the street, towards the pub. Has anyone spoken with the landlord? It's likely they have cameras.'

'Not yet, but they're on our list.'

'I think—' Karen stopped mid-sentence as she saw Tim Farthing stand up and march towards her.

'Found something?' Rick asked.

Tim Farthing grunted, a stony look on his face. 'Pretty sure it's not going be important, but DS Hart wanted me to search the drain.'

He held out a clear plastic evidence bag. Karen took it. Inside the bag was a playing card. She turned the bag over: the Queen of Hearts. Apart from being smeared with mud, it was in good condition. It couldn't have been in the drain for long.

'Just general rubbish?' the inspector suggested.

'Possibly,' Karen said.

'*Probably* more like. And I'm filthy.' Tim wiped his dirty blue nitrile gloves on a cleansing wipe. But they remained stubbornly coated in a layer of black grime.

'Anything else down there?' Karen asked.

'Oh yes.' He gestured behind him and a female SOCO came forward, face flushed, looking uncomfortable. 'Well, show her,' Tim urged.

She held out another evidence bag. This time it contained an old, faded wrapper. It had clearly been in the drain a long time, so was highly unlikely to have any relevance to the abduction.

Karen took the bag. 'Monster Munch?'

'Yes.' Tim smirked and waited for Karen's response. He thought he was being clever. 'Well, you did want *everything*. I wouldn't want to be accused of not being thorough.'

'Great. Log them both please. Thanks for taking the drain cover up,' Karen said, handing back the evidence bags.

Tim turned away. 'Waste of time if you ask me,' he mumbled, loud enough for Karen to hear.

No one did ask him, Karen thought, but she let it go.

Rick frowned. 'What was all that about?'

'Personality clash, I think,' Karen said.

'You think the rubbish is important?'

'Not the crisp packet, but the playing card is odd. I don't know if it's significant, but we really don't have much else to go on at this stage.'

Inspector Travis was called away by one of his officers.

'Let's hope we can get some security footage. Someone is bound to have it around here,' Rick said. 'What did you make of the witness?'

'Like the inspector said, she's very young.'

'Yes, I know, but what did your instinct tell you?'

'Honestly, I'm not sure,' Karen said. 'Molly is adamant she's telling the truth, but her mother had been watching a soap where a character was abducted – while Molly was in the room.'

Rick grimaced. 'Kids that age are easily influenced by stuff like that.'

'Right, and it's possible she might not understand what's real and what isn't. She could *think* she's telling the truth. But she reminded me of Tilly in a way.'

Rick put a hand on Karen's arm. 'Oh, Sarge, I didn't think. You should have assigned me to speak to her.'

'It's my job. It wasn't a hardship. She's a great kid.'

'Yes, but, it must be hard . . .'

'Rick, I can't avoid talking to children for the rest of my life. Besides, sometimes it's good to remember. Molly's got the same type of imagination Tilly had – always making up new games, unusual stories – but I think, like Tilly did, she knows what's real and what isn't. I think Molly McCarthy witnessed an abduction.'

Rick rubbed his chin, looking in the direction of the McCarthy house. 'Did she give you any more details on the van?'

'Just that it's like her dad's, so presumably a Transit, and there's no writing on the side.'

'So we're looking for a plain white Transit.'

'Yes.'

Rick sighed. 'Needle in a haystack.'

'Worse than that. A piece of hay in a haystack.'

'So what's next?' Rick asked.

Karen checked the time. Morgan would still be on his course. The next move was up to her. 'I'm going to call Sophie and ask her to look for any reports of missing women locally. Then I think we should help out Inspector Travis's team with the door-to-door. We need more information, and that's our best chance of getting it.'

CHAPTER FIVE

Karen and Rick visited five houses without success. At two of the homes, there was no one in, and the residents of Aubourn who had opened the door denied seeing anything unusual that morning.

It was looking more and more like they were on a wild goose chase, but Karen couldn't forget the stubborn certainty in young Molly McCarthy's eyes.

After they received no answer from yet another residence, they were called over by Inspector Travis. 'I think you should come along and talk to the lady at number sixty,' he said, pointing out a semi-detached house.

'Did the occupants witness something?'

The inspector rattled off the details. 'Mrs Chelsea, lives alone, widow, seventy-six. She said she was in the kitchen at the back of the house at the time the child said she witnessed the abduction.'

'But?' Karen prompted, eager for him to get to the point.

'But she does have a security system. Her son installed it, worried about his mother living alone after his father died.'

'And the camera caught the abduction?'

'Not the abduction, no, but it did capture a white van.' He paused, rubbed his chin. 'In fact, the van didn't fit in the frame, just half of it.'

'Right,' Karen said, 'I suppose that's a start. Thanks. We'll have a word with Mrs Chelsea.'

They swung open the gate and walked up the path to number sixty. The door was answered by a lady with a warm smile and grey curly hair.

Karen could hear voices coming from inside.

'I'm Detective Sergeant Karen Hart, and this is my colleague, DC Rick Cooper. We understand you have some security footage of a white van parked near your house this morning.'

'More police. Goodness, I am popular this morning. It must be important. Has the owner of the van committed a crime?'

'We're not sure yet,' Rick said. 'Would you mind if we took a look at the recording?'

'Of course, come in.' She shut the door behind them and ushered them into the hallway.

The smell of bacon wafted from the kitchen.

'Can I get you a bacon sandwich?' she said, as they stepped into the kitchen. 'I think there's some left. Luckily I bought a large supply of bacon yesterday. It was on offer. Your colleagues are already eating.'

'So I see,' Karen said dryly, looking at three uniformed officers clustered around the small table in the kitchen. In the centre of the round table was a large plate stacked with doorstop-sized white bread and bacon sandwiches. Bottles of tomato ketchup and brown sauce stood next to the plate.

The officers sheepishly looked up from their sandwiches.

'Sorry, we didn't like to refuse. It seemed rude,' the officer closest to Karen said. 'We didn't intend to put you to any trouble, Mrs Chelsea.'

'Oh, it's no trouble at all. It's nice to have the company,' she said. 'Are you sure you wouldn't like one? There are plenty left.' She looked at Karen and Rick.

'I'm fine, thanks,' Karen said, at the same time as Rick said, 'Oh, yes please!'

'Could we get a look at the footage? I take it you've already seen it?' Karen directed the second question to the uniformed officers.

'Yes, we told Inspector Travis, and he went to find you. Since we were just waiting for you to take over, we thought there was no harm in a little bacon sandwich and a cup of tea. It's cold out there this morning.'

'It's on my phone,' Mrs Chelsea said, reaching for her reading glasses and then a large, almost tablet-sized mobile phone.

She peered at the screen, squinting, then tapped a few buttons on the display to open up the app. She moved closer to Karen and pressed play.

Karen watched the scene unfold on the mobile phone.

The view was of in front of the property. Most of the garden was visible, as was half the road. The recording started just as the nose of a white Transit van pulled up. It stopped at the curb, but less than half the van was in the frame. As it had angled into the curb, there was a brief moment when Karen thought the number plate might be about to come into view, but the angle was too acute. It was hard to be sure on such a small screen. Maybe Harinder would be able to get something from it with his technical wizardry. The seconds ticked by, then the recording cut out.

Karen looked up. 'Is that it?'

'No,' Mrs Chelsea said. 'There's another video when the van moves off again. The camera is motion-sensitive, so I'm afraid it didn't record the whole time the van was parked outside the house.'

'What time was this video recorded?'

Mrs Chelsea squinted again as she scrolled through the app's menu. 'Eight fourteen. And then the van left at eight twenty-four. You can see that here.'

She opened the second video, and Karen watched closely. It was hard to see into the cab of the van. The dreary light didn't help. There was a shadowy shape in the position she'd expect the driver to be, but it was hard to make out any details. Perhaps the video could be enhanced.

'This could be really helpful,' Karen said to Mrs Chelsea. 'Could we get a copy?'

'We've got one,' one of the officers said, speaking with his mouth full, but at least putting his hand over his mouth.

'We worked out how to download it,' one of the other officers chipped in, looking very pleased with himself. 'We can send it to you.'

'Thanks, I'd appreciate it,' Karen said.

Mrs Chelsea held out a cup of black tea. 'At least have a cup of tea, dear. You need to keep warm on a day like this.'

Karen took the cup. 'Thanks.'

'Milk? Sugar?'

'A little milk please.' She held out her cup, and Mrs Chelsea added the milk.

Karen then gratefully wrapped her fingers around the cup, enjoying the warmth, as Rick tucked into a bacon sandwich.

'Do you know anyone around here who owns a white van?' Karen asked.

'There are quite a few in the area. There's one usually parked in the drive opposite me. Mr McCarthy, he's a nice chap. Others I've seen around the village, but I don't pay much attention to them. I don't know who owns them, I'm afraid.'

'You didn't hear anything unusual this morning? No shouting? Loud voices?' Karen asked.

'No, nothing. It was just a normal morning for me until police officers turned up on my doorstep. We don't usually get that sort of thing around here. If you don't mind me asking, what has happened? Is it anything I should worry about? I live on my own nowadays.' She tugged nervously at the collar of her blouse.

'I don't think you should worry. There was a report of a woman getting into the back of a white van. We need to make sure she isn't in danger.'

'Oh, goodness. I hope she's all right. Is it one of my neighbours?'

'We're not sure who the woman is. That's why we need to look at security footage and speak to people who might have seen something.'

'That's if a woman really has gone missing,' one of the officers said.

Karen shot him a look that told him very clearly his input was not required.

'Oh, so she might not be missing?' Mrs Chelsea frowned.

'We're still looking into it. It's early days,' Karen said. 'Do you know if any of your neighbours would have been home at eight fifteen this morning?'

Mrs Chelsea thought for a minute and then said, 'Possibly, but I'm sorry, most of my time is spent in the kitchen in the morning. I don't know what time my neighbours go to work. I don't even go into the front room until the afternoon. Otherwise I find I tend to sit in the armchair and waste the day.' She smiled apologetically.

'Thank you very much, Mrs Chelsea,' Karen said. 'For the tea and for feeding the five thousand.' She nodded at the other officers, who were busy stuffing their faces.

Mrs Chelsea beamed. 'It's my pleasure.'

◆ ◆ ◆

Rick drove back to Nettleham station, so Karen used the opportunity to place a call to Sophie and ask whether she'd uncovered any reports of missing women locally.

If a woman had been abducted, someone else must have noticed.

But Sophie wasn't at her desk, so Karen left a message with DC Farzana Shah.

After she hung up, Karen looked at Rick. 'You've got a little something just there,' she said, gesturing to the corner of his mouth. 'Looks like sauce.'

'Thanks,' Rick said, wiping his mouth with the back of his hand. 'Can't have a bacon sarnie without brown sauce.'

Karen, who wasn't a big fan of brown sauce, pulled a face.

Rick chuckled.

'What?'

'I was just thinking of that uniformed officer's face after you tore strips out of him for suggesting the abduction hadn't happened.'

'He deserved it,' Karen said. 'He needs to learn never to make comments like that in front of a witness.'

'I think he learned his lesson. He won't be doing that again in a hurry.'

'Is everything all right with you?' Karen asked. 'I've been meaning to have a chat, but it's hard to get a spare five minutes at the station without people interrupting. You know you can tell me if you need a bit of extra time off.'

'Thanks, Sarge,' Rick said with a smile. 'But I've nearly used all my leave, and we're only at the start of the year.'

'If it's related to caring for your mum, I'm sure there's something we can sort out.'

Anyone else might have been taken in by Rick's smile, but Karen caught the tense lines around his eyes, and noticed how the smile seemed to take a big effort. Perhaps Rick would have fooled someone else, but Karen knew him too well. He was struggling.

'I don't want to pry, Rick. Tell me to mind my own business if you like, but I'm worried about you.'

'You know me, Sarge. Takes a lot to bring me down. I'm fine,' he said, attempting to turn on his trademark grin, but failing. They sat in silence for a couple of minutes until Rick stopped at the traffic lights. Looking straight ahead, he said, 'To be honest, I'm not doing that great.'

'Your mum?'

'Yeah, and the thing is, it's not going to improve. There's nothing I can do that will make her any better.'

Karen didn't reply straightaway. It was easy to dole out the platitudes, but she didn't know what it was like to live with someone you loved as they slowly slipped away. His mother's dementia meant she unknowingly made increasing demands on his time. Demands that couldn't reasonably be met when he was also trying to hold down a full-time job.

'How is your sister coping?'

'It's hard on her, too. She doesn't live with Mum, but she's got a job and kids.' He let out a long breath and pulled away from the lights.

'Priya still with you?' Karen asked, referring to the home carer who'd been helping out.

She worked five days a week, and Rick took over the caring when he got home.

'Yes, and she's great,' Rick said. 'I don't know what I'd do without her. We did get a bit of respite care last week. Someone came around to help in the evenings as well, but it just made Mum more distressed because she doesn't know them, and she panics . . .'

Karen nodded. It was an impossible situation.

'Maybe you could take a sabbatical?'

'I can't afford it. If I don't work, I have no money to pay Priya's wages. The only option is to put Mum in a home, and I just don't want to do that.'

'I understand,' Karen said.

'I know they're pretty good these days, and other people I know who have elderly relatives in care homes say they're happy, but I just feel like I'm letting her down.'

'It must be incredibly hard,' Karen said. 'If she was in a local place, you could still see her every evening and on weekends.'

Rick didn't reply, and Karen guessed she had said the wrong thing. It was such a deeply personal decision.

'I don't know if there's anything I can do. Rick, I want to help. I really do. But I don't know how.'

'It's not your problem,' Rick said as he pulled into a parking space outside the station and switched off the engine.

'I might not be able to solve your problems, but I can listen – and you know I'll do what I can to help if you need me.'

'Thanks, Sarge,' Rick said, but his tone and body language communicated he didn't want to talk about it anymore.

As they walked up to the entrance, Rick said, 'I've been thinking about that playing card you asked that moody SOCO to get out of the drain. Weird thing to find down there. Didn't look like it had been there long.'

Karen smiled, pleased it wasn't only her who'd noticed the tetchiness of the new scenes of crime officer. 'Yes, it is odd. I was thinking some kind of calling card, but I'm probably only thinking that because I went with Sophie last night to hear Dr Michaels's talk.'

Rick grimaced. 'Yes, Sophie's been telling me all about it.'

'And I bet you found that incredibly enjoyable,' Karen joked.

'*Enjoyable* isn't quite the word I'd use,' Rick said, grinning and looking a bit more like his old self.

CHAPTER SIX

Karen and Rick went straight to the CID office, but Sophie wasn't at her desk.

Farzana waved to get Karen's attention. 'There's a phone call for you,' she said, holding up the handset on her desk. 'I was just about to take a message, but I can put it through to you now.'

'Thanks,' Karen said as the phone on her desk chirped.

She picked it up. 'DS Karen Hart.'

'Hi there, this is Dr Michaels. Remember me?'

'Of course, Dr Michaels. How can I help?' Karen leaned on her desk, trying to peer into Morgan's office to see if he was back from his course yet.

'I thought you might have called. I wondered if I missed you?'

'Sorry?' Karen said.

'Well, I thought you might have phoned to arrange my visit. We talked about it last night.'

'Right, the thing is, we are quite busy today, so—'

'I wouldn't take up much of your time. I'd just sit and observe. I'll be as quiet as a mouse.'

Karen rolled her eyes. She really didn't need this right now. 'I'm sure, but we've got a potential abduction on our hands at the moment, and I really need to focus on that.'

'Now a visit to your station sounds even more attractive. Why don't you use me?'

'Use you?'

'Yes, like a resource. My brain is at your disposal.'

Karen waited a beat, took a deep breath, and then said, 'Thank you very much for the offer, but today is not going to be suitable. I'm sorry.'

'Maybe I could persuade you with the offer of lunch?'

Did this man never take a hint? After having to deal with Tim Farthing earlier, she could really do without another overconfident egotist today.

'Sorry, I have to go now. Goodbye,' she said quickly, and hung up.

Rick lifted his eyebrows. It was clear he'd been earwigging on Karen's conversation.

'That was Dr Michaels,' Karen said. 'He wants to come and observe, see how our police station is run here. But I told him it wasn't a good time.'

'Sophie will be disappointed,' Rick said.

'That's true.' Karen frowned. 'But where is Sophie?'

At that moment Sophie walked in, carrying a pile of files. Arnie Hodgson was with her.

Karen liked Arnie now that she had got to know him. At first, she'd found him lazy and very messy, and occasionally a bit old-fashioned. But she soon realised he was a decent man, and despite appearances, he got things done when he put his mind to it.

'Sophie, did you find anything on missing women locally?'

'Yes,' Sophie said, unloading the files on to her desk and pushing her curly hair back from her face. 'I tried to call you, but it just went straight to answerphone. So I emailed you the details.'

'What did you find out?'

'One report seems most likely to match our abduction victim. A woman who lives in Aubourn. Her name is Tamara Lomax, aged thirty-three. She was reported missing by her husband, Aiden Lomax. Apparently, she didn't turn up for work this morning, and her boss was worried and called her husband.'

'When was she last seen?'

'Eight o'clock this morning. That's when she left for work.'

'Who's spoken to the husband?'

'No one in person yet. It's only been a few hours, and until the report of the abduction there was no reason to think she was in danger. It wasn't an immediate priority.'

'Right,' Karen said. 'I'm going to go and speak to Aiden Lomax. Can you get me his address and details?'

'I've already done it,' Sophie said, plucking a sheet of A4 off her desk. 'I've also emailed it to you.'

Karen should have known Sophie would be on the ball. She should have checked her emails earlier.

'Good work.'

Arnie plopped himself down behind his desk as Rick filled Sophie in on the case so far. Karen did a cursory check of her emails to make sure she wasn't missing anything else.

Sophie slid into her own seat and rested her elbows on the desk. 'Was there any physical evidence at the scene?'

'Not much,' Rick said. 'Possible tyre tracks. Part of the van was caught on camera. I've sent the footage to Harinder. Hopefully he'll be able to get some identifying features of the van from the video even if he can't make out the number plate. Oh, and also a playing card down the drain, along with an empty packet of Monster Munch.'

'A playing card?' Sophie rested her chin on her hand. 'That's fascinating.'

'Why?' Rick asked with a frown.

'Playing cards were used in one of Dr Michaels's old cases. It was the calling card for a killer he tracked.'

'If it was a calling card,' Rick said, 'then why would it be down the drain where nobody would look for it?'

Sophie was silent for a second or two, and then shrugged and said, 'Well, somebody looked for it, because we found it.'

'Thanks to Sarge,' Rick said. 'She spotted it. The new scenes of crime guy didn't want to get his hands dirty.'

'That doesn't sound like a scenes of crime officer.'

'No. It was the new SOCO, Tim Farthing. He was convinced there hadn't been an abduction and pretty much told us we were wasting our time.'

'Imagine if it was a sign . . . It could be just like one of Dr Michaels's cases,' Sophie said.

Rick scoffed. 'Really? What about the empty packet of Monster Munch then? Is that a calling card too? The Monster Munch Mutilator?' He laughed at his own joke.

Sophie narrowed her eyes. 'Actually—' she began, but Arnie interrupted, rubbing his stomach.

'Oh, I could murder a packet of Monster Munch. I love them. Pickled onion, the best flavour in the world.'

'Anyway,' Karen said, standing up. 'Back to the case. I'm heading to see Aiden Lomax. Who's coming with me?'

'Me!' Sophie said eagerly.

'Are you all right to stay here, Rick? You can start on local traffic cameras and coordinate any findings. And let me know when Morgan gets back, would you?'

'Absolutely, Sarge. You can rely on me.'

'That's if the Monster Munch Mutilator doesn't get him first,' Arnie said, standing up and chuckling.

'Honestly,' Sophie said with a huff, as she reached for her coat.

'I can't believe Rick and Arnie,' she said to Karen as they made their way to the car. 'A woman is missing. It's no laughing matter, and the card could be important.'

'It's just how they handle things. It's their way of letting off steam,' Karen said. 'It's nothing personal.'

'It's easy for you to say that, but it's always me they make fun of.'

Karen got into the driver's seat, wishing she could be focusing on the questions she was going to ask Aiden Lomax instead of dealing with Sophie's hurt feelings.

'When the card turns out to be significant, they'll be laughing on the other side of their faces,' Sophie said.

Karen turned on the engine, but before she reversed out of the parking spot she asked, 'You really think it's significant then?'

'Almost certainly.'

'The fact is, it was found down the drain, so if it was a calling card, or a clue to taunt us, it's a pretty poor one. It should have been left in plain view for someone to find.'

Sophie thought about that for a moment, then sighed. 'So you think it was just discarded rubbish then?'

'Possibly. But we don't know anything for sure yet, so we have to focus on what we do know, and that is that Aiden Lomax has reported his wife missing. Now, what did you uncover about Mr Lomax?'

As they headed to Aubourn, Sophie filled Karen in on what she had found out about the Lomaxes so far.

They were a couple with no children and had married four years ago. Aiden Lomax said there had been no arguments between him and his wife recently. He insisted his wife's behaviour had been completely normal and that he had waved her off to work at eight o'clock that morning.

'And what do we know about Tamara's boss?'

'Not much,' Sophie said. 'But I thought we could get her boss's details from Aiden.'

Karen nodded. 'All right. I suppose he's rung around friends and family?'

'I don't think so,' Sophie said. 'I didn't ask him. Sorry, I should have thought of that.'

'Well, we can ask him in person.'

'He did say he tried to call her multiple times, but her phone was switched off.'

That didn't bode well. Karen slowed the car as they approached the Lomax home. It was a large, detached house in the centre of Aubourn.

Two cars were parked on the driveway. A dark blue Lexus and a white Mini. Karen parked behind the Mini and switched off the engine.

She looked at Sophie. 'Ready?'

Sophie nodded.

'I'm sure I don't need to say this, but don't mention playing cards . . . or Monster Munch. All right?'

Sophie reached for the door handle. 'Do you want me just to take notes, keep quiet?'

'Leave the first couple of questions to me, but then you can ask questions too. You might pick up on something I miss.'

As they walked, Karen looked up at the modern red-brick house Tamara Lomax had left that morning. She'd been heading for work, just like she would have done every weekday, with no idea what fate had in store for her. Just as Karen's husband, Josh, had put Tilly in her car seat then driven away from their house unaware of the malevolent presence that had been waiting to end their lives.

She now had to talk to Tamara's husband, a man whose life was in the process of being turned upside down. Karen knew what that was like better than most.

CHAPTER SEVEN

'Here, let me move those out of the way for you,' Aiden Lomax said, lunging forward to grab a pile of fresh laundry that had been folded and was sitting on the arm of a chair.

'Sorry.' He ran a hand through his hair. 'I was supposed to put the washing away this morning, but with everything that happened . . .' He looked around the living room helplessly.

Aiden Lomax was thirty-five, tall, good-looking, and incredibly nervous; he hadn't stopped pacing since he'd let them in.

Karen sat on the red sofa, while Sophie took the matching armchair.

'Can I get you a cup of tea?' The question was asked on autopilot – practised politeness – though Karen doubted his hands could stop trembling long enough to boil the kettle.

He placed the clothes on the coffee table and rubbed a hand over his face. Then he folded his arms over his chest. He was decidedly out of his comfort zone and didn't know how to behave. Karen felt for him.

'We're fine, Mr Lomax,' Karen said. 'Why don't you sit down, and we can ask you some questions if that's okay?'

'Uh, okay. Of course.'

He sank down into a green velvet chair beside a well-stocked bookcase. A reading light arced forward over the chair, and he shoved it roughly away.

'When did you first realise Tamara was missing?' Karen asked.

He licked his lips. 'It was when her boss, Mr Casey, called me. It was nine thirty and she hadn't turned up. She was meant to be at work by nine. He was worried. It's not like her, you see.' His words were rushed, tumbling over themselves.

'Is there any reason why your wife might not have gone to work today?'

'No,' he said quickly, looking at Karen wide-eyed. 'She left the house and was going to work.'

'Was her routine any different this morning?'

'How do you mean?'

'Did she get up at the same time as usual? Wear the same type of clothes?'

'She wore . . . I can't really remember, but yes, they were just normal work clothes. I think trousers, grey ones, and a blouse. Maybe cream . . . Or it could have been white.' His head dipped forward. 'Sorry, I'm not being much help.'

'You are,' Sophie said encouragingly. 'This information is very helpful.'

'And your wife left for work the same time she normally does?' Karen asked.

'Yes, like I said, eight o'clock.'

'Does she usually drive?'

'No, only if the weather is really bad. She prefers to walk.'

'It is her car parked on the drive?'

'Yes, the Mini. It's not been driven for a couple of days.'

'Has there been anything bothering Tamara? Any problems she may have mentioned to you?'

'No, she's been completely normal. Something must have happened to her. She wouldn't just leave like this, making me worry. It's not like her.'

'And how has work been going? Does she enjoy it?' Sophie asked.

Aiden blinked and looked at Sophie, as though he couldn't understand why that would be important in the current situation.

'I suppose so.'

'How long has she been working there?' Karen asked.

'Since just before we got married, so four years.'

'Do you have a white Transit van?' Karen asked the question casually, but Aiden's reaction was extreme.

He gripped the arms of the chair and leaned forward so fast his head connected with the edge of the reading lamp. He swatted at it angrily. 'A white Transit van? Why do you ask that?'

Though Karen knew the question would make him worry, it had to be asked. Tamara could have been abducted by a stranger, but it was equally likely to be someone she knew, or at least had met in the past.

'There have been reports of a white Transit van in the village this morning. There may not be a connection,' Karen said, trying to minimise his fears.

It was a difficult dance. Though it seemed cruel to withhold information from a frantic husband, they still didn't have concrete evidence Tamara was the woman Molly saw bundled into the back of the van.

'Have you called close friends and family to see if Tamara's contacted them?' Karen asked, quickly moving on so he didn't dwell on the van.

Aiden nodded. 'I spoke to Julie Wainwright. She works with Tamara, but she hasn't heard from her.' He put his hands on his thighs, gripping them, breathing hard. 'Sorry, it's just . . . I can't believe this is happening.'

'Take your time,' Karen said.

'I could get you a glass of water,' Sophie offered, but he shook his head.

'Her sister, Rachel. She sees her quite a bit.'

'Have you spoken to Rachel?' Karen asked.

'No, I didn't want to worry her unnecessarily.'

'It might be a good idea to call her,' Karen said. 'Just in case she's heard from Tamara.'

'Right.' He just sat there. Then looked up. 'Oh, you mean I should call her now.'

'If you're up to it,' Karen said. 'We can wait.'

He stood up and pulled a mobile phone from his back pocket, stared at it for a moment and then looked at Karen. 'It's just . . . Tamara and Rachel's parents died recently. Just two months ago. Car crash. So I didn't want to . . .'

'You didn't want to scare Rachel if there was nothing wrong.'

'Exactly.'

'It's kind of you to consider her feelings,' Karen said. 'But I really think you should call her. We need to find your wife, and Rachel might know something.'

His hand shook slightly as he lifted his mobile. He swallowed hard. 'You think something's happened to her, don't you? Not an accident, but you think someone's *done* something to her.' He looked at Karen and then to Sophie, whose head was bent over her notebook.

'That would be the worst-case scenario. Right now we need to try to find Tamara as soon as possible.'

He took a deep breath and then placed the call.

Karen observed him as he did so. He paced the room, stopping beside the log burner and in front of the green velvet chair and bookcase. The shelves were full of paperbacks: Val McDermid, Ann Cleeves, Peter James. Either Tamara or Aiden, or both, was a fan of crime fiction. There was also a large collection of true crime books.

Karen's eyes skimmed the bookshelf as Aiden spoke.

'Rachel, it's Aiden. Look, I don't want to worry you, but I don't know where Tamara is. She didn't turn up for work this morning. Have you heard from her?'

He paused, listening.

'I'm sure it's nothing. I mean, she's probably fine. It's just that the police are here with me now.'

Karen could hear the raised voice of Tamara's sister on the other end of the line, but she couldn't work out what she was saying.

'You don't have to. It's all right.' Another pause. 'All right then. See you soon.'

Aiden hung up and put the phone back in his pocket. 'She's coming round. She'll be here in a few minutes.'

'Aiden, what do you think has happened to Tamara?' Karen asked.

Aiden looked lost for words. He chewed his lower lip and then collapsed back into the armchair. He put his hands over his face. 'I don't know. I just don't know.'

There were photographs framed with silver and crystals on the walls. 'Is this Tamara?' Karen asked, standing and moving towards one of the pictures.

Aiden looked up. 'Yes, and there's one on the mantelpiece of her and Rachel.'

Karen looked closely at the photographs.

The one of Tamara on her own had probably been taken on holiday. She had her back to the sea. Her light blonde, almost white, hair blew across her tanned face.

The photo had been taken while she was laughing, her head tilted back. She wore a thin gold chain around her neck.

In the second photograph, taken with her sister, Karen observed the close resemblance. They could almost be twins. It was only after careful study that the differences became clear. Rachel was a fraction shorter and had a narrower nose, slightly thinner lips and hair just a shade or two darker, though still blonde. She had a line of four moles on her right cheek, and high-arched brows. Tamara's features were broader, softer. Her eyebrows were less arched and looked more natural. Behind them were an older man and woman. 'Their parents?' Karen asked.

Aiden nodded.

Next to the framed photo on the mantel was an odd-looking carved wooden owl. Karen couldn't tell if it was intentionally deformed or the result of bad workmanship. The eyes were misshapen – one larger than the other – and the beak was open and crooked, as though the creature were screaming. Maybe it was modern art and supposed to make the viewer uncomfortable. It was creepy.

'She looks very happy here,' Karen said, pointing to the photograph of Tamara on her own.

'Honeymoon,' Aiden said. 'We were both happy.'

He wrenched his eyes away from the photographs and stared at the floor.

Karen spoke to Aiden while Sophie went into the kitchen to make tea. She had just brought three mugs into the living room when there was a knock at the door.

Aiden got to his feet. 'That's probably Rachel. I'll get it.'

Karen and Sophie stood up just as Rachel rushed in. She was recognisable from the photograph, though she had put on a little weight, which made her face rounder, more attractive. She looked pale and panicked.

'What's going on?'

Karen introduced herself and Sophie. 'Aiden reported Tamara missing this morning after she didn't turn up for work. When did you last see your sister?'

'A couple of days ago. Oh no, hang on, that's not right.' She looked at Aiden. 'A week last Sunday. I came over for Sunday lunch, didn't I?'

'Yes, that's right,' Aiden said. 'The three of us had lunch together here.'

Rachel nodded. 'We had roast lamb. That's Tamara's favourite . . . I'm sorry, that's not relevant or important.' She pressed a hand to her forehead. Then she looked back at Aiden. 'I don't understand what's happening. Where has she gone?'

'I don't know.'

'Why wouldn't she go to work?'

'I don't know,' Aiden said again and fell back into the green chair.

'Do you want a drink, Rachel?' Sophie asked. 'Tea? Coffee? I can make it for you.'

Rachel's hands clenched and unclenched repeatedly. 'No, thank you. You've tried ringing her, I guess?'

'Of course,' Aiden said. 'Her phone's switched off.'

'But you can trace it, can't you?' Rachel said, turning to Karen.

'We can certainly try,' Karen said. She didn't add that that wouldn't necessarily lead them to Tamara if the phone had been dumped.

Rachel shoved her hands in the back pockets of her jeans. 'Right, that's good. What if she's had an accident? Can you check the hospitals?'

'We have checked,' Sophie said. 'No one matching Tamara's description has been admitted to any Lincolnshire hospitals this morning.'

'But she could have had a car accident . . . Maybe she's gone off the road somewhere and is trapped.'

'Rach, they're professionals. Let them deal with it. Besides, her car is on the drive. You must have just walked past it.'

Rachel recoiled as though she'd been slapped. 'Sorry, I'm just trying to help.'

'I understand,' Karen said. 'This has come as a terrible shock, but maybe you can give us some idea where she might have gone. A favourite place she goes walking, perhaps? Or coffee shops she frequents?'

Rachel's lower lip trembled. The woman was close to tears. 'I don't know. She likes going to that garden centre, Pennells. Do you know it?'

'I do,' Karen said. 'We'll look into that.'

'She's hardly likely to have gone shopping for plants and left us all to worry,' Aiden snapped.

'We'll look into every possibility,' Karen said.

Karen and Sophie spent the next twenty minutes talking Aiden through what would happen next, and after promising to be in touch very soon, they left Aiden and Rachel to their anxious wait.

CHAPTER EIGHT

Karen checked her watch for the third time. She had been sitting with Sophie in the reception area of a converted barn – the office building owned by Tamara Lomax's boss – for the past fifteen minutes.

The receptionist sat at her desk opposite them, typing away on her computer, occasionally shooting them an apologetic smile.

Karen got to her feet and stretched.

It wouldn't be so bad if they hadn't called ahead to let Tamara's boss know they were on the way. Was there really something so important that he couldn't delay it to talk about his missing employee?

Karen walked over to the desk. 'Do you think you could chase him up, please? We have a lot of other people to talk to today.'

The receptionist looked horrified at the idea. She lifted her hands from the keyboard and then shot a look over her shoulder. 'I'm not sure. Mr Casey wouldn't appreciate that.'

'I'm not concerned with what Mr Casey would appreciate,' Karen said, keeping her tone polite because it wasn't the receptionist's fault they were being kept waiting. 'Talking to us is more important than whatever business Mr Casey is getting up to right now.'

The receptionist sucked in her lower lip, reached for the handset on her desk, and then hesitated. 'It's just that he doesn't like to be interrupted during meetings.'

'What's your name?' Karen asked.

'Sarah.'

'Sarah, one of your colleagues is missing. Tamara could be in danger, and so I'm not content to sit around here and wait for your boss to finish his meeting. Do you really think whatever he's doing is more urgent than finding Tamara?'

'Oh, no, of course not. It's just I haven't been in this job long. I don't want to lose it.'

'I'll deal with it,' Karen said. 'Put me through. I'll tell him I forced you to do it.'

Sarah picked up the handset and passed it to Karen, then pressed a couple of buttons. The phone rang once and was abruptly answered by a stern male voice.

'I told you, no interruptions,' he barked.

'This is Detective Sergeant Karen Hart, Mr Casey. I don't appreciate being kept waiting. If you prefer, we can escort you to the station now to answer our questions.'

There was an audible breath and then a pause.

'I was just on my way to come and greet you,' he said. There was a click as he hung up.

Karen gave a satisfied smile and passed the handset back to the receptionist.

Less than thirty seconds later, the door behind the reception desk opened, and a balding man, wearing a grey suit, walked towards them. He stopped very close to Karen, invading her personal space, and looked down at her disapprovingly.

She guessed he was in his late forties or early fifties. What was left of his hair was turning grey at the edges.

'DS Karen Hart. My colleague, DC Sophie Jones.' They both produced their warrant cards.

'Right. This is about Tamara,' he said.

'That's right. You were the first person to notice she was missing. Can we go to your office and ask you a few questions? Alternatively, you could accompany us to the station?'

'That won't be necessary.' He turned and scowled at the receptionist. 'I'm sorry you weren't properly looked after by my staff. There must've been some misunderstanding.'

'No, Sarah was very helpful,' Karen said. 'I insisted she call you again.'

He huffed. 'I'm sorry I kept you waiting,' he said, not sounding sorry in the least. 'But I'm a busy man. I had meetings this morning. I can't just stop everything because—'

'—because one of your staff is missing and may be in danger?' Sophie asked. She didn't even attempt to keep the disapproval from her voice.

He stiffened, perhaps becoming aware of how callously he was behaving.

'I'm just trying to keep my business running,' he said. 'With Tamara missing, we are very short-staffed.'

'And I'm sure you can understand that we are very busy too, Mr Casey,' Karen said, marvelling at the man's selfishness. 'Any delays could have serious consequences.'

'Yes, well, I have apologised.' He pushed open the door to his office.

It was a large room dominated by a huge mahogany desk, and the padded chair behind it looked more like a throne. The two visitors' chairs in front of the desk looked decidedly less comfortable.

'Take a seat,' he urged, offering a weak smile.

Karen and Sophie sat as he lowered himself into the majestic, plump chair. He pushed himself back, getting comfortable, then crossed his arms.

'So what is it you want to know?'

'You reported Tamara missing this morning?' Karen asked.

'No,' he said. 'I didn't. I just called her husband when she didn't turn up for work. I thought she'd overslept. We had important work on today, a meeting with new clients. Tamara is my right-hand woman, as it were. I needed her here.'

'What time did you call her husband?'

He thought for a moment, stroking his chin. 'Just about nine thirty. *After* the meeting was supposed to start, and I was standing around like an idiot waiting for her.' He scowled again.

It was all about him, Karen thought. Did he really not have any compassion for Tamara?

'Had you noticed any changes in Tamara's behaviour recently?'

'No,' he said. 'Nothing out of the ordinary.'

'Any bad feeling at the office? Arguments?'

'No,' he said again. 'And before you imply anything else, I'd like to state we had a perfectly civil working relationship. Nothing else. She has been working here for years. She was a good assistant.'

'Was?' Karen asked, immediately picking up on his use of the past tense.

'Of course. I'm not going to be keeping her on now. This morning she's cost me over a quarter of a million pounds' worth of business.'

Sophie looked up from her notebook. 'Mr Casey, Tamara could be in danger. She may have had an accident, or someone may have deliberately hurt her, and you've decided to fire her?'

He huffed out a breath and rubbed his hands over his face. 'Yes, well, I realise how that must sound. I was angry. I still am.

This morning was incredibly embarrassing, but I'm not heartless. Obviously I don't want her to be in danger or injured.'

While Sophie asked some more questions, Karen thought about Casey's reactions. He was a thoroughly selfish and unlikeable man, but Karen had to push her feelings aside and focus on his responses. His insistence that they had a working relationship and nothing else triggered alarm bells. Had he tried it on with Tamara, perhaps been rebuffed? She was a young, attractive woman. Was he the type of boss to try to use his powerful position to put pressure on her? Karen couldn't rule it out.

When she'd spoken to Aiden Lomax, Karen had got the impression that Tamara's boss had been worried about her, but now, talking to Casey, she had the distinct impression he was more annoyed than concerned. That led her to think perhaps Tamara had turned up late for work on more than one occasion.

'So what makes you think that she'd purposely not turn up for an important meeting?' Karen asked.

Casey fiddled with a piece of paper on his desk. 'She has overslept a few times in the past. And once she phoned in sick, and I later found out she'd gone to Wimbledon! So it isn't as though her past behaviour is exemplary.'

'You said she was a good assistant.'

'She is,' he said, this time taking care to use the present tense. 'When she's here, but she can be flighty and unreliable at times.'

'Is there anyone here she gets on well with, perhaps may have confided in?' Karen asked.

'She gets on fine with all of them.'

'And how many people work here?'

'Eight of us,' he said. 'That's why if one of the staff goes missing it's a big deal. Besides, we don't have great staff retention here. They come and go. It's impossible to get good reliable staff these days.'

Karen thought that was probably down to his attitude.

He pushed the piece of paper he'd been playing with away from him. 'Look, I hope she's all right, I really do, but I'm sorry, I can't tell you anything else. I don't know anything about her personal life.'

'What about her husband? You spoke to him this morning. Have you met him before?'

'Once or twice at company events. But I don't know him, not really.'

'Anything you can tell us about Tamara could help. If she'd been seeing someone else perhaps?'

'I think you should ask her husband about that. I wouldn't know anything about it.'

'You've worked with her for more than four years. There must be something you can tell us.'

'I can't tell you anything personal. She was good at her job, very good. That's why I hadn't got rid of her after the Wimbledon thing. She seemed to get on well with everyone here, but I wouldn't say she was close to anyone.'

Karen glanced at Sophie, who was busy making notes. They weren't getting anything helpful from Casey. They needed to talk to people who really knew Tamara. There had to be someone here she chatted to, perhaps confided in, as they gathered around the coffee machine during their breaks.

'Do any of your employees drive a white Transit van?' Karen asked.

'No, no one has a van as far as I'm aware.'

'Does the company own any vehicles?'

'No.' He leaned forward, elbows on his desk, trying to peer at Sophie's notes. 'What are you writing?'

'A record of this meeting,' Sophie replied, surprised at the question.

'I hope you haven't put something down about me taking too long to talk to you. That was a misunderstanding. I didn't realise it was so serious.'

'Why would two police officers be visiting your place of work to ask you questions if it wasn't serious?' Sophie's voice had a barbed edge to it, but her innocent, almost cherub-like face made it seem like a perfectly innocent enquiry.

'I don't know.' He leaned back in his chair. 'I didn't give it much thought. I had an incredibly busy morning. Very stressful.'

'I think we've all had a stressful morning,' Karen said, thinking, *especially Tamara*.

'Well, are we done now?' He put his hands flat on the desk, pushing himself up.

'I suppose we are. For now,' Karen said. 'I'll leave my card in case you think of anything else that could be important.'

He took the offered card, glanced at it and then placed it face down on his desk, presumably never to be looked at again.

'But we'd like to talk to the other members of staff. Particularly anyone who worked closely with Tamara.'

He groaned. 'That will absolutely ruin the working day. They'll never settle to do any work after this.'

'I think you need to get your priorities in order, Mr Casey,' Karen said. 'Tamara Lomax is missing. I'm not concerned about your lack of productivity today. I care about locating Tamara.'

'Fine,' he said grumpily. 'I'll take you down to the main office and introduce you, but if you could keep it as short as possible, I'd be very grateful.'

Karen shook her head in disbelief as he led them out into the corridor.

'It will take as long as it takes, Mr Casey.'

He grunted and grumbled under his breath as he led them out of his office.

CHAPTER NINE

After some persuasion, Mr Casey arranged to have the contents removed from a room he'd been using for storage, so they could interview the rest of the staff in private. Though he called it an office, Karen thought it looked more like a storage cupboard.

With some difficulty, they managed to fit a small desk and a couple of chairs into the space. Karen sat behind the desk, while Sophie remained standing, leaning against the wall. The office hadn't been completely emptied, and there was a pile of boxes stacked perilously on top of the tall filing cabinet in the corner.

Before they called in the first member of staff, Karen put a call through to Morgan, who had finally finished with his course. He gave her an update on the white van that had been used in the abduction.

Unfortunately, it wasn't good news. Traffic cameras in the area around Aubourn had picked up a total of fifteen white vans within half an hour. Harinder had not yet been able to extract any more information from the video they had from Mrs Chelsea's security system. Morgan had assigned a family liaison officer to wait with Aiden Lomax and try to get him to open up, but so far they'd had no success on that front either.

'What did you make of Aiden Lomax?' Morgan asked.

'Difficult to say. He was really nervous and edgy, but of course that was understandable because his wife is missing.'

'I've asked the family liaison officer to keep a close eye on him.'

'Good. He told us they hadn't been having any marital problems, but then again he also said his wife had no trouble at work, but according to her boss she'd been late and unreliable on numerous occasions, and he was close to firing her.'

'Interesting,' Morgan said, with typical understatement.

'Other than that, Tamara's boss hasn't been very helpful. I'm planning to stay here and speak to other members of staff to see if any of them can tell us more about Tamara. I've also asked Mr Casey for the CCTV that's set up outside his office block, focused on the car park. Just in case Tamara did turn up here for work.'

'You think Casey is lying?'

'I'm not sure, but reporting her missing would be a good alibi. And he's definitely the type of person to lie if it would save his own skin.'

Morgan gave a rare chuckle. 'You didn't warm to him then?'

'No. He isn't worried that Tamara is missing. All he's bothered about is missing out on some work this morning. He's focused on revenue. I can't tell whether he doesn't understand the importance of the situation or genuinely doesn't care.'

'Sounds like a great bloke,' Morgan said dryly. 'I'll let you know if we get any more on the van. At least we've managed to narrow it down to fifteen possibles.'

'Unless the van took a different route out of Aubourn that wasn't monitored by traffic cameras. Has Rick looked into that?'

'Yes, we should be okay. All roads monitored. Unless the van took off on a private road, we should have caught it on one of the cameras.'

'All right. We'll head back to the station after these interviews,' Karen said. 'Hopefully it won't take long.'

After she hung up, Karen turned to Sophie. 'Ready?'

Sophie nodded. 'Yes. Shall I bring the first one in?'

'Yes, thanks.'

Karen shuffled the personnel files Casey had given her. As Sophie reached for the door handle, she said, 'There's not much chance of Tamara turning up unharmed now, is there?'

Karen paused, then said, 'I don't think so. I hope she does. But I've had a bad feeling about this case from the moment I spoke to Molly McCarthy.' Others had suggested Molly's description of the abduction had been make-believe, but after speaking to the little girl, Karen's instinct told her to trust Molly's account. 'Anyway, let's bring in Tamara's first colleague.' Karen nodded towards the door.

Sophie squared her shoulders and walked out.

In the short time Sophie was gone, Karen flipped through all the personnel files. Casey had forgotten to give her Tamara's. Or had he omitted it on purpose?

Sophie came back into the room with a young man. He was dressed in a navy suit and a red tie with white spots. He cleared his throat nervously.

'Noah Hillock,' he said, holding out his hand. 'She's not in any trouble, is she? Tamara, I mean.'

'Tamara was reported missing this morning when she didn't turn up for work. We are a bit worried about her.'

'Oh, I see,' he said, sitting down and then nodding distractedly.

'Did she mention anything to you about planning to miss work today?' Karen asked.

'No, not to me, but then she wouldn't. We're not really that close.' Karen allowed the silence to stretch out in the hope he would say something else, and he did. 'My desk is opposite hers, so we talk occasionally, but that's it.' He ran his hand through his hair.

His face was plump, the skin unlined. He had a youthful face, but his hair was thinning prematurely. He continued: 'We just talk about normal things, you know. How bad the weather has been, moaning about paperwork, that sort of thing.'

Again, Karen let the pause tease more from him.

'Actually, we talk about my kids sometimes. I've got two. Boy and a girl.'

He began to dig around in his jacket pocket. *He isn't really going to show me photographs of his children right now, is he?* Karen wondered. *Oh, yes, he is.*

He pulled out his wallet, flipped it open and proudly showed Karen two small pictures of his children.

'Lovely,' Karen said. 'You were telling me about Tamara . . .'

'Of course. Sorry,' he said, shoving his wallet back in his pocket. 'She's worked here longer than me. I started here about three years ago. She's always friendly, always smiling. She does a good job. I think Mr Casey relies on her more than he does the rest of us.' He looked down at his hands. 'They were always huddled away in Mr Casey's office.'

Karen raised an eyebrow.

Noah flushed when he saw it. 'Oh, I didn't mean like that! Just that, you know, she's always helping him with work things.'

'I see,' Karen said. 'Have you met Tamara's husband?'

'Yes, a couple of times, I think. He's always at the Christmas party.' He looked up and to the right, focusing on the ceiling tiles as he tried to remember. 'I think he came to one of Mr Casey's barbecues last summer. He held it for all the staff and their partners when he landed a big contract. I didn't really speak to him much – Tamara's husband, I mean. We've not really got much in common I wouldn't think.'

'Why do you say that?' Karen asked.

'Oh, he's just one of those physical types. He looks like one of those men who go to the gym a lot.' He looked down at his own physique, waving a hand. 'I don't, as you can probably tell.'

'Do you know who Tamara was close to? Anyone she might have confided in?'

He sucked in a breath through his teeth. 'I don't, no. We all get on all right in the office, have a bit of a laugh sometimes, but we don't see much of each other outside work. It isn't really that sort of place.'

The door suddenly opened. It was Mr Casey.

Noah straightened in his seat, spine stiff as a board.

'Is everything all right?' Casey asked, looking at Noah meaningfully and then at Karen and Sophie.

'Everything is fine,' Karen said. 'We're just trying to get on with the interviews.'

His gaze swept around the room. 'Well . . . just thought I'd check if you needed anything.'

'As I said, we're fine, thank you.'

Reluctantly, Casey turned away and left, but he didn't close the door behind him. Sophie pushed off from the wall, leaned over and shut the door.

'How do you find working for Mr Casey?' Karen asked. 'Is he a difficult boss to work for?'

Noah shifted in his seat. 'He's just a stickler for preciseness, and he doesn't suffer fools gladly,' he said, as though he was repeating a well-rehearsed phrase. Perhaps one he'd heard from Casey himself. It was the type of thing the man would boast about. Noah probably thought Casey would approve of that description.

'Honestly, though,' Karen said, leaning forward. 'Anything you tell us won't get back to him.'

Noah looked very uncomfortable. 'He's fine. Just a boss. I'm happy enough. I've got a nine-to-five job and it pays the bills.'

'Thank you for your time,' Karen said and nodded to Sophie.

Noah couldn't leave the room fast enough, and Karen was starting to think there was something strange going on at this office. The dynamic was very unbalanced. What was Noah afraid of?

Was Noah simply scared of losing his job, or was something else going on?

The other members of staff they spoke to acted in a similar way, intensifying the alarm bells ringing in Karen's mind. They all seemed cowed by Mr Casey, but they wouldn't say a bad word against him. Karen found that very odd because, if he was her boss, she would certainly have a lot to say. He didn't appear to be the type of man to inspire such loyalty. It certainly hadn't been earned through kindness, understanding and the good treatment of his employees.

The final member of staff they interviewed was Julie Wainwright, the woman Aiden Lomax had mentioned. She was young, only twenty-five, with long dark hair, neatly tied back, and pale skin.

She sat in the chair in front of the desk, hands clasped tightly together over her knees. She smiled nervously when Karen introduced herself.

'Did you know Tamara well?' Karen asked.

'Yeah, pretty well.'

Karen looked up, surprised. Julie was the first member of staff to admit to knowing Tamara well, rather than trying to insist they knew nothing about her despite the fact they'd shared a workspace for years.

'Do you have any idea what might've happened to her this morning?'

Julie shook her head.

'Did she mention anything she was doing today? Anything out of the ordinary?'

'No, she didn't say anything.'

'Mr Casey said she's done this sort of thing before, just disappeared.'

Julie pulled a face. 'Hardly. She did it once, and that was because she got tickets to Wimbledon. She didn't want to pass them up, but she also knew that Mr Casey would tell her no, she couldn't go, because she hadn't given him enough notice. So she decided to call in sick.' Julie spoke quietly, and constantly looked over her shoulder to make sure the door was firmly shut.

'Is he a bit of an ogre to work for?' Karen asked.

'He's not the easiest boss I've ever had,' Julie said diplomatically.

'When was the last time you saw Tamara?'

'Yesterday, at work.'

'Do you know her husband, Aiden?'

'Yes, but not that well.'

'Had he and Tamara been getting on okay recently?'

Julie hesitated.

'I know you don't want to tell tales about your friend, but it could be important, Julie.'

The young woman stared down at her fingers. 'I think they'd been having problems recently. Arguing.'

'Do you know what they were arguing about?'

Julie shook her head. 'I'm not sure. I think she thought Aiden might be playing away, or maybe . . .' She paused, took a deep breath. 'I don't think I should be saying any of this.'

'Julie . . .'

'I know.' Julie put her hands over her face. 'It could be important. It's not like I'm grassing her up.' She was clearly having an internal conflict.

'We are not here to judge anybody. We just need to find her,' Karen said.

Julie nodded slowly. 'I'm not saying this because I think Aiden would have done anything. I don't know him that well, but from how Tamara talked about him, it wasn't like she was scared. I don't think there was ever any domestic violence involved. I think I would have picked up on that.'

Karen waited for the woman to continue.

'I think Tamara might have been seeing someone else. As a kind of revenge, because Aiden had been playing around.'

Karen sat back in her chair. She had half expected the first suspect to be someone close to Tamara. It usually was. Stranger abductions were rare. If Tamara had been abducted, it was most likely by someone that she knew. Aiden had been nervous this morning. Because he was worried about his wife? Or because he had committed a crime and was trying to cover it up? But why bundle his own wife into the back of a van? It didn't make sense.

'What makes you think she was seeing someone else? Did she tell you?'

'No, but one day last week she told Aiden she was out with me and when he couldn't get through to Tamara, he called me on my mobile. I felt like a right mug. She hadn't even warned me! I didn't know what to say on the phone.'

'Was he angry?'

'I just blagged it. After saying she wasn't with me, I backtracked and told him she was in the shower. I made out like I got confused and thought he was someone else calling for a different friend. I'm not sure he believed me.'

Karen wasn't surprised. It didn't sound like a believable scenario in the slightest.

'What happened?'

'I called Tamara and told her what happened. She just laughed it off. Said it would be fine and she'd make up some excuse.'

'And was it fine?'

'As far as I know. She came into work the next day laughing about it.'

After asking Julie if she knew anyone Tamara was connected with who owned a white van and getting a negative response, Karen said, 'Thanks very much, Julie. We'll probably be in touch again to ask more questions, but you've been really helpful.'

The woman's eyes widened. 'Is that it, then?'

Karen nodded, stood up and squeezed behind the desk so she could open the door. After Julie left, she turned to Sophie. 'I think we need to have another chat with Aiden Lomax.'

CHAPTER TEN

Sophie and Karen were just around the corner from the Lomaxes' house when Sophie took a call.

'Hi, Rick.' She groaned. 'Really? Now? All right. I'll tell her.' She hung up.

'What was all that about?' Karen asked.

'Apparently Churchill wants us back at the station now for an in-person briefing. He was *displeased* when Rick gave him an update because he'd expected *you* to keep him abreast of all developments.'

'So he's unhappy I haven't checked in with him?'

'That's about the size of it.'

'There's not much point updating him until after we've spoken to Tamara's husband,' Karen said. She had a lot of questions for Aiden Lomax. He'd given no indication he and Tamara were suffering from marital problems. There was a good reason for that – it made him look guilty.

Karen slowed as she approached the junction. 'I'm making an executive decision. We are going to see Aiden first. It won't take long, and we'll have more information ready for the briefing.'

Sophie bit her lower lip. 'Are you sure, Sarge? DCI Churchill will blow his top; you know what he's like.'

Karen took the turning and then glanced at Sophie. 'I thought you were getting on better with him now?'

'I am. Well, I'm trying to. It looks like he's here to stay now, and he's taken DI Morgan's position as head of our team, so it looks like I don't have any choice but to get along with him.'

'I'm following Arnie's advice,' Karen said.

'I'm not sure that's a good idea!'

Karen grinned at the shocked look on Sophie's face. 'He's been working with Churchill for a while, and he says he knows how to handle him. Basically, agree with the DCI, but do things on your own schedule. We'll get back for the briefing, but we'll speak to Aiden first.'

'But what if he finds out we didn't go straight back to the station and blames me for not passing on the message? I'll get in trouble.'

'No, Sophie, you won't. If he finds out, then I'll tell him I made the decision. All right?'

Sophie tilted her head, thinking about it. 'I suppose so, but I do feel a bit uncomfortable going against authority.'

'It'll be fine.'

'Sorry, Sarge, I know you think I'm being a big baby about it.'

'Sophie, following the rules closely is who you are. I wouldn't have you any other way.'

'Really?'

'Yes, but we're still stopping at the Lomaxes' house.'

'All right,' Sophie said, sounding a little more confident.

'It's important we speak to him as soon as possible if he is involved in his wife's disappearance. He could have set this whole thing up.'

'You mean he might have killed her? Then pretended she disappeared? Abducted her himself?'

'That's exactly what I mean.'

Most female murder victims were killed by a so-called loved one or family member.

'Aiden did seem worried though, didn't he?'

'Yes, but what if he was worried about getting caught rather than the fact his wife was missing?' Karen suggested.

'If that's true,' Sophie said, 'what about the card? The Queen of Hearts?'

'That could be nothing, completely unrelated. It was found down the drain, after all.'

Sophie was quiet for a moment, digesting the information.

Karen pulled up outside the Lomax house. 'It looks like Rachel is still here,' she said, noticing the blue Astra parked behind Tamara's white Mini.

'Imagine how she'll feel if Aiden has done something to her sister. She's here to offer him support and he might have—'

'Don't get carried away,' Karen said. 'We don't know yet if he's guilty. That's why we need to ask questions, right?'

Sophie nodded.

It was Rachel who answered the door. She looked as though she'd been crying.

'Is there any news?' she asked quickly.

'I'm afraid we don't have much of an update yet,' Karen said. 'But we need speak to Aiden again.'

'Then you'd better come in,' she said, looking even paler than she had earlier. There were small dents in her lower lip where she'd been biting down on it.

Aiden came out into the hallway. His whole body was tense. 'Have you found something?'

'We've only come to ask more questions, I'm afraid, Aiden,' Karen said. 'Can we come inside?'

He nodded dully and led them into the living room.

Karen and Sophie took a seat on the sofa, just as they had before, but Rachel didn't sit down. Aiden sank into the green velvet chair while Rachel hovered behind him.

'We've spoken to Tamara's boss,' Karen said, not wanting to waste any time. She knew she was already taking a chance by stopping off at the Lomax house before going back to the station. She didn't want to anger Churchill by delaying the briefing any longer than absolutely necessary.

'Did he tell you anything?' Rachel asked.

'He did say that Tamara hadn't been getting on well at work. In fact, he came close to firing her. She skipped work on a few occasions, once for Wimbledon.'

'The Wimbledon thing?' Aiden rolled his eyes. 'I'd forgotten all about that. It was just a one-off. No big deal. Mr Casey is just uptight. I don't even know his first name. His staff all have to call him Mr Casey. Weird, right?'

'I don't see why this is important,' Rachel said. 'How is this meant to help us find Tamara?'

'Calm down, Rachel,' Aiden snapped.

Her body jolted as though she'd received an electric shock, and she gave Aiden a wounded look.

'We interviewed all of Tamara's colleagues, and although they all spoke warmly of her, they also told us something that we need to discuss, Aiden. You may want to do this in private,' Karen said, giving him the chance to ask Rachel to leave the room.

They would also need to ask Rachel if she was aware of Tamara or Aiden seeing other people, but it seemed cruel to spring it on Aiden in front of his sister-in-law.

There was a chance that he really was simply a worried husband.

Aiden frowned. He looked at Rachel and then back to Karen. 'Why?' His tone was guarded.

'We have some sensitive questions, and you might feel more comfortable answering them alone.'

'You don't mind me being here, do you, Aiden? He hasn't got any secrets, have you?' Rachel gripped the back of the chair as she looked down at her brother-in-law.

'No, of course not,' Aiden said, but he had started to sweat.

'Maybe you could make some tea,' Sophie suggested, smiling at Rachel.

'I don't want a cup of tea!' Rachel's temper exploded. 'I want you to tell us what is going on!'

Karen looked at Aiden for confirmation she should proceed with Rachel present.

He nodded. 'Yeah, just ask your questions. Get on with it.'

'When I spoke to your wife's colleagues, someone mentioned they thought you'd been seeing someone else.'

For a moment, the room was completely silent. Neither Aiden nor Rachel moved. Aiden seemed to have stopped breathing. Then he suddenly became animated.

He stood up, his fists clenched at his sides. 'How dare you! Who said that? Tell me!'

Rachel blinked, and then stepped forward and put a tentative hand on his arm. 'Don't worry, Aiden. It's obviously nonsense. It must be someone spreading gossip. An evil person, whoever they are.'

Karen said nothing, just waited.

'Well, are you going to tell me who's been saying these horrible things?' Aiden demanded.

'No, I can't do that,' Karen said slowly. 'What I'm doing is giving you the chance to tell me the truth.'

He looked up at the ceiling and laughed. 'I can't believe this. My wife is missing, and you're asking me if I played around?'

'Did you?' Karen asked.

'No,' he said, then hit the side of his fist against the bookshelf. 'No, I didn't.'

He didn't meet Karen's gaze when he replied. A sign of guilt, perhaps? It was hard to tell. After more than a decade in the job, instinct told her Aiden was holding out on them.

'Was Tamara seeing someone else?' Karen asked.

His head whipped around, this time looking Karen directly in the eye. 'I can't believe you would ask that question right now.'

'It's important, Aiden. If Tamara was seeing someone else, we need to question them. Maybe you had an open relationship. If either of you had affairs, I'm not judging you. No one is. But if you are holding anything back, you need to tell us, because even if it's embarrassing, it could help find her.'

Aiden sank back down into his seat.

'I think it's disgusting,' Rachel said in a strangled voice. 'We're going to be putting in a complaint.'

She put her hand on Aiden's shoulder, but he shrugged it off. 'Get off, Rachel. Stop fussing. I can't stand it.'

Rachel took a step back and then burst into tears.

Sophie stood and gently put an arm around Rachel. 'Why don't we go into the kitchen now and make some tea?' she suggested kindly.

'I don't want tea,' Rachel said tearfully.

'All right, but I think you could both do with a bit of a breather.'

Rachel allowed Sophie to lead her out of the room.

Karen leaned forward until she was sitting on the very edge of the sofa. 'Aiden, this is your chance. I need you to be completely honest with me because I'm going to be honest with you. If we discover you've been lying, whether it's because you don't think it's any of my business, or because you think I'll treat you differently . . . whatever the reason, if you lie to me, you go straight to the top of the suspect list. Do you understand?'

Aiden blinked. 'Why would I be a suspect? I'm the victim here. My wife is missing.' He looked distraught. His hands were trembling. Karen searched his face for any sign he might be lying, but he genuinely seemed upset.

'Aiden, I'm sorry, but I have to ask these questions. It's part of my job. This is how we find Tamara.'

His eyes filled with tears, and he bowed his head. 'Right, but I don't know what to do. I never wanted any of this to happen.'

He rested his face in his hands, so Karen could no longer study his expression. His shoulders shook. He was crying, but was he putting it on? It was so difficult to tell. This part of the job wasn't easy. It felt natural in this situation to offer sympathy and support and to treat the husband as a victim, but experience warned Karen that she could be looking at their prime suspect.

A couple of minutes later, Sophie and Rachel came back into the living room. Rachel was now dry-eyed, but she still wore a stony expression, and glared at Karen, who obviously wasn't topping her favourites list at the moment.

'We have to head back to the station now,' Karen said. 'But we'll keep you updated. By the way, where is your family liaison officer?'

'I sent her away,' Rachel said. 'She kept hanging around, getting in the way.'

Karen noted that Aiden had been annoyed with Rachel for doing the same thing.

'Well, let me know if you'd like to have the family liaison officer back again. They can be very helpful. I know it's difficult at the moment and you want your privacy, but it's a good way to keep you constantly updated.'

Rachel lifted her chin and studiously ignored Karen.

'Right, we'll be on our way. You've got my number if you need to get in touch, Aiden.'

He nodded but didn't look up.

As Karen stood and put her mobile in her pocket, Aiden took a sharp breath. 'I forgot to tell you, someone put something through the letterbox earlier. It's probably nothing, but I thought it was a bit weird.'

'What was it?' Karen asked.

'You didn't tell me,' Rachel said.

'I'll get it,' Aiden said. 'It's on the hall table with the rest of the mail.'

Karen and Sophie followed him out of the living room and into the hall.

He plucked something small and rectangular from the top of a stack of letters, then held it out to Karen.

Her throat tightened when she saw what he was holding: a Queen of Hearts playing card.

CHAPTER ELEVEN

Churchill sat at the head of the table, ready to lord it over everyone. He plucked a thread from the arm of his suit jacket and dropped it to the floor.

'Shall I make a start?' Karen said, impatient to get the briefing over and done with.

'No, not everyone is here yet,' Churchill said, looking around the room. 'We're missing DS Hodgson. DC Cooper, would you mind finding out where he is, please?'

'Right,' Rick said, smothering a yawn as he got up from the table.

Before Rick could get to the door, Arnie burst in. 'Sorry I'm late, folks. Apologies for keeping you all waiting.' He slid into a seat at the opposite end of the table to Churchill, while Rick trudged back to his own chair.

'Now can I make a start?' Karen asked, trying but failing to keep the impatience from her voice.

Churchill inclined his head. 'Go on.'

Karen looked down at her notes. She needed to be methodical and precise, but fast, so they could get on with tracking down Tamara Lomax.

She started with the most recent – and in her opinion, most important – discovery: the Queen of Hearts playing card that had been pushed through the letterbox at the Lomaxes' house.

'If you look at item 8a,' Karen said, 'you'll see the image of the playing card Aiden Lomax told us was pushed through his letter-box. It's with Forensics at the moment, and we're hoping to get some prints or other evidence from it. We're unlikely to get much with the one found in the drain. I think we'll have more luck with this one.'

'What time was it delivered?' Churchill asked.

'He's not sure. It wasn't there when we visited him earlier today, but he ignored the mail when it was first delivered. When he went to pick it up at three p.m., the playing card was on top of the letters.'

'But we're assuming it didn't get delivered with the other post.'

'Exactly. There's no security cameras at the house, but presumably the card was hand-delivered.'

Churchill nodded at Arnie. 'Look into it. See if we can get an image of whoever delivered the card.'

'Yes, boss.' Arnie scribbled something down on the pad in front of him.

'Do we have any info on the cards themselves? Do we know where they were purchased?' Churchill directed his question to Karen.

'No,' Karen said. 'Unfortunately not. They're cheap, generic cards, and I don't think we're going to be able to trace where they were purchased. They're pretty ubiquitous, even sold in supermarkets.'

'And you visited Tamara's workplace?' Churchill prompted.

'We did. There seems to be some bad feeling between George Casey and Tamara Lomax.'

'What do you mean by *bad feeling*?'

'I got the impression there was tension between them. He was irritated with her attitude towards her job.'

'How much tension? Could he have been violent?'

'I don't know. He was annoyed at her for being late for work on occasions, but that doesn't suggest he's got violent tendencies. There's nothing we've uncovered that makes me think Casey would abduct Tamara, but I don't think he's someone we should ignore.' Karen filled them in on the interviews with the rest of Tamara's colleagues, then moved on to what Julie Wainwright had told them. 'She's the only one who admitted a close friendship with Tamara. She believes both Tamara and Aiden had been having affairs. She doesn't know who with, which obviously isn't helpful, but that's something we need to find out fast.'

'Agreed,' Churchill said.

Rick told everyone how they were progressing with the CCTV and traffic cameras, and then Morgan cut in.

'With your permission,' he said to Churchill, 'I thought Rick and I should talk to the van owners in person. The ones we've contacted by phone give good reasons for being in the area, but a face-to-face could spot out any potential holes in their stories.'

'Yes, that's a good idea,' Churchill conceded. 'What about the vehicles registered to businesses?'

'That's proved a little trickier,' Morgan said. 'Two of the companies have made it difficult to find out which of their employees would have been driving the van at the time of the abduction. They've been giving us the runaround.'

'Okay.' Churchill turned to Karen. 'You and Sophie need to chase up the businesses. We have to find out who was driving those vans. It's our strongest lead.'

'The thing is—' Karen started to say.

Churchill sighed. 'Please, DS Hart, no objections. You're not in charge of this investigation.'

89

Karen hadn't even voiced her opinion yet. Churchill had no idea what she was about to say. And okay, she *had* been about to object to the role he'd assigned to her, but he didn't know that.

She paused and took a breath, struggling to control her temper. 'I don't have a problem with that. I just wanted to say let's not forget these extramarital affairs. We all know the kind of emotions they can generate. We've seen the fallout before.'

'So you're suggesting the husband is a strong suspect?' Churchill enquired, raising an eyebrow.

'Absolutely,' Karen said. 'I think we'd be stupid not to think so at this stage.'

Too late, she realised she'd implied that Churchill was stupid. She sank slightly lower in her chair. 'I didn't mean . . .'

'No, you're right, we can't rule him out. We can't discount anything yet.' He glanced down at the briefing notes in front of him. 'This playing card, what does it say to you?' He looked directly at Karen, as did everyone else in the briefing room.

She hesitated. 'It looks like a calling card. A message left by whoever abducted Tamara.'

Churchill thought on that for a moment, stroking his chin. 'And another was sent to her home address – why? To drive the message home?'

'Possibly. Perhaps the abductor noticed the first card went down the drain and didn't want us to miss it?'

'So the abductor is trying to send some sort of message,' Churchill mused.

'I agree,' Sophie said.

'You would,' muttered Rick, earning him a glare from Sophie.

She was undeterred. 'Honestly, I think we should reach out to Dr Michaels.' She put her hands flat on the table and looked at everyone in turn. 'He has experience with a killer who left a similar message in the US. The Playing Card Killer.'

'Was it the Queen of Hearts?' Churchill asked.

'Um, no,' Sophie said. 'I think it was actually the Ace of Diamonds. I need to reread the book. I'll do it tonight. But I think we should call Dr Michaels and ask him to come in as a consultant.' She looked at Churchill. 'If you think that would help?'

But Churchill didn't answer straightaway; he was still looking down at his briefing notes.

Finally, as people began to shift uncomfortably in their chairs, and Karen started to wonder if Churchill had fallen asleep with his eyes open, he said, 'It can't hurt. I'll talk to the superintendent about it.'

After making a statement, summarising where they stood in the investigation and assigning more tasks, he called the briefing to a close and stood. 'Everyone knows what they have to do?'

Around the room there were murmurs of 'Yes, sir' as everyone trailed out.

'You know,' Arnie Hodgson said to Karen as they walked back to the office, 'you just need to learn how to handle him.'

'You've said that before, Arnie,' Karen said. 'But I'm obviously not a fast learner when it comes to DCI Churchill.'

'You're doing all right,' he said. 'You're just too sensitive. You need to grow a thicker skin.'

'Maybe it's not that I'm too sensitive,' Karen said. 'Maybe it's just that you've got a hide like a rhinoceros.'

Arnie threw back his head and laughed. 'You might have a point there.'

◆ ◆ ◆

Karen was sitting at her computer, scrolling through the details of the businesses who owned the white Transit vans seen in the vicinity around the time Tamara was abducted, when DC Shah appeared at her shoulder. 'Karen, sorry to interrupt – the superintendent is asking to speak to you and Detective Inspector Morgan.'

'Thanks,' Karen said. She looked past DC Shah to peer through the glass into Morgan's office. He was focused on his computer. 'I'll tell Morgan and we'll head straight up there.'

She rapped on Morgan's door. 'Super wants to see us.'

'Now?'

'Yes.'

Morgan stood. 'Do you know what it's about?'

'Not a clue.'

Pamela was sitting at her desk outside the superintendent's office as usual. She waved them in. 'Go ahead. She's expecting you.'

Karen tried to gauge the superintendent's mood by Pamela's expression, but the woman's face was serene as she smiled at them. She never gave anything away.

Superintendent Murray was filling in paperwork. She looked up from her desk as Morgan and Karen entered the office. Behind her were sweeping views of the Lincolnshire countryside. Every time she came up here, Karen was reminded of how beautiful the county of Lincolnshire was.

'Take a seat,' the superintendent said. 'Dr Michaels – what's your opinion of him?' Superintendent Murray wasn't one for beating around the bush.

Churchill must have already been to see her. He didn't waste any time either.

Karen was reluctant to bring him on board but didn't want to voice that to the superintendent or to Morgan. It was as though, by letting Dr Michaels into the investigation, they were admitting they had an extremely unpredictable case on their hands. The thought was terrifying. And after everything the team had been through, including betrayal by fellow officers two months earlier, Karen didn't even want to entertain the possibility that they were dealing with a criminal who was taunting the police with messages again.

The superintendent raised an eyebrow. 'Neither of you have an opinion?'

'I don't know that much about him, ma'am,' Morgan admitted. 'I know he's an American. Used to work with the FBI. He works on high-profile cases in the States. Sophie is probably the person you want to speak to. She's a big fan.'

The superintendent nodded. 'I'm aware,' she said, which made Karen think that Sophie had even been bending the superintendent's ear about the talk.

'You saw him last night, correct?' the superintendent asked, looking at Karen.

'Yes, I did. I spoke to him briefly too. He gave a very interesting talk and came across as a professional with a talent for apprehending some of the worst sorts of criminals.' Karen could have told the super that Dr Michaels was keen to visit the station, but his motive gave her pause. Why was he so keen to look around their station and observe them at work? If he wanted to visit a police force, why not the Met? They were far bigger, with more officers, more cases . . . Why was Dr Michaels so interested in them?

'I'm sensing some reluctance here, Karen,' the superintendent said. 'What's wrong?'

'Dr Michaels called and suggested we use his expertise.'

The super raised an eyebrow. 'Well, that's good, isn't it?'

'I can't help wondering why he's so keen to get involved.'

'Isn't that what he does? He works with the police and the FBI in the States, doesn't he?'

'Yes, but . . .' Karen tried to articulate her reticence without sounding paranoid. 'We don't know that much about him.'

'I've asked Churchill to contact someone in Washington who has worked with him in the past. But I want to know if you think he'll be reliable?' the superintendent asked. 'I don't want to bring in somebody who is going to waste our time or use up precious resources.'

'That's understandable, ma'am,' Karen said.

'So, what do you think? Should I invite him to consult?'

Morgan hesitated, clearly waiting for Karen to speak. She understood why. After all, she was the one who'd heard him talk, but there was something holding her back. There was no doubt he was good at his job. His record spoke to that, so why was Karen reluctant to bring him in?

She was out of her depth. Two months ago, she had come very close to losing her life. She had to admit that now, if she walked down a dark street, she was constantly looking over her shoulder and always on her guard. It felt like evil was lurking around every corner. If she invited Dr Michaels into their world, it was admitting that evil could strike again. His eagerness unnerved her. Incidents in her recent past had made it hard for Karen to trust people. She had always been wary of newcomers, but were her suspicions warranted in this case?

The super had a point. Karen had to be practical.

It was now looking less and less likely that Tamara Lomax would turn up unharmed. The playing cards, if they were as significant as they seemed, certainly suggested the abductor viewed this as some kind of game.

The people who committed these types of crimes didn't usually stop at one, which meant they needed all the help they could get to stop him.

'I think it's a good idea to bring him on board,' Karen finally said. 'We could use his expertise and advice. We don't necessarily have to follow his suggestions, but I think it's a good idea to ask for his help.'

'All right,' the superintendent said. 'I'll give DCI Churchill permission to contact him.'

Then she nodded, letting Morgan and Karen know they were dismissed.

As they left the office, Karen had a sinking feeling in her stomach, as though she'd just triggered an irreversible action. There was no turning back now.

CHAPTER TWELVE

As directed, Karen got straight to work trying to chase up one of the owners of the white Transit vans picked up on cameras immediately before and after Tamara's abduction. She telephoned Branston Chickens, a small firm based less than a mile from her house.

Unfortunately, the staff she was trying to get answers from appeared determined to put as many obstacles in her way as possible.

Was it really feasible they didn't know which employee was driving the van today?

Karen was passed from pillar to post. First, a member of the admin staff would be able to tell her; then no, they couldn't help, so she would have to speak to the works team; then no, she'd need to speak to someone who had the password to access the system. Again and again, her simple questions went unanswered. Finally, she was told the person she needed to talk to had gone for a tea break and could she call back in ten minutes.

'Ten minutes? I've already spent ten minutes being transferred to different people.'

Branston Chickens was a relatively small outfit. How could they have so many unhelpful staff?

'Can I speak to the owner?'

'Sorry, I believe Mr Greaves is away from his desk right now,' the woman said.

'You *believe*? Could you check please? See if he really is away from his desk? And if he is, can you track him down? This is important.'

'I'm afraid not. We aren't in the same building. The company outsources administration work.'

'So, let me get this straight – I'm talking to you, but you're not physically located in Branston.'

'That's correct. I'm in Leeds.'

Karen gritted her teeth and stabbed the pad in front of her with her pencil, breaking the lead. 'Then can you phone him?'

'I've tried, but he's not picking up. That's why I think he's away from his desk.'

'He must have a mobile?'

'I don't have that number. Sorry I couldn't be of assistance. Is there anything else I can help you with today?' she asked in a sing-song voice.

'Yes. Could you *please* put me through to someone who is actually working at Branston Chickens?'

'Of course, happy to help. I'll just put you on hold for a moment.'

'No!' Karen said, but it was too late. Tinny classical music played down the line.

When she finally put down the phone, without managing to speak to an employee who could tell her anything about the van, Karen was cursing under her breath.

She stood and stretched, deciding she would have to go and speak to the owner of this company in person. It wouldn't be so easy for them to fob her off then.

But first, she needed coffee.

On the way back from the canteen, she spotted some familiar figures ahead of her. She was desperately trying not to spill her coffee, as the cup was full to the brim. It was the machine's fault. She'd only turned away for a second as the stream of hot coffee was deposited in the cup until it overflowed. What a waste of perfectly good coffee.

Dr Michaels and Zane Dwight had stopped ahead of her in the corridor. In front of them, Sophie stood with her hands clasped. Karen recognised the pose. Sophie was clearly anxious.

Zane said, 'Really, it's not your fault.'

Dr Michaels said something inaudible in reply.

Then Zane put his hand on Dr Michaels's shoulder and said, 'No, you mustn't blame yourself.'

'What's going on?' Karen asked as she reached them.

All three turned to face Karen. Dr Michaels arranged his features into a professional smile.

'DS Hart, how lovely to see you again. I didn't think I would have the pleasure.' His smile widened and he forced a little laugh, which indicated to Karen that he'd taken her earlier rebuff personally.

Karen switched her overfilled cup to her other hand, as her fingers were starting to burn. 'Shall we get started?'

'I was just taking them to DI Morgan's office,' Sophie said. 'I think DCI Churchill is there.'

Then they're in for a treat, Karen thought. But if Churchill was going to deal with Dr Michaels personally, that meant Karen could get out and visit the owner of Branston Chickens.

'Oh, hello again.'

Karen turned to see the photographer, Nicholas Finney, emerge from the gents' toilets. He gave her a wide smile, before approaching Zane with his hands outstretched.

Zane handed him a large camera bag.

'Why is there a photographer here?' Karen asked, looking to Sophie for answers.

'I said it would be okay,' Sophie started to say, and then wilted a little under Karen's gaze.

'No photographers,' Karen said firmly.

Nicholas was a big man, but he hunched his shoulders and shrank back. 'It's only a few snaps. I'm the official—'

'You're the official photographer for the book tour, I know, you told me, but we're not having a photographer in the station. We didn't authorise that.'

'That's my fault,' Sophie said. 'I thought it would be okay.'

'I'm sure it's not a problem.' Dr Michaels delivered a megawatt smile. 'DS Hart is right to be cautious, but Nicholas won't be privy to any sensitive information.'

As Karen fumed, they all watched her expectantly.

What was Sophie thinking? Had she lost her mind? Or was she so desperate to impress Dr Michaels she didn't want to tell him no? Karen had no qualms about that. She returned Dr Michaels's smile. 'I said no photographers.'

Nicholas clutched the camera case to his chest. 'I don't want to cause any trouble.'

'You haven't, buddy.' Dr Michaels put a hand on Nicholas's shoulder. 'It's not a problem. We'll get it sorted. I just need to speak to . . . It's Superintendent Murray, isn't it?' He looked at Karen innocently, as though he wasn't really threatening to go over her head.

'You can speak to whoever you like,' Karen said coolly, 'but Nicholas is leaving.'

'Aw, c'mon,' Zane said. 'He's just here to take some pictures of Dr Michaels. He's not interested in you.'

Karen turned to look at Zane, her patience growing thin. 'Then you can arrange for Nicholas to take photos of Dr Michaels elsewhere.'

Zane and Dr Michaels looked like a pair of sulky toddlers. Sophie was mortified, sending an apologetic glance to each of them, which only annoyed Karen further.

Nicholas looked as though he'd quite like the floor to swallow him up. 'I'll go,' he said, looking down at his shoes. 'I didn't mean to cause any issues.'

Karen switched her coffee cup to her other hand again. It was still too hot, and she was already regretting recommending bringing Dr Michaels on board.

'You can take Nicholas back to reception,' Karen said to Sophie.

'But what about Dr Michaels?'

'You can leave him to me.' It sounded more threatening than she'd intended, but the coffee was burning her fingers and she was incensed at Dr Michaels thinking he'd get the superintendent to overrule her.

Sophie nodded meekly and escorted Nicholas back along the corridor.

'Follow me,' Karen said, leading Dr Michaels and Zane to Morgan's office. After a quick scan inside, she said, 'Sorry, DCI Churchill must have gone back up to his own office.'

'I'll take them,' Arnie said cheerfully. 'I was just on my way up there.' He held out a hand to Dr Michaels. 'It's a pleasure to meet you. I'm DS Arnie Hodgson.'

Arnie wandered off with Dr Michaels and Zane, chatting away like he'd known them forever.

When Sophie returned, looking sheepish, Karen asked, 'What was going on in the corridor?'

'I'm sorry. I didn't think the photographer would be a problem. They said they always had a photographer on tour.'

'I mean before that. Before Nicholas Finney came out of the gents, there was something going on.'

'Oh, right. Yes, Dr Michaels was upset. There've been some stories published about him in the US press. They're all completely inaccurate.'

'What sort of stories?'

'The daughter of one of the victims in a previous case has accused him of selling details to the tabloids in order to get notoriety and sell copies of his book. It's clearly not true,' she added hurriedly. 'But he's really upset. Zane was trying to comfort him. He just received a call from the victim's daughter. He explained the articles were nothing to do with him, but she didn't believe him. I could hear her yelling at him down the phone.'

'I suppose the victim's daughter is traumatised,' Karen said. 'Does she have any evidence it was Dr Michaels selling the details to the press?'

'Of course not, because he didn't.'

'Which case was it?'

'The Playing Card Killer, in Washington, about twenty years ago. The killer abducted his victims. Then cut their throats and dumped their bodies in public places. One of them was Mary Munro. It's her daughter Angela who is blaming Dr Michaels, even though he was the one who brought the killer to justice.'

Karen paused, thinking. A playing card killer. That was quite a coincidence. Dr Michaels just happened to be in the UK during a case with very striking similarities?

'What are you thinking?' Sophie asked.

Sophie wouldn't take kindly to Karen's suspicions about her idol, so she simply replied, 'I'm not surprised Angela's angry if the tabloids are filled with personal details of her mother's case.'

'That's what Dr Michaels said – her reaction was perfectly understandable. But he looked crushed – so disappointed that he wasn't able to persuade her he hadn't been selling stories. He told her he doesn't sell his books to make money but for the benefit of law enforcement officers, so they can learn from his experience.'

Karen raised an eyebrow.

'What?' Sophie said.

'I'm sure he's a very altruistic man,' Karen said. 'But you have to admit he likely makes quite a lot of money from his books.'

'He regularly donates to victims' charities. At least, that's what Zane said.'

'Zane is his right-hand man. He's probably good at PR, don't you think?'

'I think Dr Michaels has done a brilliant job helping victims of crime, and without him, there'd be a lot more nasty criminals on the loose.'

'I'm sure you're right,' Karen said. 'I just think it's possible for him to want to catch bad guys and also want to make a profit at the same time.'

'I suppose.'

'Why did you think bringing a photographer into the station was a good idea?'

'I . . . well, I didn't really. He was just there with Dr Michaels and Zane, and they said they always had a photographer and it wasn't a big deal.' She looked up at Karen. 'Sorry, you're right. I should at least have cleared it with you. I just didn't want to . . .' She trailed off.

'You didn't want to disappoint Dr Michaels?' Karen guessed.

Sophie nodded miserably and then returned to her desk.

Karen took another sip of coffee. She hoped Sophie wasn't about to discover her hero had feet of clay.

Karen had just drained the last of her coffee and was reaching for her coat when Churchill called another briefing. This time, Dr Michaels took centre stage.

Although Churchill sat in his usual spot at the head of the briefing table, all eyes were on Dr Michaels, who was sitting opposite Karen.

He had a stack of notes in front of him that Sophie had prepared, to bring him up to date with the investigation.

'I haven't had as much time to focus on your findings as I would like, but I can share my initial profile. Though it's a shame I wasn't brought on board earlier.' He looked directly at Karen.

'We are very grateful you could spare the time, Dr Michaels,' Morgan said. 'And we'd be interested in your thoughts.'

It was a gentle but stern nudge to Dr Michaels to get on with it, for which Karen was grateful.

'As I'm sure you're all aware, the Queen of Hearts is being used as a calling card by our unsub . . .' He paused, looking around the room. 'Sorry, I should clarify. By *unsub*, I mean the unknown perpetrator of this crime.'

'Yes, we're all familiar with the term,' Karen said, wondering if it was possible for the man to be any more condescending.

'Ah, good,' he continued. 'One card was found at the scene, and another posted through the victim's mailbox. Sadly, I have experience of a very similar case. A total of seven women were abducted and murdered in Washington, in 1999, although those victims were taken late at night and the calling card was the Ace of Diamonds. I believe your perpetrator will have a lot in common with the Ace of Diamonds killer.'

'Do you think we could be dealing with a copycat?' Rick asked.

Dr Michaels frowned at the interruption.

'Sorry,' Rick added quickly.

'No, it's a good question,' Dr Michaels conceded. 'The Ace of Diamonds case was all over the media in the US, and my books do sell very well over here in the UK.' He smiled broadly. 'The Brits obviously have very good taste. You've read my books?'

Rick squirmed in his seat. 'Well, no . . .'

Sophie straightened in her chair, and Karen imagined a younger Sophie, at school, straining, her arm in the air so that the teacher would pick her to answer a question. 'I've read them. All of them, except the new one that's just come out.'

Dr Michaels gave Sophie a wide smile and then looked at Karen. 'Perhaps you picked up one of my books last night?'

'No, I had a look through them, but couldn't decide. I thought I'd order it online once I took Sophie's advice on which one to get.'

'Ah, I see.' Dr Michaels looked crestfallen. Ridiculously, Karen felt guilty. 'Anyway, a copycat is a possibility. The case was well publicised. I will, of course, prepare a full profile for you, but for now I can give you some pointers. I believe we are looking for a man between twenty-five and fifty-five. He could live alone, but he also could live with family, either a female relative or a wife. This behaviour – the abduction of women – is something he would hide. He's probably well practised at hiding his tendencies. This isn't something new to him. He is likely to have committed previous misdemeanours. Perhaps not violent or sexually deviant crimes, but there's a high probability he's had contact with law enforcement in the past. His actions suggest he is either local or he knows the area very well from working there. He could have recently moved away from the area, but local knowledge is important. I'd also say that the playing card is almost certainly a taunt directed at the police.'

Karen spoke up. 'I think we'd all agree that the playing card seems to be important, now that one was delivered to the Lomax house, but what I don't understand is why the first one was found in a drain. It wasn't left in an obvious place. We could have missed it.'

Dr Michaels smiled. 'Yes, I see how you could find that confusing.' Perhaps he was trying to be kind, but the words did come off as slightly patronising. 'I think the card was likely left at the scene to be found, but then was perhaps blown down the drain or kicked down there during the struggle. It's possible the unsub even saw this happening, and that's why he delivered another card to the victim's address.'

Karen nodded. 'We are trying to get hold of witnesses and CCTV in the area of the Lomaxes' house from this afternoon. Visiting the victim's house in the middle of the day was certainly a confident move.'

'Exactly. He's enjoying this, and believes he is in charge. He thinks he's too clever to get caught.'

'Hopefully we'll get some forensic evidence from the card shortly and prove him wrong,' Karen said.

'I don't think you will,' Dr Michaels replied. 'I think you're dealing with someone pretty smart. They will have taken precautions. I doubt you'll find any fingerprints or DNA on the card.'

'That's unfortunate,' Churchill said. 'We are chasing down all white Transit vans seen in the area around the time of the abduction. And we've narrowed it down to two – isn't that right, DI Morgan?'

'Most of the drivers we've contacted had legitimate reasons for being in the vicinity. That said, we haven't ruled them all out definitively.'

Churchill gave an irritated huff. 'Then let's make sure we do rule them out *definitively*.'

Morgan remained silent, but Karen could almost feel the tension rolling off him.

'Identifying the vehicle is vital,' Dr Michaels said. 'Again, I would emphasise that the suspect will be familiar with the surroundings. They are going to know the layout of the area, which streets they could carry out the abduction on without being spotted – or where brave members of the public are unlikely to intervene.'

'Do you think she was being stalked?' Karen asked. 'He snatched her in the morning, walking to work. It was unlikely he was just waiting for any passing woman.'

'Yes, I'd agree with that,' Dr Michaels said. 'He's likely to have been following her for some time and knows her movements, what time she leaves for work, what time she gets home, when she's home alone . . .'

'That makes sense,' Karen said. 'He knew her address. He put the second card through her letterbox.'

'Exactly,' Dr Michaels said, slapping his palm on the table. 'We are dealing with an incredibly intelligent criminal.'

Karen thought the way he said *intelligent* almost made it sound like he admired the abductor. She thought back to Rick's suggestion of a copycat and scribbled a doodle in the margin of her notepad. Her suspicions about the doctor's eagerness to help hadn't gone away. Was it possible that Dr Michaels was involved? Perhaps re-enacting his old cases? Reliving the thrill? This time as the perpetrator?

Unlikely. Why would he take the risk? And besides, other than the similarities between the cases, there was no evidence linking him to this new crime.

'DS Hart?' Churchill barked.

She looked up to see all the faces in the room turned to her. 'Sorry?'

'I'll do it,' Sophie said quickly. She swivelled in her seat to face Karen and said quietly, 'DCI Churchill suggested we work with Dr

Michaels and provide him with the notes from our interviews with Tamara Lomax's work colleagues.'

Karen nodded her agreement. 'Good idea.'

Dr Michaels ran through a few more details, but he didn't give them anything concrete to go on. It was mostly conjecture, though that was the point of a profile. It was a guide. It wasn't cast in stone. If she was being cynical, she'd say it wasn't much better than guesswork. Some called it pseudoscience.

She couldn't see how his analysis was superior to an officer following their gut instinct. Though Sophie would insist there was a lot of data behind Dr Michaels's reasoning, Karen wasn't entirely convinced. In fact, his profile had about as much legitimacy as her own suspicions about him.

She glanced at the clock on the wall behind Churchill. Branston Chickens would be closing soon, and she needed to get out there and track down that van.

Despite her urgency to get out of the room, when Dr Michaels drew the meeting to a close, Karen couldn't help adding, 'I think we still need to keep some focus on Aiden and keep reaching out to people who knew Tamara. Julie Wainwright said she thought they were both cheating, and we know from experience that can cause extreme behaviour.'

Everyone nodded and murmured agreement, except Dr Michaels, who gave a small shrug.

'I'm sure that's true for your usual low-profile cases, but I'm afraid this is going to be the biggest case of your careers.' He looked around the room at the officers, who had been in the process of gathering their papers and leaving but had stopped when he started talking. 'It will be like nothing you've experienced before.' After Dr Michaels had paused for dramatic effect, he carried on talking. 'The husband just doesn't meet the profile, I'm afraid. Our unsub treats his victims like prey. He stalks them. He won't target anyone close to him. Focusing on the husband will be a waste of time.'

'I'm not saying it's necessarily the husband,' Karen said, 'but a profile is no guarantee. The abductor could be the man Tamara was having an affair with.'

'You're looking for connections. Relationships. I understand. Because you're used to dealing with small investigations. You're not prepared for a case like this.'

To Karen's surprise, before she could reply, Churchill intervened. 'We're not ruling anything out at this stage. We'll keep reaching out to Tamara's friends and uncover whether or not Julie Wainwright was telling the truth when she said the pair of them were carrying on with other people. We can't ignore any lines of enquiry.'

Dr Michaels gave a gentle nod and a tight smile, as though to indicate he wasn't bothered, but Karen could tell by the tension in his jaw that he was put out.

Even if he was right about the suspect, good police work meant never overlooking the obvious. It was a bad idea to focus all of their attention on one possible lead: a stranger abduction.

In an attempt to make amends and show Dr Michaels his opinion was valuable to the investigation, Karen said, 'If the abductor has been stalking her, Tamara may have told her friends, or the person she was having an affair with. That's why we need to follow up.'

That earned another, slightly warmer, smile from Dr Michaels.

After everyone filed out of the room, Dr Michaels caught up with Karen by her desk.

'I have my own computer, but the office they've assigned to me doesn't have an internet connection. Can you help?'

Karen put down her coat, resigned to never getting to Branston Chickens before it closed. 'Of course, I'll call IT and get it sorted.'

'Oh, I can do that,' Sophie said, darting over to Karen's desk, eager to be helpful.

'Thanks,' Karen said gratefully. She picked up her coat again.

'Now, look,' Dr Michaels said as he perched on the edge of Karen's desk. 'I don't want to overstep the line here, but I've picked up on some tension.'

'Tension?' Karen repeated blankly.

'Yes – you don't trust me.'

'It's not that,' Karen said.

'Yes, it is.'

She tensed. Was he purposefully trying to wind her up? 'I just think we need to keep open minds during this point in the enquiry.'

'Of course, and I completely agree,' Dr Michaels said, even though he had disagreed during the briefing in front of everyone else. 'The thing is, as you may know, I studied psychology. I've got a master's. Did you know that?'

He was so needy. 'No, I didn't.'

'Oh. Well, I have. After I got my doctorate in criminology.'

'I'm pleased for you,' Karen said. 'I'm supposed to be chasing down the vehicle potentially involved in the abduction, so I need to get a move on.'

He didn't take the hint. 'What happened in your past?' He leaned forward slightly to peer into her eyes.

Karen took a step back. 'Sorry?'

'Something happened to make you very mistrustful. What was it?'

None of your business, Karen thought, as stress tightened the muscles between her shoulder blades and worked its way down her spine. Slowly, she said, 'Nothing happened.'

He straightened, so he was no longer staring creepily into her eyes. 'I understand if you don't want to talk about it, but something happened to make you distrust me.'

Karen felt a sudden urge to shove him off the edge of her desk. It gave her some pleasure to imagine him falling over backwards.

'If that's all? I really need to get on.'

'Sure,' he said with a smile.

'Oh, I meant to ask. Did you speak to Superintendent Murray about getting your photographer back?' Karen asked.

He stiffened slightly, his smile fading just a little. 'I did.'

'And what did she say?'

'She agreed with you. No photographers inside the station.' He raised his hands. 'It's not a big deal. I just wanted to help Nicholas. He's freelance. I don't think work has been easy to come by lately. What can I say? I'm a soft touch.'

Karen narrowed her eyes. Now he was trying to make her feel guilty by suggesting she'd ruined Nicholas Finney's chance at a paid job, but Zane had already told her Nicholas was working for free and hoping to sell his pictures and report later.

'Surely you'll still pay him?' Karen raised an eyebrow.

Dr Michaels shrugged. 'Oh, Zane deals with all that. I just do all the talking.'

Annoyingly, he didn't leave. Karen grabbed her bag. If he wanted to remain sitting on her desk, he could, but she wouldn't be there.

But before she stepped away, Churchill appeared by her shoulder.

Would she ever get the chance to track down this van?

'Karen,' he said, using her first name. He didn't usually do that. He called her DS Hart, which made it sound like he was telling her off, like when her mother had used her full name when she'd misbehaved as a child.

'Yes?'

'Do you want to bring him in?'

'Who?'

110

'Aiden Lomax.'

'I don't think that's—' Dr Michaels started to say, but to Churchill's credit he held up a hand to silence the doctor.

Karen almost smiled. In that moment, she nearly liked Churchill.

'Well?' he prompted. 'You could bring him in for questioning, and Dr Michaels can observe.'

Now Karen did smile. 'All right, yes, let's do it.'

CHAPTER THIRTEEN

When Karen and Rick arrived at the Lomax house, they were disappointed to see press outside. The reporters hadn't entered the front garden but were lingering on the pavement.

As soon as they opened the car doors, the braying pack surrounded them, shouting questions. A woman with a bright-yellow belted coat thrust her phone into Karen's face. It was recording.

Karen scowled at the woman, instantly recognising her. Her name was Cindy Connor. Karen had had dealings with her in the past, and they'd never been pleasant.

Cindy was in such a rush to keep up with Karen that she jabbed the photographer to her left with her elbow when he didn't move out of the way. Karen blinked in surprise when she realised it was Nicholas Finney. He didn't hold his ground, moving back so Cindy could claim her position right beside Karen.

'I saw that! What's wrong with you?' Karen demanded, glaring at Cindy. 'Calm down.'

Nicholas held his ribs and, despite his size advantage, seemed to cower away from Cindy.

'Are you okay?' Karen asked him.

He nodded. Nicholas hadn't wasted any time. He clearly wanted in on this story one way or another.

'I'm surprised to see you again so soon.'

He smiled. 'Sorry about earlier. I didn't mean to cause any problems. You don't mind me covering the story with the rest of the press pack, do you?'

Karen would have preferred the press pack to go away and give Tamara's family some peace, and let the police get on with their jobs. But she could hardly ban Nicholas from a public place.

'It's fine.'

Other photographers crowded around them.

Cindy shouted, 'What's the latest on the missing woman? Can you give us an update? Are local women at risk?'

'We're not giving a statement at this time,' Karen snapped. 'And if you had any decency, you'd leave the family alone.'

Cindy wasn't put off in the slightest. 'Keep taking photos, Nicholas!' She glared at him and then turned back to Karen. 'Do you suspect the husband?'

Karen stopped dead. How did she know that? Lucky guess? Or did Cindy know someone in the force who was feeding her information?

'No comment,' Karen said as she marched on, following Rick.

The story would be all over the local news tomorrow. The press would have photographs of Aiden being led out of his home and put into a police car. Not a bad thing if he was involved in his wife's disappearance, but if he was an innocent victim, this would do some serious damage to his reputation.

They'd hoped to surprise Aiden, but she saw him standing in the living room watching them through the window. He knew they were coming.

He was prepared.

◆ ◆ ◆

Aiden Lomax sat in the interview room opposite Morgan and Karen. He'd waived his right to legal representation, either because he was innocent and didn't think he needed it, or because he was very cocky.

He didn't look overly confident right now. It annoyed Karen that she still couldn't get a proper read on him.

When they'd picked him up, he'd been angry, really angry. He'd punched a hole in the wall of his hallway, and it had taken some stern words to calm him down.

Karen had made it clear that they wanted to question him at the station, but he wasn't being arrested. She had been glad to have an officer of Rick's experience with her. When Rick had placed a strong hand on Aiden Lomax's shoulder, it reminded him it would be a very stupid idea to throw any more punches.

Now, in the interview room, Aiden was a completely different man. He stared stonily ahead, morose and quiet. They'd been asking him questions for several minutes but not got very far.

His answers were monosyllabic.

Dr Michaels and DCI Churchill were watching the interview from upstairs in Churchill's office. The camera was on the ceiling to the right of Karen's head and it focused on Aiden's face, which was now pretty unreadable. Karen would be impressed if Dr Michaels could get anything from his facial expression.

'You know you need to tell us everything, don't you?' Karen was playing the part of good cop, trying to reassure Aiden and persuade him they were on his side.

Morgan took the opposing role. He wasn't aggressive or rude, but his tone was hard and cold.

'I've told you everything,' Aiden said, not bothering to look at either of them.

'So why would one of Tamara's colleagues tell us that you were cheating?' Karen asked reasonably.

'I don't know. I told you, they must have the wrong end of the stick. Neither of us were cheating.'

'You're absolutely sure that Tamara wasn't seeing anyone?' Morgan's tone was disbelieving.

Aiden shook his head firmly.

'Perhaps Tamara believed you were and acted out of revenge,' Karen suggested.

'No, she wouldn't do that.'

Karen went back over the timeline, asking again where Aiden had been when he received the call from Mr Casey, and whether he had access to a white van.

'Why are you always asking about a white van? What has that got to do with it? You think whoever took Tamara has a white van, don't you?' Aiden was finally becoming more animated.

'It's something we're looking into, yes,' Karen admitted. 'What do you think happened to her?'

'I don't know. Something bad must've happened to her because she hasn't been able to get home. Maybe she's had an accident, or was hit by a car when she was walking to work.'

'She didn't walk down any country lanes,' Karen said softly. 'She used residential roads with pavements. If she'd been hit by a car, I think someone would have heard or seen her.'

He shrugged. 'I don't know, maybe someone hit her and then put her in their car or van. Have you looked into that?'

He looked so distressed that Karen started to feel guilty for pressuring him like this. She knew how she would feel if it was one of her loved ones missing and the police were hounding her with questions, but it was her job. She knew better than to be sentimental.

Aiden bowed his head, sniffed, and wiped away a tear.

Morgan pushed forward a packet of tissues. 'Dry your eyes, son,' he said. 'We've still got questions.'

Aiden looked at Morgan with intense hatred. 'You lot are heartless.'

'All I care about right now is finding your wife,' Morgan said. 'And it's looking more and more like you're not telling us the truth. As that's the case, I have to ask myself why not? What do you have to hide, Mr Lomax?' He leaned forward, forearms resting on the table. 'What happened at home this morning? Did you argue?'

Aiden pushed himself back in his chair, looking horrified.

'Arguments can get out of hand,' Morgan continued. 'I know you didn't mean it to happen. She probably just went on and on, wouldn't shut up, kept pushing, and then what happened? Did she tell you she'd been fooling around with someone else? You must have been very angry.'

Aiden was breathing heavily. He put his hands flat on the table. 'No. I don't have to listen to this,' he said through gritted teeth.

'It's better for you to say something now. You need to tell us everything,' Morgan said. 'It's all going to come out in the end.'

'You're just focusing on me because I'm an easy target. Because you lot are so bad at your jobs, you haven't identified any other suspects! You should be out there looking for her.' Aiden pointed towards the door. 'Both of you are in here wasting time with me, when Tamara is out there somewhere.'

He wrapped his arms around his stomach and rocked forward, looking as though he was trying not to cry.

He was convincing. Very convincing.

Karen's stomach churned with guilt and shame. But she hadn't chosen to do this job because it was easy. Her priority was Tamara. And she was still missing.

There was a balance to be found, but they needed to press Aiden hard right now. Because if he had something to do with his wife's disappearance, they had to act quickly. There was a possibility Tamara was still alive and in danger. If Aiden wasn't telling

116

them the identity of the man Tamara had been seeing out of some misguided sense of loyalty, they needed to apply pressure until he cracked.

'I . . . I just want her back,' Aiden said.

'That's what we want too, Aiden,' Karen said, tilting her head to try to make eye contact with him. 'You need to tell us who else she had a relationship with, because that is vital to finding her.'

'I . . .' He hesitated. They were close to getting the information out of him.

'Aiden, you *have* to tell us,' Karen said gently.

'No, she wasn't seeing anyone else!'

'How do you know for sure?' Morgan asked.

He threw up his hands. 'I just do.'

'It probably didn't mean anything to her,' Morgan continued. 'She preferred you, didn't she? We just need to know who it was, so we can talk to them. You understand that, don't you? Why should you cover for *them*?'

Aiden pressed his lips together and shook his head. After running his hands through his hair, he said, 'I don't understand anything at the moment.'

'If you can't help us, we can speak to your boss, your work colleagues,' Morgan said coldly.

Aiden looked up sharply. 'My boss? Why?'

'If you won't tell us the truth, we'll have to speak to all your colleagues, your mates down the pub. We'll find out somehow.'

Aiden was sweating. 'You can't do that!'

'Of course we can,' Morgan said. 'Don't be so naive. You might think they're a loyal bunch, but one of them will spill the details. Not many people will keep quiet just to cover for you. I guess you'll find out who your real friends are.'

Aiden's mouth hung open. He shook his head. 'Why are you treating me like I'm the one who's done something wrong?'

117

'Because you're lying to us,' Morgan said. 'I told you. If you don't tell the truth, it makes you look guilty.'

Aiden put his hands over his face. It was hard for Karen to see him broken and vulnerable.

She wanted to apologise, walk out and give the man some privacy to lick his emotional wounds, but there was something telling her that he was holding back, so they had to press on.

They kept at it for another ten minutes until there was a knock at the door. It was Rick.

'Sorry to interrupt. The DCI would like a word.'

Both Karen and Morgan stepped out of the room.

'What does he want?' Morgan asked.

'He said that's enough for now.'

'He wants to end the interview? But Lomax is holding something back.'

'Yes, I thought so too, but apparently Dr Michaels has seen enough and wants to give you his verdict. Churchill said to go back to your workstations, and he'll call you when Dr Michaels is ready to present his information.'

'And what are we supposed to do with Aiden Lomax in the meantime?' Karen asked, nodding at the closed door to the interview room.

'He's distressed,' Morgan added. 'It's not a good idea for him to be on his own at the moment.'

'I'll take him home and stay with him if his sister-in-law isn't around,' Rick said.

Together, Karen and Morgan headed back to the open-plan office area.

'That was a hard interview,' Karen said.

'I felt like a right callous so-and-so, to be honest,' Morgan said. 'But I'm sure he's holding something back.'

'Yes, I feel it too. But no matter how hard we pressed, he refused to tell us everything. He must have a really good reason for that, don't you think?'

'Yes, definitely. I've no idea what it is, though. You?'

Karen shook her head. 'Do you think he'll put in a complaint?'

'I don't know, but if he's hiding something, I doubt it. He won't want to draw any more attention.'

'I don't understand why he doesn't just tell us. It's an affair. They happen all the time. Why not tell us who it is?'

'Your guess is as good as mine.'

It took almost an hour and a half for Churchill to call down and tell Morgan and Karen to come up to his office. Fortunately, DC Farzana Shah had agreed to chase up Branston Chickens on Karen's behalf.

They found Churchill leaning back in his chair, listening to Dr Michaels, who looked incredibly at home, lounging comfortably in a second padded chair.

'Take a seat,' Churchill said, gesturing to the two other chairs in the room – which didn't look as comfortable as the ones Churchill and Dr Michaels were using.

'We watched the interview,' Dr Michaels said without preamble. 'And I can tell you unequivocally that Aiden Lomax isn't your man.'

'With respect—' Karen started to say but was cut off.

'It's my professional opinion. He's upset, genuinely devastated. He doesn't know where his wife is.'

'I'm not sure you can say that with absolute certainty,' Karen said.

'It's psychology,' Dr Michaels said. 'Of course, you can't be expected to know that. It takes training. It's not only body language, but sentence pattern, emphasis on certain words. It's the way he looks down at his hands, defeated, broken. If he knew anything, he would tell you. That interview has torn him apart.'

119

Karen experienced another pang of guilt. 'We had to press him hard,' she said.

'No one is criticising you, Karen,' Churchill said, and again she was struck by the use of her first name. 'But we don't want to pursue Aiden at the expense of everything else. I think you're right. Both he and his wife probably had affairs at some point.'

'Then why won't he offer up any names? It's not illegal to have an affair,' Karen said.

'I think I can answer that,' Dr Michaels said. 'Aiden is experiencing a shame so strong it's crushing him. His affair has left him wracked with guilt. He can't admit to it – not to you, or even to himself.'

'He's in denial?' Morgan asked.

That made a certain amount of sense, Karen thought, although not enough for them to stop viewing Aiden Lomax as a person of interest. 'But we know there was at least one other person with a very strong connection to Tamara. We need to identify them. We can't just let it drop.'

'Actually,' Churchill said. 'I think that's exactly what we need to do for now. We've put enough pressure on Aiden. We'll assign another family liaison officer, someone who can restore his trust.'

'So it's our fault if Aiden doesn't talk, because we broke his trust?' Karen asked, irritated because she'd been doing exactly what Churchill had suggested. They'd been through the interview plan before she and Morgan went in to talk to Aiden.

Churchill folded his arms over his chest. 'This isn't personal. You both did a good job in there. But it's my call. And I say we've put enough pressure on him for now, all right?'

Both Morgan and Karen nodded.

The door burst open, and Sophie appeared. She hadn't bothered to knock. Her face was pale. She blurted out, 'You've got to come downstairs, quickly. Another woman's been snatched off the street.'

CHAPTER FOURTEEN

The evening air was cold and sharp as Karen exited her car at six thirty. She shivered, fastening up her coat. Washingborough wasn't far from her own home in Branston. The thought of someone snatching women off the streets here was unnerving.

The second abduction shared similarities with the first. The victim was a blonde woman, and again she'd been forced into the back of a white van.

Fortunately, this time they had a number of witnesses. The woman had been grabbed outside a small shopping arcade in Washingborough. There was also a post office, which was closed at the time, a Chinese restaurant that had just opened, a fish and chip shop, and a Co-op.

There were lots of people milling around. Too many. The place was packed full of interested locals. Uniformed officers were struggling to deal with the curious members of the public. It was only natural that everyone wanted to know what had gone on, and word had spread quickly around the village.

Karen sighed heavily when she realised Tim Farthing was the scenes of crime officer in charge. She saw him plodding towards her, dressed in his white paper suit. She wasn't sure she'd be able to recognise him without it.

'I don't want to hear *I told you so*.' He put a hand on his hip, which made his suit rustle.

He passed her a transparent evidence bag, and Karen knew what it contained before she examined it. Another Queen of Hearts.

'I take it this one wasn't found down a drain?' she asked.

The small amount of Tim Farthing's face that was visible reddened. He grunted and shook his head.

'It was found there.' He pointed to a section of road beyond the crime-scene tape. 'On the pavement this time. We think the van pulled up just beside the curb.'

Karen scanned the area, taking in all the parked cars, and the houses opposite. Then she looked back towards the shops. 'At least we should have the vehicle on camera this time.'

'Yes, it's much more populated round here.'

'Yes,' Karen said. 'I don't like it.'

'Why? Should make your job easier. You'll be back at the station munching donuts before you know it.'

Karen gave him a withering look.

He raised his hands. 'Touchy! It was just a joke.'

'You're right,' Karen said, glancing around the area again.

'I am?' She caught the note of surprise in his voice. 'Well, yes. You should be able to take a joke.'

'Not that,' she snapped, only just managing to refrain from calling him a name peppered with expletives. 'You're right about the area being more built up, with more people around, and it's worrying.'

'It is?'

She nodded. 'So many things could have gone wrong attempting an abduction in an area like this. His confidence must be growing.'

This was an escalation – a fast one.

Another SOCO called Tim away. Karen moved on, looking for the two officers who'd been first on the scene. She found one of them remonstrating with a man who was trying to get under the cordon to access the Co-op.

'I just need to get some fish fingers for my kid's tea,' the man said. 'It won't take a minute.'

'I'm sorry, sir,' the officer said. 'But you can't gain access this way.'

'How else am I supposed to get there? You've blocked off the whole arcade.'

'I'm sorry. You'll have to go to another shop this evening.'

The man huffed and shoved his hands into his pockets, turning away and trudging back up the street, muttering his discontent to a passer-by.

Karen introduced herself to the uniformed officer. 'DS Karen Hart. I worked on the abduction this morning.'

'PC David Norris,' he said. 'I was one of the officers first on the scene.'

'What can you tell me about what happened here?'

'Multiple reports of a woman being attacked and forcibly put into the back of a white van. It happened approximately half an hour ago. We've already spoken to all the retail outlets here, and have gained access to their security camera footage.' He swallowed hard. 'It was a pretty violent attack. She put up a fight, by all accounts.'

'How many witnesses do we have?'

'Three who managed to get a good, close-up view. One of them actually tried to help. A woman called Mandeep Singh. She had contact with the attacker, too. Grabbed on to him and got a really good look at him.'

'She could have some material evidence on her hands or under her nails,' Karen said. 'I'll ask one of the SOCOs to process her. Where is she?'

'I thought of that,' Norris said, puffing out his chest and standing a little straighter. 'She's already been seen by one of the scenes of crime crew. They took scrapings from her fingernails and swabs of her hands.'

'Excellent,' Karen said. 'And have you taken statements?'

'Briefly.' He pulled out his notebook. 'I jotted a few things down.'

'Great, I'll take a look later. I'd like to talk to the witnesses myself if they're still around?'

'Yes, they're in the fish and chip shop. They kindly let us use the seating area inside. The three main witnesses are in there having a cup of tea. They were all quite shaken by the incident. Mrs Singh especially.'

'That's understandable,' Karen said as she followed PC Norris to the fish and chip shop.

Though she was glad the witnesses had been kept in the area, she was disappointed that they were all gathered together. It was only natural after a traumatic event that they would want to talk through what had happened, and without meaning to, their stories would merge.

When talking to witnesses, it was important to get a fresh take as soon as possible, without the influence of others. It was amazing how recollections could change and become part of the group experience, rather than individuals directly reporting what they'd seen with their own eyes.

'I've spoken to the Co-op staff, and they're happy for you to use the store to talk to the witnesses individually. I guessed you'd want to do that, as there's not much room in the fish and chip shop.'

'That's very good thinking,' Karen said, impressed. 'Somewhere quiet where I can talk to them individually is ideal.'

He beamed. 'That's what I thought.'

Though the staff had turned off the fryers, the shop was still warm and smelled of chips and hot vinegar. All three of the witnesses sat on orange plastic chairs, cradling mugs of tea.

PC Norris introduced Karen to the witnesses, and then left her to it.

Karen asked Mandeep Singh if she'd mind coming along with her to the Co-op so she could ask a few questions.

Mandeep followed Karen out into the cold.

'This won't take long, will it? Only, my son is home alone.'

'It shouldn't do. How old is your son?' Karen asked.

'Fifteen. Old enough to be at home alone, of course. It's just after what's happened . . .'

'I understand,' Karen said. 'I'll be as quick as I can.'

They stepped into the Co-op and Mandeep blinked at the bright artificial light.

One of the Co-op staff smiled. 'Are you the police?'

Karen showed her ID. 'It's still okay to use one of your rooms to interview some witnesses?'

'Sure. It's only a tiny room at the back. We use it for breaks.'

'I'm sure it will be fine,' Karen said. 'Thank you.'

But the woman's eyes were fixed on Mandeep. 'What you did was so brave.'

'Oh, I'm sure anyone would have done the same . . .'

The woman led Karen and Mandeep past the produce aisle towards the fridges at the back of the store, and then took a left through a set of double doors that led into a dimly lit, windowless corridor. 'It's just up here.'

She pushed open a blue door and let them enter the small room, which contained four padded chairs, a number of health and safety posters on the wall, and a minuscule kitchen area with a sink and a kettle.

'Is it okay?'

'It's perfect. Thanks very much.'

Once the door was shut, they both sat down. 'Your name is Mandeep Singh, is that right?'

The woman nodded. Her long hair fell forward, and she tucked it behind her ears.

'You must have had quite a shock tonight. Are you doing okay?'

Another nod.

'Can you tell me what happened? In your own words?'

Mandeep took a deep breath. She was still holding her mug of tea, but Karen noticed she hadn't been drinking it. The mug was full.

'I was walking up to the arcade to get some shopping. I'd run out of a few things. Milk and bread, and I couldn't be bothered to go all the way to Tesco—'

Karen interrupted. 'Sorry, to be clear . . . what direction were you coming from?'

'Just up the hill. I'd reached the steps when I noticed a man. He was standing beside his van, and there was something about him that drew my attention.'

When Mandeep paused, Karen nodded encouragement but didn't say anything, just waited for her to continue.

'He seemed agitated, and I don't know . . . I found his behaviour suspicious somehow, I suppose.'

'Why did you find him suspicious?'

'He was bundled up, wearing a knitted hat and a big scarf that covered his face. I know it's cold tonight, but it seemed to me he was deliberately hiding. He was dressed all in black and was pacing back and forth by the side of his van. He just stood out. He didn't look like he was there to go to the shops or pick up some chips. I thought maybe he was about to rob the Co-op. So I watched him for a while from outside the shop. Then I got a text message from my son asking me if we could have chips for tea. I said no, but said

I'd pick up some potatoes and we could make our own.' She shook her head. 'That's not relevant. Sorry. Anyway, I was looking at my phone, so I didn't really see what happened at the beginning . . . I didn't see the woman approach, but all of a sudden, I heard her scream. I knew it was him. He'd grabbed her, pulling her towards the back of his van. I didn't know what to do.' She looked down at her lap. 'I wasn't quick enough. I couldn't decide whether to phone for help or to help her . . .' She looked up at Karen. 'I should have moved faster, but it was all such a shock. You don't expect to see that sort of thing. My brain wouldn't process it. I thought it had to be a joke. Maybe they were messing around. But she was screaming and kicking so hard, and then, when I realised he was trying to put her in the van . . . I don't really know what happened next. I remember running up towards them, trying to stop him. He was too strong though. I pulled on his jacket. I really tried to stop him . . .' She trailed off.

'It *was* very brave,' Karen said.

'It didn't do much good though, did it?'

'I don't know. It may have slowed him down. There may be trace evidence on your hands that the SOCOs have collected. And the most important thing is you tried.'

'I really did.' Mandeep shook her head. 'He shoved me and then pushed her into the van and slammed the doors. And by the time I got up, he was behind the wheel and driving off.'

'Were there other people around?'

'Yes, a couple of people were close, but no one was quick enough. No one could help.' Mandeep sniffed and rubbed her nose. 'It was awful. I mean, you read about these things happening, but to actually see it . . . And she was so scared. I could hear it in her voice.'

'It must have been extremely scary for you too. Not many people would put themselves at risk like that.'

'I didn't really think about it,' Mandeep said. 'I think if I had, I probably would have chickened out, to be honest. But the way she screamed . . . She was petrified.' She pressed a hand to her chest. 'Do you know who she is?'

'I'm afraid we don't yet,' Karen said. 'Can you give me a description of the man?'

Mandeep blew out a long breath. 'I can't tell you much. He was wearing a knitted hat that was either black or navy blue, and it was pulled down very low. He had a bomber jacket on, which was black and made of a sort of shiny material. Black jeans, I think. He was tall, well-built but slim. And he was strong.'

'Could you tell his ethnicity?'

'I think he was white.'

'What about the van? Was there any writing on it? Or did you catch a glimpse of the licence plate?'

Mandeep leaned back in her chair and looked up at the ceiling. 'I don't really remember much about the van, other than it was white and had doors at the back. I did look at the van as it drove off, thinking I needed to get the number plate, but the back plate was covered with mud. I couldn't make out any letters or numbers.'

Karen's stomach sank. That didn't sound promising.

'Sorry, I've not been much help, have I?'

'You've been incredibly helpful. It's not easy to focus on details in the heat of the moment. Can you tell me anything about the woman? Did you recognise her?'

'She had long blonde hair. It came to about here.' Mandeep pointed to a spot in the middle of her bicep. 'She had a big coat on, and that's all I remember.'

'The colour of the coat?'

Mandeep shook her head. 'It was dark. Black, navy, dark green, I'm not sure.'

Karen asked a few more questions and then wrapped things up.

Mandeep rummaged in her handbag as her phone began to ring. 'It's my son. I need to take this. He's going to be worried and wondering what's taking me so long.' She answered the phone. 'Hello, love. I know. I'm sorry. I got held up. Everything is fine, and I'll be home soon. Why don't we order pizza for dinner?'

Karen followed Mandeep out of the Co-op and waved her off. Then she walked back towards the fish and chip shop. There were lots of cameras available. If they were high-enough resolution, they might be able to get a good look at the suspect. Though the clothing Mandeep had described suggested that identification was going to be difficult. And the number plate on the van being obscured with mud sounded deliberate.

Though it was hard to admit, it was looking increasingly likely that Dr Michaels was right. Whoever was doing this was using the Queen of Hearts as some kind of message. But Karen had no idea what it could mean. Perhaps the queen signified a female. He was targeting women. Did he feel he'd been treated badly by them in the past? Hearts could signify love or relationships.

She shook her head. Soon she'd be creating her own profile.

CHAPTER FIFTEEN

The other two witnesses were waiting in the fish and chip shop: one man and one woman.

'Can I go next?' the woman asked, standing up. 'I'm Naomi. I'm neighbours with Mandeep. We only live three doors apart.' She looked at the bald man still sitting on his orange chair. 'You don't mind, do you?'

He shook his head.

'Right, come with me,' Karen said.

As they walked towards the Co-op, Karen asked some general questions. 'Is anyone waiting for you to get home?'

'Yes, three kids under five, and my husband, Jamie. Do him good to look after them for a while. He escapes out to work all day. Thinks my job is easy!'

'What were you doing out this evening?'

'What? Aren't I allowed out? I haven't done anything wrong.' She was defensive. A difficult character.

'Of course. I just wondered what you were doing.'

Naomi shrugged. 'I needed to post a letter and then get some milk.' She held up her bag for life in one hand. It was green and decorated with pictures of vegetables.

Karen saved the rest of the questions until they were in the break room at the back of the Co-op.

'Can you tell me what you saw?' Karen asked simply as they both sank into their chairs.

Naomi put her bag on the floor between her legs. 'I'd just come out of the shop when I saw the van. I don't think it was there when I went in. Although, it could have been. I wasn't paying that much attention. I was focused on getting my shopping.'

'Can you describe what you saw?'

'I was putting my purse in my handbag. I heard her scream before I saw anything. There was a big commotion by the van. At first, I thought it was two men having a fight, so I walked back down to the steps, keeping to the far left to avoid any trouble. When I got closer, I saw the woman. She was blonde and making an unholy racket. Really screeching. I thought they were having a domestic, and then I saw him dragging her towards the van. That was when I realised something really bad was happening. Then Mandeep flew at him. She jumped on him, but he pushed her off. Shoved her really hard, pushing her over. I shouted out, telling him to stop, but of course he didn't. The woman was really kicking him hard, but he managed to get her in the back of the van. That's when I got my phone, to ring 999. But I dropped it. By the time I picked it up again, the woman was in the van, and he was climbing into the driver's seat.' She chewed her lip. 'I called for help, and the first police car got here pretty quickly. The officers asked me a few questions and then asked me to wait in the fish and chip shop. Then you arrived. Are you in charge?'

'I'm working on the investigation,' Karen said, 'but I'm not in charge. Can you tell me any identifying details? Anything you noticed about the man, the woman he attacked, or the vehicle?'

Naomi puffed out a breath. 'It was dark, and I was some distance away when I first noticed what was going on. The van was white. I know that for sure. And it was quite big, maybe a Transit.

But the man was dressed in dark colours, and he had a hat on. I can't tell you much about him.'

'How tall do you think he was?'

'I'd say about as tall as my husband. So about six foot two. He was broad-shouldered, quite fit-looking. I think he was quite young.'

'What do you mean by *young*?'

'I can't say for certain, but the way he moved made me think he was probably under forty. Though I didn't get a good look at his face.'

'What about the number plate on the van?'

'Sorry, I know it's ridiculous – it's the first thing I should have looked at, but it was happening really fast, and I was concentrating on getting my phone to call the police, and when I looked up again, the van was already heading off.'

'Did you see what route it took?'

'Straight down the street and then left at the bottom.'

'Thanks, that's really helpful.'

'Do you think it was some disgruntled ex or something like that? I keep thinking of the woman. How scared she sounded.'

'I'm not sure,' Karen said. 'At this stage we're looking into all options, but was there a reason you thought he might be a disgruntled ex?'

'I don't know.' Naomi shrugged. 'That sort of thing happens a lot though, doesn't it?'

'More often than it should,' Karen said. 'Was there anything about the woman that stood out?'

'I might have recognised her. Seen her before, anyway. Never chatted to her, though. I've lived here all my life and know a lot of the other locals. It's hard to tell because in this weather everyone is bundled up, aren't they? She was about my height and had long blonde hair. And she was wearing a jacket with a hood. I think it was dark green.'

'Anything else?'

Naomi thought for a moment, chewing her lip. 'Yes, she was wearing heels. Just low ones, maybe two inches. I'm not sure if they were boots or shoes. I remember because she was kicking him, and I thought what a shame the heels weren't a bit longer, because then they could have done some real damage.' She nodded to herself. 'Yes, higher heels really would have hurt him. Such a shame.'

The final witness was a man called Paul Broxton. Compared to the other two witnesses, he'd had the worst view of the incident. He'd been inside the Co-op when he heard someone shout that a woman was being attacked.

Paul sat opposite Karen. He rubbed his hands over his hair-free scalp, and his bushy dark eyebrows met in the middle as he frowned.

'What did you see as you came out of the shop?' Karen asked.

'It was mayhem. I wasn't sure what was going on,' he said. 'There were two women ahead of me. They blocked my view a bit. Then I heard a woman screaming. I think she was the one being attacked. I started running, you know, to try and help her. It was such an awful noise. I've heard women screaming before, like on the TV, but this was different. It was pure terror.'

'So you ran towards her?'

'Yes, towards the screams. I saw a man getting into the driver's seat of a white van, and then he drove off.'

'So you didn't see the woman at all?'

'No, I only heard her.'

'Did you see anyone else in the van?'

'No.'

'Do you remember who shouted that someone was being attacked?'

He shook his head. 'I didn't actually see them. I heard them when I was standing by the fruit and veg. I needed to get a bag of salad for dinner.'

He was still holding his now-empty mug.

'Can you give me a description of the man you saw?'

'I'm really sorry, but I didn't get a good look at him. He was wearing dark clothes. Maybe a puffer jacket.'

'Could you tell his ethnicity?'

Paul shook his head. 'I wasn't close enough. He was tall, over six foot, I'd say, and athletic.'

'Did you manage to get a look at the number plate? Or did you see anything printed on the side of the van?'

Again, he shook his head. 'I couldn't swear to it, but I don't think the van had a sign. As for the number plate, no chance, sorry.'

'That's okay. Thanks, Paul. We'll be in touch. We have your details, don't we?'

He nodded. 'Yes, I gave them to the first officer I spoke to.'

When Karen left the shop, she stopped in the middle of the square and watched the white-suited scenes of crime officers as they finished gathering evidence. Their large floodlights illuminated the area.

Karen looked up. The sky was cloudless, and stars, only faintly visible against the background light pollution, dotted the blackness.

She exhaled, her breath curling up to the sky. She tried to sort through the facts in her mind, but one question kept pushing itself to the front of her brain.

If this man needed a fresh victim, what did that mean for the first woman he'd taken?

She knew the answer, of course. It meant Tamara Lomax was probably dead.

CHAPTER SIXTEEN

Rick and Sophie got straight to work at the station, sifting through all the camera footage. This time, they had the opposite problem they'd had with the first abduction. The amount of footage was going to take a great deal of time and manpower to examine thoroughly.

But they had made a good start. When Karen went to check on how they were getting on, they'd already isolated relevant sections, making clips and getting screenshots.

'There's good news and bad news,' Rick said.

Karen stood at the end of his desk. 'All right. Give me the good news first.'

'The abduction was caught on camera. A number of different cameras, actually. One was council-owned, and another belonged to the Co-op. They've given us the best footage. Both cameras were directed towards Park Lane.'

'That's excellent news.'

Rick pressed a button on his keyboard, and Karen watched the action unfold on his computer monitor. It was dark. The footage was in black-and-white, and the white van was clearly visible. Although the nose of the van was just out of shot, it was a good enough picture to see that the wheels were muddy.

Karen's gaze was drawn to the dark figure standing beside the back wheel arch. She immediately saw what Mandeep had meant when she'd said the man looked agitated. He shifted his weight from foot to foot and kept glancing up and down the road. There was something about him that didn't quite fit. But Karen wasn't sure what that was yet. His appearance lined up with the witness statements. He looked to be slightly over six foot tall, with a strong, athletic build, just as everyone had described.

As she watched him, it slowly dawned what was bothering her. He was nervous.

He wasn't the confident, cunning man she'd expected from Dr Michaels's profile. He didn't look like he was enjoying playing a game – he appeared stressed. She imagined him worrying someone was about to approach and ask what he was doing.

He also hadn't managed to avoid any of the cameras, and that was a very obvious error. Parking just a little further up the street would have reduced the amount of footage they had of him.

Karen moved closer to the monitor, leaning on Rick's desk to get a better look. This wasn't adding up the way she'd expected it to.

To the left of the screen, a blonde woman walked into view. She was in profile; her hair was loose and her face was hidden from the camera.

Again, the witness statements had been pretty accurate. She had long fair hair. Her hands were in the pockets of her dark coat, her shoulders were hunched against the cold, and her head was bowed. She wasn't paying attention to her surroundings.

'Can you zoom in?' Karen asked.

'A little, but not too much because it goes all blurry.' Rick pressed a couple of buttons and the picture enlarged. He was right. There was no way they'd be able to see much more detail at this resolution. The small section of the man's face that wasn't covered was pixelated and blurred.

'Harinder might be able to do something with it,' Sophie suggested. Karen hadn't noticed her move behind them because she'd been so intent on the screen.

Karen nodded, but she was doubtful. There was a limit even to Harinder's technical wizardry. 'Zoom back out and keep playing,' she said.

It was horrible, watching the footage back, knowing that the unsuspecting victim, innocently walking home, was about to meet her attacker.

Karen held her breath as the woman approached the back of the van. Something seemed to alert her to the danger. She lifted her head. Perhaps the man had said something?

There was no way they could see her face, but she walked closer. Maybe she felt safe in a residential area with so many people around.

When she was almost level with him, she raised an arm. Was it a protective move? Self-defence? But she didn't run or even turn and walk away. Instead, she stopped beside him. It looked like they were talking, but then he grabbed her, pinning her arms to her sides.

It was then that the shock and panic kicked in. The woman bucked in his arms and kicked out.

Karen found herself willing the woman to break free, even though she knew the outcome. If only she could reach up and scratch his face, marking him out as a suspect. Perhaps that would be enough to arouse suspicion in people who knew him. Enough for them to report him to the police before he claimed another victim.

He had the woman in a bear hug and towered over her by almost a foot, making a mockery of her ineffective struggle.

He'd just managed to get one of the doors at the back of the van open when Mandeep Singh appeared.

She streaked across the screen, fists raised, and she actually jumped on him. Clambering on to his back, she looped her arm around his neck.

For a moment, it looked like it might be enough for him to loosen his grip on his victim, but then with a shrug of his shoulders and a flick of one of his arms, he sent Mandeep careering to the ground.

Mandeep got to her knees, bent double, obviously winded. The man took the opportunity to shove the blonde woman into the back of the van and lock the doors. He ran around to the driver's side, climbed in and pulled sharply away from the curb within seconds.

Karen saw the back of Paul's bald head as he jogged into view, but the van was already making its way up the road.

The back number plate of the van was covered in mud. It was impossible to work out. Again, they'd have to ask Harinder if he could enhance the image, but Karen didn't like their chances.

She sighed. 'I think I can see the bad news for myself. There's no way we're going to get a good picture of his face from that, is there?'

'It doesn't look likely, Sarge,' Rick said. 'Between the hat and the scarf there's not much of his face visible anyway.'

Karen thought for a moment. 'We could ask Mandeep to work with an artist, but I don't hold out much hope for success. What's the other video like?'

'Worse than this one,' Rick said. 'The angle of the camera is more acute.'

'Have you managed to track the van's route via traffic cameras?'

'We're working on it. So far it looks like he took Fen Road.'

'Right. Well, that's a top priority. We need to know where that van went. If we manage to track it down fast enough, we might be able to save her. And we need to identify this woman. It might be a while before she's reported missing. We need any other camera footage you can get your hands on. Ideally we'll track her route from home or work and find someone who can ID her.' Karen paused for a breath and to collect her thoughts. 'Do you know if DC Shah managed to speak to the owner of Branston Chickens? That was the only van seen in the area at the time of the first abduction that we haven't tracked down yet.'

'She did try,' Sophie said. 'They wouldn't give out any information over the phone. Said they needed a warrant.'

'Right, well, let's get one. In the meantime, I'm going to pay them a visit and see if I can wrangle the name of the driver from them.' She checked the time. It was unlikely anyone would be there now, as it was outside working hours, but she had to try.

'All right,' Sophie said. 'I'll organise the warrant and ask DCI Churchill to get it signed off.'

CHAPTER SEVENTEEN

Branston Chickens was situated on a large acreage on Mere Road in Branston. It was relatively isolated. There were no residential dwellings for over half a mile in either direction, apart from one small bungalow, which Karen guessed was owned by the company.

Behind the premises and on the opposite side of the road were large open fields.

As Karen drew level with the entrance, her car's headlights illuminated a wide iron gate. The site looked dark and abandoned. As she couldn't get any closer in her vehicle, she parked by the side of the gate and got out. Somewhere in the distance, an owl screeched.

Karen shivered, then told herself it was just because she was cold.

Though she'd passed the place many times, it felt different tonight, standing there alone in the dark.

She walked towards the gate and saw with irritation that a metal chain had been looped through the posts of the gate and padlocked, preventing entry.

She looked towards the large low-rise buildings, which she assumed held the birds. There was a tall feed container and beside it was a small, squat bungalow. She checked her watch.

Sophie was going to call her as soon the warrant was issued. But standing here, alone in the silent darkness, Karen was aware of just how suitable this place would be for the abductor to take his victims.

At night he wouldn't be disturbed. During the day, though? There would be staff around. Had he risked bringing Tamara and his second victim here?

She needed to get inside and find out. There was a chance the van they were looking for was on the grounds, and even if he hadn't kept the women here, the van would provide material evidence.

She rattled the gate in frustration, and a bright beam from a torch swung around and shone directly in her face.

Karen put up a hand to shield her eyes.

'What do you want?' a gruff voice asked.

She fumbled for her warrant card. 'Police. DS Karen Hart. I need to speak to whoever is in charge here.'

He lowered the torch, which allowed Karen to see him for the first time. A middle-aged man wearing a blue security guard's uniform. He had dark curly hair and a heavyset build. His mouth turned down at the corners. He looked Karen up and down.

'What's all this about?' he asked.

'Are you in charge?'

'No, that'll be Mr Greaves.'

'Is he here?'

The security guard nodded. 'He's working late. Always does.'

'What's your name?'

'Travis Deacon.'

'Right, Travis Deacon, can you take me to see Mr Greaves, please?'

He hesitated, and for a second Karen thought he might be about to refuse. But then he shrugged. 'I don't have the padlock key.'

'Who does?'

'Mr Greaves.'

'Then can you get it?' Karen asked.

'Could do, but it's easier if you come round here.' He shone his torch at a spot a few metres away, where there was a small gap in the hedge.

'You want me to get through there?' Karen asked, thinking the padlocked gate wasn't much use if there was a way to get through the hedge.

He shrugged. 'It would be easier,' he said again.

For a split second, she imagined getting back into her car and driving it full throttle at the gate. She'd definitely developed anger issues. Put that down to the stupidity of other people rather than a fault of her own.

'Fine.' She stepped carefully over the verge and headed towards the gap.

The security guard kept the beam from the torch on the hedge as Karen squeezed through the gap in the prickly hawthorn. She felt the spiky branches tug at her coat.

Once on the other side, she said, 'Right, where is he?'

'Over there,' the security guard said, pointing towards the bungalow.

They trudged towards it over the hard, frozen ground.

'Sorry about that,' he said, nodding back to the gate as they walked. 'When I spotted you, I thought you might be one of those animal-rights types. We had a couple creeping in here to take videos of inside the main building.'

'I guess the chickens aren't free-range then?' Karen asked, looking up at the ominous dark buildings.

'Don't ask me,' he said. 'I'm just security.'

He rapped on the door and a cheerful voice told them to enter. The security guard held the door open for Karen and then shut it behind her.

Mr Greaves was a short man. He wasn't much over five foot two, Karen guessed. Though it was hard to be sure when he was sitting behind a desk. He was bald on top, but his dark red hair was long around his ears and the base of his skull. It was an unusual look.

He smiled widely. 'How can I help?'

'Hello, Mr Greaves. I apologise for disturbing you, but—'

'Not at all,' he said. 'You can call me Greavsie. All my mates do.'

I'd rather not, Karen thought. He seemed more like the cliché of the second-hand car dealer than a chicken farmer. 'We're looking for a white van. As you probably know from the numerous phone calls I've placed to your business today.' She read off the licence plate number. 'I need to know who was driving the vehicle this morning around eight a.m., and also who had it this evening at around six p.m.'

'Ah,' he said slowly, leaning back in his chair. 'I think you better sit down.'

Karen took a seat in a rather grubby-looking chair in front of Mr Greaves's desk.

'I'd like to help,' he said, 'but there's a bit of a problem.'

'We can get a warrant, Mr Greaves. I understand you want to protect your staff's privacy. But two women have been abducted, and this is a very time-sensitive enquiry.' Karen laid it all out, so he could see how important it was. Most people were reasonable if they knew why the police needed the information. 'Their lives are in danger, and we believe this vehicle is incredibly important to our investigation. You need to tell me who was driving it.'

'Oh, it's not about warrants,' Mr Greaves said, even though that was exactly what DC Shah had been told on the phone. 'I want to cooperate with the police, of course. I'm a law-abiding citizen, and I pay my taxes. I've never had any trouble with the law.'

'Then what exactly is the problem?' Karen asked, losing patience. She shifted in her seat and noticed what looked like scratch marks on the chair legs.

143

'Everyone who takes one of the vans out has to sign the log-book.' He flipped open a large navy-blue hardback book and pushed it across the desk to Karen.

A number of handwritten columns were visible. Times and dates were listed alongside signatures.

Mr Greaves ran his finger down one of the columns. 'After I got your call earlier, I looked the vehicle up in the logbook. We keep excellent records here, DS Hart.'

'Great. So who had the vehicle?'

He prodded the page. 'Tony.'

'Tony who?'

'Tony Hickman. Lovely guy, salt-of-the-earth type of bloke. I can promise you he won't be involved in these abductions.'

'Tony had the vehicle all day?'

'No. You see, that's where it gets complicated.'

'Please, Mr Greaves—'

'I told you, call me Greavsie.'

Karen jolted as a marmalade cat appeared from under the desk and began to wind its way around her ankles. She guessed that explained the scratch marks on the chair legs.

'Please, Greavsie, could you tell me who had the van today?'

'That's just it. I don't know.'

'You don't know?'

'No.' He held out his hands, palms up, and shrugged. 'It's been stolen.'

Karen stared at him blankly. 'You're telling me the van we're interested in has been stolen? Then why hasn't it been reported missing?'

'Well, we haven't had a chance to report it yet.'

This was unbelievable. 'I'm sorry, Mr Greaves, but this sounds very suspicious. Perhaps we should be looking at you as a suspect in this investigation?'

His jaw dropped. 'Me? Why would you do that? I didn't have the van.'

'You're the owner of the vehicle. Whoever had the van today abducted two women. If you won't tell us who that was, I have to assume it was you.'

'But that's hardly fair. I don't think I've ever driven that van.'

He was panicking, his leg bobbing up and down under the desk.

'You're telling me now it was stolen? That seems very convenient timing.'

'Hold your horses. You're being ridiculous. I wouldn't hurt a fly. Let's be logical. I'm helping you, aren't I? I showed you the logbook.'

'But the logbook doesn't help me, does it? It tells me Tony's got the van, but you're telling me it was stolen.'

'It was.'

'How do you know it was stolen?'

'Because Tony told me.'

'When did he tell you?'

'When I called him. Look, I heard from you lot, asking me about the van, so I checked in the logbook and saw Tony had booked it out. I thought he'd been a bit naughty, perhaps got caught speeding or parking in the wrong place, and to be honest, I was a bit annoyed at him using the van, because he told me he was off sick. So I gave him a ring, and he said the van's been parked outside his house all day, but then he goes to look while he's still on the phone to me and says, *Oh, it's not there anymore.* So I said, *What do you mean, it's not there anymore?* And he said, *I think it's been nicked.*'

Karen rubbed her forehead, trying to process the convoluted information without losing her temper. 'Right, well, I need to speak to Tony. Can you give me his address?'

'Of course, he won't mind. He's a good bloke, and I can assure you he's not involved.'

'Thank you for your opinion, but I think I'll judge that for myself.'

'Sure, no problem. I wouldn't dream of telling you how to do your job. Just like you wouldn't tell me how to raise chickens.' He actually winked at her.

◆ ◆ ◆

Blood boiling, Karen walked back to her car with her security-guard escort. They didn't even trust her to go back to her car without snooping around. The security guard watched closely as she squeezed back through the gap in the hedge.

Once she got into the car, to annoy the security guard, she didn't reverse out on to the main road straightaway, but instead placed a call to Sophie, who was still at the station.

'Sorry, Sophie. I know it's a late one.'

'No problem, Sarge. I'd stay here all night if it meant we got them back.'

Deep down, Karen was almost certain they wouldn't get Tamara back. The second woman's abduction indicated that Tamara was likely dead already, but she didn't voice her fears. Instead she said, 'Annoyingly, Mr Greaves of Branston Chickens is still giving us the runaround.'

'Can't you bring him in?' Sophie asked. 'We could put some pressure on.' The eagerness in Sophie's voice made Karen smile.

'I think that might be a waste of time. He's told me that the van was stolen from outside one of his employees' houses, and apparently they only realised after we called them to ask about it today.'

'Well, that sounds dodgy.'

'That's what I thought, but I've checked it out, and an employee called Tony Hickman had the van. I'm going to go to his house now. He's been off work sick, which is his excuse for not realising the van had been taken.'

'If he's been off work, he may have had the opportunity to do both abductions . . .'

'Yes, so it's important I speak with him tonight. Any more luck with the camera footage? Any clues to the woman's identity?'

'Not yet. DC Morrison is helping me on that, as Rick has gone home now. Priya stayed late, but she couldn't stay all night.'

'Okay, let me know any developments, and I'll—'

'Oh, Sarge, hang on a minute.' Karen heard someone else talking to Sophie and then Sophie's voice came back on the line. 'DCI Churchill wants to speak to you.'

'DS Hart. How are you getting on?'

'Not great,' she said. 'Mr Greaves, the owner of Branston Chickens, said the van we're interested in was stolen. It was in the possession of an employee called Tony Hickman at the time, so I'm just on my way to call in at his house now. As luck would have it, he lives in Nettleham, close to the station.'

'Right, pick me up on the way,' Churchill said.

Karen was shocked into silence.

'DS Hart, are you still there?'

'Yes, sorry. Did you just say you wanted me to pick you up?'

'Yes, that's right. I want to come with you and be there when you talk to Tony Hickman.'

'Okay, depending on traffic, I should be about twenty minutes. Meet you outside?'

'Yes.' He hung up.

Karen tossed her phone on to the passenger seat and then yawned. It had been a long day.

The security guard was still watching her from behind the gate. She waved and then backed out on to Mere Road.

She headed to the crossing, then turned left on to Lincoln Road. A minute later, she was driving past her own house. She gave it a wistful look, imagining Mike inside, perhaps tucking into dinner and a glass of wine, with Sandy companionably lying at his side. She'd sent him a text earlier to tell him she'd be working late.

The road was quiet as she got to the new roundabout and headed right. The bypass certainly made it easier to get to Nettleham now.

She had no idea why Churchill wanted to come with her to speak to Tony Hickman, but hoped he wouldn't get in the way.

There was a lot of pressure to get answers from Hickman, and she wasn't used to working side by side with Churchill when questioning witnesses or suspects. He could mess things up. Ruin the flow. She'd much rather have Morgan by her side, or Rick, or Sophie. But she could hardly refuse Churchill. He was the DCI, after all. Karen hoped he would at least let her lead the questioning.

Ideally, she wanted to pin Tony Hickman down quickly, so he had no time to prepare an elaborate story. But she wasn't stupid. She had no doubt Mr Greaves had picked up the phone to warn Tony as soon as she'd left his office. So she needed to be sharp. A lot would depend on her chat with Mr Hickman.

CHAPTER EIGHTEEN

Rick set up his laptop at the kitchen table. He'd pushed his half-eaten dinner aside. A microwaveable ready-meal of sweet and sour chicken and egg-fried rice wasn't too bad when it was piping hot, but after being called by his mother twice, it had grown cold, and he'd lost his appetite.

It was such a fuss to cook something from scratch just for him, and his mother never wanted to eat anything except soup these days.

He opened the web browser and navigated to Tamara's Facebook page. They'd had no hits from her mobile phone, so wherever it was, it was likely the battery and SIM card had been removed.

She hadn't made her page private, so he scrolled through her friends list and interests to see if anything jumped out at him.

She followed a number of true crime authors, including Dr Michaels. *Interesting.* She also seemed to be a big fan of forensic TV shows and detective series, judging by the pages she'd liked. She'd commented on a recent post for a US cop show to say that she couldn't wait for the next series.

Rick sighed. He bet Tamara could never have anticipated being the victim in a real-life case that would have fitted into the true crime books and series she liked so much.

He heard a noise, a movement, and paused. Another sound – a wardrobe door opening?

Rick walked out into the hallway to find his mother wearing her coat and slippers. 'What are you doing, Mum?'

'I've got to go to the library. My books are overdue, but I can't find them.'

'It's night-time. The library is shut. Why don't we do it tomorrow?'

His heart broke at the confusion on his mother's face. 'They're late. I'll get a fine. And I can't find them!'

'It's all right,' Rick said. 'I know where they are. I'll take them in the morning.'

There were no books. His mother hadn't been to the library in over a year.

'You will?' She looked at him sceptically. 'But what about the fine?'

'They'll let us off,' he said, gently leading his mother back to her room.

'How can you be sure?' She let Rick ease off her coat.

He pulled the duvet back for her. 'Because they know I'm a police officer. Perk of the job.'

His mother sat on the bed and stared at him, then she started to giggle. 'Oh, Rick, you mustn't tell tales.'

'What do you mean?'

She lay back against her pillows, still smiling. 'You take them in for me on the way to school in the morning. There's money in my purse for the fine.'

Rick swallowed hard. 'Okay, Mum.' He leaned forward to kiss her forehead. 'Love you. Sleep tight.'

'Night, darling.'

He hung up her coat, and softly closed the bedroom door. Then he went back to the kitchen to set the alarm.

The alarm wasn't used in the typical sense. It wasn't to keep people out, but rather to keep his mother in. If she opened a window or a door when Rick was sleeping, it would go off, alerting him before anything bad could happen. That was the idea, anyway. But all Rick could think as he inputted the numbers was that he was locking his mum in her home, just like the disease had locked her into a confused mind.

He sat back down at the kitchen table and buried his head in his hands.

'So,' Karen said as Churchill slid into the passenger seat. 'How exactly do you want to do this?'

He frowned. 'What do you mean?' he asked, buckling up.

Karen began to back out of the parking space outside the station. 'Do you want to make an interview plan or leave it up to me to ask the questions?'

'Oh, I see what you mean. Yes, you can ask the questions.'

'You're content to take a back seat?' Karen asked. Her scepticism came through in her tone.

'Yes, I'm just observing your work.'

'No pressure then,' Karen muttered as she pulled out on to the road.

'It's part of your assessment. Didn't I mention it?'

'No, you didn't. What assessment?'

'Your personal assessment. We have to do them every year.'

'DI Morgan normally does them.'

'Well, this time, it's going to be me,' Churchill said, and Karen thought he looked smug.

It took less than five minutes to drive to Tony Hickman's house. But a further two minutes just to find somewhere to park.

'What number did you say it was again?' Churchill asked, craning his neck to look out of Karen's side of the car.

'Thirty-two.'

'You've passed it. Number thirty-two is back there.'

Karen's hands gripped the steering wheel tightly. 'I know, but I need to find somewhere to park. I can't just leave the car in the middle of the road.'

'Why can't you park there?'

'The space is too small.'

'No, I'm sure you could manage it. You just need to reverse park.'

Karen pressed the brake and turned to look at him. She said nothing. Her glare told him everything he needed to know.

'All right.' He put his hands up. 'I'll stop talking.'

Eventually, she found a suitable spot and parked, then grabbed her mobile and put it in her pocket.

She double-checked with Churchill. 'So you're really all right with me leading the questions? You're only there to observe?'

'Yes.'

Karen led the way back up the small hill towards number thirty-two.

'You really did park a long distance away,' Churchill said when they were halfway there.

Karen ignored him and continued marching on, wishing she'd come on her own.

Number thirty-two had a blue door with a brass knocker. It was a terraced house, and Karen guessed it would be a two- or three-bedroom place. At the front of the house was a small garden rather than a driveway. It was the same as most of the houses in the street, which was a shame because driveways would go a long way to solving the parking problem.

Karen rang the doorbell.

A harassed-looking woman opened the door. She had straw-berry-blonde hair scraped back into a ponytail, but a few strands had escaped and hung loosely about her face. 'Yeah?' A small child grabbed on to her leg.

Karen held up her warrant card. 'DS Karen Hart, and this is DCI Churchill. We've come to speak to Tony Hickman please.'

'What do you want with Tony?' the woman asked, but before waiting for an answer, she stepped back and called up the stairs. 'Tony! It's for you. It's the police.' She looked back at Karen with narrowed eyes. 'You'd better come in.'

Karen and Churchill stepped into the small hallway just as a tall, gangly man appeared at the top of the stairs. 'Police?' he asked in a reedy voice.

He was dressed in a pale blue dressing gown. His thin calves poked out of the bottom, and he hobbled barefoot down the stairs. His hair was mussed up, as though he'd been in bed.

'Tony Hickman?'

'That's me. What's wrong? Has something happened?'

'We need to have a chat,' Karen said. 'Can we come inside and sit down?'

'Of course.'

He looked nervously at his wife and child.

'You've not got anything to hide, have you, Tony?' his wife asked in a cold voice.

'No,' he said quickly. He winced as he sank down on to the sofa.

Churchill and Karen took the two armchairs opposite.

'You couldn't make us a cup of tea, could you, love?' Tony shot a pleading glance at his wife.

She regarded him suspiciously, but then nodded. 'Can I get you anything?' She looked at Karen and Churchill.

'No, thank you. I'm fine,' Karen said.

'Nothing for me, thank you,' Churchill said.

The woman turned to leave the room and said, 'Come on, Tilly, let's give Daddy some privacy.'

Karen felt like the air had been sucked from her lungs. She stared after the little girl. Her mouth grew dry, and she felt dizzy. She continued staring even after the little girl had left the room.

It's just a name, she told herself. *Focus.*

'So, what's all this about then?' Tony asked.

Karen blinked and turned her attention back to him. She could feel Churchill's eyes burning into her but studiously ignored them. She tried to get her thoughts in order, but everything was jumbled. All she could think about was *Tilly*.

The little girl didn't even look like Karen's daughter, but hearing the name when she hadn't expected it made her feel like someone had punched a hole in her chest and was squeezing her heart.

It hurt more than when she'd noticed the similarities between Molly and Tilly. The name made it feel more real.

She needed to get a grip. Some assessment this was going to be. Churchill would probably delight in giving her a terrible score.

She needed to push it out of her mind for now and deal with it later. She wouldn't mention it to Mike. He'd understand, of course, but he worried about her too much as it was.

Maybe she'd bring it up at the next group counselling session. She'd surprised herself over the past month by becoming more open with them. They were a good bunch, too. An unlikely group. Lorry driver Boris, who had a shiny bald head but a long ginger beard that reached his ample stomach, and Gloria, who'd started dating again in her eighties after losing her husband, and enjoyed sharing stories about her romantic liaisons. Karen was sure she exaggerated some of her exploits to try to embarrass the others.

Karen clenched her fists, feeling a sharp stab of pain as her fingernails pressed into her skin. *Concentrate.* There wasn't time for this.

Tony Hickman was looking at her expectantly, and she didn't dare glance at Churchill.

'It's about the van,' Karen managed to say.

'Oh, of course,' he said, slapping a hand to his forehead. 'Yes, it was stolen. Sorry, I should have realised. But I didn't think you'd actually come around in person over a stolen vehicle. I thought I'd just have to go into a local station and file a report.'

'The reason we're interested in the van, Tony, is because we believe it's been involved in a crime.'

'Yeah, well, I expected as much. That's what they do, isn't it? They steal vans and then use them for a robbery or something like that – a smash-and-grab – and then dump the van somewhere. Have you found it?'

'Not yet. In this case, the crime is very serious. We believe it was used by a man who abducted two women today. One this morning, and another early this evening.'

'Abducted?' Tony looked genuinely shocked.

'Yes. When did you first notice it was missing?'

'When Greavsie gave me a ring this afternoon. It had been parked outside, just up the street. I normally leave it there, and it's safe enough around here.' He rubbed the back of his neck. 'It's got an alarm and everything. I didn't hear a thing, though. I hope you catch them quickly.'

'Tony, can you tell me where you were at eight o'clock this morning and at six thirty this evening?'

He paled. 'I can't believe you think I was involved.'

His wife came in, holding a mug of tea. She put it down on the coffee table.

'I was here, wasn't I, love? I've been home all day.'

'Yes, I can vouch for that. He's been getting under my feet.'

Tony shot her a hurt look. 'I haven't,' he said. 'I've been in bed. Shingles. The pain is awful. I've never known anything like it. I've

155

got a rash on my side and intense stabbing pains. I haven't left the house in three days.'

'He is telling you the truth,' his wife said.

Tony pressed his fingers to his eyes. 'My head is banging. Could you get me the painkillers, love?'

His wife nodded and turned to go back into the kitchen.

Tony leaned forward and picked up his mug of tea. 'I'd like to help you, but I don't know anything about how the van was stolen, or who took it. It's nothing to do with me.'

The small child had wandered back into the room. Karen tried to ignore her and keep her focus on Tony. But her gaze was drawn magnetically to the little girl.

See, she told herself, *she doesn't look anything like Tilly.*

She was holding a toy train in one hand and a red truck in the other, which made Karen think about Molly McCarthy and her exuberant imagination. An abduction was a distressing thing for anyone to witness, let alone a child. When the case was over, Karen decided she would pay Molly another visit and let her know they'd managed to catch the bad guy.

Tilly's face was smeared with chocolate. She wandered up to Churchill and held out the train, as though she wanted him to play with her.

Wouldn't it be a shame if some of that chocolate found its way on to Churchill's pristine white shirt, Karen thought.

'I can't find them. Where did you put them?' Tony's wife called out.

'Excuse me,' Tony said, getting to his feet, tightening his dressing gown cord and then hobbling out towards the kitchen.

Karen nodded at Churchill and then stood up and followed Tony. She turned just as she left the room to see the child resting chocolate-covered fingers on Churchill's knee. She smiled.

The kitchen was quite a large room and must have been extended at some point.

Tony began opening all the cupboards. 'They were here earlier.'

'We always put them in the cupboards up high because of Tilly,' Tony's wife said.

'Of course,' Karen said. 'Very sensible.'

'Ah, here they are!' He grabbed a box of prescription medication and held it up to Karen. 'These are strong. I'm not allowed to drive when taking them. So there's another reason it can't be me.'

'Are you the only one who had the keys to the van?' Karen asked.

'I think there's a spare at the office,' Tony said.

'Do you still have yours?'

'Oh, I didn't think of that.' He looked around the kitchen. 'Have you seen them, love?'

'Why are you asking me?' His wife rolled her eyes. 'They should be in the little pot on the telephone table. That's where we're supposed to put the keys, so we don't lose them.'

Tony walked past Karen and back into the living room. She followed him and saw with delight that Churchill was now on his hands and knees, constructing a wooden train track. She was surprised to realise he actually looked in his element. She couldn't believe he would risk creasing his trousers by crawling around on the floor.

'They're not here,' Tony said from the hallway. 'Like my wife said, I always leave the keys here.'

'Could you have put them down somewhere else?' Karen asked.

He frowned. 'I don't think so. Although I have been a bit spaced out with the drugs, and haven't needed them for three days, but I always put them down there.'

He looked to his wife, who suddenly seemed more worried than short-tempered. 'Do you think someone came inside the house and took the keys?'

'Has anything else gone missing?' Karen asked.

They both shook their heads.

'Not that I've noticed,' Tony said. 'We've never had any trouble before.'

'Has anyone else visited the house in the last three days?'

'No one.' Tony rubbed a hand over his face. 'I've been ill. Not up to visitors. I read that some chancers put a bit of wire through the letterbox and grab the keys that way. I bet that's what happened.'

'Maybe,' Karen said, though she was doubtful. She thought it was much more likely to have been taken by someone on the property. Perhaps they'd left the door open just for a few minutes while they were unloading shopping. Thirty seconds was all it took to scope a place out and grab a set of keys.

She asked the couple some more questions, but it was looking more and more likely that Tony was telling the truth. He even opened up his dressing gown to show them his shingles rash, which Karen quickly protested he didn't need to do.

They said their goodbyes, and Karen was very satisfied when she saw a child-sized handprint of chocolate on Churchill's dark grey trousers. 'Oh dear. It looks like you got a little something just there.' She pointed out the mark, and he began dabbing at it with a handkerchief as they walked back to the car.

'I think Tony was telling us the truth,' Karen said. 'Someone pinched the keys and took the van. We could set up a door-to-door to see if anyone noticed anything. One of the neighbours might have seen when the van was moved.'

'Yes, that's a good idea,' Churchill said. 'There's an alert out on the van. But I think our abductor will know that. I'd expect the van to be dumped soon. He'll steal a new one if he plans to do it again.'

Karen suppressed a shudder at the suggestion of another abduction.

'I think this means we can take the pressure off Tamara Lomax's husband for now,' Churchill continued.

Karen's hands were freezing. She shoved them in her pockets. 'I'm not sure. Remember, we didn't have Aiden in custody when the second abduction occurred, and he was still refusing to let a family liaison officer stay with him.'

'Wouldn't you have recognised him in the footage?'

'Honestly, no. The man in the footage was a similar height and build. His face was pixelated and partially obscured. It's impossible to exclude him based on that.'

'So you think after your interview he decided to go out and abduct another woman?'

'I just think we can't rule him out.'

Churchill shoved the soiled handkerchief into his trouser pocket and straightened. 'I admire tenacity, Karen, but not foolhardiness.'

'I don't think it's being foolhardy. Just open-minded.'

'And I think you need to accept when to let things go. I don't mind you having drive, or challenging authority now and again. You seem to enjoy that.'

'Not really,' Karen said. 'But we need to deal with facts. And as facts go, Aiden Lomax doesn't have an alibi for either abduction.'

Churchill grunted. 'I think Aiden Lomax is a broken man, and we'd better be careful. If we don't treat him with kid gloves from now on, we could have a complaint on our hands.'

Karen's phone rang when they were halfway to the car. She didn't recognise the number.

'DS Hart.'

'Oh, er, this is Tony Hickman. You were just here.'

Karen turned back to the house. 'Did you remember something else?'

'Not exactly. We found the keys. They were in Tilly's toy box. She must have been playing with them. Sorry.'

Karen and Churchill went back and collected the keys, putting them in an evidence bag. It was unlikely to be material evidence, but it paid to be cautious.

When they finally got back to the car, Churchill asked, 'Would you mind dropping me at home?'

Karen raised her eyebrows. He lived in Boston. Surely he didn't expect her to drive all the way there and back tonight?

But she could hardly refuse. This had better not be part of her personal assessment.

'What's your address?'

'Uphill Lincoln,' he said. 'We moved up last week. So it's not too far out of your way.'

'Oh, right,' Karen said.

The traffic was light, and it didn't take long to get to the Uphill area. It was one of the poshest and nicest areas in Lincoln. She dropped Churchill off on a leafy street in front of a very large detached house.

'Nice,' Karen commented. 'You've moved here permanently, then, have you? You're planning to stay in our department?'

'Yes. The superintendent has offered me a permanent post. You don't have a problem with that, do you?' It looked very much like Churchill was trying to hide a smirk.

'Of course not,' Karen said, perhaps a bit too quickly. 'I was just making conversation. It's a nice house.'

'Yes, just renting for now.' He opened the car door. 'See you tomorrow.'

Karen drove off but came to a stop at the end of the road. She parked up to call Colin Greaves at Branston Chickens. He checked for the spare key to the van and confirmed it was missing.

Then she called Sophie to check on things.

There was still no sign of the van, but Sophie reassured her that DI Morrison would be taking over and working through the night.

Karen thanked Sophie and hung up. When working cases like this, it was difficult to slow down and take time off. No matter how long she'd been doing the job, going home in the middle of an important case still made her feel guilty. But if she didn't get any rest, she'd be useless on the job tomorrow. She sent Mike a message to let him know she was on her way.

It took twenty minutes to drive home. She kissed Mike on the cheek when she saw he'd made Bolognese for dinner along with garlic bread.

He offered her a glass of wine.

'I'd better not,' she said. 'I'm trying to keep a clear head.'

'Tough day at work?'

'You wouldn't believe it,' Karen said. 'I had to pay a visit to Branston Chickens.'

Mike looked bewildered. 'Crimes against chickens were keeping you working this late?'

She smiled. 'No, the vehicle we're looking for is tied to the company.'

As Mike warmed the Bolognese on the stove, Karen grabbed her laptop and sat at the kitchen table. First, she did a quick search on local Facebook groups for anything she could find on Branston Chickens. But there were only a few complaints about the noise of the transport trucks. Then she looked up Tony Hickman's Facebook page.

He'd made a couple of updates over the last two days, telling everyone how rough he was feeling. There were lots of get-well wishes in response. He'd even uploaded a picture of his shingles rash. Sometimes, Karen thought, social media had a lot to answer for.

She brought up Tamara's Facebook page – though Rick was already focusing on Tamara's online presence, searching for potential friends and contacts in the hope of discovering the identity of the mystery man she'd been seeing.

There was nothing new.

She stared at Tamara's profile photo and had the strange feeling she was missing something. She sat back thoughtfully, and then quickly closed the laptop as Mike began to plate up the Bolognese.

She tucked into dinner. The garlic bread was hot and deliciously buttery, and she dipped it in the Bolognese sauce.

'This is delicious,' she said. 'I'm sorry I was so late.'

'It was easily reheated,' Mike said. 'We were all right, weren't we, Sandy?'

Sandy looked up from her basket in the corner of the kitchen. She really was a sweet, well-behaved dog, never begging for food or lingering by the table when they were eating. Though it wasn't a surprise, since she was an ex-police dog and Mike's job had involved training them.

'We watched a very interesting programme about squirrels earlier,' Mike continued. 'It's a whole series. You should have seen Sandy. She had her nose six inches from the TV screen throughout. She was transfixed.'

Karen chuckled. She began to relax as Mike talked about his day. He'd been doing some training as well as working at the rescue centre. It was nice to switch off and think about normal things again.

'I think I'm going to take a bath and then go to bed,' Karen said after Mike asked if there was anything she wanted to watch on TV.

'Are you sure?' Mike asked. 'The squirrel programme is compelling viewing – just ask Sandy.'

Karen laughed again, but stood up to put the plates in the dishwasher. She leaned down to make a fuss of Sandy, whose tail thumped against her basket. 'How are you, gorgeous girl? I missed you today.' There was something about the spaniel's unquestioning loyalty and love that helped the tensions of the day melt away. 'As tempting as your squirrel programme sounds,' she said, looking over her shoulder at Mike, 'I'm absolutely beat, and if we're going to get to the bottom of this case, I'm going to need a very early start tomorrow.'

CHAPTER NINETEEN

Sophie rubbed her eyes. They were gritty and sore after staring at her computer monitor for so long. Rick had gone home, but Morgan was still working in his office.

Sophie had shared information with DI Morrison, who would be taking over as SIO tonight. They had no ID on the second victim yet, but Sophie hoped that would change overnight. The van involved in the abduction appeared to have vanished into thin air, too. They had it on camera as far as Fen Road. But after that, they had nothing.

A solid object couldn't disappear, so it had to have taken one of the small single tracks or private lanes.

The fact it hadn't been flagged again after that suggested to Sophie that the van was on private land somewhere. Even the helicopter hadn't spotted it, despite flying over the local fields. The trouble with Lincolnshire was that there was a lot of private land – large barns and outbuildings, as well as warehouses. If nothing turned up on the cameras tonight, then tomorrow they would need to start searching private premises in the area. That was a big job.

Despite the fact that other officers would be working through the night on the case, Sophie felt a pang of guilt as she packed up her belongings. It felt wrong to be going home when Tamara and the second victim were still in danger.

Logically, she knew she had to get home, eat something and get some sleep to be able to function tomorrow.

She'd hitched her handbag up on to her shoulder when her mobile phone started to buzz.

She answered it. It was Zane Dwight, Dr Michaels's assistant.

'Hi,' Sophie said. 'What's up?' She assumed it was something to do with the case as it was so late.

'Hey,' Zane said. 'If you haven't eaten yet, would you like to join us?'

She felt excitement bubble up in her chest as she looked at the clock on the wall. She was hardly likely to turn down dinner with one of the men she admired most in world. It was ten thirty p.m. Late, but she hadn't eaten. Her stomach rumbled.

'Where are you?' she asked, wondering what restaurant would be taking new diners at this time of night.

'We're at the hotel,' he said. 'Dr Michaels has a suite, and the chef has agreed to keep the kitchen open for us. It's the Bishop's Palace. Do you know it?'

'I do,' Sophie said. 'I can be there in about ten minutes.'

'Perfect.'

Sophie grinned. 'Can't wait!'

'All right, see you soon,' Zane said and hung up.

Sophie stared at the screen for a moment and gave a little shiver. Dinner with Dr Michaels and his assistant. She only hoped she didn't embarrass herself. She had so many questions for him. Of course, she'd read all the books, but that wasn't the same as having a one-on-one and being able to pick his brain.

She threw her phone into her bag, grabbed her coat and rushed out. She didn't want to miss a minute of her evening with Dr Michaels. Just think of all the investigative techniques she could ask him about! It wasn't every day an opportunity like this came along.

The evening started off very well. Sophie had delicately poached haddock, new potatoes coated in butter, and salad with a balsamic dressing. Zane and Dr Michaels both ate burgers with skinny truffle fries.

She watched as Zane tucked into his fries, and wondered where he put it all. There wasn't an ounce of fat on him.

By the time they'd finished the main course, Sophie had already asked a lot of questions.

Dr Michaels had just put his fork to one side of his plate when his phone rang.

'I'm sorry,' he said. He pulled his mobile out of his jacket pocket. 'I'll switch it off. It's probably one of my colleagues across the pond forgetting the time difference.' But when he looked at the screen, the smile slid from his face. 'On second thoughts, I'd better take this.'

'Of course,' Sophie said, distracted by the dessert trolley that was being wheeled into the suite by a smartly dressed waiter. Her mouth watered at the sight of chocolate brownies, raspberry pavlova and lemon tart.

Dr Michaels walked to the other side of the room and answered the call.

The area they were dining in had a huge table and a large sofa in front of a flat-screen television. Opposite the table there was a door, which presumably led to the bedroom, and to the right of that there were large windows that looked out over the illuminated cathedral and castle.

The lights were dim in Dr Michaels's suite, and after the large meal, Sophie was beginning to feel very sleepy.

Zane kept his gaze fixed on Dr Michaels as he spoke on the phone, resisting Sophie's attempts at conversation. In the end, she gave up.

When Dr Michaels walked back to the table, Sophie was just polishing off the last bite of her deliciously fudgy brownie and vanilla ice cream. 'That was so good,' she said, sighing with pleasure. But when she caught sight of Dr Michaels's pale face, she stopped smiling. 'Is everything all right?'

'That was Angela Munro,' he said.

'Not again,' Zane said scornfully. 'You need to block her number.'

'I can't do that,' Dr Michaels said. 'She's hurting.'

'She might be hurting, but I'm more concerned with the fact she's trying to hurt you.'

'What's she doing?' Sophie asked.

Dr Michaels sat down. 'She's the daughter of a serial killer's victim.'

'The one with all the stories in the press at the moment?' Sophie asked, though she already knew most of the details. Angela's mother had been killed by the Ace of Diamonds killer. The parallels with their current case were disturbing. Angela's mother had been snatched off the street, and her body was discovered two days later in a park. She'd had her throat cut, like all the Ace of Diamond killer's victims.

Dr Michaels nodded. 'Yes.'

'You must have developed quite a bond with her when you were working the case?'

'I did. Angela was very young when her mother was murdered. Fifteen. She put a lot of trust in me to bring her mother's killer to justice, and I did. I did it for her and the other families. But now these articles have been published in the press, and she thinks it's me telling them all the inappropriate details.'

Sophie rested her elbows on the table and pushed her dessert plate out of the way. 'What sort of details?'

Zane looked at her sharply.

'Sorry,' Sophie said, raising a hand. 'Ignore me. I'm tired. My usual politeness filter is off.'

'No, it's a fair enough question. The sort of question an excellent law enforcement officer would ask,' Dr Michaels said with a smile. 'During the investigation, it was revealed that Angela's mother was a sex worker. She'd managed to keep it secret from her family, and when it was revealed, Angela was very upset. We'd managed to keep it out of the press until now.'

'If the crime happened years ago, why would the press care about the private life of one of the victims now?' Sophie asked.

'You'd have to ask them. But I suppose the salacious stuff sells.' Dr Michaels despondently toyed with his napkin. 'Angela is a good person. She doesn't want that part of her mother's life to be what people remember about her.'

'But why does she think it's you selling the stories?'

'Because she's crazy,' Zane said, with such passion he almost spilled his wine.

'That's not fair, Zane,' Dr Michaels said. 'She's been through a lot. She trusted me. I'm one of the few people who knew these details, so I guess I'm a logical choice.'

'Why would she think you would spill the details now, after all this time?'

'Honestly, you give her far too much attention,' Zane said. 'It's ruining the evening. We should change the subject.'

But Dr Michaels ignored Zane, and said, 'She thinks I'm using the articles for publicity to sell my new book.'

'And to be fair, it *is* generating publicity.' Zane took a long sip of wine. 'And, as they say, no publicity is bad publicity.' He frowned. 'Or am I getting that muddled?'

'I don't want book sales if they come at Angela's expense,' Dr Michaels said, and then excused himself. 'My phone's out of battery. I need to put it on charge.'

He went into what Sophie assumed was the bedroom and shut the door behind him. She leaned towards Zane. 'He seems devastated by this.'

Zane topped up his wine. 'I know. It's awful. She's been hounding him all week.'

'Can't you do anything about it?'

'He won't listen to me. He just needs to block her number.'

He gave Sophie a sideways glance and took a sip of his wine, then smiled conspiratorially. 'And I know he says he doesn't care about book sales, but in Washington his books are selling like crazy right now.'

'That's not much consolation if people believe he betrayed Angela and is cashing in on the victims.'

'No.' Zane wafted a hand in dismissal. 'Nobody will remember any of that. They'll only remember his name, and then they'll see his book in stores and buy a copy.' He put his wine glass down and rested his arms on the table. Meeting Sophie's gaze with a twinkle in his eye, he said, 'I'll let you in on a secret. I've already been fielding calls for major talk shows, and I mean *major*. Two words. *Mornings with Anne*.'

'That's three words.'

Zane giggled. 'So it is. Must be the wine.'

'*Mornings with Anne*? I'm not sure I've heard of that.'

Zane rolled his eyes. 'It's probably because you're English and don't know anything about American talk shows. It's got huge ratings in Washington.'

'Are you sure Dr Michaels will want to do the talk shows? I mean, they'll probably want to ask him questions about Angela's mother, and he wouldn't want to put her through that.'

Zane gave an exaggerated sigh. 'Look, it's obviously a really awful thing that happened to Angela's mother. But Dr Michaels deserves credit. He's helped so many families and brought so many killers to justice.'

'Oh, I know,' Sophie said hurriedly. 'I've read all of his books, except his latest, but I'll get to that soon.'

'It's a good read,' Zane said, 'and I'm not just saying that because it's my job.'

He stretched and then smothered a yawn with the back of his hand. 'I've got another busy day tomorrow. I need to work on the publicity for the final stage of the book tour. We'll be moving on soon.'

'I thought Dr Michaels was hanging around for a while to act as a consultant on our case,' Sophie said.

Zane shrugged. 'He is, but he's got a talk scheduled in Cambridge on Monday. So, by Sunday night we'll be out of here. You'll be on your own.'

Sophie hoped the case would be wrapped up by then. 'It must be exciting to work with Dr Michaels,' she said. 'Do you act as his assistant while he's tracking the killers?'

Zane shuddered. 'No! And besides, working for him isn't as glamorous as you might think. I have to deal with crazy fans, irritating journalists and ridiculously antiquated booking systems.'

'I hope you don't consider me a crazy fan.' Sophie laughed nervously.

Zane grinned. He was playing with his phone. He had it flat on the table and was twirling it around, so it spun on the tablecloth. But as a message flashed up on the screen, he quickly picked it up. Sophie had the definite impression he didn't want her to see the message.

And she hadn't. At least, not the whole thing. She did see the sender's name though – *Genius News*.

Zane now seemed transfixed by his phone.

'I don't mind if you need to do some work,' she said. 'I'm happy to wait here until Dr Michaels gets back. You don't need to babysit me.'

He peered at her over his phone screen. 'Honey, that's not happening. It's a major part of my job description. Dr Michaels doesn't have dinners with women on his own.'

'Why not?'

'Because there are certain women out there who'd target him.'

'Is he really that famous?'

'You'd be surprised. Some women have a weird attraction to people involved with cases like the ones Dr Michaels works on.' Zane shrugged. 'I don't understand it, but it's my job to make sure no women spending time with Dr Michaels get the wrong idea.'

Sophie felt her cheeks grow hot.

Dr Michaels returned to the table and said, 'What did I miss?'

'Nothing,' Sophie said hurriedly. 'We were just talking about how much work we had to do tomorrow.'

'Oh, yeah. I have a feeling it's going to be a busy day. Say, I've been meaning to ask you, how do you find working for DS Hart?'

'Karen? I love it. She's brilliant. She's taught me everything I know.'

It wasn't what Dr Michaels said, because he didn't actually say anything, but he looked at Sophie in a way that suggested he thought she wasn't telling the whole truth. He nodded sympathetically.

'No, really. She's great. Understanding, patient. I can be a bit of a swot sometimes.' Sophie gave a nervous smile. 'But Karen always appreciates the effort I put in . . . Why? Did she say something to you? Did I do something wrong?'

'What could she possibly have said?' Dr Michaels flashed his white teeth. 'I can tell you're an incredibly hard worker.'

Sophie beamed at the praise from her hero.

'It's just . . .' Dr Michaels began, grimacing as though what he was about to say pained him. 'I picked up on something. Some animosity from Karen.'

Sophie shook her head. 'There's no animosity. She just has her methods. She's used to doing things her way, and we don't often work with profilers.'

'Yes,' Dr Michaels mused. 'But she was very reluctant to accept my help, and that leads me to believe something in her past has hardened her, made her distrustful of others.'

Sophie opened her mouth to reply. She was about to tell Dr Michaels and Zane how Karen's family had been targeted, and her husband driven off the road with their five-year-old daughter in the back of the car, all because someone had a grudge against Karen. The fact the crime had been covered up by a network of corrupt officers could certainly explain any hardness and distrust Karen had.

But in Sophie's opinion, Karen wasn't hard. She was still compassionate, patient, and did the job because she believed in helping others.

Besides, telling Dr Michaels about Karen's past behind her back felt like a betrayal.

Dr Michaels was Sophie's idol. But Karen had taught her so much. She was the one who'd supported Sophie's development at work, even though Sophie was aware her perfectionism – or what Rick might call her *acting like a swot* – could sometimes be a little irritating to others. Karen never dismissed her. She always made time if Sophie needed help.

And it was Karen who'd tried to save Sophie, despite the risk to her own life, when they'd been trapped in the snow with two killers.

Sophie's tone was cool when she said, 'I have to disagree. Karen is an excellent officer, but she isn't afraid to share her opinion when she thinks the investigation is heading in the wrong direction.'

'Is that what you think? Do you think I was wrong about the profile? I think it's becoming clearer now that I was right.'

'I don't think you're wrong, and I don't think Karen was necessarily disagreeing with your profile.'

'Really?' Dr Michaels raised his eyebrows and flicked his shiny hair back from his face. 'She had the husband brought in for questioning. I remember her saying she thought it was him.'

'No,' Sophie insisted. 'She didn't say that. She said we couldn't discount the husband. That's different.'

'But no one was asking her to,' Dr Michaels said, holding up his hands and making his words sound so reasonable. 'Karen just had a problem with my profile and taking my expertise on board.'

'No, I don't think she did.'

'Did you know she turned me down when I called to arrange a visit?'

Sophie was speechless. She looked at Zane, who nodded to confirm.

'I didn't know that.'

'Yes, it was only after DCI Churchill got in touch that I was brought on to the case.'

Sophie shook her head. 'I hadn't realised you'd called before that.'

'She said you were all too busy. Maybe that was the truth, but it makes me ask myself if there's a reason Karen doesn't want me involved.'

Sophie blinked. This had caught her off guard. Why had Karen not told her Dr Michaels had called to arrange a visit? She knew what a big fan Sophie was. Okay, so it wasn't Sophie's decision whether or not Dr Michaels could visit the station, but Karen knew how thrilled Sophie would have been to give him a quick tour.

'Sorry,' Dr Michaels said. 'I didn't mean to cause any bad feeling between you and your boss.'

'Oh, you haven't,' Sophie said. 'I'm sure Karen simply forgot to tell me about it.'

'I'm sure that's it,' Dr Michaels said with a smile. Then he clapped his hands together and nodded at the dining table. 'I've put this on my tab. So dinner is on me.'

'Thanks, that's very kind,' Sophie said, reaching for her bag. 'I'd better head home.'

Sophie left the hotel feeling confused and conflicted, but by the time she'd driven home, she'd reached the conclusion that Karen had forgotten to tell her about Dr Michaels trying to arrange a visit.

Of course, it would have been a massive distraction during the abduction case, so it was perfectly reasonable that Karen had put him off.

◆ ◆ ◆

Back home, tucked up in bed, Sophie used her iPad to look up some of the stories in the press about Dr Michaels. Zane had been right. There were a number of very lurid and derogatory descriptions of Angela's mother. No wonder Angela was upset, Sophie thought, as she flicked through the news articles.

After a few minutes, she put the iPad on her nightstand and reached for Dr Michaels's new book. She balanced it on her knees as she thought back to the briefing earlier that day. Rick had suggested perhaps the killer was a copycat of Dr Michaels's infamous Playing Card Killer. Dr Michaels hadn't warmed to the idea of a copycat, but if there was one thing Sophie had learned from Karen, it was that it was important not to dismiss any options until they were absolutely sure.

Five minutes later, Sophie was sound asleep, the book resting on her lap.

CHAPTER TWENTY

Karen was at the station by six a.m. She'd woken early, and rather than turning over and going back to sleep, decided to get up and on with the day. There was a lot of work ahead of them.

She regretted leaving the warmth of her bed as she stepped outside into the freezing air and her feet crunched over the frost-coated gravel on the way to the car. She had to leave the engine running for two minutes before she could see through the windscreen, and her fingers had turned numb as she tried to hurry things along by scraping off the ice.

She'd hoped that progress had been made on the case overnight, but on checking her emails and messages, she discovered that the Transit van had disappeared again, which was infuriating and perplexing when there were so many traffic cameras on the main roads. And even worse, there was still no ID on the second victim.

A search from the air had been fruitless too, which meant they now had to search the woods and look at properties in the area that had the capacity to hide a van. They'd need to speak to the owners first to get permission, which wasn't always easy when it came to buildings on farmland.

The early hour meant the CID offices were quiet as DI Morrison updated Karen over coffee. One new discovery piqued her interest. The executor handling Tamara's parents' estate had sent over some legal paperwork.

Tamara and her sister, Rachel, were the main beneficiaries for the estate, which had not yet been settled. According to the Grant of Probate, the estate was valued at just over a million pounds. Even divided two ways, that was a lot of money. Karen skimmed the details. They had put in a request for a copy of the will from the probate court.

'Over a million pounds,' Karen commented as she flicked through the documents.

'It's a fair amount,' DI Morrison said. 'I've known people to kill for a lot less than that.'

Karen nodded thoughtfully. It was possible the abductor was motivated by money, but there had been no ransom demand, and Tamara didn't have access to the funds yet.

Most murder cases Karen had worked were driven by a limited number of motives – money, love or revenge. Access to half a million pounds made a good motive. The money that had been due to Tamara would now go to her husband. Yet another reason not to put Aiden out of the frame just yet.

When DI Morrison left, Karen checked her email and saw that Churchill had scheduled a briefing for nine a.m. They'd probably spend the time going over old ground, looking for things they'd missed, but she'd mention the will. That could be important.

She looked up from her screen as DI Morrison strolled back into the office.

'Forgotten something?' Karen asked.

'There's someone downstairs asking to speak to you.'

Karen put her coffee cup down. 'Who?'

'Julie Wainwright. Says she spoke to you yesterday. But there's something else she wants to tell you.' He shrugged. 'She wouldn't tell me what it was.'

'Right. Thanks. I'll come down.'

Karen stepped into the reception area, and the desk sergeant smiled. 'She's outside. Chain smoker.' He pointed to the double doors. 'Seems jumpy,' he added before turning his attention back to his monitor.

'Right,' Karen said. 'Thanks.'

As the desk sergeant had indicated, she found Julie outside. She wore a long black wool coat and was pacing back and forth with a cigarette in her right hand. Her lips were moving silently as though she was playing out a conversation in her head.

'Julie?'

She looked up, startled, and Karen got the impression she'd quite like to run away. The desk sergeant's assessment had been spot on.

'Is everything all right?' Karen said, trying not to shiver as the cold air nipped at her hands and face. 'It's freezing out here. Do you want to come in, maybe get a coffee?'

Julie looked over her shoulder, towards the car park. Then she took a deep breath, put out her cigarette and nodded.

Karen was intrigued. They could really do with a breakthrough in this case, and she hoped Julie Wainwright might be about to provide one. But her instinct told her not to push too hard. Julie was skittish, and could have second thoughts and decide to leave without revealing what she knew.

Karen got two coffees from the machine as the canteen wasn't yet open, and then led Julie into an unoccupied interview room.

Julie eyed the recording equipment and then glanced up at the camera in the corner of the room.

Karen put the coffees down on the large table.

'It's just somewhere to chat,' she said. 'Nothing formal. None of the recording stuff is on.'

'Right,' Julie said, pulling out a chair and sitting down. She didn't unbutton her coat, and she put her large tote bag on her lap as though she could hide behind it.

'Is everything all right? You seem nervous. Has something happened?' Karen asked.

'Not really,' Julie began tentatively, 'but last night I couldn't sleep. I kept going over what I told you and . . . what I *hadn't* told you.'

'And what hadn't you told me?' Karen asked, keeping her tone light and friendly.

'Well, I said Tamara was worried that Aiden was seeing someone, and that I thought maybe she'd been playing around as well?'

Karen nodded. 'Yes, I remember.'

'The thing is' – Julie hugged her bag to her chest – 'I think I might lose my job over this.'

'I'm sure you won't,' Karen said. 'What is it?'

Julie was silent for a full ten seconds, then blurted out, 'I think Tamara might have been having a fling with Mr Casey.'

'Your boss?'

Julie nodded and bit down on her bottom lip.

'Why do you think that, Julie?'

'I thought it was a coincidence at first. Because Mr Casey would pull the blinds down in his office some afternoons and say he wasn't to be disturbed. On one occasion Mark from supplies went up there, tried to get in, and the door was locked. Mr Casey was furious. Mark needed some papers and thought he heard Mr Casey say come in, but he obviously hadn't. I suppose we all knew *something* was going on.'

'Why Tamara?'

'Because I could never find her when Mr Casey shut himself in his office. At first, I thought she just took the opportunity to skive off – you know, while the boss wasn't paying attention. But now I think about it . . .'

'You think Tamara was in the office with Mr Casey?' Karen asked.

Julie nodded. 'Yes.' She hugged her bag tighter to her chest. 'I don't know. Maybe.'

Karen picked up her coffee and took a sip, watching Julie carefully. 'Is there anything else that makes you believe Tamara would have been having a relationship with Mr Casey?'

Julie exhaled a long breath and shook her head.

Rick had been through Tamara's phone records, and there'd been no text messages or calls between her and Mr Casey. No way of arranging illicit meetups in his office. Unless Tamara had a second phone.

There was no evidence of that, but it was certainly a possibility and something to look into.

When Karen had finished questioning Julie, she led her back down to reception.

'You won't tell Mr Casey I said anything, will you?' Julie tugged her bag higher on to her shoulder. 'He'd go mental if he found out this came from me.'

'I'll keep your name out of it as best I can,' Karen assured the woman, though if George Casey was involved in Tamara's abduction, she intended to use everything she knew to get the truth from him.

CHAPTER TWENTY-ONE

George Casey didn't look so confident now. He sat across the table from Morgan and Karen in interview room three. Dr Michaels and DCI Churchill were observing from upstairs.

'You weren't completely honest with me when I spoke to you yesterday, Mr Casey,' Karen said.

Casey frowned and rubbed his nose. 'I have no idea what you're talking about. I've agreed to come along to the station. I've waived my right to legal representation because I have done nothing wrong,' he said. He spoke loudly, trying to convey confidence, but Karen caught the slight tremor in his voice. 'Now, if you wouldn't mind telling me what all of this is about?' He waved a hand at Morgan and Karen.

'Of course, Mr Casey,' Karen said. 'We're investigating the abduction of Tamara Lomax.'

'Yes, yes. I know all that,' Casey said impatiently. 'But what's that got to do with *me*? I'm trying to run a business. Yet another day wasted. Will I get reimbursed for this? My productivity is vital to my company's income.'

'I think your productivity is the least of your worries at the moment,' Morgan said dryly.

Casey's eyes narrowed. 'What do you mean?' he asked, suddenly wary.

'Perhaps you'd like to tell us more about your relationship with Tamara Lomax,' Karen said.

'Relationship?' He shrugged. 'I told you everything yesterday. I was completely open, and very helpful I might add.' He leaned forward, talking into the recorder. 'I offered the use of my premises while you interviewed my staff. Of course, that cuts into my bottom line, but I thought finding Tamara was more important than money.'

He hadn't thought that at all. He was just trying to make himself sound good now.

'Yes, I'm aware of that,' Karen said. 'I was there, but more information has come to light.'

'What sort of information?'

'Information that your relationship with Tamara Lomax was not strictly professional.'

Mr Casey looked aghast. After a moment, as he seemed to be struck dumb, he put a hand to the collar of his shirt and tugged at it. 'I don't know what you're talking about,' he said quietly.

'I think you do, Mr Casey,' Morgan said. 'I think it's time for these games to stop and for you to be honest with us.'

'But I was being . . . I mean, I *am* being honest.' He looked around as though expecting someone else in the room to step in and save him.

'Would you like to describe your relationship with Tamara again, Mr Casey?' Karen asked.

'Not particularly,' he said. 'I really don't see why any of this is relevant, and I—' He broke off with an irritated huff. 'Tamara worked for me. That is all.'

Both Karen and Morgan said nothing, letting the silence stretch uncomfortably until Casey felt compelled to talk again.

'Look, I'm telling you the truth. Tamara was a good worker most of the time. We had our disagreements when she missed work without permission, but there was nothing else between us if that's what you're implying.'

'That is contrary to what we've been told.' Karen looked down at the papers in front of her, pretending to consult her notes.

'Contrary to what?' He leaned forward, desperate to see the notes. 'I don't . . . Who's told you this?'

'Were you having a romantic relationship with Tamara Lomax?' Karen asked.

He put his hands flat on the table. 'No, I was not,' he said emphatically.

'Are you sure about that,' Morgan asked, 'because that's not what we've been told.'

'I don't care what you've been told. It's not true. I haven't had a relationship with Tamara, other than a strictly professional employer-employee relationship.'

'So, you're suggesting the person who provided this information is lying?'

'Yes, they must be.'

'Why would they want to imply you're having a relationship with Tamara when you're not?' Karen asked.

Casey's cheeks flushed red. 'I don't know. You'll have to ask them, but I'm not. I wasn't. Ever.'

'So you locking the door to your office, pulling down the blinds a few afternoons a week. What is that all about?'

Casey's cheeks burned even redder. 'I hardly see that's any of your business,' he said.

'I think you'll find it's very much our business if it relates to Tamara Lomax's disappearance.'

'It doesn't,' Casey insisted, loosening his tie. 'Actually, I think I will need a lawyer, after all.'

'Very well,' Karen said. 'Do you have a solicitor, or do you want us to arrange for the duty solicitor to come in?'

He put his hands over his face. 'I don't know. I mean, yes, I've got a solicitor. But is there really any need for this? I'm cooperating, and I promise you I did not have a romantic relationship with Tamara Lomax.'

'The trouble is, Mr Casey, we need to be convinced, and right now it's your word against somebody else's. So, unless you can give us some—'

'All right, fine. I do sometimes lock the office door and close the blinds, but it is nothing to do with Tamara.'

'Then why do you do it?'

'To get some privacy.'

'And why do you need privacy? Are you having a romantic relationship with somebody else in your office?'

Mr Casey went very still and then he nodded.

'Okay. Who?' Morgan asked.

'Noah Hillock,' Mr Casey said in a strangled whisper.

'Noah?' Karen stared at him. Noah's interview had been odd. But she'd assumed he was afraid of Casey and worried about losing his job.

'Yes. I'm only telling you this because you've completely got the wrong end of the stick. But yes, I'm gay, and I don't want it to come out, because Noah's married. He's not ready for anything to be made public.'

Karen put down her pen and sat back in her chair. How had she missed that? 'So this has nothing to do with Tamara?'

Mr Casey shook his head. 'I can see perhaps why someone else might have thought that. I'm not stupid. I know she used to use the opportunity while I was distracted to skive off. Another reason she deserved to lose her job.'

'To be fair, you and Noah were skiving off at the same time,' Karen said.

'That's completely different. It was the only time we had together. We're in love. Tamara, on the other hand, is simply an opportunist.'

Karen resisted the urge to roll her eyes.

CHAPTER TWENTY-TWO

'He's not involved.' They were the first words out of Dr Michaels's mouth when Karen and Morgan entered DCI Churchill's office.

Karen gave a tight smile as she sat down. 'You seem very sure, Dr Michaels.'

'I am. As sure as I can be, anyway.'

Karen had to grudgingly agree. It looked like another lead was slipping through their fingers. Another dead end.

'It was worth getting him in,' Churchill said. 'You were right. He was hiding something.'

'There is still a chance he's involved,' Morgan said.

Everyone turned to look at him. 'If you look at the situation from Casey's point of view. He was having an affair. One that he didn't want to come to light. What if Tamara had found out and tried to blackmail him?'

'That's an interesting possibility,' Karen said.

'No,' Dr Michaels said. 'He wasn't involved in Tamara's abduction.'

'Can you elaborate?' Churchill asked.

'It's the way he holds himself, his posture. The way he talks. He's guarded when he talks about the affair, but not when he talks about Tamara. That's important. He might not be a likeable character—'

'You can say that again,' Karen murmured.

'But I don't think he has any feelings towards Tamara other than mild irritation because she failed to turn up for work on a few occasions.'

'He didn't seem to be worried when she went missing,' Karen said. 'Perhaps that's because he knows what happened to her.'

Dr Michaels shook his head. 'No, he doesn't know anything. I'm afraid we're wasting time with him.'

'Then what about Noah?' Karen asked. 'He had an even stronger motive for keeping his affair quiet. He would be vulnerable to blackmail.'

'What do we know about him?' Churchill asked.

'He's married, two young children,' Karen said. 'I thought the dynamic between him and Casey was a bit odd, but I didn't pick up on the affair. I thought he was worried about losing his job if word got out he'd been badmouthing Casey.'

Morgan nodded. 'What did you think of him? Could you believe he would have gone as far as abducting Tamara to cover up his relationship with Casey?'

Karen blew out a long breath, thinking back, analysing her interactions with George Casey and Noah Hillock. 'To be honest, Noah Hillock didn't ring alarm bells. That said, I missed the affair. I hadn't picked up on the undercurrent that was obviously there.'

'All right,' Churchill said. 'Morgan, why don't you follow up with Noah Hillock? Talk to him. Go to see him at home.'

'If his wife is at home that might make him reluctant to talk,' Morgan said.

'On the contrary, I think a visit from the police is just what he needs to drive home the need to cooperate.'

'All right,' Morgan agreed.

'And I'd like to go and talk to Aiden again,' Karen said.

Dr Michaels turned, resting his intense gaze on Karen. 'You still think there's more to him than the traumatised husband.'

'It's possible.'

'I think it's very unlikely he's involved though,' Dr Michaels said, 'especially now another woman has gone missing. I understand the need to look for relationships, for connections when you're working on a case. But when it comes to these types of crimes, there aren't the usual motives.'

Karen knew she was being stubborn but couldn't seem to help it. She didn't want to rule out Aiden. Not when he didn't have an alibi for the time of either abduction.

'The fact is, he had the opportunity to do it. For all we know, this second abduction could be his way of distracting us from the truth.'

'That's a long shot,' Dr Michaels said, with a confident smile that bordered on a smirk. 'If a woman is killed by a partner, it's usually a hot-headed, spur-of-the-moment thing – perhaps evolving from an argument. There is also typically a history of domestic violence, which isn't the case here, is it?'

Karen shook her head. 'No. At least, not reported.'

'It's unlikely he would have cold-bloodedly gone out and abducted another woman just to get the police off his tail. I've never experienced anything like that in my long career.'

'Aiden doesn't want a family liaison officer,' Karen pointed out. 'He's restless when we're there.' She shook her head, frustrated. 'He's hiding something.'

'As I mentioned before,' Churchill said, clicking his ballpoint pen multiple times for no other reason Karen could ascertain other than to be annoying, 'I admire tenacity, Karen, but pursuit of one suspect at the expense of everything else is folly.'

Before Karen could respond and describe an imaginative way he could utilise his pen, he moved on.

'Anyway,' Churchill said with another click of his pen. 'Morgan, you're going to speak to Noah. Karen, you can pay Aiden Lomax another visit, but take Dr Michaels with you. Let's see if he concurs with your hunch that Aiden is hiding something from us.'

As they left Churchill's office, Dr Michaels said, 'I'm sorry, Karen, I hope you didn't take offence at me sharing my views.'

'Not at all,' Karen said. 'You're just doing your job.'

'And you're just doing yours. You're looking at relationships, but we've got two abductions now, and the second woman changes things. You see that, don't you?'

Karen reluctantly nodded. 'What do you think our chances are of finding both women alive? Our abductor might be keeping them somewhere,' she suggested.

'I don't think the chances are good, to be honest.'

She had expected that answer, but it still stung.

'It's frustrating we haven't identified the second victim yet,' Karen said. 'That would give us more to go on.'

'Not necessarily. You're still thinking there will be a link between the victims, but it's possible the only link between the two women is the man who targeted them.'

'Are you ready to go and visit Aiden now?' Karen asked, checking her watch.

'Yes, just give me a minute to tell Zane where I'm going. I'll meet you at the car.'

'All right,' Karen said, heading for her desk to collect her coat. She had warmed a little to Dr Michaels. She might not want to believe him when he said it was unlikely either woman was still alive, but she had to admit that he had more knowledge and tools at his disposal for dealing with this type of crime than Karen and her team. He had experience of crimes beyond anything Karen had ever dealt with. It would be interesting to get his take on Aiden Lomax, because she was sure Tamara's husband was holding something back.

CHAPTER TWENTY-THREE

'I thought you were supposed to call before coming around,' Aiden said. His large frame blocked the doorway, and one hand gripped the door as though he was scared Karen was going to push it open and rush inside.

'Sorry, Aiden. We just have a few more questions. Is it all right if we come in?'

He glared at Karen with pure hatred. She couldn't really blame him. They really had put him through the wringer during questioning. As Dr Michaels had said, it was no surprise the man didn't trust them.

'Really, Aiden, we're just here to ask questions,' she said.

'Seems to me like you're looking to frame me,' he spat.

'That's not true. We just want answers. We want to know what happened to Tamara.'

'So do I,' Aiden said. 'That's what I want, too.'

'Then we're on the same page. Can we come in?'

'Who's this?' Aiden said, refusing to let go of the door and jutting his chin at Dr Michaels.

'He's a consultant with the police who's helping us on this investigation. His name is Dr Michaels.'

'That name sounds familiar,' Aiden said, regarding the doctor with narrowed eyes. 'Did you mention him before?'

'I don't think so,' Karen said, clutching her coat tightly around her body. 'Look, it's freezing out here, Aiden. Are you going to let us in?'

With a sigh, he stepped back. 'All right.' He watched them carefully as they entered.

They went into the front room, and Karen noticed Aiden shoot a quick glance over his shoulder towards the stairs.

'We weren't interrupting anything, were we, Aiden?' Karen asked.

'No, I've just been waiting for news.'

'Rachel not here today?'

'No, she's busy.' Aiden must have seen the look of surprise on Karen's face as she took a seat on the sofa. 'She's looking after her parents' property.'

'They passed away recently, didn't they? Your mother- and father-in-law?'

Aiden nodded. 'Yeah, two months ago.'

'Tamara was due to inherit quite a bit of money, I understand.'

Aiden whirled around, his eyes blazing. 'You'd better not start down that line. If you're implying that somehow I abducted Tamara to get my hands on the money—'

'I didn't say that, Aiden,' Karen said.

'I know this must feel like a personal attack,' Dr Michaels said, his soothing, warm tones acting like a balm on Aiden's temper. 'I can't imagine what you're going through. It must feel like you're being attacked from all sides.'

Aiden leaned heavily on the mantelpiece, his fingers touching the photo of Tamara and Rachel right next to the creepy wooden owl.

'I'm trying to help, but it feels like everyone thinks I'm involved,' he said.

'Not everyone, Aiden,' Dr Michaels said.

Karen shot him a look. They hadn't really discussed much of an interview plan on the way over, but she had expected him to keep quiet and let her lead. She didn't want Aiden to think he was in the clear. She wanted to keep the pressure on. It might seem cruel at the moment, but sometimes that was a necessity.

'So, Rachel is at her parents' place?' Karen asked.

'I think so. She has to check on it regularly for insurance purposes.'

'I see,' Karen said.

'It's not like Tamara can do it now, is it?' Aiden said bitterly.

'No,' Dr Michaels said. 'That must be really hard. Have you got anyone else to support you?'

'I don't need anyone else.'

'No other family?'

'No, my family are in Yorkshire, but we don't really get on.' He shrugged. 'They didn't like Tamara, so we had a falling-out. They didn't come to the wedding.'

'I'm sorry to hear that,' Karen said. 'Was Tamara close to her parents?'

'Yeah, very.'

'And her sister?'

'Yeah. We saw Rachel at least a couple of times a week. They had their fallings-out occasionally, like sisters do. Squabbling and stuff.'

'Do you have brothers and sisters?' Karen asked.

'No, only child. I was close to my cousins when we were growing up, but we drifted apart as I got older.'

'What about friends?' Karen asked.

He looked wary. 'Are you asking me because you're concerned about me, or are you just trying to find out who else you can pressure because you think they'll spill the beans, dob me in?'

189

'If you haven't done anything, Aiden, you don't need to worry about being dobbed in, as you put it.'

'We're genuinely concerned,' Dr Michaels cut in. 'This is one of the hardest things you'll ever have to go through.'

Aiden sank down into the green velvet easy chair, resting his forearms on his knees and bowing his head. 'It really is,' he said. 'I just want it all to be over.'

'Have any of your friends called around since the incident?' Karen said.

'No. I suppose I don't have that many mates I'm really close to. I go out with a couple of the lads to the local pub, usually on Friday nights. Tamara goes out with Julie from work. The rest of the time it's just me and Tamara. We've got into a routine. We're used to each other's company. Don't need anyone else,' he said, shooting another look at the photo on the mantelpiece.

'Could I get a glass of water?' Dr Michaels asked.

'Yes.' Aiden got to his feet. 'Would you like something?' he asked Karen.

'No, I'm fine thanks,' Karen said. She waited until Aiden had left the room and then turned to Dr Michaels, who stood and walked over to the mantelpiece. Curious, Karen joined him.

'You noticed him looking over here too?' she asked softly.

Dr Michaels nodded. 'Yes, it's interesting.' He rubbed his chin and peered closely at the images. 'What's motivating him? Guilt? Sadness?'

Karen didn't know. Throughout their conversation, Aiden had kept looking over at the objects on the mantelpiece. Perhaps it wasn't surprising. There was a framed photograph of his wife, but it was a photograph of Tamara *and* Rachel. There were plenty of other pictures of his wife in the room. One of their wedding day, and another of Tamara on holiday. So why this one? Why was this one significant to Aiden?

She pulled out her mobile phone and took a quick picture.

'I don't know why he keeps looking at this photograph, but it's significant,' Dr Michaels said.

Karen agreed. 'I won't be long. I just want to check something out. Keep him busy.' Without waiting for a reply, she walked out into the hall. 'Is it all right if I use your toilet?' she called out to Aiden.

There was no response from Aiden, and Karen at first thought he hadn't heard, but then he appeared in the kitchen doorway. 'Sorry, what?'

He looked pale.

'Your toilet. All right if I use it?' Karen asked. 'Upstairs, is it?'

He nodded. 'Yeah, but . . .'

'There's not something up there you don't want me to see, is there?' Karen asked.

'Of course not,' he said gruffly. 'Top of the stairs, second on the right.'

Karen headed upstairs. Instead of taking the door to the bathroom, she walked ahead to the master bedroom and looked around. It was pristine. The bed was made, and a grey throw was draped over the white duvet. Light grey chenille curtains were drawn back on loops studded with tiny crystals.

She'd expected a mess. A room to reflect Aiden's state of mind.

She was looking for something, but unfortunately she didn't know exactly what it was she was looking for.

Perhaps a book belonging to Dr Michaels, detailing the Playing Card Killer's crimes. But that would be too easy. Besides, it was a bestseller, so it would be easy to explain away its presence.

There were two bedside tables. On one, which she presumed was Tamara's, was hand cream, lip salve and an Agatha Christie mystery. On Aiden's side of the bed, the nightstand was empty.

Not exactly damning evidence.

She scanned the room again, but everything looked very ordinary. He'd been so nervous. She'd seen him glance upstairs, so what was he afraid of her finding? She opened the wardrobe door. It was packed. Three-quarters of the space was filled with Tamara's clothes, the rest filled with Aiden's. It didn't look like anything was missing. She glanced down at the shoes. No obvious bloody clothing stashed at the bottom of the wardrobe.

She closed the door with a click and then headed out into the next bedroom. This was obviously used as a spare room and was pretty bare apart from a large double bed and two nightstands, and a large print of a tropical seascape above the bed.

She went into the bathroom, flushed the chain, washed her hands and then walked downstairs. The bathroom had smelled faintly of bleach. Surprising Aiden would focus on keeping the bathroom clean at the moment. The living room was understandably a bit neglected. He obviously hadn't taken the time to keep up with the cleaning there. So why the bedrooms and bathroom?

Was he trying to hide something – to get rid of something, destroy DNA evidence?

Karen hadn't found anything related to material evidence upstairs, but what she'd seen certainly hadn't decreased her suspicions of Aiden Lomax.

'We'll leave you to it now, Aiden. If you think of anything else, or you have any questions, you can call me. You've still got my number, right?' Karen said.

Aiden nodded.

'And I don't think you should be alone. I'll organise a family liaison officer to come and stay with you for a few hours.'

He shook his head. 'No, I told you. I don't want anyone here.'

'What about Rachel then? You need support, Aiden.'

'I don't see why you're worried about my support now. You weren't too worried about me yesterday.'

'I'm sorry. It's not personal,' Karen said. It wasn't her job to support Aiden emotionally through this. It was her job to find out what had happened to Tamara.

'DS Hart is right,' Dr Michaels said. 'You really need somebody here with you.'

'I'm fine,' Aiden snapped. 'I'm better on my own.' He looked again at the mantelpiece.

'All right. Well, if you change your mind . . .' Karen said as Aiden led them to the door.

'I won't,' Aiden said firmly as he closed the door on them.

◆ ◆ ◆

'So, what did you think?' Karen asked when they were back in the car. 'He's edgy, isn't he?'

Dr Michaels mused on that for a moment. 'You know, I think you're right. There's something he's holding back.'

Karen smiled. 'I knew it.'

'That doesn't mean I agree with you. I still don't think he has anything to do with his wife's abduction.'

'Then what is he trying to hide?'

'I don't know. Maybe he smokes marijuana to wind down in the evening? Maybe he's got some dope stashed in the house?' Dr Michaels shrugged and turned his palms upwards. 'It could be anything.'

'But you don't think it's related to Tamara?'

'I don't. I think he's paranoid after his interview yesterday.'

'You think we went too hard on him, don't you?'

'It's not really my place to say.'

'But you're going to say it anyway?'

He smiled. 'Well, I probably wouldn't have pushed quite as hard.'

'I just can't shake the feeling that he's holding something back from us, and it's important to the case. Why did he keep looking at the photograph of Rachel and Tamara on the mantelpiece?'

Dr Michaels nodded. 'I was surprised by that, actually.'

'Why surprised?'

'Well, from what you told me about your meeting with Rachel, and from the notes I read, I thought Tamara and Rachel had a more competitive relationship. It's something you see in siblings, sometimes. Mainly due to the way the parents have played one off against the other. They always feel like they have to impress – they have to compete for affection.'

'And you got that impression from the notes on Rachel?'

He nodded. 'Yes, it intrigued me. So it interests me that Aiden doesn't mention any rivalry, and he kept looking at that particular photograph – the one with *both* sisters in the frame.'

Karen pulled out her mobile and zoomed in on the picture she'd taken on her phone. 'They look happy enough,' she said, holding up the phone for Dr Michaels to have a closer look.

He nodded. 'They do.'

'So are you saying you think there's something going on between the two sisters, or between Aiden and Rachel?'

'What did you think? You saw them both together.'

'I thought Aiden seemed a bit fed up with Rachel, to be honest, like she was irritating him.'

'Interesting,' Dr Michaels said.

'It is?'

'Yes, very.'

'You think it has a bearing on the case?'

'Oh, I doubt it.'

Karen frowned. Just when she thought they were getting somewhere! Dr Michaels was not an easy man to understand. Sometimes she suspected he was dropping hints and words of wisdom that could be interpreted in different ways, so at the end of the case he could claim victory without actually giving them anything helpful.

'I hope you didn't resent me coming with you today to see Aiden.'

'Resent you? No, of course not,' Karen said. 'It's helpful to get your opinion.'

'Even if you don't listen to it?'

'I do listen to it,' Karen qualified. 'I like to keep our options open. That's all. I don't think we can discount Aiden.'

'Does he strike you as a killer?'

'Not really,' Karen said honestly, 'but you can't always tell.'

'No,' Dr Michaels said, gazing back at the Lomax house as Karen pulled out on to the road. 'I only wish it were that easy.'

CHAPTER TWENTY-FOUR

Morgan left the Hillocks' house, feeling Noah's wife's eyes boring into his back. He'd been as discreet as possible, but Noah Hillock wasn't a natural-born liar. His wife knew something was up.

She had at least confirmed Noah had been at home for the times of both abductions, and Noah had given Morgan permission to check his mobile phone data to confirm.

Noah was, not unsurprisingly, desperate to hide his relationship with his boss, but Morgan was as sure as he could be at this stage that the man wasn't involved in the abductions.

He got back into his car and wondered how Karen was getting on with Dr Michaels. Their theories and ideas on how to handle the case didn't currently line up.

On the one hand, Dr Michaels had vast experience, a PhD in criminology, a forensic mind and a history of tracking some of the most prolific killers in the US. On the other hand, Karen was . . . well, Karen. He smiled. Dr Michaels probably hadn't come across anyone quite like her before. If Morgan was a betting man, he'd put money on Dr Michaels coming around to her way of thinking by the time the case was over.

◆　◆　◆

Colin Greaves smothered a burp and pushed away his empty plate. He always started the day with a takeaway bacon bap from the local café. He was just about to get started on some paperwork when there was a knock at the door.

It was Travis, the night security guard.

'I thought you'd knocked off already,' Mr Greaves said.

'I was about to leave, but then I thought I'd ask you when the van turned up.'

'The van? What van?'

'The one that went missing. The one the police were looking for.'

'It's here?'

'Yeah, out the back.'

Greaves walked to the back of his office and opened up the blinds. It was a murky, grey morning, but sure enough, he saw the missing white Transit. There was mud splatter up the side and the back, but he could just about make out part of the number plate where the dirt had flaked off.

'How long's it been there?'

Travis shrugged. 'It wasn't there last night. It must have been dropped off this morning.'

Greaves's eyes narrowed. 'Are you sure it wasn't there last night?'

'Well . . . I don't think so.' He scratched the back of his neck and shuffled about nervously.

'I'm only going to ask you this once, Travis. Were you napping last night when you were supposed to be guarding my premises?'

'It's not my fault,' he whined. 'It's these long hours. I'm not used to it. I'm used to the day shift.'

Greaves slammed a fist on to the desk. The fact that he was only a fraction over five foot and the security guard was six foot two had no bearing on the power dynamic. Greaves could be a vicious man and he was in a foul mood.

Travis began to shake. 'I'm really sorry. It'll never happen again.'

'Do you realise what this is going to look like? I'm going to have to tell the police, aren't I? I'll have to ring up and say that the van's turned up, and we didn't notice who dropped it off. That's going to make us look like idiots – or worse, like suspects.'

'Not me, though,' Travis said quickly. 'I mean, I've been here all the time. I've got an alibi.'

Greaves's eyes turned cold. 'That's no alibi. You could have snuck off anytime. Nobody else was here to confirm you stayed put all night.'

'Oh . . . I'm really sorry, Mr Greaves. Please don't tell the police. I—'

Greaves held up a hand. 'I don't want to hear it.'

'I really need this job, though. Please, I . . .'

'We'll talk about it later.' He stalked past the security guard, down the steps and around the back of the building, and there it was.

The white van was parked neatly next to the others.

Why would the scumbag who took it bring it back to Branston Chickens, though? They'd stolen it from outside Tony Hickman's house, so why not take it back there?

Or why not just dump it somewhere to reduce the risk of getting caught?

He scratched his head and looked around the yard. The ground was muddy and wet, and he could hear the chickens clucking.

He gritted his teeth. It had been brought back because whoever took it wanted to make him look bad. Maybe they were even trying to frame him. Well, he'd see about that. He'd tell the police. He'd give them a ring in a minute, let them know the van they were looking for had turned up, and then they could do all that fancy forensic stuff and work out who took it.

Greaves had his suspicions. He didn't think it was the security guard. Travis wasn't bright enough to pull anything like this off.

And Greaves suspected he'd probably spent most of the night having a kip, so it was hardly surprising someone had managed to drive in and park up the van and leave again without Travis noticing.

He pinched the bridge of his nose, frustrated. It must have been one of his men, because they'd had to have taken the keys from his office. Tony was still off sick, and the others . . . Well, they'd worked for him for years. If they needed to use the van, they would have asked. It wasn't unheard of for him to allow people to use the vehicles. He wasn't an ogre. So, why would one of them have taken the van without asking? It didn't make any sense.

Unless . . . Greaves thought back. There was one other person who'd popped in to visit. But surely not. Why would *he* want the van?

Greaves pondered over the problem as he walked closer to the van. No, his brother definitely would have asked if he'd wanted to use the van. There was no way Mr Perfect would have just taken it.

But then again, he never came by if he could avoid it. Said the smell of chicken poop made him ill. Big baby. He'd always been the soft one. Mummy's favourite. The spoilt brother who was packed off to university while Greaves was given no such favours but built up his own business from scratch.

He trudged up to the driver's-side door. The keys were on the driver's seat and the door was open. He frowned. They'd have it on camera, at least, and see it coming in the main gate. Or would they? He took a step back and walked around the van, inspecting the tyre tracks.

Then it hit him. Of course. That was why they'd brought it back here, he realised. They didn't come in the main gates. They'd taken the private lane, the one that led through the trees and was overgrown, so no one would see them. It cut in from Fen Road.

Clearly, someone had taken the van to do something illegal, and they didn't want to be seen.

He clenched his teeth, furious that someone would use one of his vehicles to do their dirty work, and that it was likely one of his employees.

Well, they were about to realise that his loyalty only went so far, because he was quite prepared to tell the police the van had turned up and let them deal with it.

He wasn't protecting any criminals, especially if they'd been involved in the abduction of a young woman. The thought was abhorrent, and he still found it hard to believe one of his lads was involved in such a crime.

He opened the van's back doors. Greaves wasn't expecting to find much. But the sight that greeted him made him go dizzy.

He clapped a hand over his mouth, smothered a string of expletives, and then his stomach rolled and he began to heave.

It was the smell that got to him. Coppery, salty. The normally white interior walls were splattered with red, and the floor of the van was slick with blood.

CHAPTER TWENTY-FIVE

Branston Chickens was no more attractive during the daytime. Grey clouds hung low in the sky over the similarly grey buildings. Even the ground was a greyish-brown mud.

Though it was cold, the frost had thawed, and Karen's low-heeled boots squelched in the mud as she walked towards the small bungalow.

A uniformed officer stood outside. Karen held up her warrant card. 'Is Mr Greaves in here?'

'Yes, he's a bit shaken up,' the uniformed officer said, opening the door for Karen.

She found Mr Greaves in his office, perching on the edge of his large, padded chair and looking smaller and more vulnerable than he had last night.

He looked up at Karen with haunted eyes, and a flutter of recognition crossed his face. 'I didn't think you'd be back so soon,' he said, attempting a grin. It stretched across his face and then quickly disappeared.

Karen pulled up a chair close to him. 'How are you doing?'

He looked surprised at the question and blinked at Karen, but she recognised the symptoms of shock. He was pale, clammy, and his hands were clenched tightly in his lap, but even that didn't stop them trembling.

'I don't mind saying it was a bit of a shock,' he said. 'It really knocked me for six.'

'Were you the only person who went into the back of the van?'

He shook his head. 'I didn't actually go in,' he said. 'I opened the driver's door, saw the key on the seat and then opened the back doors . . .' He trailed off and shook his head. 'There was so much blood.' His skin had taken on a greenish tint. 'I'm sorry to say I threw up. I know, it's not nice for you to have to work in it. I'm sorry.'

'It's a very human reaction,' Karen said. He was talking, which was a good sign. She'd be more worried if he was quiet. Shock was not uncommon in witnesses who'd stumbled across crime scenes like Mr Greaves had. 'Do you know what time the van was brought back here? It wasn't here when I paid you a visit last night.'

He shook his head. 'No, it definitely wasn't. I came in this morning about seven thirty and noticed it was parked up shortly after that.'

'You have security working overnight, don't you?'

'Yeah, you met him last night. That's Travis. Travis Deacon. Unfortunately, it seems I've been paying that useless layabout to have a snooze.'

'So he was asleep?'

'That's about the size of it. He doesn't know when it turned up. He actually came to me and asked when the van had been returned. To be honest, I hadn't noticed when I'd arrived myself at seven thirty. Presumably, it was already parked up around the back, but, you see, I park around the front because the mud is bad.'

'Yes,' Karen said, looking down at her mud-encased boots. She'd tried to scrape most of it off before entering the bungalow.

He gave her a nervous smile. 'I'm sorry I can't be more help. I suppose someone dropped it off last night.'

'Do you have security cameras?'

He hesitated. 'We do on the main gate, but the thing is, I noticed the tyre tracks leading up to the van make it look like they've come in the back way, via the old lane. It isn't paved or tarmacked, and isn't used very much, only for farm vehicles usually.'

'Mr Greaves—'

'Call me Greavsie,' he said, this time minus the buoyant tone he'd used the previous evening; almost like he said it out of habit. 'Did you hear the chickens?' he asked.

'Hear them?'

'Yeah,' he said. 'They're unnerved. They pick up on it – vibrations, I think. They can tell something's wrong.'

Karen had heard some clucking and squawking coming from the building housing the chickens as she'd walked up to the bungalow, but had assumed that was what they normally sounded like in the daytime.

'I'll get a map printed up,' Karen said. 'So if you could mark out the route you think the van took, we'll chase it up.'

'All right,' Greaves said. He rubbed his hands over his arms. 'Really cold today, isn't it?'

In fact, though it was still cold – a typical February day – it wasn't as cold as it had been yesterday. 'I think you've had a bit of a shock, Mr Greaves. Maybe a nice hot cup of tea with some sugar in it.'

'Oh yes, good idea. Can I get you anything?' he asked, but Karen had already turned to leave.

'No thanks. I'm going to go and see how our scenes of crime officers are getting on.'

◆ ◆ ◆

The area was being processed by Tim Farthing and his team. As Karen gingerly approached, keeping carefully to the marked walkway area, Tim spotted her and trudged toward her.

'Chicken excrement,' he said.

'Sorry?'

'The place is covered with it,' he said, sniffing the air. 'Can't you smell it?'

'Yeah, a bit. So, what have you got for me?'

'So far, a lot of blood, and inside there's a metal pole, possibly a bit of scaffolding, which looks like it might be the murder weapon.'

'Murder then?'

Tim tilted his head and gave Karen a scathing look. 'I hardly think it likely that anyone could survive that much blood loss, do you?'

Karen bit back a retort. She needed Tim onside. 'Good point,' she managed to say after unclenching her jaw. 'I'd be interested in your ideas. I know you have a lot of experience.'

Tim raised an eyebrow.

Karen continued, stroking his ego. 'You've attended so many crime scenes in your career, I thought you may have some ideas as to whether the murder was carried out in the back of the van.' She gave him what she hoped was an encouraging smile.

Tim puffed out his chest. 'Yes, well, I've seen plenty of scenes with blood spatter. You're right about that.'

Was he really waiting for more flattery? Hadn't that been enough? He was so needy. She was tempted to pull rank and order his cooperation, but he would likely sulk and be as unhelpful as possible if she did.

'Did you learn anything from the blood spatter? I'd really value your opinion.'

He tilted his head, waiting for her to continue. He was enjoying this. 'Would you really?'

'Of course. We don't come across SOCOs with such a breadth of experience as yours very often.' *Or as annoying*, Karen mentally added. 'Your input would be very helpful.'

He gave a smug smile. 'Yes, I suppose in London we get more of the action.' He chuckled, then turned in the direction of the van. 'There's a small amount of blood spatter on the surfaces inside the back of the van, and the floor is covered with blood. But I'd say there isn't enough spatter to conclude the victim was killed in the van. In my opinion, the victim was beaten and then put in the van, where they bled out. And you're right about my *vast* experience, but I'm not a blood spatter expert. This is opinion only.'

'Of course,' Karen said, thinking that no matter how many times he said he wasn't an expert, he clearly viewed himself as such. 'We can bring in an expert to study the spatter patterns. But it's very helpful to get your initial take.'

He inclined his head regally.

'Does the blood give us any clues to the victim?'

'We've run a quick blood group test. It matches Tamara's, but we won't know for sure until we've analysed the DNA.'

'Right,' Karen said, looking at the van and processing the new information.

A crime scene photographer was standing by the door, leaning down and adjusting their camera lens to get a good shot.

'Anything else?' Karen asked.

'Well, we've not found a Queen of Hearts playing card this time. Maybe he's got tired of that little game.' Tim looked down at his boots. 'My toes are numb,' he said. He lifted one boot slowly, and the mud made a sucking sound as he extracted the sole. 'This is not the most pleasant scene to process.'

'No,' Karen said, looking at the red-spattered interior of the van, covered in what was likely to be Tamara's blood. But she had a feeling Tim was referring to the mud. 'What about the route the van took? The owner of Branston Chickens suggested that it came along a private lane, rather than coming in the front gates, which is why they don't have the van on camera.'

'Yeah, the mud means we've got some deep tracks, so we can see it certainly looks like they drove in from over there.' He pointed to a spot behind the buildings, along the tree line. 'There's a single track there, but I'm not sure where it comes out.'

'We'll look into that,' Karen said. 'If it borders a farm or another private lane, that's likely why we didn't pick it up on any traffic cameras. If he has access to private land, he must be familiar with the area.'

She looked off into the distance where there were clumps of trees and shrubs. They could easily have camouflaged the van. 'What about footprints around the van?'

'Not much to go on there,' he said. 'There's too many of them, one on top of the other. I'll probably get a good set from Mr Greaves since he was the one to find the van, but we'll take some photographs – some casts if we can get them.'

'Fingerprints?'

'We're looking. There are some, although most of them will probably belong to people who were legitimately using the van. Not necessarily your suspect.'

'Right. We'll definitely need Greaves's and Hickman's prints for elimination purposes. And I'll ask Mr Greaves who else has had access to the van in the last few weeks.'

Tim nodded.

'Keep me updated?' Karen asked.

Tim nodded again and then set off back towards the van, his feet squelching with each step.

◆　◆　◆

Karen caught up with Morgan as he walked back from the private-lane entrance.

Morgan said, 'I think we should fingerprint everyone who's had access to that van so we can eliminate them.'

Karen nodded. 'I'd just said as much to Tim Farthing. You know, the spare van keys were taken from inside the bungalow. It's likely to be someone who works here who took the keys and the van, don't you think?'

Morgan shoved his hands in his pockets and stared at the large feed containers. 'Yes, makes sense.'

'I think we should get Rick and Sophie to interview everyone who works here – everyone who had access to the keys, authorised or not.'

'Agreed,' Morgan said. 'Whoever it was certainly knew the area. If they brought the van back at night, it would have been pitch-black. Only headlights along that single-track road, which is probably not the easiest drive in daylight. I want to initiate a search of local properties that lead off from that lane. It looks like we could be too late to save them, but we still need to recover the bodies.'

Karen buried her face in her scarf. 'Yes,' she said quietly. 'We do.'

Morgan stared down at his shoes, which looked to be in a worse state than Karen's boots.

'I hope this is just mud,' he said. He checked his watch. 'Churchill wants a briefing at nine, and—' He was interrupted by his mobile phone ringing. He pulled it out of his pocket. 'Morgan.' He was quiet for a moment, and his gaze flickered over to Karen. A muscle in his jaw tensed. 'Right. Okay, we'll be right there,' he said and hung up.

Karen asked, 'News?'

'It looks like Churchill's briefing is going to have to wait for a while. A farmer has found a body in one of his fields.'

Karen felt a chill run along her spine. They'd been expecting this, of course, but despite everything, she'd been hoping that the madman was keeping the abducted women alive.

'Adult female?' Karen asked.

Morgan nodded as they started to walk back towards the car. 'Yes.'

'Well, if it's her blood in that van,' Karen said, pointing back towards the Transit, 'then the body could be in a pretty bad state.'

'Yes.'

'Has she been identified? Is it Tamara?'

'They didn't give me that information,' Morgan said.

Karen turned to look over her shoulder as they reached the car. 'It's one of those fields, isn't it? Along there?' She pointed in the direction of the single-track path that the van had taken. It looked likely that the van had come through the fields, dumped the body and then returned to park up at Branston Chickens.

Karen had been here last night. But she hadn't been able to stop this horrendous murder.

'I think so. They're emailing me the location. Why not just dump the van in the field?' Morgan wondered aloud. 'It seems like an extra risk.'

'I don't know. I suppose the van would be more visible in the middle of a field. Along the single track there'd be no cameras, and less chance of him being spotted by anyone,' Karen said.

They both stared at the wooded area.

Morgan's phone pinged, and he opened the email containing the location of the body. 'I think it's quicker to drive around,' he said. 'Access the field from the other side.'

They both got into the car, and Morgan started the engine. 'You know,' he said. 'I was really hoping it wouldn't come to this.'

CHAPTER TWENTY-SIX

The hardy tufts of grass at the edge of the field were easier to walk on than the mud slick at Branston Chickens.

Though Karen and Morgan had headed straight there once Morgan got the location, a white tent had already been erected in the middle of the field. As they walked towards it, they were approached by a crime scene officer whom Karen had worked with many times before, Deidre Meadows.

'DI Morgan, DS Hart,' she said, nodding at them both. She held out a plastic evidence bag.

'Queen of Hearts,' Karen murmured, her skin prickling with revulsion at the sight of the now all-too-familiar playing card. 'Is the victim recognisable?'

'Most of the injuries are on the back of her head, some on her arms, presumably defensive wounds,' Deidre said. 'One thing you might find interesting is the woman was fully clothed. Even her coat was zipped up.'

'No signs of sexual assault?'

'The pathologist would be the one to ask about that. But I thought you'd want to know about the clothing. Photographs have been taken, of course.'

'Is the pathologist here yet?'

'Raj is on his way.' She nodded behind them, and when Karen turned, she saw Raj daintily picking his way over the field, holding his kit bag.

Karen looked down at the playing card. Poor Tamara Lomax. It seemed a cruel twist of fate that she would end up the victim of a killer who'd fit into one of the true crime books she was so fond of reading.

Once Raj had taken an initial view of the body, he came out to talk to Karen and Morgan.

'Blunt force trauma,' he said sadly. 'Multiple blows to the back of the head and upper region of the back. Some broken bones, but it will have been the head injuries that killed her. She wasn't killed here. Not enough blood at the scene, though her clothing is soaked with blood,' he said. 'I also noticed some small fragments of what looked like rust around the wounds. It could be the murder weapon was a metal object.'

'Like part of a scaffolding pole?' Karen suggested.

He looked at her, his dark eyes bright with curiosity. 'That would fit,' he said. 'Have you already found the murder weapon?'

'We think so. A scaffolding pole was found in the back of a Transit van that we believe was used to transport the body.'

Raj nodded slowly and thoughtfully. 'Yes,' he finally said, pursing his lips so his moustache twitched. 'A scaffolding pole could inflict similar injuries.'

'Deidre said the victim was found fully clothed,' Morgan said. 'Was there evidence of a sexual assault?'

'Nothing immediately obvious. But I'll be able to give you a more accurate answer later. Would you like to see the body *in situ*?' he asked.

Karen went in first, ducking through the entrance to the tent and carefully keeping to the marked areas so as not to contaminate the scene.

The back of the woman's head was a bloody mess. Her blonde hair had been soaked to a dark red, her scalp lacerated. She wore dark trousers, and her jacket, dark green with a hood was stained with blood.

Karen crouched so she was closer to the victim. She studied the dead woman's face. Her left cheek was pressed to the cold ground. Four small moles dotted her right cheek.

Karen drew back in surprise. The woman wasn't Tamara Lomax. It was her sister. Rachel.

Karen darted out of the tent. 'Morgan, that's not Tamara. It's Rachel – Rachel Brooke, Tamara's sister.'

'*Rachel?* Are you sure?'

'Positive. She's got moles on her cheek, and her hair is slightly darker than Tamara's. I know it's hard to see with the blood, but yes, I'm sure it's Rachel Brooke.'

'Has Rachel been reported missing?' he asked.

Karen shook her head. 'Not as far as I know.'

'When was the last time you saw her?'

'Yesterday, when we first went to visit Tamara's husband, Aiden.'

Morgan turned to Raj. 'Do you have an approximate time of death?'

'Rough guess,' he said, 'probably early evening.'

Karen thought hard.

Nothing made sense.

'So, Rachel was likely to be the second abduction victim, taken from outside the Co-op. The woman had blonde hair, wearing a coat with a hood.' She turned to Morgan. 'That means he's targeted two sisters.' She shook her head. 'But if he's killed Rachel, then where's Tamara?'

'Good question,' Morgan said. 'Dr Michaels might need to adjust his profile. Sisters. Surely it has to be someone who knows them, or has at least interacted with them before.' He frowned. 'Who's in line to inherit their parents' estate if both Tamara and Rachel are dead?'

'Most likely Aiden.' Karen bit down on her lip. 'I've just had a thought. What if Rachel's left her share of the money to Tamara? That might be motive for killing Rachel first and then Tamara. Maybe Tamara's still alive. Maybe he's kept her somewhere.'

'I suppose it's possible,' Morgan said slowly. 'Let's not jump to conclusions.'

'I'm not,' Karen said, irritated. 'You sounded just like Churchill when you said that.'

Morgan looked wounded. 'We need to talk to Aiden again and search the house.'

'Sorry to interrupt,' Raj said, nodding back at the tent. 'But if you're happy, we'll take the body away now.'

Happy was certainly not the word Karen would have chosen, but Morgan nodded his assent.

'Are you *absolutely* sure?' Churchill asked Karen, looking at her as though she was trying to convince him Father Christmas was real.

The team were all sitting around the large table in the briefing room.

'Yes,' Karen said slowly, trying to keep her temper. 'It was definitely Rachel Brooke.'

'And not Tamara Lomax? Because I've seen the photographs, and they do look very similar.'

'They do,' Karen acknowledged, feeling the start of a tension headache building behind her eyes, 'but they're not twins. Rachel had four moles on her cheek.' Karen pulled out her mobile phone and zoomed in on the snap she'd taken of the framed photograph of Rachel and Tamara. 'See, nothing on Tamara's cheek. Four small moles on Rachel's.'

Churchill nodded. 'And she hasn't been reported missing?'

'Apparently she didn't turn up for a meeting at work this morning,' Sophie said.

'And where's work?' Churchill whirled around in his seat to face Sophie.

'She works at a private school, the Devonshire Academy, Uphill Lincoln.'

Churchill raised his eyebrows. 'That's my son's school,' he said. 'He's only just started there.'

'She didn't turn up for the meeting this morning, and it was reported when they weren't able to get in touch.'

'They were quick to report on that,' Churchill commented.

'Yes, the head reported it. She said they'd actually been quite worried about Rachel. She'd been very down after the death of her parents, understandably, and with her sister missing, they were very concerned she might have done something to harm herself.'

'Well, she certainly came to some harm,' Churchill said, 'although I doubt she managed to inflict those injuries herself.'

Karen frowned at his flippancy. 'I'd like to get a warrant to search the Lomax house. I think we should all agree now that Aiden is a major suspect. He has clear links with both women, and if both sisters die, I believe he's due to inherit a lot of money.'

'Do we know if Rachel left a will?' Churchill asked.

'We don't yet,' Karen said, 'but Tamara was her only living relative after her parents passed away, so it seems logical that as the next of kin she'd leave everything to Tamara.'

Churchill rubbed his chin thoughtfully. 'We've not kept our cards very close to our chest when it comes to Aiden Lomax. He's likely to put in a complaint after his last interview. I don't want to rush in like a bull in a china shop unless we're absolutely sure.'

'There's a chance Tamara could still be alive,' Karen said, and explained her theory that if Aiden wanted to inherit all the money, then Tamara surely would have to die *after* her sister.

'That's quite convoluted.' Churchill leaned back in his chair. 'Wouldn't he just stay married to his wife, and inherit that way? Even if he divorced her, he'd still get some of it, wouldn't he? A lot easier than going to these extremes.'

'I have to agree,' Dr Michaels said. He had the type of voice that was calming yet magnetic; it made people take notice. He wasn't domineering. He didn't shout, but he commanded attention. 'I'm sorry, Karen,' he said. 'I can see what's driving you to examine Aiden Lomax carefully, but I still feel we're dealing with someone from outside the family. It's possible that the fact the women are sisters is important. In fact, I'd say it's very likely this figures into some kind of fantasy the killer has. I'm sorry to say that, in my opinion, it's most likely Tamara Lomax is already dead, but the body hasn't been discovered yet.'

For a moment, no one said anything. His words made sense. The suspect was very probably from outside the family. And yet there was something about Aiden that niggled away at Karen. It wasn't as though he came across as some kind of psychopathic mastermind, but Karen knew when someone was hiding something – when they were holding something back – and Aiden Lomax was certainly keeping some things to himself.

'All right. If we can't get a warrant to search his property,' Karen said slowly and carefully, 'then I'd like to go and visit him again, give him an update. He needs to know his sister-in-law has been killed. The way he reacts could tell us a lot.'

Churchill stared hard at Karen. Finally, he conceded, 'Right. But it has to be done sensitively. I don't want any complaints. Understood?'

'Understood,' Karen said.

'I'd like to go with you,' Dr Michaels said.

Churchill raised an eyebrow and looked at Karen.

'It's fine by me,' Karen said and then turned to face Dr Michaels. 'It will be good to get your take on how Aiden reacts to the news.'

'Right. Good. Moving on. Where are we with the van and the murder weapon?' Churchill asked.

'Still being processed. Rick is at Branston Chickens now, taking prints of every member of staff, including the security guard, and interviewing them. We know someone took the keys from the office. It's likely to be someone who works there.'

Sophie looked up from her notepad. 'I was working on that too,' she said. 'DI Morgan thought it would be a good idea to dig and see if I could find a link between Aiden Lomax and Branston Chickens.'

'Is there a link?' Churchill asked.

'Yes, he worked there for six months, three years ago, as a part-time labourer on a temporary contract.'

Karen folded her arms. 'I specifically asked Mr Greaves if he knew Aiden Lomax or Tamara. And he said no. But I still think we should look into Greaves's history. He seemed genuinely shocked by the state of the van, but he could be a very good actor.'

'It's possible he didn't come into contact with Aiden,' Sophie suggested.

'But ultimately he's in charge of hiring, and the farm doesn't have that many employees.'

'Perhaps he knows Aiden well, and didn't want to get him into trouble,' Morgan suggested.

'Maybe. It certainly puts Aiden more firmly into the frame, in my opinion. It means he had access to the keys.'

'Well, not necessarily,' Churchill said. 'Strictly speaking he isn't currently employed there.'

'No, but he would have known where the keys were kept, how to access them, and the best time of day to take the keys,' Karen insisted. 'It's looking more and more likely that Aiden knows a lot more than he's letting on.'

'All right. Go and speak to him,' Churchill said and wrapped up the meeting.

Chairs scraped on the floor as everyone got up to leave.

'When you get back, we need to go through your personal assessment, Karen.'

She stopped halfway to the door and turned to look at Churchill. Was he serious? They were in the middle of a major investigation. Surely that could wait.

Her thoughts must have been conveyed in her expression as Churchill hurriedly added, 'Yes, all right. I suppose it can wait. We'll do it later.'

'Right. Ready?' Karen asked, looking at Dr Michaels.

As Dr Michaels stood up, Karen's phone beeped twice. She pulled it out of her pocket and then saw it was just social media notifications. Nothing that couldn't be dealt with later. She shoved it back into her pocket and headed out of the briefing room with Dr Michaels.

CHAPTER TWENTY-SEVEN

Karen went to her workstation to collect her coat. As she did so, she passed Sophie, who was looking intently at her phone.

'Everything all right?' Karen asked. 'You know what you've got to do?'

Sophie looked up with a guilty expression as she quickly put her mobile face down beside her keyboard. 'Yes, of course,' she said. 'I'm just getting to it now.'

Well, that was weird, Karen thought. Was Sophie trying to hide something?

'Are you sure everything's all right?' Karen asked. 'I can spare a couple of minutes if you need to talk something through.'

'No. No, you go. Everything's fine. There's nothing wrong at all,' Sophie said, sitting down behind her computer and studiously refusing to look at Karen.

Karen shrugged on her coat. 'All right then. Well, ring me if there are any developments. I'm going to go and talk to Aiden now.'

'Okay, bye,' Sophie said, and still didn't look up.

Karen didn't have time to analyse Sophie's strange behaviour. She needed to focus on Aiden Lomax. There was a small chance, minuscule really, that Tamara was still alive. And if they got to Aiden and made him talk, there was a chance they could save her.

She met Dr Michaels at the entrance to the stairs.

'Do you mind if I ask a few questions this time?' he asked, giving Karen a charming smile as he held open the door.

Karen thought for a moment. She didn't want to make him feel that his input was unwanted, because it wasn't. She realised he had abilities outside her skill set, but she needed to spring this information on Aiden in a controlled way, because they only had one chance to view his first reaction to the news about Rachel. That could provide crucial information and they had one shot.

'I don't mind,' Karen said slowly, 'but I'd appreciate it if you save your questions until after I've told Aiden about his sister-in-law. Deal?'

Dr Michaels smiled again. 'Deal.'

The traffic was heavy, irritating Karen as they headed to Aubourn. They got stuck behind a tractor, and then an HGV. Why was it whenever she wanted to get somewhere quickly in Lincolnshire she got stuck behind a tractor?

When they pulled up outside Aiden Lomax's house, Karen's phone began to ring. She turned off the engine and answered it straight-away, expecting it to be Sophie or Rick calling with fresh developments. But it wasn't. It was Karen's sister, Emma.

'Is it you they're talking about?'

'Sorry, what?' Karen replied, noticing that the living room light was on in Aiden's house.

'All the articles. Are they about you?'

'Sorry, Emma, I've got to go. I'm in the middle of a—'

'No, don't hang up. Have you seen them?'

'What are you talking about?' She turned to Dr Michaels and mouthed, 'Sorry.'

He nodded politely and got out of the car to give Karen some privacy.

'Seriously, Emma, I'm at work. I'm in the middle of a really important case.'

'I know, because it's all over the internet.'

'What?' Karen began to get a very uneasy feeling.

'Yes, that's why I'm calling. I tagged you in a couple of tweets. They actually named you. They've got a picture. Mum and Dad have seen it.'

Karen rolled her eyes. 'How have *they* seen it?'

'Well, I sent them a link,' Emma admitted, 'but even if I hadn't, they would have seen it eventually.'

'Right, okay. Why have they got my picture?'

'Because it's a hatchet job, Karen. The papers are saying it's your fault a woman has died.'

'What?'

'I know. That's why I'm calling you.'

'Right. Look, Emma, thanks. I'm going to have to go.'

'Have a look at the articles. I sent you a link.'

'All right, I will.'

Cursing under her breath, Karen quickly opened the message from her sister. It was a link to a local online news site. At least it wasn't one of the mainstream ones.

The headline was typically ghoulish.

Woman slaughtered after cocky cop ignores US profiler.

Karen gritted her teeth and glanced out of the window at Dr Michaels. He was standing casually beside the small wall that bordered the Lomaxes' garden.

She swore under her breath as she skimmed the rest of the article. They'd named her and said it was her fault that Rachel had died, though thankfully they didn't give the name of the victim. They'd even used a photo of Karen looking stressed and angry. The credit beneath the photograph was Nicholas Finney, and the article byline was Cindy Connor. She swore again.

'This is the last thing I need.' She got out of the car and slammed the door. 'Is this anything to do with you?' she asked, holding up her phone so Dr Michaels could skim the content.

'Sorry. What?' he asked, taking Karen's phone. 'Oh.' His eyes widened as he read. 'That's unfortunate. I see the tabloids are the same everywhere.'

'Where did they get the information? That's what I want to know.'

'It was nothing to do with me,' he said quickly.

'Where else would they get it from? I mean, you have to admit, it puts you in a pretty good light. It even mentions your new book at the end of the article!'

'Well, I can see it looks pretty incriminating.'

'You're right. It does,' Karen snapped. She took her phone back. 'We don't have time to get into it now, but this isn't over. All right?'

Dr Michaels put up his hands, and Karen stalked past him heading for Aiden Lomax's front door.

◆　◆　◆

As soon as Karen walked out of the office, Sophie picked up her phone. Cindy Connor's story had been recycled and rehashed on lots of news sites, all of them derogatory towards Karen, saying what a terrible job she'd done and how a woman's blood was now on her hands. *If only she'd listened to the intelligent, wonderful Dr Michaels.*

Ugh. Sophie put her mobile away. This was awful. Everyone Karen knew would read these articles. They were all over social media.

She'd already had two friends texting to say, *Isn't this your boss?*

She should have told Karen about the stories straightaway. She knew that, but she was a coward. She didn't want to be the one to tell Karen about the nasty lies, because Karen was bound to think Dr Michaels was behind it. There was even a plug for his book in Cindy Connor's article. It certainly looked bad, but Sophie knew he couldn't be behind it. He was too honourable for that.

She stood up, left her desk, and walked along the corridor until she reached the small office Dr Michaels and Zane had been assigned.

Dr Michaels, of course, was out with Karen, but Zane was sprawled in a chair, scrolling on his phone.

'Oh, Sophie,' he said as she stepped into the doorway. 'Be an angel and make me a coffee, would you? I can't seem to work out that dumb machine.'

'I'm a bit busy,' Sophie said, folding her arms.

Zane narrowed his eyes and shrugged. 'Then what are you doing here?'

'I need to have a word with you.'

'All right.' He looked up expectantly. 'What about?'

'About Karen. About all these stories in the press about how terrible she is at her job, and how if only she'd listened to Dr Michaels everything would have been fine.'

He smiled. 'Oh, did you see those? I didn't think they'd be so popular. The first article has already had two thousand retweets,' he said.

'It was you, Zane. I know it was you.'

'What are you talking about?' he said, leaning forward and raising his hands. 'It could have been anyone.'

'But it wasn't anyone. It was you. It's blatantly obvious. You're the only one who gets any benefit from these kinds of articles.'

'That's not strictly true now, is it?' Zane said. 'Dr Michaels is the one who benefits.'

Sophie shook her head. 'He wasn't the one who provided the story though.'

'Are you sure?' Zane asked with a grin.

'Yes, it was you.'

'You don't have any evidence.'

'Actually, I do.'

The smile slid from Zane's face. 'What?'

'You've done this before, haven't you? You've got a talent for sneakily feeding stories to the media.'

'You don't know what you're talking about. You'd better be careful, throwing accusations around like that,' Zane said, his tone growing cold.

'I wonder what Dr Michaels would think if he knew those stories about Angela's mother were coming from you.'

Zane froze. 'You've got no proof. And anyway, those articles did him a favour. They got him publicity.'

'I don't need proof,' Sophie said. 'Although I'm sure I could get it if I tried. I'm going to tell you what's going to happen next. You're going to email your resignation to Dr Michaels. You're not going to be working with him again. And you're going to leave the station right now.'

Zane was silent. He glared at her, motionless.

'Is that understood?' Sophie said.

'Why should I agree to that?' Zane asked, his voice low.

'Because, Zane, I saw the message from Genius News flash up on your phone yesterday. I know you're the one feeding the stories. If you don't agree to resign, I'll tell Dr Michaels it was you providing information about Angela's mother.'

Zane sat up straight. 'He'd *never* fire me.'

'Are you sure? I think he would. You've betrayed him.'

'I have not! You don't know the first thing about us.'

Sophie narrowed her eyes. On the surface, Zane was flippant, and yet his relationship with Dr Michaels was intense. 'So tell me – what don't I understand?'

'I only did it to help him. He doesn't realise what the world's really like. All that nonsense about helping people. No one cares. You have to make your own success. Do you really think Angela cares about him? She wants to ruin his career over a few articles after everything he did to bring her mother's killer to justice.' Zane was trembling with rage.

'But surely you can see that information was private, hurtful. Angela Munro felt betrayed.'

Zane shook his head. 'You're naive. Just like him. I've tried to help, but if my work isn't appreciated then I'm done. I'm out of here.'

He stood up so fast that he knocked his chair to the floor. He grabbed his phone and his coat. 'The whole thing is pathetic. We were supposed to be on a literary tour. I expected London, Paris, Frankfurt. Not this kind of backwater town.'

'It's a city actually,' Sophie said, following Zane out of the office.

'You don't have to follow me. I'm going,' he snapped.

'Sorry, but you're not to be trusted. I'm following you to make sure you leave and you hand in your ID pass.'

He turned, snatching the lanyard from around his neck and thrusting it at Sophie. 'Take it!'

She trailed him to the exit where he turned around again, swore at her and then marched off just as it started to rain.

Sophie looked up at the dark grey clouds and hoped the rain would get heavier.

CHAPTER TWENTY-EIGHT

Karen was halfway to the Aiden Lomax's front door when her mobile rang again. With a sigh of frustration, she pulled it from her pocket. It was a number she didn't recognise, probably her sister calling from work this time.

She answered it. 'What now?'

There was a pause on the other end of the line, followed by, 'DS Hart? That's not a professional way to answer a call.'

It was DCI Churchill.

'Sorry, sir,' Karen said. 'I thought you were someone else.'

'Who?'

'My sister.'

'You shouldn't be taking personal calls on work time, especially in the middle of such an important case.'

'I'm aware of that, sir. I'm too busy to take calls, which was why I was trying to get rid of her.'

Karen was too busy for Churchill's interruptions too, if he only wanted to lecture her on how to answer a phone call.

She wanted to get in there and question Aiden. Was that really too much to ask?

Apparently so.

'I don't care how busy you are. I want you back at the station now,' Churchill barked.

'But we're at Aiden's house. I'm a few feet from his front door. Can we just—'

'No! You are to return to the station immediately and come to my office.'

'Could we—'

'No!' Churchill shouted and ended the call.

'I take it that wasn't good news,' Dr Michaels said.

Karen shot a glance at Aiden's house. The light was on in the living room, but the curtains were all still closed. 'No, it's not,' Karen said. 'I have to go back to the station.'

'Why?'

'*Churchill*,' Karen said, as though that explained everything.

'Well, should I talk to Aiden on my own?' Dr Michaels suggested.

'No, definitely not,' Karen said, then saw the look of wounded pride on Dr Michaels's face. 'Sorry, I didn't mean to imply you weren't capable of doing it, but legally one of us should be with you.'

'I understand,' Dr Michaels said. 'So, back to the station then?'

Karen took one last regretful look at Aiden's front door and nodded. 'Yes, back to the station.'

◆ ◆ ◆

When they got back to Nettleham HQ there was a scrum of people around the entrance. Karen waited for a moment before getting out of the car and scanning their faces. 'Oh great,' she said.

'What is it?' Dr Michaels asked as he unbuckled his seatbelt.

'Press,' Karen said.

'Press?' Dr Michaels said. 'I can't see any TV crews.'

'Oh, it's just the local journalists,' Karen said. 'It's not an important enough story, I guess, for the six o'clock news. Well, we'd better face the music.'

They got out of the car, and were halfway across the car park when one of the journalists spotted Karen.

'There she is,' the woman yelled. She had a neat blonde bob and bright-pink lipstick. Cindy Connor.

Cindy had risen up through the ranks after starting her own gossip blog, and was now given some of the important local stories, although she always managed to work in a gossip angle.

Occasionally the stories were good and in the public interest – attacking the local councils for wasting money by abandoning projects that had been paid for, for instance, or for awarding contracts to family members.

But in this case, Karen sensed that an officer who had a complicated personal history was a more attractive target for a hit piece than a corrupt politician was. It was a dream story for reporters like Cindy. An officer's mistake, leading to the death of an innocent woman, was a much better story than the truth.

They jostled around Karen. Cameras started clicking and whirring. She put her hand up to her face.

'Is it true, DS Hart? Was your decision responsible for the death of a young woman? Do you have a name for the victim?' Cindy yelled.

Nicholas Finney lowered his camera. He gave a small, shy smile directed at Dr Michaels. 'Hope things are going well. My source says you've been a great help to the police.'

'Too kind.' Dr Michaels gave him a charming smile.

'Anything you'd like to say, Doctor? My source—'

Cindy snorted. 'Your source? Oh, please. You're here to take photographs, Nicholas.'

Nicholas's shoulders slumped, and he stepped back as Cindy thrust her phone towards Karen. 'What about the victim? We need a name. The public deserves to know the truth.'

'Especially if her death was your fault!' another member of the throng shouted. He stood at the back – dark hair, leather jacket and a deeply lined face.

'It wasn't . . .' Karen started to say, then thought better of it. 'No comment.' She pushed her way through the melee.

Dr Michaels followed at a much slower pace, still wearing his professional, charming smile.

Cindy turned her sharp eyes on him. 'Dr Michaels, your expertise as a *profiler* is known around the world? How does it feel to have your book topping the charts this week?'

'It feels pretty good, ma'am,' he said, giving her his full attention.

Cindy giggled. Actually giggled. 'I've bought a copy.'

'How kind,' Dr Michaels said. 'Thank you for your support.'

'I bought one too,' Nicholas said, but he was quickly pushed aside by the journalists and other photographers. It was clear where he was in the pecking order.

'Could you spare a few minutes, Dr Michaels? Give us the lowdown on what's happening?' Cindy asked.

'No, he couldn't,' Karen snapped before Dr Michaels had a chance to reply. 'We're busy. There'll be a statement released shortly.'

They headed inside, and Karen let out a long breath as the doors shut behind them. She nodded to the desk sergeant.

'They've been making a pain of themselves for the past half an hour. I tried to get rid of them,' the desk sergeant said, 'but you know what they're like once they get a whiff of a story.'

Karen nodded. 'Yes, I do. And sometimes I think they don't even care if it's not true.'

'Do you want me to come with you?' Dr Michaels said as they pushed their way through the double doors and headed for the stairs. 'To speak to Churchill? Maybe I could help smooth things over.'

'Thanks, but I'm not sure anything could help me at the moment. I'd better face him alone.'

'All right.'

◆ ◆ ◆

Churchill sat behind his desk tapping a pen vigorously on an A4 pad. The pen left deep indentations on the paper.

'Sir,' Karen said as she entered and sat down.

'Don't you have anything to say?'

'Are you talking about the newspaper articles?' Karen asked.

'Yes I'm talking about the newspaper articles. I sat here looking like an idiot with the superintendent on the phone asking me what's going on. Of course, I don't know, because nobody thought to tell *me*,' he said, speaking in a furious rush. He slapped the pen down on the pad. 'It's not good enough, Karen.'

'I'm sorry. I only found out myself when we were on the way to speak to Aiden.' She sighed. 'It's just the news. It'll be fish-and-chip wrappings tomorrow.'

'No, it won't. I don't know what world you're living in, but we don't use newspaper to wrap fish and chips anymore. And—'

'It's just a saying, sir,' Karen said. 'What I meant was there'll be another news story to catch their attention tomorrow.'

'I don't think you understand. This isn't going away. It's all over social media. It's gone viral.' He raked a hand through his hair. 'I don't understand why you're not more upset. You're the one they're pointing the finger at.'

'Yes, I know.'

'And where's Dr Michaels?' he said. 'I don't think it's a coincidence he comes up smelling of roses in all this, do you?'

'No, I don't.'

'It's another way to hawk his book. I can't believe I was taken in. I really thought he wanted to help. I thought he was a professional. I should have listened to you,' Churchill said. 'You didn't want him on this case from the start.'

Karen sat back in her chair, not quite sure what to make of that. Churchill telling her she was right all along! Of course, she had to then go and ruin it, rather than savour the moment.

'Actually, sir, I'm not sure it was him.'

'But it makes sense. He puts us down to make himself look good. Then he sells more copies of his books.'

'Yes, that was how I reacted at first as well, but . . .' Before Karen could say any more there was a rap at the door.

'Come in,' Churchill snapped.

The door opened, and Sophie entered, followed by Dr Michaels.

'Sorry to interrupt,' Sophie said. She gave Karen a small smile. 'But I thought I should tell you that Zane Dwight was behind the stories. He's given Dr Michaels his resignation. I made sure he handed in his entry card, and the desk sergeant knows Zane's not permitted to access the station anymore.'

Dr Michaels held up his mobile. 'She's right. I've just checked my emails. I'm really so sorry.'

'Come in and shut the door,' Churchill said, flinging a hand in the direction of two other chairs.

Sophie and Churchill sat.

'What I don't understand,' Churchill said, running his finger over the dents in his pad, 'is that you're supposed to be an expert on human behaviour. You've spent your career tracking down criminals, and yet Zane was able to trick you like a second-rate con artist.'

Dr Michaels leaned forward and held up his hands. 'You're right. I should have seen it coming. Zane has had troubles in the past, but I'm close to his family. I thought I could help him.'

'So,' Karen said slowly, 'Zane sold a story on me to make you look good.'

'That's about the size of it. He thought he was helping me.'

'And what about the other stories, in the American press?'

'That's what made me sure it was Zane,' Sophie said. 'When the story came out, I knew it wasn't Dr Michaels, so there was only really one person it could be. Zane. He'd got the details from Dr Michaels's files and sold the story to Genius News, an outlet that runs gossip and news blogs in the US. Angela, of course, thought that it was Dr Michaels selling the stories, as he was one of the few people with all the details.'

'You didn't suspect anything?' Karen said to Dr Michaels.

He paused, looking down at his interlinked fingers in his lap. 'I didn't think he'd go as far as he did, and he hadn't given me any reason not to trust him.'

Karen could understand Dr Michaels's desire to help, especially as Zane was the son of a family friend. But all the same, he had let Zane have access to a very sensitive enquiry.

'I know what you're thinking. I shouldn't have brought him on board if I had any doubts at all. I did keep things from him. I told him he wasn't to come to the briefings. I kept the information separate, and I didn't give him access to any files. So, the story he sold is what he's picked up from hearing people talk at the station.'

'The story he sold is pretty much made up,' Karen said.

'Right,' Dr Michaels acknowledged with a meek nod. 'You're right, of course. I can only apologise and leave you to it. I've not been much help so far. It looks like Karen was right. There is a link between the victims. Two sisters were targeted, and I didn't see that coming. I was convinced Aiden didn't have the right personality type to commit these crimes, but perhaps I was wrong about that too.' He stood up.

'No, wait,' Karen said. She looked at Churchill. 'I don't think Dr Michaels should go. We've had differences of opinion, but I value his input.' She turned to Dr Michaels. 'I understand your point. Aiden doesn't strike me as a killer, either. I know that it's not always possible to tell, but I think there's more going on here.' She shrugged, feeling uncomfortable with Dr Michaels's penetrating gaze. 'We could really do with your help.'

Sophie couldn't hide her delight. 'Yes, we really could. Zane was definitely a mistake, but there's no denying your expertise in this area.'

Both Karen and Sophie looked at Churchill.

He grunted, 'Right. Well.' He looked down and straightened his navy-blue tie. 'I suppose we'll go on as before.'

CHAPTER TWENTY-NINE

'If we're picking up where we left off,' Karen said, 'I'll go back to Aiden's house.' She checked her watch. It was fast approaching lunchtime already.

'No,' Churchill said. 'We need to do the logical thing.'

Karen frowned. 'Which is?'

'We need to look at Rachel's life. Friends and work colleagues. Visit the parents' property. That's where Aiden thought she was going yesterday.' He glanced at Sophie. 'She worked at the secondary school in Uphill Lincoln?'

Sophie nodded. 'That's right. Devonshire Academy.'

'Then, Karen, I want you to check out her parents' place. Then you and Morgan speak to her colleagues at the school. If she was stalked before her murder, there's a chance they noticed something. Rachel may have confided in one of them.'

'But Aiden—'

'No,' Churchill said. 'Aiden is still a person of interest, of course, but he's not opened up. Perhaps we applied too much pressure at the wrong time. Right now, our priority is background on Rachel, our murder victim. Understood?'

Karen gritted her teeth. 'Understood.'

'Sophie, you can deliver the news to Aiden with Dr Michaels. Tell him we've found Rachel, and see how he responds.' Churchill turned to Dr Michaels. 'You don't have a problem with that?'

'No, I think it's very sensible.'

'Right.' Churchill nodded at Karen.

'Okay,' she said. It was getting harder and harder to hide her frustration, but maybe Churchill was right. She knew Aiden Lomax was withholding something, but they hadn't managed to find out what it was, despite heavy questioning, so perhaps coming at this from another angle made sense.

Back downstairs, Karen stepped into the open doorway to Morgan's office.

'Sorry to interrupt. Churchill's requested you come with me to Rachel Brooke's school to talk to her colleagues later. I've got to check out the parents' property first though.'

Morgan nodded. 'No problem. I'll call the school and let them know to expect us. I've just been chasing up phone records. Nothing on Tamara's. Still waiting on Rachel's. Did you get anything from Aiden?'

'I didn't even get to *talk* to Aiden,' Karen said, and explained what had happened.

'I saw the articles,' Morgan said. His face was impassive. 'Very unfair.'

'They usually are,' Karen said. 'This one's particularly so, as they named me. They even used a frightful photograph. It must have been snapped as I was telling them to get out of the way. My mouth's open and I look deranged. Not very flattering.'

'Let's hope we catch our killer, and they'll have something else to write about.'

◆ ◆ ◆

Sophie got out of the car and gave Dr Michaels a nervous smile. She was in charge, the lead officer. Churchill had entrusted her to break the news to Aiden Lomax that his sister-in-law, Rachel, had been murdered. She was teaming up with Dr Michaels to gauge Aiden's reaction to the news.

They were later than expected, as Churchill had wanted to go through things in detail. Sophie was worried the news would break before they had a chance to tell Aiden about Rachel, but she understood Churchill's reasoning behind making a plan.

So much depended on this. His reaction could tell them a lot, but Sophie had to admit she felt out of her depth.

Her previous experience with Aiden hadn't yielded much in the way of progress. Karen had been sure he was hiding something, but Sophie had just seen a grieving husband. Though she was worried that she might screw this up, at least she had Dr Michaels at her side. Now he really was an expert. She could rely on him to delve into the psychology of Aiden Lomax.

Churchill had asked them to stay with Aiden for as long as they could. He was still refusing a family liaison officer, so she and Dr Michaels were supposed to stay and observe. When Sophie had asked, 'How long for?' Churchill had replied, 'Until he kicks you out.'

'Have you heard from Zane?' Sophie asked Dr Michaels. She'd half expected to see the former PR man hanging around the station as they left, ready to declare his innocence and tell Dr Michaels that Sophie had made up the accusations.

There had been no sign of him since he stormed out, but Sophie was still concerned. It had been easy to get rid of Zane. Too easy.

'No, I've heard nothing since the email. I haven't called him yet either. I'll probably do that later. He's done the wrong thing, I know that, but he's still away from home and vulnerable.'

Sophie raised her eyebrows. It was hard to think of Zane as vulnerable. He always appeared to be out for number one. The short time she'd known him had shown that. How could Dr Michaels be so knowledgeable, and yet so trusting when it came to Zane? It didn't make sense.

Together they walked up the path towards the Lomaxes' house.

Sophie took a deep breath. 'Once we're inside I'll break the news,' she said. 'If you could watch him carefully for any reactions, that would be really helpful. Any signs at all could be important.'

Dr Michaels's mouth twitched into a half-smile. 'I have done this before, Sophie.'

'Of course you have, sorry. I'm just nervous. Karen thinks Aiden's reaction when we tell him about Rachel could reveal key information.'

'Yes, and she's right. But don't worry. I'll be watching him very carefully.'

'Thanks,' Sophie said. That did make her feel better.

She rang the doorbell, and had to do so twice before the front door was opened by Aiden Lomax.

He looked much worse than the first time Sophie had seen him. The first time he'd been agitated and anxious, stressed. His hands had been fluttering about. He'd been clenching his jaw; his gaze had never seemed settled on anything for long. But today he moved slowly – lethargy in every movement. His eyes looked red and puffy. He wore an old T-shirt with a hole near the collar and a pair of baggy tracksuit bottoms.

He said nothing, just stared at them.

'I don't know if you remember me,' Sophie said. 'I'm DC Jones and this is my colleague Dr Michaels. There have been some developments, and we'd like to talk to you. Can we come in?'

She'd expected him to ask immediately about Tamara, and the fact that he didn't and just simply stepped back, allowing them to enter, struck her as odd.

They went into the living room. Sophie and Dr Michaels took the sofa, and Aiden padded slowly over to his green velvet chair.

'What's happened?' he asked, his voice hoarse and quiet.

Sophie looked at Dr Michaels for reassurance, but he was staring intently at Aiden.

'I'm afraid I have some bad news. It's your sister-in-law, Rachel Brooke. She . . .'

The words died in Sophie's throat as Aiden looked up and his gaze locked with hers. She could only see pain, no guilt. 'I'm very sorry, Aiden, but Rachel was found dead this morning. She's been murdered.'

For a long time, Aiden said nothing. Then he lowered his head. 'Right,' he said. 'I see.'

'This must have come as an awful shock to you,' Sophie said. 'I know you were expecting news on Tamara, and this isn't the ideal time to ask you questions, but we need to ask you if you have any idea why someone may have wanted to target both sisters.'

He stared blankly at the floor. Was he in shock?

That would be understandable, perhaps explaining why he wasn't asking any further questions. Sophie had expected him to demand to know what exactly had happened to Rachel – where she was found, why Tamara wasn't with her, and why there had been a delay in giving him the news.

But instead Aiden sat in front of them like a broken man, curled in on himself.

Finally, he shook his head. 'No, I don't know why anyone would want to hurt either of them.'

'I'm afraid my next question is quite a delicate one, and I don't want you to take offence, but I need to ask.'

He lifted his head slowly and swung his gaze to Sophie.

'Do you know who inherits the money Rachel was left by her parents?'

He shook his head. 'I don't think she'd even sorted the estate. I don't think she's had the money from her parents yet. As far as I know, Rachel was acting as executor of the will.'

'Not Tamara.'

He shook his head. 'No, they'd named both as executors. But it was too much for Tamara. She didn't want to do it. She wanted to hand it all over to a solicitor, but Rachel said no, she wanted to do it, and she was quite prepared to handle it all herself.'

'I see. So you don't know whether Rachel had made a will?'

He let out a breath. 'Yes, I think she did. Tamara did too, after their parents died. I suppose it just reminded them of their own mortality.'

'I see. We'll look into it.'

He looked up sharply, her words finally getting through the hazy fog that seemed to surround him. 'Why are you asking about wills?' he asked.

'It's just routine.'

'You mean you need another reason to suspect me of being involved?' he said. 'Well, I can save you some paperwork. Everything belonging to Tamara would come to me, as her husband.'

'And Rachel?'

'I don't know. I think she left everything to Tamara.' He shrugged.

'So, that means if something happened to Tamara, you would end up with all of the inheritance?' Sophie suggested, trying to keep her tone light and non-accusatory.

He shook his head and gave a cold laugh. 'I should have known you'd try to pin it on me. Why not? I suppose it makes life simple for you. Nice, easy investigation.'

He twisted away so he was no longer facing Sophie.

She looked at Dr Michaels, wondering what he'd been able to gather from Aiden's reaction. He was difficult to read. To Sophie, he'd seemed like a genuinely distraught husband when Tamara had first gone missing. But she had to admit his strange response to the news about Rachel was unsettling.

For most people, being told something like that would lead to an emotional response. Most people would ask questions. But perhaps Aiden Lomax wasn't like most people. Maybe his grieving-husband bit was all an act?

CHAPTER THIRTY

Rachel and Tamara's parents' property was a relatively modest-looking bungalow with a lot of land. As it was worth a million pounds, Karen had been expecting something a bit fancy – a huge, modern house maybe. She parked on the gravel drive and walked along the path between two large flower beds, now filled with brown, stick-like plants.

She'd spoken briefly with Sophie, who'd told her Aiden Lomax had given his permission for the property to be searched. He'd said the spare key was hidden beneath the windowsill to the right of the front door.

Karen crouched down and saw the key secured to the underside of the sill by a magnet. It was an improvement on the usual method of hiding a key under a flowerpot, but it still wasn't advisable.

She grasped the key and then noticed a movement to her right. She straightened and turned.

'Can I help you?' The voice belonged to a woman with shoulder-length grey hair. Karen judged her to be in her mid-fifties. She wore purple gardening gloves, a blue body warmer and green wellington boots.

'DS Karen Hart,' she said, showing her ID. 'I've got permission from Aiden Lomax to take a look around.'

'Aiden?' The woman raised an eyebrow. 'No one told me.'

'And you are?'

'Gretchen. Gretchen Chambers. I help run the sanctuary.'

'The sanctuary?'

'Yes, around the back here. Did you want to take a look?'

Karen nodded and followed the woman, carefully stepping over clumps of grass growing out between the paving stones. From the side of the property, the bungalow appeared much larger than it did from the front.

The garden was huge and full of mature shrubs and trees. At the end of the lawn was a wooden gate.

'Do you mind me asking if Rachel knows you're here?'

Karen hesitated. Would Sophie have had a chance to tell Aiden by now? Probably.

'I'm very sorry to have to tell you this, Gretchen, but we discovered Rachel's body this morning.'

Gretchen stopped walking suddenly. 'You found a body?' Her voice sounded raw. 'Rachel's body? But no, that can't be right. Don't you mean Tamara?'

'No, Tamara is still missing, and sadly we found Rachel early this morning.'

'Oh, that's . . . awful.' She looked up at the pale grey sky, blinking away tears.

After a moment, she carried on walking. 'Rachel and Tamara's parents set up the wildlife sanctuary about twenty years ago. They found an injured owl and nursed it back to health,' Gretchen said. 'Since then, things have grown. They take in all sorts of animals, and after the deaths of their parents, Rachel and Tamara have been trying to keep things going. They're such good . . .' She looked at Karen. 'I know you told me Rachel is gone now, but it's going to take a while to sink in.' Her face crumpled, and she turned away from Karen to roughly wipe her cheeks with the back of a gloved hand.

She stopped beside the gate and pointed. Karen read the sign. There was a line drawing of an owl beside the words *Tamra Wildlife Sanctuary*.

'Tamra?' Karen asked.

'It's from the girls' names, Tamara and Rachel. They were involved in it, both of them, when they were growing up. They would help out at weekends and after school. At one stage, there was quite a menagerie here. Two donkeys, a whole aviary of birds being nursed back to health. Even foxes, although they don't go down well with the birds.' She smiled. 'They were kept separately, but they could sense the danger while the foxes were here.'

Karen looked beyond the gate at the fenced-off areas and wire cages.

'We aim to release them all eventually, unless they're unable to survive in the wild. Very few of them are kept, but some just can't fend for themselves, so they stay here. Obviously, it costs quite a bit – vet bills, feed, that sort of thing.'

She opened the gate, and Karen walked through. Immediately in front of them were two large wire cages, approximately eight by twelve feet. There were branches and bits of wood stuck into the earth at the centre, like miniature trees. A magpie chattered loudly, hopping around.

'We've had him for a while,' Gretchen said. 'He had a broken wing. It's been fixed, but he still doesn't like to fly.' She shrugged. 'It's difficult. You want him to have his freedom back, but at the same time, he's a sitting duck for any predators.'

The magpie croaked in agreement as it hopped its way to the top of the branch, watching them with bright, dark eyes.

The rhyme about magpies pushed its way to the front of Karen's mind. One for sorrow, two for joy . . . She shivered.

'There aren't many animals here at the moment. Sad, really. We've been turning them away. The thing is, Rachel works full-time at the school. I mean . . .' She pushed her hair from her face with the back of her hand. 'Rachel worked full-time at the school, and Tamara, well, she's been brilliant. She's always popping in and out to do the feeds, clean the cages and make sure the animals are all right. I don't know how she manages it. She must have a very understanding boss.'

Karen smiled, thinking of Mr Casey. At least that explained where Tamara had been sneaking off to while George Casey and Noah Hillock had their sneaky get-togethers.

'And are you working here full-time?' Karen asked.

'No, I took early retirement,' Gretchen said. 'I'm a volunteer, but it's taking up a lot of time. As you can imagine, there's no one else. It's just me at the moment. I'm hoping Tamara comes back.' She looked at Karen, hoping for reassurance.

It was so tempting to say the words she wanted to hear, but Karen couldn't bring herself to lie. The chances of Tamara being alive at this stage were very slight.

'You said it takes a fair bit of money to keep this place running,' Karen said. 'Were Tamara and Rachel using money from the estate?'

Gretchen nodded. 'Yes, their father made quite a bit of money back in the day. He had some luck in the dot-com boom, and he bought this place. But things are complicated until the estate is settled. Not all the bills have been paid, as most of the money is tied up in the house. If the bungalow is sold, I don't know what will happen to the sanctuary.' She sighed. 'Right now, we've only got the magpie, a couple of pigeons and an underweight hedgehog, who's refusing to hibernate.' She smiled. 'We sent some of the animals out to other sanctuaries and released the ones we could after we got the vet's clearance. But others, like the magpie, will have to stay.'

Karen looked back at the gate. 'The picture of the owl on the gate. Is that symbolic because the first creature they saved was an owl?'

'Yes, I think so.' Gretchen looked thoughtful. 'There were some awful tales around here when I was a girl. Certain people used to think that owls were able to keep evil spirits away. They'd nail them to barn doors to protect the animals inside, and the crops.' She shivered. 'Thankfully, that doesn't happen anymore.'

Karen folded her arms, suddenly feeling the cold more intensely. 'Do you know if Tamara or Rachel were having trouble with anyone? Any relationships, or things they were worried about?'

Gretchen shook her head. 'No, I spoke to both girls nearly every day. There was nothing bothering them other than the obvious. Their parents were gone, and they were struggling to come to terms with it and work out what to do with this place.' She glanced back at Karen. 'There was one thing I found strange. I'm sure it was nothing, though.'

'Go on.'

'They usually got on well, but over the last week or so I didn't see them together.'

'And that was odd?'

'Yes. Probably my imagination, but I did wonder if they were avoiding each other.'

'And has there been any history of stalking or angry ex-boyfriends, anything like that?' Karen asked.

Gretchen shook her head. 'No, not that I know of, and I've known both girls for a long time.'

'What do you think of Aiden?'

'Tamara's husband?'

Karen nodded.

Gretchen pulled a face. 'Well, he's not really the outdoor type. He never comes by to help with the sanctuary or anything like that,' she said, as though that immediately should tell Karen everything she needed to know about Aiden. 'Bit of a city boy if you ask me.' She smiled. 'But I don't know him well.'

'Do you think they were going to sell the place?' Karen asked, thinking Gretchen could be emotionally attached to the sanctuary. Though she seemed like a very sensible woman in her fifties, unlikely to commit murder just to save her volunteer role at a wildlife sanctuary.

'They didn't want to sell. They were hoping to keep things going, raise some more donations, that sort of thing. Get some more volunteers to help out. I think they'd had a few people interested and did some interviews.'

'Do you have any names or contact details for those people?'

Gretchen shook her head. 'I'm afraid not. You might find some notes or something like that inside in the office.' She nodded towards the bungalow. 'They'd been doing all sorts – set up a new website, did interviews with the local press. And they were talking about having an open day for people to come in, see the sort of work the sanctuary does and raise some money at the same time.'

'I'll take a look in the office as you suggested,' Karen said.

Gretchen looked wary, as though she wanted to stop Karen going into the bungalow, which was precisely why Karen didn't ask if it was okay. Gretchen wasn't family, and Aiden had already given her permission to look through the bungalow. There could be something in there that would give her a clue as to what had happened to both women.

'Okay,' Gretchen said. 'You can go in the front if you've got the key, but the back's open if you want to come in with me. I was just going to make a cup of tea. Would you like one?'

'That would be nice, thanks,' Karen said. Her hands and feet were already numb.

Gretchen made the tea while Karen got to work. The bungalow was much bigger inside than she'd expected, and it was nicely decorated in a modern style with pale walls and warm wood. Each bedroom had a cream-tiled en suite with a walk-in shower, and the living area was open-plan, with a massive kitchen that included an eight-seat dining table as well as two sofas. The view from the double doors at the back of the house looked directly out onto the sanctuary. Karen saw the magpie leaping from its branch. It was an athletic little thing, even if it couldn't fly.

She turned her attention back to the search. The office was the first place she looked. There was a filing cabinet full of bills and invoices relating to the wildlife sanctuary. In the second drawer, she found the list of recent interviewees the women had seen when they were searching for new volunteers. It could be useful, but there would be a lot of work involved in tracking them all down.

There was a cork pinboard in the office. Lists of animal feed and supplies were pinned to the cork, along with the number for a vet and an article from the local press. Both Rachel and Tamara were in the image accompanying the text. The article was an appeal for donations. Both women smiled confidently at the camera as they stood by the gate to the sanctuary. They looked so vital and alive.

Karen pulled out her phone and took a photograph of the article.

She went on to search the other rooms, looking specifically for notes or diaries. There was nothing.

There were no visible signs of blood anywhere to indicate this had been the scene of Rachel's murder.

The loft was empty, except for a few boxes of photo albums and a pair of old garden lounger chairs.

There were lots of pictures of Tamara and Rachel scattered about the place. A couple showing a very young Rachel holding up trophies for dancing and gymnastics – with Tamara in the background, looking on, unsmiling – took pride of place on the walls in the living area.

Maybe it was Karen's imagination, but the young Tamara seemed to have the gleam of envy in her eyes. Had Tamara been jealous of her sister?

She spent an hour searching the bungalow and didn't find anything she thought would lead to a real breakthrough. It wasn't a proper search, but manpower was short. Every day, there were difficult decisions to make about how to allocate resources.

When she'd finished her search, she went back outside and found Gretchen again.

'Thanks for your help,' Karen said. 'I'm going to head back to the station. I'm taking the key with me. Under the circumstances, I don't think it's wise to leave it in its usual hiding spot.'

Gretchen nodded. 'You'll let me know if there's any developments?'

'We're in touch with Aiden frequently,' Karen said. 'Would he let you know if there was news?'

'Yes, I think so,' Gretchen said. 'I really hope Tamara's okay.' The woman's eyes filled with tears. 'Do you think she is?' Her eyes searched Karen's face.

'I don't know,' Karen said honestly. 'I'm sorry. This must be very hard for you.'

Gretchen sniffed. 'I've known them since they were tiny.'

Karen waited until Gretchen had regained her composure and then said, 'I've got one more question for you about the girls.'

Gretchen nodded tearfully. 'What do you want to know?'

'Were they close, or was there some rivalry between them?'

Gretchen smiled. 'Rivalry? Oh, they were competitive, but that was when they were younger, not so much now,' she said.

Karen thanked Gretchen and walked back to her car, remembering the images of Tamara looking covetously at her sister's trophies.

CHAPTER THIRTY-ONE

Devonshire Academy was a private school for eleven- to sixteen-year-olds, located near the cathedral. It had been founded in 1960.

It must have been lesson changeover time because, as they drove into the entrance, children wearing dark blue blazers paired with grey skirts or trousers milled about looking bored.

'Apparently it costs twenty thousand pounds a year to come here.'

Morgan gave a low whistle. 'You're kidding?'

'No. It would certainly add up over the years.'

'Yes. How the other half live, eh?' he said. 'Rachel must have had a good salary then?'

Karen nodded. 'Yes. Her parents were both teachers, so I guess teaching runs in the family.'

'Not for Tamara, though.'

'No, although both sisters held well-paid jobs. No long periods of unemployment. Steady, reliable. Not usually the type of people to get mixed up in criminal activities.'

They got out of the car and followed the signs to reception.

The receptionist ushered them into a staffroom that smelled of stale coffee. There were large windows that looked out on to the playing fields.

After a couple of minutes, they were joined by Ms Devonshire, the head teacher at the school. She wore a dark green tweed skirt-suit with a cream blouse, and a discreet string of pearls and matching pearl earrings. Old money, Karen guessed.

She smiled pleasantly with the confidence of one who had never been on the wrong side of the law and was prepared to help, up to a point.

'Good afternoon,' she said. 'It's absolutely terrible news about Rachel. We're all devastated. We're having an assembly this afternoon as a way for us to pay our respects, and to allow the children to process their grief.'

She flicked a bit of fluff from her dress and sat down. Her words rang with insincerity. Karen's first impression of Ms Devonshire was that she was an officious type. Not a woman to allow anyone at the school to suffer anything as impractical as grief.

Ms Devonshire crossed her legs. 'Now, of course we want to help in any way that we can. I understand you'd like to talk to some of the staff.'

'That's right. We'd like to find out if anyone noticed anything unusual over the past few days or weeks. And we'd also like to know more about Rachel. Is there anyone here Rachel was particularly close to?' Morgan asked.

'Oh, yes. She got on well with one or two of the other female staff members. I believe they went out to a wine bar in Lincoln occasionally.' She wrinkled her nose, as though that was somehow distasteful. 'But she wasn't a heavy drinker. I don't mean to give you that impression.' She gave an affected laugh. 'No, Rachel was a good teacher. She was well liked by both the staff and the pupils.'

'What classes did she teach?' Morgan asked.

'Classes? Oh, she was Humanities. Her specialty was Geography.'

'Right. GCSE?'

'She taught all year groups, but mostly GCSE and A level. She was a form tutor as well. Her form were year sevens, so very young. It's quite a shock for them, as you can understand.'

'Yes.'

'We have someone filling in temporarily. We'll have to advertise her post, of course.' She went on: 'Very difficult to fill a vacancy partway through the academic year, as I'm sure you can appreciate.'

'What about friends or family? Do you know much about them?' Karen asked, trying to direct the conversation away from Ms Devonshire's distress over the vacancy and back to Rachel and her life.

Ms Devonshire paused, then said, 'Rachel had recently lost both parents. A car accident, I believe. She was upset – devastated, really. Took compassionate leave. She'd only recently come back to full-time duties.' Ms Devonshire smoothed her fingers over her hair. 'Then, with her sister going missing, I think it must have proved too much. When she didn't show up for work this morning, or answer our telephone calls, I was worried she might have harmed herself.'

'Had she done anything like that before?' Karen asked.

'No, not to my knowledge, but she was very depressed, and it's something we're trained to watch out for in children. External pressures that lead to depression – feelings of hopelessness.'

'And in your opinion, Rachel was depressed?' Morgan asked.

'I think she was struggling. I'm not a medical professional, but yes, she had certainly changed in the last two months. She was withdrawn, anxious, quite a different character. Not the teacher we all knew and loved.'

Morgan shifted in his chair, leaning forward. 'And that's why you were quick to report her missing when she didn't come to work this morning?'

'Yes. We had arranged a meeting early this morning to discuss some of the changes planned for next year. Renovations will take place when the school closes for the summer break. We wanted to get the teachers' input. She didn't show up for that, and I assumed she had forgotten the meeting. But then she still wasn't here when it was time for her form tutorial, and that's not like her at all. So, I tried her mobile and got no answer. I then tried her home phone number with no luck, and her next of kin is listed as her sister. Obviously, that was no help.' She spread her hands. 'I thought perhaps it had all got too much for Rachel, and that's why I called the police. I wanted them to check her home and make sure she was all right. I never thought that something like this would happen.'

'No.'

Momentarily, Ms Devonshire appeared to be genuinely affected by Rachel's death. She blinked rapidly and cleared her throat.

Perhaps Karen had judged her too harshly. Her cool exterior could be a protective front. Most people went into self-preservation mode when confronted with news like this.

Ms Devonshire reached up to touch the string of pearls around her neck. 'The school has lost an excellent teacher.'

CHAPTER THIRTY-TWO

'Hailey McIntosh is probably the best person to start with,' Ms Devonshire said, still fiddling with her pearls. 'She was close to Rachel. They spent time together outside work and weren't too far apart in age. Hailey's a few years younger, and Rachel had taken her under her wing.'

'Yes, she sounds like the best person to interview first,' Morgan said.

'She's actually taking a class at the moment, so I'll look after the children while you're talking to her. If you send her back to me when you're done, I'll arrange for the other members of staff to talk to you in turn.'

'Thank you very much, Ms Devonshire,' Morgan said. 'We appreciate your cooperation.'

'Of course. It's no problem. Like all of us here, I'm devastated about what's happened.' She uncrossed her legs, stood up and nodded at them both. 'I won't keep you waiting long. Can I offer you tea or coffee?'

'No, thank you. We're fine,' Morgan said.

Hailey McIntosh looked young for her age. She had dark brown hair that reached her shoulders and had a heavy fringe. She had large brown eyes that were red; it looked like she'd been crying.

She shut the door behind her. 'I'm Hailey,' she said. 'Hailey McIntosh. Ms Devonshire sent me to see you.'

'Have a seat, Hailey,' Karen said. 'I'm sorry. I know this is a difficult time, but we'd like to ask you some questions about Rachel.'

'Of course. Anything I can do to help,' Hailey said, sinking down into one of the armchairs. She didn't sit back but remained perched forward on the cushion, hands clutched in her lap. Her cheeks were blotchy, and she rubbed away a tear.

'Sorry. I'm trying to keep it together for the children, but every time I think about Rachel . . .' Her eyes brimmed with tears.

'It must be incredibly hard,' Karen said. 'Do you know what happened?'

'They said she was murdered. Did she suffer?'

It wasn't easy to answer that question. Rachel had been bludgeoned to death with a metal pole, and probably bled out in the back of a Transit van. She most certainly had suffered. 'We're not aware of the full details yet. We hoped you could provide us with a little more information about Rachel.'

'Such as?'

'Was she seeing anyone at the moment, romantically?'

'No, I don't think so. She had a steady boyfriend when I started here, which was about two years ago, but they went their separate ways. I don't think there was any bad feeling. His name was Tim something. Montgomery, I think. He left to take a job in America. As far as I know he's still there.'

'Right. And there hadn't been anyone else on the scene since him?' Karen asked.

Hailey shook her head. 'No.'

'Would she have told you if there was?'

'I think so. We talked about most things. She was very kind to me when I started working here. I was out of my depth. It was only my second teaching job – and, well, the children here can be . . .' She smiled. 'Well, let's just say they can be a bit difficult at times.'

'Did you see Rachel outside work?'

'Um, once or twice a week we would go out, either for a meal or for a drink. Just talk about life and things. We hadn't been out that much recently though.'

'And why was that?'

'Well, it was after her parents were in the car crash. She was devastated, of course, and she didn't really feel like going out, which was understandable. She just wanted to deal with things in her own way.'

'Would you say she was depressed?' Morgan asked.

'I think she was very sad,' Hailey said. 'She was close to her parents. She adored them. She was the apple of their eye. She had lots of things to do, I think, with the estate – looking after her parents' property. They owned a wildlife sanctuary. That was a lot to sort out.'

'Did you ever meet Rachel's sister, Tamara?'

'Yes. I think they were quite close, but they had a sibling-rivalry thing going on.'

'What sort of rivalry?' Karen asked.

'Oh, just sisters, I suppose. Just a bit competitive. But they were both close to their parents. I think Rachel had seen more of Tamara after their parents died. She said something to me about wanting to keep her sister close because Tamara was all she had left.' She twirled a lock of hair around her finger. 'Sorry, it's one of those things she mentioned in passing. I didn't really pay as much attention as I should have. When her sister went missing, it would have been the last straw. If I'd known what was going to happen, if it was going to be like this, then . . .' Hailey trailed off.

'I'm sure Rachel valued your friendship,' Karen said. 'She didn't take her own life.'

'I know, but I wish I'd given her more support.'

'It sounds like you were a good friend to Rachel,' Morgan said. 'Had you noticed anyone hanging around the school, or had Rachel mentioned to you she was worried about anything?'

'You mean like a stalker?' Hailey asked. She bit her lower lip and shook her head. 'No, I didn't notice anything, and Rachel hadn't said anything to me.'

'Can you think of anything unusual that happened in the past few weeks?' Karen asked. 'Even something mundane might be important.'

Hailey looked up at the ceiling, blinking. 'I'm sorry. I don't know who would want to hurt Rachel. She was the nicest, kindest woman, and she was always really good to me. I mean, after Tamara went missing all she was worried about was Aiden.'

'She was? You spoke to her?'

Hailey nodded. 'Yes. She went home from work yesterday after she heard Tamara was missing. Ms Devonshire said only to come back when she was ready, but Rachel insisted she would come in for the staff meeting this morning. Rachel was hoping to get her ideas for the renovations recognised. I told her to forget the building work. She had more important things to worry about, but she insisted she wanted to come, which was why it was so strange when she didn't turn up.'

'When was the last time you spoke to her?'

'Yesterday lunchtime. She said Aiden was acting strangely, and she was really worried.'

'Did she say she was worried about Aiden, or just that he was acting strangely and that worried her?' Karen asked.

'Um, I'm not really sure. Is there a difference?' Hailey asked, frowning.

'Yes,' Morgan said slowly. 'Please try to remember exactly what she said.'

'Okay.' She was quiet for a moment, staring down at the floor, hands clenched tightly in her lap. 'I asked how she was doing, and she told me not so good. I asked if she needed anything and if she wanted me to come round after work. She said no because she was going to go back to Tamara and Aiden's house because she was worried.'

'Those were her exact words?' Morgan pressed.

'Um, no. I think she said, *no, you're all right, Hay*. She called me Hay.' Hailey smiled. 'Then she said, *I'm going back to my sister's. Aiden is worrying me.*'

'Did she say why?'

'No. I asked, but she said she had to go because there was another caller trying to get through. I wish I'd gone around to hers anyway after work. I never expected this. I thought maybe she'd taken some sleeping tablets or—'

'Was she taking sleeping tablets?' Morgan interrupted.

'She had a prescription from her GP. After her parents died, she was having trouble sleeping. I kept telling her that things would get better with time, and now . . .' Her voice broke and tears rolled down her cheeks.

'You've been really helpful, Hailey,' Karen said. She'd spotted a box of tissues near the kettle, and offered one to the young woman.

Hailey sniffed and clutched the crumpled white tissue in her hand. 'I tried to be,' she said.

'Did you ever meet Aiden?' Karen asked.

'I met him on a couple of occasions. Once when Rachel and I had gone out for a drink and bumped into him and Tamara, and once when I visited the family's wildlife sanctuary.'

'What did you think of him?'

'Er, I don't know. They seemed nice.'

'Was Aiden—'

'Why do you keep mentioning Aiden?' Hailey cut in, looking at Karen and then Morgan. 'Do you think he was the one who . . . the one who . . .' She couldn't say the words, but her expression said it all. Wide-eyed and stammering, she finally whispered, 'The one who hurt Rachel?'

'We're looking carefully at all possibilities. Why – did anything about him worry you?' Morgan asked.

Hailey stared down at her lap; her breathing rate had increased. 'No, I don't think so. I didn't notice anything, but we didn't speak for long.'

'Was Rachel close to any of the other members of staff here?'

'She got on with most of us. She was quite close to Mr Price. He's the head of drama. And Mr Fisher, the French master. Would you like to speak to one of them next?'

'Yes, please.'

'Should I get one of them for you?'

'I think Ms Devonshire wanted you to go back to your class-room. Then she said she would bring the next member of staff to us,' Morgan explained.

Hailey stood up. 'Right. Okay then.'

'Thank you for your help, Hailey,' Morgan said. 'I'm sorry for the loss of your friend.'

'Thank you,' Hailey said quietly, and walked quickly out of the room.

CHAPTER THIRTY-THREE

A few minutes later Ms Devonshire brought in the head of French, Brian Fisher. He was an older man, balding, with a trim figure and a Midlands accent. He confirmed Hailey's description of Rachel's time off and grief over her parents' deaths. He didn't know anything about her previous boyfriend and wasn't aware if Rachel was dating anyone currently.

Mr Fisher was not as helpful as Hailey.

Morgan and Karen went through the procedure with another four members of staff who Ms Devonshire said were particularly close to Rachel.

When the penultimate teacher left the staffroom, Morgan turned to Karen. 'We're not getting anywhere with this.'

Karen checked the time. 'I know. I keep coming back to Rachel and Aiden and Tamara. It's Aiden we need to speak to, but Churchill—'

'I know. He's worried about offending Aiden again and getting a complaint. He's concentrating on impressing the superintendent in his first role as a permanent DCI. Understandable, I suppose,' Morgan said.

'I'm sure the superintendent would be much more impressed if we actually solved the case.' Karen took a deep breath. 'Rachel sounds like she was a really good person.'

Morgan nodded thoughtfully. 'She does, doesn't she? Good at her job, well liked, supported her parents' wildlife sanctuary. Then she was targeted by a maniac killer.'

'If she had a stalker, then either she hadn't noticed, or she decided not to mention it.'

'Perhaps she mentioned it to Tamara, her sister.'

Karen sighed and nodded. 'Yes. Sadly we can't talk to her either.'

Ms Devonshire came back into the room. 'Well, that's almost everyone who had a close working relationship with Rachel. There's just Mr Price left. Would you mind terribly if you spoke to him in the hall?'

'No, that should be fine,' Karen said, getting to her feet.

'What should we do with Rachel's things? There are a few items in the staffroom.' Ms Devonshire glanced over at the piles of mugs on the draining board. 'I'm sure no one will be demanding her coffee cup back, but there are a few items of clothing in her staff locker. Perhaps her family would . . .'

Karen nodded. 'Yes, I see. Perhaps we could take the items.'

It was difficult. Tamara was Rachel's immediate next of kin, and they didn't know where she was, or if she was even still alive.

Ms Devonshire showed them the contents of Rachel's locker: a grey hoodie, a pair of purple and silver trainers, and a water bottle. There were three paperbacks, all crime fiction. It seemed Rachel shared a love of all things crime-related with her sister.

'I've read this one,' Karen said, picking up a copy of Russel D. McLean's *Ed's Dead* with a gloved hand. 'It's good.'

She flicked through the pages of the books just in case, but found nothing.

At the bottom of the locker was a phone charger and a small washbag containing a powder compact, pink lipstick and mascara in a gold tube. Nothing useful.

'Leave it with us,' Karen said. 'I'll organise someone to come collect the items.'

Ms Devonshire led them towards the hall.

'Mr Price is setting out the seats for assembly this afternoon. He's going to read out some poetry,' Ms Devonshire said. 'He's head of drama, after all,' she added, as though that explained everything.

'Has he taught here long?' Morgan asked as they walked along the corridor following Ms Devonshire.

'Yes, over twenty years.'

'Has he always been a teacher?' Morgan asked.

'No, he used to tread the boards. Shakespearean actor. He did quite well for a while, but then the work dried up, as it often does, and he ended up here. He worked for my father. My father was always a strong supporter of the arts.' Ms Devonshire came to a stop beside a set of white double doors.

She pushed them open, and they entered a large hall with a well-polished wooden floor. A tall man with grey hair swept back from his forehead was setting out chairs with a young, tall pupil.

The boy, who wore a too-small navy-blue blazer, looked older than sixteen.

'Mr Price,' Ms Devonshire called out. 'As requested, I've brought the police officers to you.' There was a definite tone of disapproval in her voice.

'Ah, thank you *so* much for accommodating me,' Mr Price said. He threw his arms wide. 'We are attempting to pull something together to pay our respects to dear Rachel.'

'Do you have time to answer a few questions about Rachel?' Karen asked.

'Yes, if it will help,' he said. 'You don't mind me continuing to put chairs out as we talk, do you?'

Morgan eyed the boy in the background, who looked like he was listening in to their conversation.

'Oh, don't worry about Tristan.' He leaned forward and said confidentially, 'He's been thrown out of Maths. Happens a lot.

259

Attention problems. They always send them to me.' He turned. 'Bend at the knee, boy,' Mr Price barked. 'You'll injure your back if you're not careful.' He shook his head and turned his attention back to Morgan and Karen.

Karen debated whether or not to ask Mr Price to stay still while they talked, but he certainly seemed to be a forceful personality, and in her experience they often got more information by being accommodating.

As he walked towards a stack of blue plastic chairs, Karen asked, 'How long have you worked with Rachel?'

'Nearly six years,' he said.

'Were you close?'

'In some ways,' he answered thoughtfully, taking three chairs off the stack with a huff of exertion. 'We had a lot in common. Both fans of the theatre. Although, of course, she hadn't done any real acting. Just university plays. She didn't have experience, but she was well read and enthusiastic. She would help out behind the scenes and during rehearsals for the school's shows.

'Excuse me,' he said pointedly, and Karen took a step back so he could put a chair where she had been standing. 'Yes, it's incredibly sad,' he went on. 'I can't believe she's gone. I thought I'd do a poetry reading this afternoon, perhaps "Death, be not proud". What do you think?'

'Did Rachel like the poem?'

'She asked me for suggestions when it came to her parents' funeral service, and she seemed to like the John Donne. So it seems appropriate.'

Karen nodded. 'Do you know if Rachel was seeing anyone?'

'No, I don't know. I don't think she was at the moment, but if she was, she wouldn't have necessarily told me about it.'

'Had she had any problems with relationships as far as you were aware?' Morgan asked.

Price leaned on the stack of chairs. 'No, I don't think so. Again, she probably wouldn't have confided in me. It's Hailey you want to talk to. Hailey McIntosh.'

'Yes, we've spoken to her already,' Morgan said. 'Did you notice anything out of the ordinary recently? Anyone hanging around the school, for example. Or perhaps you noticed Rachel was acting differently?'

Price paused and thought for a moment. 'Well, her behaviour had been different lately, yes, but that was because her parents had just passed away. Tragic accident. And then, of course, yesterday, her sister going missing.' He tapped the plastic chair. 'I was going to call and see if there was anything I could do, but I didn't like to bother her at such a time. I wish I had now, though.'

He echoed Hailey McIntosh's earlier words. It was only natural to dwell on what you could have done differently. Common to wonder whether calling someone or paying them a visit might have stopped the pieces of the tragedy falling into place.

'So Rachel hadn't confided in you about anything worrying her?' Karen asked.

'No. I mean, we did talk about how she was coming to terms with the death of her parents. I think she'd made a will recently. I don't know what was in it,' he said.

'Did you ever meet Rachel's sister, Tamara?' Morgan asked.

'I did, as it happens. A couple of years ago we put on a school play and parents and families came along, and Rachel's sister came too. With her husband, I think. I can't remember his name.'

'Aiden?' Karen said.

'Oh yes. Well, I didn't speak to them, but Rachel seemed very pleased that her sister was there. I got the impression she wanted to impress Tamara, and she was so nervous when she saw them in the audience.' He smiled. 'Quite sweet really. Probably because she hadn't had real-life experience of the theatre. You thrive on nerves as an actor, you see, once you learn to handle them. It's all about channelling the energy.' He pounded on his chest. He had a deep voice that carried well, echoing about the hall.

There was something about the large room that made Karen want to whisper, to keep her voice down. The boy at the back had stopped unloading the chairs and was blatantly eavesdropping on the conversation.

'Were you a student of Rachel's?' Karen asked him.

Mr Price turned around and surveyed Tristan sternly. 'Tristan Thomas! Who told you to stop unloading the chairs?'

Tristan straightened as though Mr Price had cracked a whip, and carried on unstacking the chairs.

'No, I didn't have her as a teacher,' he said quickly and turned his back.

'What happened to her?' Mr Price asked, lowering his voice, but only to a stage whisper.

'We're still investigating,' Morgan said. 'Do you know if Rachel had any other family or close friends?'

'As far as I know it was only her sister. She was close to Hailey. I think she had some friends from university, but they live in different parts of the country now. I remember a couple of years ago she went on a hen do with one of them.' He pulled a face. 'They went to Marbella.'

'Nice,' Karen commented.

'Do you think so? I've never been particularly attracted to Marbella as a holiday destination myself. I prefer Italy. Rome, Florence, Verona.' He pushed his hair back from his face and began to quote a line from Shakespeare. *'There is no world without Verona walls, but purgatory, torture, hell itself.'*

Karen and Morgan exchanged a look and decided it was time to leave. They thanked Mr Price for his time and left the hall. He didn't offer to escort them out.

'What do you think?' Morgan asked Karen by the door. 'Do we need to talk to any more of the staff or students here?'

Karen was torn. In one respect she wanted to stay, question every-body and make sure they'd thoroughly extracted every bit of informa-tion. But on the other hand, she was desperate to get back and talk to Sophie again and see how Aiden had reacted to the news that his sister-in-law was dead. During their last conversation, when she had told Karen where to find the key to the bungalow, Sophie had been in the same room as Aiden, so it hadn't been possible to talk freely.

He had secrets. Perhaps something in his past. Gambling debts? A crime? Or had he crossed the wrong person, and Tamara had been taken as collateral until he paid up? Would he really keep that secret from them? There were so many possibilities. She couldn't guess.

Karen needed to get Aiden to open up. But the only way to make that happen was to apply more pressure, and Churchill defi-nitely wouldn't be happy about that.

'I don't know,' Karen said. 'Doesn't feel like we're getting anywhere.'

'All right. Let's ask Ms Devonshire if she feels there is anyone else we should speak with, just to make sure we've covered every angle,' Morgan said.

They were walking along the corridor when they heard 'Psst!' behind them.

They both turned to see Tristan coming after them at a half-hearted jog. 'Hang on,' he said, and then looked over his shoulder to make sure they were alone in the corridor. They were.

'Sorry,' he said when he reached them. 'I just heard you talking about Miss Brooke.'

'Yes. That's right,' Morgan said. 'You said she wasn't your teacher.'

'No, I've got Mr Price.' He gave an exaggerated grimace. 'But I heard you asking him questions.'

Karen nodded encouragingly. 'Yes – do you know something that might help us?'

'Maybe,' he said and bit down on his lower lip.

'You can tell us, Tristan,' Morgan said. 'We can ask Ms Devonshire for a quiet room if you'd prefer to have a chat privately.'

Tristan shook his head furiously. 'No. Look, I don't want to do this on record, or whatever it's called. I just wanted to tell you that I'd seen her.'

'When?'

'It was about a week ago, but she was with a man.'

'Do you know who this man was?' Karen asked.

'No. The thing is, I wasn't supposed to be there unaccompanied as I'm fifteen, but I only had a Coke.'

'It's all right, Tristan. We're not interested in that,' Karen said. 'You're not going to get in trouble. We just want to know about Miss Brooke.'

'Right. That's what I thought. So, I guessed you would want to know she was with a bloke because Mr Price said she wasn't seeing anyone.'

'You think Miss Brooke and the man you saw her with were romantically involved?' Morgan asked.

Tristan snorted. 'I'd say so, yes. He had his tongue halfway down her neck!'

'And this was a week ago?' Karen asked again, to make sure.

'Yep.'

'And it was definitely Miss Brooke.'

'A hundred per cent. She saw me, looked really embarrassed, and didn't say anything at first. But when they left the pub, she walked right past and said she hoped the pint I was holding wasn't for me.'

'You were holding a pint?' Morgan asked with the hint of a smile.

'Yes. I didn't really have a Coke. I lied about that. Sorry.' Tristan's face crumpled; his forehead beaded with sweat. Definitely not a born liar, Karen thought.

'Okay, so which pub did you see Miss Brooke and this gentleman in?' Morgan asked.

'The Tap, do you know it?'

Morgan nodded. 'The Tap and Spile? That's a bit out of the way for you.'

'I have a friend who works there.'

That made sense. Tristan looked old for his age, but eighteen was a bit of a stretch. Karen decided to leave the lecture for now; there were more important things to worry about.

Morgan asked, 'What night was it?'

'It was lunchtime. Last Wednesday. I was supposed to have PE afterwards, so I blew it off. That's why I got in trouble.' He shrugged. 'I don't like PE. It's pointless. We just run around the track, get all wheezy, and I need to take my asthma inhaler.'

'What did the man look like?' Karen asked.

'He was tall, dark hair, looked quite fit, I suppose.' Tristan shrugged and then looked again over his shoulder and around the corridor. 'Look, you won't tell Ms Devonshire or Mr Price about the pub thing, will you?'

'I don't think they need to know,' Karen said. 'But you could do us one more favour if you don't mind.' She pulled out her mobile phone, opened up the picture she'd taken of Tamara and Rachel, and showed it to Tristan. 'It was definitely her?'

'Yeah,' he pointed at Rachel. 'Definitely Miss Brooke. Is that her sister? The one that's missing?'

Karen nodded.

'Well, I hope she's all right,' he said. 'I can't believe someone would want to hurt Miss Brooke. I wish I'd had her for lessons rather than old Pricey. She was always so nice. When she supervised after-school detentions she'd talk about things, rather than make us sit there in silence. She told me even if I wasn't any good at Maths

265

or PE, it didn't matter because everyone was good at something and that I'd find my strength soon enough.'

Karen smiled, thinking of Mrs Hush, her English teacher at school, who'd been similarly encouraging. Teachers had such power over young minds. It seemed Rachel had been well aware of that. 'It sounds like she was an excellent teacher.'

'Yeah, better than Mr Price, that's for sure,' Tristan said.

'What are you doing, boy?' demanded the booming voice of Mr Price.

Tristan jumped. 'I was just . . .'

'Tristan was taking us back to Ms Devonshire's office,' Morgan said smoothly. 'Thank you again for your help, Mr Price.' He turned and put his hand on the boy's shoulder. 'Carry on, Tristan. Lead the way.'

Tristan nodded gratefully, shot a terrified look at Mr Price, and then began to lead them along the corridor.

Price watched after them, but he didn't follow.

By the time they turned into the next corridor, Tristan started to relax again, and Karen swiped through the photographs on her phone and showed him another. 'Was this the man you saw Rachel with?'

Tristan looked carefully at the photograph. 'Yeah, that's him. I'm sure that's him. Who is it?'

'You're sure they were kissing?'

'I may be fifteen, but I do know what kissing is,' Tristan said with a roll of his eyes. 'Yeah, they were all over each other.'

'Thank you, Tristan. You've been very helpful,' Karen said as she showed the photograph to Morgan, whose eyebrows shot up.

The photograph was of Aiden Lomax.

CHAPTER THIRTY-FOUR

'Is there anyone else you'd like to talk to?' Ms Devonshire asked.

But their priorities had changed. Aiden Lomax was now their major suspect.

'I don't think so, Ms Devonshire,' Karen said. 'Thank you very much for your help. We'll be in touch.'

Morgan got in the driver's seat. He slowed at the junction and flipped the indicator to turn left and head back to Nettleham.

Karen turned to him. 'Why don't we go and see Aiden now. We've done what Churchill asked. He didn't say we *couldn't* see Aiden. He said to go and talk to the teachers first.'

'I think us not visiting Aiden Lomax was implied,' Morgan said drily, but he didn't make the turn.

'He didn't explicitly say so,' Karen said. 'Besides, I'd like you to see him at home. I know we interviewed him together, but there's something about him being at home. He seems edgy, like he's worried we're going to stumble across something.'

'Like what?'

'I don't know. I went upstairs. The bedrooms were tidy, bathroom smelled of bleach.'

'Maybe he eases his stress by cleaning.'

'Unlikely. Downstairs isn't very tidy.'

'You went in their bedroom?'

'Just a peek,' Karen said defensively. 'He's definitely hiding something, Morgan.'

'All right. Persuade me. What's he hiding? Why do we need to go and see him?'

Karen hesitated, well aware what she said next could make her sound a little crazy. 'I'm thinking there's something at the house. Some evidence to do with Tamara,' she said. 'If he is responsible, and if his motive is money, then he'd want Rachel to die before Tamara.'

'So you think . . . Hang on, let me get this straight. You think he's keeping Tamara at the house, locked up in a cellar or something. Does the house even have a cellar?'

'No,' Karen said. 'I know it sounds a bit nuts, but humour me. Let's go talk to him one more time. We won't do anything but talk. It's a good idea to check on him anyway. Sophie will have told him about Rachel by now.'

'That's a good point,' Morgan conceded. 'What was Churchill planning to do about having someone there with him?'

'He wants to send a family liaison officer. Aiden keeps refusing to have one, which is suspicious if you ask me.'

'Not necessarily,' Morgan said. 'A lot of people don't want a stranger around when they're feeling their most vulnerable. They want privacy.'

Karen shrugged. She could tell Morgan's curiosity was getting the better of him. 'Come on. It'll only take an extra half an hour.'

Morgan flipped the indicator to the right instead, and grumbled, 'I must be mad.'

◆ ◆ ◆

'Watch out up there, love. A cyclist.'

Doris gripped the steering wheel, imagining it was her husband's neck. 'It's not a cyclist, Ron. It's a little boy on a scooter, and he's on the pavement next to his mother,' Doris snapped.

'Is he?' Her husband blinked. 'Oh, so he is. Maybe I need stronger glasses. I'd better get a new prescription,' Ron said.

It was like this every week. They had a lovely lunch at the golf club, catching up leisurely with friends. It was a highlight of their week. The trouble was, Doris always drove home, so Ron took the opportunity to indulge.

Today he'd had at least five pints. Usually they got on well. After being married for nearly forty years, they'd got used to each other's foibles and little irritations. But once Ron had consumed a few drinks, everything was exaggerated, particularly his comments on Doris's driving.

Last week she'd been very tempted to stop the car and order him to get out and walk the rest of the way home.

Perhaps that was a little unreasonable, but he really was—

'The lights are turning red!' Ron announced.

'I can see that, dear,' Doris said, wishing he would succumb to the alcohol and sleep for the rest of the journey home.

She liked the lunches. She didn't want them to stop, but Ron would never agree to drive, and he said taxis were too expensive. Of course, a taxi was cheaper than the five pints he'd downed at lunchtime, but Ron didn't see reason when it came to alcohol.

She stopped at the lights.

'Well, that was another lovely afternoon,' Ron said. 'It was nice to catch up with Brian and Mary, wasn't it?'

'Yes, very nice.'

Brian and Mary had been travelling overseas. They'd taken a cruise at first. It was called an *Around the World Experience*, but as they'd only made it halfway around before having to catch flights, Doris thought that defeated the object of an around-the-world cruise, although she didn't like to say so. Instead, she'd nodded enthusiastically as they'd shown everyone photographs – seemingly endless photographs – of their holiday.

There'd been at least one hundred sunsets. Doris had smiled politely at each one. Other people's holiday photographs really weren't very interesting. Doris blamed mobile phones.

Before phones were able to take pictures, she could avoid being roped into attending a slideshow at Brian and Mary's house. It was easy to avoid. But now there was no escape. People could take their photographs everywhere they went, whipping out their phones in the middle of a pleasant lunch, to give an acquaintance a detailed recap of every moment of a tour around the pyramids.

Of course, Ron had already had three pints by the time the photos were shown. He just talked over them and changed the subject, chatting to someone else about fishing. Doris was left to bear the boring holiday snaps alone.

That wasn't to say that Brian and Mary were normally bad company. They were a pleasant enough couple, and Doris was probably a bit peeved at being the one driving home again, which had put her in a bad mood.

'Let's have some music, shall we?' Ron said, ramping up the volume on the radio.

Some modern nonsense blared out of the speakers.

'No, no. That won't do at all,' Ron said, and then he began fumbling in the glovebox for a CD.

The lights turned green, and Doris pressed the accelerator.

'Remember, there's temporary traffic lights up here, love,' Ron said. 'I think you should take Fen Road. We'll get home quicker.'

'I think you should leave the driving up to me, Ron,' Doris snapped.

'There's no need to be grouchy,' Ron said as he slipped a Buddy Holly CD into the machine and then began to sing along to 'Everyday'.

'Mmmh mmmh mmmm *than a rollercoaster*,' he sang off-tune, missing half the words.

Thankfully, before they got to the roadworks, Ron's head was lolling and he was gently snoring.

'Thank goodness,' Doris muttered as she turned the music down. She had nothing against Buddy Holly. In fact, the CD was one of her favourites, but she valued her eardrums.

She turned on to Fen Road, begrudgingly agreeing that Ron was right. They'd probably get home quicker without waiting in traffic, which lately always seemed backed up from the temporary lights by the roadworks.

She'd wanted to come home a bit earlier, before the schools finished for the day, but Ron had ordered another two pints *after* Doris had suggested making a move.

They were halfway along Fen Road, with only another few minutes to get home, when a flash of colour appeared in front of the car. Doris slammed on the brakes, but it was too late. There was a horrendous dull thud.

'Oh no,' Doris whispered, breathing hard.

Ron woke up abruptly.

'What? What is it?' he said, looking around.

'I've hit something,' Doris said in a voice barely above a whisper. She unbuckled her seatbelt and hesitated just a moment, forcing back a wave of nausea before opening the car door.

She gingerly made her way to the front of the car and then covered her mouth with her hand. 'Oh, no, no, no.'

She stared down at the motionless body of a young blonde woman. Her eyes were closed as though she was sleeping, but there was blood on the road, coming from the back of her head.

Ron knelt beside the woman. Pressed his fingers to the side of her neck and lowered his head close to hers. 'She's got a pulse and she's still breathing. Quick, Doris, call for an ambulance.'

Doris darted back to the car, grabbed her handbag from the back seat, and snatched up her mobile, quickly dialling 999.

'We need an ambulance. I've knocked a young woman down with my car. I didn't see her,' Doris said, giving the operator her location. 'She came out of nowhere.'

The operator asked if the woman was conscious. Doris told her no. But at that moment, the woman's eyelids fluttered, and she groaned.

Doris moved towards her gently, 'You've been in an accident, dear. Try to keep still. There's an ambulance on the way.'

'I . . . I . . .' the woman said, her eyes now wide and wild.

'What's your name, sweetheart?' Ron asked.

'Tamara,' the woman said and winced, her hands going to her stomach.

'Okay, Tamara. You're going to be all right,' Ron said.

Doris looked at the woman's pale face and the increasing amount of blood on the tarmac, and shivered.

Tamara's gaze swung towards Doris. 'Police.'

Doris swallowed hard. 'Yes, I'll ask for them too. I'm sorry, so sorry. I just didn't see you.'

But Tamara's eyes had closed again.

'Can you hear me?' the operator was saying. 'Can you please stay on the line?'

Doris's legs were weak. She leaned heavily on the car, but her arms had started to shake too. 'Oh, Ron, what have I done?'

CHAPTER THIRTY-FIVE

Morgan and Karen stopped outside the Lomax house. Morgan nodded to a car parked on the other side of the road. 'It looks like Sophie and Dr Michaels are still here,' Morgan said. 'Are you sure you want to do this now?'

Karen nodded. Although Churchill had been clear when assigning his tasks, he hadn't actually forbidden Karen to speak to Aiden again.

'I think we hold back our knowledge of the affair,' Karen said, 'and see if he volunteers the information himself. Churchill will probably want to control how we handle this, but I'd really like you to see Aiden in his home environment and get your opinion.'

Morgan stared at the house. 'I'm not likely to give any more information than Dr Michaels. He's the profiler.'

'I know, and he's very specialised. I don't doubt he's excellent at his job. His reputation goes before him, but we *all* have biases, and I think he's too focused on suspects outside the immediate family. He's looking for a lone predator.'

'He'd probably say you were being too focused on inside the family.'

Karen shrugged. 'And he'd be right. Which is why I want your input too.'

'Fair enough,' Morgan said, 'I agree with you. Aiden's hiding something – but now we have a witness telling us he was having an affair with his sister-in-law, we know what he's been hiding. Would he murder his sister-in-law to hide the affair? Maybe he tried to persuade Rachel to keep quiet and then lost his temper. But it doesn't explain why he'd abduct his own wife, does it?'

'No, it doesn't,' Karen agreed.

'He was genuinely distraught when we interviewed him,' Morgan added.

They both got out of the car.

'Maybe he'll be more cooperative now he's learned of Rachel's death,' Karen said. 'If he had nothing to do with her murder, the news might convince him to open up and tell us everything.'

'I suppose it depends on what else he's hiding,' Morgan said as they trudged up to the front door.

Sophie opened the door. 'Hello, Sarge. Sir,' she said, nodding at them both. 'We've broken the news already,' she added in a whisper and stood back, so they could come in.

Like on previous visits, Aiden was sitting in the green velvet chair beside the bookshelves.

'Aiden. I'm very sorry. How are you holding up?' Karen asked.

He shrugged. 'Not great.'

He was quieter today. The anxiety and the jerky movements had gone. He sat perfectly still, staring ahead at nothing, barely glancing up when Karen and Morgan entered the room.

Karen held up the key and then put it on the coffee table. 'I've brought this back. It's really not a good idea to leave a key so accessible, Aiden.'

He didn't reply.

'Can you think of anyone who would want to do this to Rachel?' Karen asked.

No answer.

'We wondered whether Tamara was targeted first because she was mistaken for her sister.'

Aiden lifted his gaze to Karen. But still stayed silent.

'Do you think that's possible? They looked quite alike,' Karen persisted.

Aiden nodded glumly. 'They did.'

'So, do you know if Rachel was seeing anyone? Did she talk to you about that sort of thing?'

Aiden shifted uncomfortably in his seat but didn't look up again. 'No. Maybe she would have talked to Tamara, but not to me.'

'What did you and Rachel talk about after Tamara went missing? Was there anything that struck you as unusual?'

'Like what?'

'I don't know. Anything that made you think she could be in danger, or she might know more than she was letting on.'

'No, she was just very worried about Tamara.'

He glanced at the mantelpiece – at the picture of the sisters next to the creepy carved owl.

'She didn't deserve this,' he said.

'No,' Karen said softly. 'She didn't.'

After a pause, Karen spoke again. 'Do you have any questions for us, Aiden? While we're here?'

'I don't think so,' he said.

Karen glanced at Sophie, wondering if he'd already asked about how Rachel had died. Perhaps he hadn't wanted to know. His wife was still missing, and the idea that something like this could happen to her, while he was completely powerless to help, would be traumatic.

Karen's phone began to ring. She had switched it on to silent but felt it vibrate in her pocket.

She pulled it out. It was Churchill. *Great.*

'Sorry, Aiden, I'm going to have to take this. I'll just step outside, all right? I'll be back in a moment.'

Karen waited to answer the call until she was outside and the front door had been closed behind her.

'Sir?' Karen said.

'Where are you?' he asked without pleasantries.

'We've spoken with Rachel's colleagues at the school, and just called in to speak to Aiden Lomax on our way back to the station.' Karen winced, waiting for Churchill to launch into a full-on scolding.

But he surprised her by saying nothing.

'Sir?' she said. 'Are you still there?' She checked the screen on her phone to make sure she hadn't lost the signal.

'Yes, I'm here. There's been a development.'

Karen's skin prickled, and her stomach felt like lead.

'Tamara?' she asked. 'Has she been found?'

'Yes,' Churchill said.

Karen turned to look through the window into the living room. She couldn't see Aiden from where she stood, but saw Sophie perched on a chair, leaning forward, talking to him, and Dr Michaels, who was standing quietly off to one side, observing.

She would have to go in there now and break the news. After everything she'd put him through, Aiden was going to hate her.

'Where was she found?' Karen asked, knowing that would probably be one of the questions Aiden asked. 'Was she killed the same way as Rachel?'

'No, that's just it. She's alive. She was hit by a car on Fen Road.'

'She's alive?' Karen said, turning away from the window. She hadn't seen that coming. 'Where is she?'

'She's in Lincoln County Hospital getting checked out. Sounds like her injuries are serious. We can't speak to her yet. We'll have to wait for medical clearance,' Churchill said.

'Right. I should mention we uncovered something important at the school. Rachel Brooke had been having an affair with Aiden Lomax.'

She heard Churchill inhale a sharp breath. 'Why didn't you tell me earlier?'

'We were planning to as soon as we got back to the station. Should we bring him in?'

'Who told you about the affair?'

'A pupil. Tristan Thomas. He saw them together, kissing at a local pub.'

'Well, you'd better be sure the kid didn't mistake Rachel for her sister.'

'He said Rachel spoke to him. She was a teacher at his school. He knew what she looked like.'

Churchill sighed heavily. 'Okay, bring him in, and get Morgan to head up the interview this time. I want you to speak to Tamara. She might open up more to a female officer.'

'Right. Do you want me to go straight to the hospital?'

'I think that's a good idea,' Churchill said. 'It might mean some hanging around until she's stable enough to talk, but we need answers as soon as possible.'

'Okay, I'll tell Aiden his wife has been found and Morgan will bring him in for questioning. He doesn't—'

'He doesn't what?'

'He just doesn't strike me as the type to plan such an elaborate scheme.'

'You said he was hiding something. You were right. Perhaps he held his wife captive somewhere, and she managed to escape. Maybe he was worried he wouldn't get any of the inheritance money if Tamara found out and divorced him. Covering up the affair with his sister-in-law is a good motive, isn't it?'

'It is,' Karen conceded, 'but . . .'

'But what, DS Hart?' DCI Churchill said, his tone indicating he was losing patience rapidly.

'Nothing,' Karen said. 'We'll bring him in.'

After hanging up, she took a moment to gather her thoughts and then headed back into the Lomax house. None of this was adding up. Why would Aiden abduct his own wife? Why not attack her here in their home? Was he really so calculating? Did he plan this to make the police think she'd been abducted by a stranger? Then hold her until after he'd killed her sister?

Aiden barely glanced up as she walked back in. Did he know Tamara had escaped? Did he know the game was up? Was that why he was quiet and seemingly remorseful?

'Aiden, Tamara's been found.'

His head jerked up. Suddenly, he was animated. 'What?'

Sophie gave him a sympathetic look. 'I'm sorry, Aiden.'

'She's alive,' Karen said, and from the expressions on Sophie, Dr Michaels's and Morgan's faces, they were all as surprised by this development as Karen had been.

Aiden shook his head and put his hands on the armrests, pushing himself to his feet.

'Really?' He looked again at the photograph of Rachel and Tamara.

'She's been hit by a car and badly injured,' Karen said. 'We'll give you updates on her condition as soon as we have them.'

'I don't believe it.'

Karen closed the gap between her and Aiden and looked up into his dark eyes. Were these the eyes of a killer? Had he cold-bloodedly murdered his sister-in-law and kept his wife captive, intending to dispatch her as well? And all just to get his hands on their money?

'We're going to need to search the house, too. Just a formality.'

Aiden shot a look towards the stairs.

'What's wrong, Aiden?' Karen asked. 'Do you want to go upstairs?'

His face paled, and he swallowed hard. 'Tamara will need some clothes and her toiletries and stuff. I'll get them now.'

'I'm sorry, Aiden, but you're going to have to come to the station with us. We have more questions for you,' Karen said.

But Aiden ignored her and kept walking towards the stairs. Sophie made to stop him, but Karen gave a subtle shake of her head.

They followed Aiden into the hallway. He started to climb the stairs.

Morgan touched Karen's arm. 'What's going on?'

'I think there's something up there he doesn't want us to see.'

Aiden turned at the top of the stairs. 'There's no need for you all to come up here. I just need to get a few things for Tamara.'

Over Aiden's shoulder, Karen could see the loft hatch in the ceiling was open.

'What did you need from the loft?'

Aiden licked his lips. 'Uh, nothing. I was just going to close it.'

Morgan marched up the stairs.

'No, wait,' Aiden said as Morgan passed him and headed for the loft hatch.

'What's wrong, Aiden?' Morgan asked. 'What are we going to find up there?'

Aiden pressed his hands to his forehead. 'I don't . . . want you to go up there,' he said.

Morgan pulled the ladder down from the hatch and made sure it was locked into position. He rattled it. 'Do you want me to go?'

'No, I've got this,' Karen said, thinking if Aiden made a run for it, then Morgan would be more likely to be able to tackle him. He had a strong build.

She climbed slowly up the ladder, and at the top, fumbled around. 'Is there a light up here, Aiden?'

He didn't reply.

But Karen found the switch and turned it on.

The loft area was boarded out. Karen was quiet as she took in her surroundings.

On one side of the loft was a makeshift bed – a blow-up mattress, a duvet and a couple of pillows. There was also a beanbag, water bottles and a couple of empty crisp packets.

If he'd been keeping Tamara up here, at least he'd been feeding her.

Karen looked back down the open hatch. 'There's bedding and water, signs that he may have kept her here.'

'I didn't,' Aiden said. 'You've got it all wrong.'

But Karen looked past him to Morgan and said, 'Let's take him in.'

CHAPTER THIRTY-SIX

The hospital car park was still busy when Karen arrived. It was dark, and a steady drizzle fell from the sky. The lights shone on the wet tarmac as Karen quickly strode across to the entrance.

She had called ahead and knew that Tamara Lomax still hadn't been cleared for interview. But the driver involved in the incident was still at the hospital, and Karen wanted to have a word with her. From the initial report, it sounded as though Tamara had just stepped out in front of the woman's vehicle.

There was a group of people puffing on cigarettes huddled around the 'No Smoking' sign at the entrance to the hospital, glaring at everyone who walked past, as though daring them to comment.

Karen ducked inside, glad to be out of the rain and the cold. A blast of warm air hit her as soon as she stepped through the sliding glass doors. She stopped by the reception desk, but there was no one there. She'd probably have had more luck if she'd gone in the accident and emergency entrance. After using the large dispenser of hand sanitiser, she gave up waiting by reception. She knew Tamara had been taken to the Bluestone Ward. She followed the directions posted on the large blue signs along the winding corridors.

She walked past the empty cafe and then the chapel of rest before spotting another sign for the ward she was looking for. It was downstairs, in a newly renovated area. It looked fresher and more modern than the rest of the hospital.

She stopped by the double doors to the ward, squirted another dollop of hand sanitiser as directed by the sign on the wall, and pressed the buzzer.

After a moment, there was a click as the door lock released.

She pushed it open and stepped inside.

A nurse looked up from a computer station. 'Can I help you?'

Karen showed her warrant card. 'DS Karen Hart. I called ahead. I spoke to Sharon, is that you?'

The nurse smiled. 'Yes, that's me. I'm afraid you can't talk to her yet. They're still trying to get her stable.'

'Thanks. I was told that the couple who were involved in the accident were still here. Do you know where I might find them?'

'Yes, they're upstairs in the family room. I'll take you. I'm going up there anyway.'

The nurse showed Karen to the family room, and then left her to it.

The room was small with white walls, blue padded chairs, and a sink, kettle and microwave against the back wall.

The man in there approached with a wide smile, his hand outstretched. 'Ron Hollingford. This is my wife, Doris. How is the young woman?'

Karen noticed Ron's wife looking a little distracted.

'The doctors are trying to stabilise her condition,' Karen said. 'I'm DS Hart. Thank you for waiting.'

'She looked in a very bad way when they put her in the ambulance,' Doris said.

Ron looked back at his wife and then sat down beside her. 'It's been a terrible shock for my wife. She was driving, you see. We'd been out and I'd had a few bevvies.' He mimed drinking to further get his point across.

'I hadn't been drinking,' Doris said hurriedly. 'But I didn't see her until it was too late. She appeared out of nowhere.'

'It must have been a horrible experience for you both. I'd appreciate it if you could tell me in detail what happened,' Karen said as she took a seat opposite the couple.

They sat beside a large window. For a moment no one spoke. The only sound was the hum of the ceiling light and the tap of rain on the window.

Then Ron broke the silence. 'We'd been to lunch at the golf club.' He patted his wife's hand.

Karen glanced at the clock on the wall. 'A late lunch?'

'A long lunch. It's a perk of retirement. Our booking was for one p.m., but we do tend to linger over dessert and coffee. Our lunches tend to go on until late afternoon, don't they, Doris?' He chuckled. 'Anyway, we were driving back home, and the woman stepped into the road. She told us her name was Tamara.'

'You were driving?' Karen looked at Doris.

'Yes, I was driving. Ron was snoring. He didn't actually see her until after I'd stopped the car.'

'I'm sure the detective doesn't want to know that I was snoring, dear. I hardly think that's relevant.' Ron dropped his wife's hand and folded his arms.

Doris looked pale and her voice trembled as she spoke. 'I'd taken a diversion because there were roadworks up ahead. We thought it would be a faster route home. I was driving along Fen Road. There are no pavements along the lane, only a grass verge on the right. I took a corner, but I was going slowly. I always watch out for cyclists, you see, so I'm careful. I was going very slowly but I still couldn't stop in time.' She bowed her head.

'So you stopped the car?' Karen prompted.

'Yes, that's right. I stopped and got out to see what had happened. I couldn't believe it. She came out of nowhere,' Doris said.

'And then what happened?'

'Ron had woken up when I'd thrown the brakes on. He came to look too, and we called for an ambulance.'

'Was she conscious?' Karen asked.

'Briefly,' Doris said and then looked at her husband. 'She said her name was Tamara, and she asked us to call the police.'

'Did she say why?'

'Sorry? Why what?'

'Why she asked you to call the police, and not an ambulance?'

'Well, she already knew the ambulance was on its way because we told her that.' Doris leaned forward, her hands clasped in her lap. 'Am I going to go to prison?'

'Have you been breathalysed?'

Doris nodded. 'But I hadn't had a drop.'

'The traffic police who were at the scene will be in charge of that side of the investigation,' Karen said.

'You're not investigating the accident, then?' Ron asked, frowning.

'Not directly. The woman you hit had been reported missing. We've been looking for her.'

'I wondered if she might be having troubles,' Ron said. 'Do you think she might have jumped in front of the car on purpose?'

'Don't, Ron. I know what you're trying to do,' Doris said.

'What? I'm just saying that it probably wasn't your fault. You didn't see her. She jumped in front of the car. That sounds like someone wanting to end it all to me.'

As Doris and Ron began to gently bicker amongst themselves, Karen turned to look out of the rain-splattered window. Lights glowed in the distance, and puddles pooled on the concrete. There wasn't much of a view on this low level.

Ron had made a good point. Perhaps Tamara was in a bad way before she was hit by the car.

A search of Aiden and Tamara's house was now underway.

Had Tamara really been held captive in the loft? If so, why hadn't she called for help when the police were in the house? It didn't add up.

'Other than giving you her name and asking you to call the police,' Karen said, cutting into the couple's disagreement, 'did she say anything else?'

'Oh, I'm not sure,' Doris said, looking up at the ceiling tiles, trying to think.

Ron scratched his chin. 'Hang on a minute, this has been in the news, hasn't it? I read some articles about it on my phone when I was waiting for Doris to be checked out. She'd almost fainted after the accident, you see. The online paper said there was one woman dead and another was still missing. Was Tamara the missing woman?'

'I'm not sure which articles you read,' Karen said, hoping it wasn't the one with her photograph in it.

'Thought I recognised you!' he said. 'Was it really your fault a woman died?'

'Ron!' Doris exclaimed.

'Sorry.' He shrugged, not looking the least bit sorry.

'That article was probably referring to Tamara,' Karen said coolly.

'Was it the husband?' Doris asked. 'It usually is.' She turned to look at the door, as though she expected a killer to burst in on them.

'We're still investigating,' Karen said. 'If you think of anything else, do let me know.' She handed them her card. 'I appreciate your help.'

They said goodbye. As Karen turned away, Doris said something to Ron under her breath.

'Yes, well, I'm sorry I fell asleep,' Ron said with a huff. 'It's hardly a criminal act, Doris.'

Karen left the bickering couple alone in the family room. Despite their sniping, there was an undercurrent of love between the pair. Karen thought Doris was telling the truth when she said she'd been sober behind the wheel. If that was the case, the investigation would clear her of wrongdoing but the process would be a stressful time for the couple. They were fortunate to have each other for support.

She returned to the ward, hoping Tamara would be ready to talk.

'I'm sorry, but we're waiting for the on-call surgical registrar to give the go-ahead for an operation,' the nurse said, and she glanced at the clock. 'She needs surgery, so you won't be able to talk to her until after that is over.'

Karen unbuttoned her jacket. It was hot in the hospital. 'What can you tell me about Tamara's condition when she came in?'

'She was very distressed and in a lot of pain. She's been sedated now, so she's comfortable, but her blood pressure is very low. The surgery team believe she has internal bleeding.'

'Did she say anything when she was brought in?'

'She said the name Aiden. That's her husband, isn't it?' the nurse asked.

Karen nodded. 'Did she sound like she wanted to see Aiden, or she wanted him to stay away?'

'I really couldn't tell you that. I assumed it was because she wanted him with her.'

'Did she mention anyone called Rachel?'

'She might have done. She was babbling a bit when she first arrived, but after the painkiller kicked in, she wasn't really making much sense.' The nurse leaned on her workstation. 'Sorry, I know this is unprofessional, but is she the woman in the papers? I read about her kidnapping online.'

Karen nodded. 'Yes.'

'So her sister was . . .'

'Yes, her sister, Rachel, was murdered. So if she knows anything about her sister's death, it could be vital to us catching the killer.'

'She was very anxious, almost paranoid when she was brought up to the ward, but I put that down to the amount of pain she was in.'

'Would it be possible to see her?' Karen asked. 'I'm not going to do a full-blown interview but . . .' She checked her watch.

'Absolutely not. She's barely conscious.' The nurse pursed her lips.

'Okay. I understand,' Karen said, feeling her best chance of getting answers slipping through her fingers.

CHAPTER THIRTY-SEVEN

'Things will go easier for you if you tell us the truth,' Morgan said. He was sitting opposite Aiden Lomax in interview room three.

Above them, a light was buzzing and flickering intermittently. Dr Michaels sat on Morgan's left. He said nothing, but leaned back in his chair, his fingers interlinked and resting on his flat stomach. Always watchful.

Aiden rubbed his hands over his face. Less than an hour ago he'd been numb, in shock. Now, the anxiety was back, the nervous tension, the constant movement. 'I don't understand how it's come to this. You're trying to play some sort of psychological mind game with me.'

'There are no mind games,' Morgan said. 'Tamara is in a serious condition in hospital. You were having an affair with your sister-in-law, Rachel Brooke, before she was murdered. Did Tamara find out about the affair? Is that when you decided to act? The evidence is stacking up against you, Aiden. It's best you come clean.'

Aiden looked at Dr Michaels. 'You're meant to be some kind of amazing profiler, aren't you? Surely you can see I'm telling the truth? Can't you use one of those lie detector tests on me?'

'We don't use those here, Aiden,' Morgan said.

Aiden put his hands flat on the table. 'I'm telling the truth. I didn't kill Rachel. I wouldn't. I . . .'

Morgan showed him the images taken from the CCTV outside the arcade. 'This is you, isn't it, Aiden? Standing by the van?'

Aiden looked down at the picture and then up at Morgan's face. He shook his head.

'It *is* you,' Morgan said again, more firmly this time.

'No.'

He pulled out another picture from the folder and pushed it across the desk to Aiden. This one showed Rachel approaching the man beside the van.

'She would have trusted you.'

Aiden folded his arms over his chest, tucking his hands beneath his armpits as he looked wildly about the room. 'Look, I just—'

'Are you sure you don't need a duty solicitor, Aiden?'

'No, I . . .' He pressed his hands over his eyes. 'I need to think. I can't think.'

'The time for thinking's over, Aiden. You need to start talking,' Morgan said. 'What about the van. Let's start there. That's easy, isn't it? You took that from Branston Chickens, right? You used to work there, so it was easy enough for you to sneak in, get the keys.'

Aiden put his head in his hands and flopped down onto the desk. 'I just . . .'

'Tell us, Aiden.'

After a few seconds had passed, he pushed up from the desk. 'Okay.' He took a deep breath. 'I'll tell you everything I know – everything. You have to believe me.'

Dr Michaels leaned forward just a fraction, and Morgan stared at Aiden, waiting for him to continue.

'I had an affair with Rachel. It only lasted a few weeks. It was the stupidest thing I've ever done. Tamara found out. She hit the roof. I've been sleeping upstairs in the loft. Out of sight. It was that or move out. I didn't want to leave. I love her. It was just a mistake.'

Morgan waited a beat, then said, 'So, you're expecting us to believe it was you sleeping in the loft? Even though you have a perfectly good spare bedroom?'

Aiden sniffed and wiped his nose with the back of his hand. 'She said she didn't even want to see me. I'd just come home late and go up there. I thought after a while she'd forgive me.'

Morgan stared at him. Was he telling the truth? Instinct told him yes.

'When did Tamara find out about the affair?'

'Last week.'

'Did she confront her sister?'

'No, she was avoiding her. She was furious with her too.'

Morgan frowned. Tamara's anger was only natural. But rather than having a row with her sister, she'd held back. Did she have some other punishment in mind? Rachel had been brutally bludgeoned to death, and most perpetrators of such crimes were men, but he couldn't ignore that Tamara now had a motive for killing her sister. An idea wormed its way into his head as he stared into Aiden's pleading eyes. Could Tamara have set this up? Tamara with her love of true crime, her fury at both of them for betraying her? She could have killed Rachel and lined Aiden up to take the fall.

Perhaps she'd been hiding out somewhere, preparing to spin a story when she was found wandering on a country lane. Her plans would have come to an abrupt halt when she'd been hit by the car.

It was devious, far-fetched, and yet the theory seemed possible to Morgan. More likely, in fact, than the trembling man in front of him committing a murder and abducting his own wife.

But how would Tamara have staged her own abduction? That and a hundred other questions still needed to be answered.

Aiden was shaking as he said, 'I've changed my mind, I do need a solicitor.' He prodded the table with a finger. 'Now. I'm not saying anything else until I get one.'

Outside the interview room, Dr Michaels leaned back against the wall. 'He's not a killer.'

'How sure are you?' Morgan asked.

Dr Michaels stroked his chin thoughtfully. 'Ninety-nine per cent. I don't know what to tell you other than his profile is . . . it just doesn't fit.'

'I have a theory,' Morgan said, and filled Dr Michaels in.

'So you think Tamara killed her own sister and set the whole thing up to look like two stranger abductions?'

Morgan's gaze met Dr Michaels's. 'It's a possible scenario.'

'How would she have staged the abduction?'

'That I don't know.'

'She'd need help. A man was seen at both abductions. Aiden?'

'I'm not sure.'

'Maybe she pressured him into it. Guilt over the affair?'

'Possibly.'

Dr Michaels drew in a long breath. 'Isn't Karen with Tamara now? Has she been allowed to talk to her?'

'No, not yet. Tamara is due to have an operation. Internal bleeding. They think her spleen has been damaged.'

'You know,' Dr Michaels said, 'there was something that bothered me about the theory Aiden kept his wife in the loft against her will. There's no soundproofing up there. So that means at any time when the police were in the house she could have called out. She could have got help.'

Morgan nodded his agreement.

'Tell me this,' Dr Michaels said, 'if you were Tamara, and you heard voices in the house, voices other than your husband's, wouldn't you call for help?'

'Yes,' Morgan said. 'So where does that leave us? They're in cahoots? Working together?'

'I think that's the most likely scenario. But' – Dr Michaels paused – 'I'd say Aiden isn't the one in charge of their relationship.'

'Then Tamara could be behind her own abduction.'

'Exactly.'

Morgan reached for his mobile. 'Karen's there alone. I need to warn her.'

'It sounds as though Tamara is incapacitated, and at the hospital they'll have security guards, surely?'

'She's unprepared,' Morgan said, dialling Karen's number.

Zane strolled into the hospital. Nobody asked him who he was or what he was doing there. It was a very different type of hospital to the ones he was used to. In New York City, you certainly couldn't walk in off the street and visit anyone you wanted. No, they would want to take your name and find out who you were visiting before they let you in.

Here, it was surprisingly easy to get in.

There were a couple of people wandering about – a cleaner, a couple of nurses chatting – but nobody paid him any attention, which suited him just fine.

He'd called earlier, giving the name DC Rick Cooper and telling the switchboard he needed to know what ward Tamara Lomax was on.

They'd believed him. Why wouldn't they? They had no reason to be suspicious.

Though they should be.

He approached the ward, peered in the small square window in the door, and then breathed in sharply, pulling away. DS Karen Hart was there, sitting opposite the nurses' station.

It was infuriating. And had completely ruined his plans. He needed to get in there and talk to Tamara. He was going to get the scoop of the century, and if he spun it right, he'd make it look like Dr Michaels had solved everything.

With enough good publicity, and a huge boost to book sales, Dr Michaels would come around to Zane's way of thinking. Of course he would. He'd know Zane had always been looking out for what was best for him.

He'd done it all to help Dr Michaels's career.

And if it hadn't been for that irritating British detective, Sophie Jones, they'd still be working together.

Zane shoved his hands in his pockets and peered through the window again. She was still there, looking down at her phone.

He tried to think of a way to get rid of her. He only needed her distracted long enough to get past her and into the ward.

It was imperative that he talk to Tamara as soon as possible. You always had to be two steps ahead when dealing with the media.

He usually didn't care if his story wasn't in print. Most people got their news online these days anyway, and it would soon spread with social media. But his new contact at the local paper would surely be able to pull a few strings. They might even make the front page. That was something he couldn't resist. Front-page and an online viral story. Best of both worlds.

He'd drop a few hints to his colleagues in the States, and then Dr Michaels would be a hero again. No one would remember that stupid Angela. It was all her fault, meddling and complaining. After Dr Michaels had done everything he could to help her track down her mother's killer, Angela had begrudged him a small amount of publicity. Some people were incredibly ungrateful.

Of course, Dr Michaels would be so pleased, he'd apologise for doubting Zane, and welcome him back with open arms.

Zane leaned back against the wall as a porter came past, wheeling a trolley. 'All right, mate?' the porter asked.

'Yes, thanks. I'm just visiting,' Zane said. 'My mom. Doctor's seeing her now,' he added. The lies spilled easily off his tongue.

'Hope she's on the mend soon, mate,' the porter said, and carried on wheeling the trolley with its squeaky wheel along the corridor.

Zane looked back through the window again just in time to see Karen getting to her feet and turning his way.

She was coming towards him. She was coming out into the corridor, and he had nowhere to hide!

His gaze darted left and right, and then he ran to the other end of the corridor where he'd seen the porter emerge from. There was a cupboard, thankfully unlocked.

He slid into it just as Karen exited the ward. She was answering a call.

'Hello. Yes, I'm here now,' she said.

This was his chance. She had her back to him. The door was closing slowly. He darted out of the cupboard, along the corridor and slid into the ward.

As luck would have it, there was no nurse at the nurses' station either. *Unbelievable security*, he thought.

He walked confidently into the ward. There were multiple side rooms leading off from a wide corridor. Tamara had to be in one of these. A gaggle of doctors and nurses was in the first room. He slipped by unnoticed.

In the second room on the left, he spotted Tamara. He recognised her from the photograph they'd had pinned to the whiteboard at the police station. There were three other beds in the side room. No one was conscious. Machines were beeping as he strolled over to Tamara. She was connected to two IVs. Cannulas in both arms.

He tried to put on a British accent. 'Hello, Tamara, can you hear me?'

No response.

He walked to the other side of her bed, so he could keep an eye on the door, in case a nurse came back – or worse, Karen.

He prodded her arm. 'Tamara!'

Still nothing.

He gritted his teeth. All this effort for nothing. This was a high-dependency ward. A nurse or doctor would be here before long.

Another poke, harder this time, but no response. He swore. Then had an idea.

He pulled out his cell phone, held it up and took a couple of snaps of Tamara in her hospital bed. He could make up the story. The picture would be the real scoop.

Feeling very pleased with himself, he walked out of the side room and straight into a nurse.

The nurse frowned. 'I don't recognise you. What are you doing here?'

CHAPTER THIRTY-EIGHT

Karen hung up the phone and slipped her mobile back into her jacket pocket. Morgan had called with an unsettling theory.

According to Dr Michaels's profile, Aiden's behaviour didn't fit that of a killer. He wasn't a leader. He wasn't the type to come up with an audacious plan like this and expect to get away with it. Was Tamara?

They didn't know. And they still couldn't talk to her.

Things were starting to make sense, but they were still a long way from putting all the pieces of the puzzle together. The affair explained why Karen had always had the feeling that Aiden was holding something back, but had he helped his wife with Rachel's murder?

When they spoke to Aiden, was Tamara simply hiding out in the loft, laughing at them as they tried to find her?

Karen looked back towards the ward. All was quiet. It was dark outside. She pulled out her mobile again and then dialled a different number.

'I'm a bit busy at the moment.' Tim Farthing's voice came down the line.

'I'm sorry to interrupt, Tim, but I have a quick question for you,' Karen said.

'Like I said, a bit busy. Can you call back later?'

It was eight o'clock at night, and she appreciated the fact he was still working, but his dismissal irritated her. 'No, I can't, Tim. This is incredibly important.' After a moment's hesitation she added, 'I need your help.'

That was the right phrase to use. His tone softened. 'Oh, you do? Well, I suppose it's nice to be wanted. What do you need?'

'The van you were working on. The blood spatter.'

'Yes, what about it?'

'Has an expert taken a look at it yet?'

'No, not yet. That'll be tomorrow. Why? Is it important? I might be able to help. As you know, I do have some experience analysing blood spatter.' She imagined him puffing out his chest.

'I know you thought the spatter had been created when the victim was moved to the van, but I wondered if there was any way of telling from the marks on the wall of the Transit how tall the killer was. I really want to know if you can tell me if the killer is more likely to be five foot two, versus six foot three?'

Tim was quiet for a moment. 'I'm sorry, Karen. But the blood spatter in the van won't be able to tell us anything about the height of her attacker.'

'I see. I suppose it was a long shot.'

'If you find the murder scene, then I'll be able to help. Bearing in mind, of course, that the killer could have been in different positions – crouching, bending, as they attacked the victim.'

'Right,' Karen said, the disappointment heavy in her voice.

'I thought you had Aiden Lomax, Tamara's husband, in the frame,' Tim said.

'We did,' Karen said. 'Do you think it's possible a woman could have bludgeoned Rachel to death?'

He sucked in a breath. 'It's possible, yes.'

'Is there anything else that might identify the killer as a woman?'

'Not so far,' Tim said, 'but it's early days. I suppose one thing that might suggest the killer's height in a very inaccurate way would be how far back the driver's seat was when the van was dumped.'

'And?'

'Well, of course it could have been changed to throw us off the scent, but from the seat position, I'd say the driver was closer to your taller estimate.'

'Right. Thanks, Tim. And one other thing. We need the Lomaxes' bathrooms gone over thoroughly. If they were involved, that's likely to be where they tried to wash Rachel's blood off. And their clothes must be somewhere. They must have disposed of them.'

'I'm at the Lomax house now actually,' Tim said, 'working the scene.'

'Great,' Karen said. 'Anything to go on?'

'There are traces of blood in the bathroom sink, but not enough to suggest they'd come back covered with blood. It could be explained by something as simple as Aiden cutting himself while shaving. We've collected samples, hopefully suitable for DNA analysis. If we're lucky, they'll match Rachel Brooke's DNA profile.'

'Right. Thanks, Tim,' Karen said. 'Let me know if you find anything else.'

'Yeah, I'll get back to you with the details,' Tim said. 'But if you need my gut reaction . . .'

'Yes, that would be good,' Karen said.

'Rachel wasn't killed here.'

'Thanks, Tim. That's very helpful.' Karen hung up, thinking the surly SOCO could be quite an asset when he chose to be. If heaping on the praise got results, Karen supposed she could get used to it.

As Tim said, they needed to locate the murder scene, because that would be crucial to cracking the case.

Morgan was on his way, and he'd asked her not to approach Tamara alone, but according to the medical staff Karen had spoken with, Tamara was in a serious condition, on a heavy dose of drugs, and wouldn't be going anywhere in a hurry.

The nurse was back at the station, and she gave Karen a prim nod.

'How's Tamara doing?' Karen asked.

'She's much the same,' the nurse said. 'She's scheduled for surgery in the next twenty minutes.'

'Right.'

'You know you'd probably be better off coming back tomorrow,' the nurse said. 'The poor woman could do with a break. The last thing she needs is being put through rounds of questioning when she's coming around from surgery.'

Karen swallowed a retort. The nurse didn't know the whole story. She didn't realise that Tamara was now a suspect, possibly responsible for bludgeoning her own sister to death.

Karen tried a smile and said, 'Well, I won't bother her, but we're going to keep a police presence here tonight.'

'Fine,' the nurse snapped.

Karen scrolled through the pictures on her phone, selecting the one of Tamara and Rachel, and zoomed in.

There'd been some tension between the sisters, a bit of sibling rivalry, but surely that wasn't enough to drive someone to murder. The only explanation Karen could see was that when Tamara had discovered the affair between Aiden and her sister, it had tipped her over the edge.

Even so, most people would be content with a shouting match, and perhaps chopping up their husband's clothes. They wouldn't be angry enough to do something like this.

It meant that urge to kill had likely always been in Tamara. Perhaps that was why she was so fascinated with true crime. Of course, not everyone who read true crime was a closet serial killer. Take Sophie, for example. She was just fascinated by the psychology of it, by the chase, and by the triumph of justice over evil.

But maybe Tamara hadn't been looking at the cases like that. Maybe she was looking at the true crime books to feed her fascination. Maybe she identified with the evil, rather than the justice.

Karen's phone rang again. This time it was Sophie.

'Sarge, I'm going through what was found on the laptop and other electronic devices at the Lomax house. They owned all of Dr Michaels's books as e-books. And, get this, the Playing Card Killer e-book has been bookmarked and highlighted.'

'That's good work, Sophie,' Karen said. 'Whose account were the books under?'

'Tamara's,' Sophie said. 'Have you spoken to Dr Michaels? He's suggested Tamara may have killed Rachel. He said the existing tension could have been amplified when Tamara discovered Rachel was having an affair with her husband. He thinks it was enough to drive the sibling rivalry into something far darker.'

'Morgan told me. I'm at the hospital now, but there's no chance of me being able to speak to her tonight,' Karen said in hushed tones, after the nurse glared at her.

A few minutes later, a male nurse entered the ward, carrying two mugs of coffee. He gave one to his colleague at the computer station and then turned to Karen. 'I'm sorry, did you want one?'

'No, I'm fine. Thank you,' Karen said.

The first nurse got to her feet and said to her colleague, 'Keep an eye on her.'

'Right,' the male nurse said, pulling a sympathetic face at Karen as soon as his colleague's back was turned.

'You must have done something to upset her,' he said as the nurse strode off into one of the side rooms.

'I wanted to interview Tamara Lomax,' Karen said. 'Still do. I'm hoping to talk to her as soon as she's out of surgery.'

'Well, I suppose you wouldn't be here if it wasn't important,' he said.

'No, I wouldn't,' Karen agreed.

'But I can understand why she's peeved. We caught someone wandering around the ward earlier. Said he was police too.'

Karen stood up. 'Who?'

'Said he was your partner.'

'There shouldn't be anyone else here,' Karen said slowly, wondering if it had been a traffic officer. But if so, why would he say he was Karen's *partner*? She walked up to the desk. 'Did he give a name?'

'Said his name was Rick something. Rick Cooper maybe. Does that ring a bell?'

Karen didn't answer immediately. It wouldn't be Rick. She was sure of that. The word *partner* gave her pause. In the UK, the police would be more likely to use the word *colleague*. British detectives didn't have partners as they did in the US. *Partner* was a word more likely to be used by an American.

'I don't suppose he was caught on camera?' Karen asked.

CHAPTER THIRTY-NINE

Zane left the hospital almost skipping with relief. That had been a close call. Giving them the name Rick Cooper had been a stroke of genius.

They'd practically chased him out of there. But it didn't matter. He had what he needed. The photograph. Now he just needed to meet up with his contact at the paper, and the plan would roll into action. His contact would have the type of story that launched journalists' careers to the stratosphere, and Zane would have the sort of publicity for Dr Michaels that money couldn't buy. Not that he deserved it after so readily accepting Zane's resignation. Before returning to work, Zane would make him grovel. It wasn't the first time he'd let Zane down.

Yes, he thought, as he flagged down a taxi, today was a good day. He was about to embarrass the squad at Lincoln Police, and they deserved everything they had coming to them.

◆　◆　◆

After viewing the hospital security camera feed, the first person Karen called was Rick. She filled him in on how Zane Dwight had been at the hospital, impersonating him.

'The cheeky little—'

'*Cheeky*'s one word for it,' Karen said. 'But he's gone too far. We need him brought in and charged for impersonating an officer. We can't have him sabotaging this case. Ask Dr Michaels if he knows where he is.'

'Will do, boss. I can't get over his nerve. Why do you think he was there?'

'Going by his previous actions, probably trying to dig up some dirt to sell to the media outlets to discredit us.' Karen sighed. She could do without Zane's irritating meddling.

'I'm on it, Sarge. Leave it to me.'

'Thanks, Rick. Everything okay your end?'

'I've spoken to one of the crime scene team,' Rick said. 'He explained they've managed to track the Transit van's route, and as we thought, it did come from that single-track road at the back of the property.'

'Right,' Karen said. 'Good.'

'And there are a few properties in the vicinity. Now, they're off the main grid, so the van could have been stashed there, which is why it didn't pop up on the traffic cameras,' Rick said. 'I'm thinking perhaps Rachel could have been kept around here somewhere too.'

'How many properties are there?'

'Five in total. We've managed to contact the owners for two of them, and they don't seem likely candidates. I was just about to head to one of the others with DI Morgan. And Sophie is going to take another one with Dr Michaels.'

'So that leaves one for me to check out?'

'Yes, if you think you've got the time. I'll send you over the map. They're all within a mile of each other, so the DI and I could do an extra one if you'd prefer to stay at the hospital and wait for Tamara to recover.'

'No, it's driving me mad being sat here not doing anything,' Karen said. 'Send me over the details via email. Tamara's being prepped for surgery. I'm not going to be able to speak to her for hours. Can you arrange for a uniform to come down, though? I don't want to leave her alone, but there's no point in me sitting around twiddling my thumbs.'

'No problem, Sarge,' Rick said. 'I'll get someone sent over to replace you now. Oh, hang on a minute. DI Morgan wants a word.'

He passed the phone over and Karen heard DI Morgan's level tones. 'Karen, any news?'

'Nothing, sadly. They're prepping her for surgery. She's had a big dose of painkillers as well, so I wasn't able to talk to her beforehand either. It's going to be at least a few hours, so I'm planning to check out one of the properties at the back of Branston Chickens. Rick's sending me the details.'

'Yeah. About that. Would you mind taking Dr Michaels with you?'

Karen hesitated. 'No, but I thought he was going with Sophie?'

'Change of plan. Sophie's going to go with Rick, and I get the pleasure of Churchill's company.'

'Oh, he's keen to get his hands dirty on this case.'

'It forms part of my assessment, apparently,' Morgan said.

'Lucky you. I'd forgotten about that. He hasn't mentioned anything else about mine, so I hope it's slipped his mind.'

'Can I tell Dr Michaels to expect you?'

'Yes, but I have to wait for an officer to take my place here, so I'll be a good thirty minutes.'

'Right. I'll tell him.'

Morgan handed the phone back to Rick, who again promised Karen he would forward her the details of the property she needed to check out.

Fifteen minutes later she was in her car, engine on, heaters blasting as she tried to warm herself up.

It was always too hot in hospitals, but that made it feel so much colder when she went outside again, she thought, rubbing her hands together.

She'd taken the details from Rick's email and plugged them into the satnav, although it was very unlikely to work, Karen thought. The satnav often produced ridiculous routes in rural Lincolnshire, sometimes over fields and through hedges. But it should send her in the right general direction. She knew the way to Branston Chickens, but the tracks and lanes behind it were a mystery to her, especially in the dark.

CHAPTER FORTY

Dr Michaels sat in the passenger seat, his fingers tapping out a rhythm on his thigh, though there was no music playing and the radio was off.

'Have you heard from Zane?' Karen asked, still miffed that he'd allowed a viper into the nest.

Dr Michaels turned his penetrating gaze on Karen. She'd never get used to that. Every time he looked at her, she felt it was like he was trying to psychoanalyse her, wondering what her motivation was for tucking her hair behind her ears or covering her mouth when she yawned.

She felt *observed*. And she didn't like it.

'Actually, I wanted to discuss the matter with you.'

'Really,' Karen said, indicating left and turning onto Moor Lane.

'Yes, I should apologise again, and I feel I owe you an explanation.'

'Well, I suppose you didn't really do anything wrong. It was Zane. I'm surprised he managed to hoodwink you, though.'

'You're right. I should have been more on my guard, and I would have been if it was anyone else, I think. I wanted to see the best in him.'

'Why?'

Dr Michaels smiled. 'You don't beat around the bush, do you?'

'I don't really see the point, no,' Karen said, slowing as a tractor chugged along at ten miles an hour in front of them. 'So, how did he fool you so easily?'

'I knew his mother,' Dr Michaels said.

'Zane's mother?'

'Yes. A long time ago, over twenty years, and she had some . . . issues. When Zane was eighteen, she told me he was my son.'

'Zane is your *son*? Why didn't you mention it before?'

'Because she lied. He isn't, but we spent a year getting to know each other on that pretence. Then I had some doubts, so I did a DNA test without his knowledge. I'm not very proud of that.'

'And he wasn't your son after all?'

'No. But I didn't feel I could just cut him off. That wouldn't have been fair. He was at a very vulnerable stage in his life. He'd been let down badly by his mother.'

'And the man he'd thought was his long-lost father had gone behind his back and taken a DNA test?' Karen suggested.

'Ouch.' Dr Michaels had the decency to blush. 'Yes.'

'Did you tell Zane the truth?'

'I did, just after his nineteenth birthday, but I told him I'd still like to be part of his life and that I would try to help him as best I could. It didn't go down well at first, and he cut me off for a while. But he'd been following my career, and he turned up six months ago, saying he needed a job and could I help him out.'

'Didn't you think with his difficult past he might not be the best person to give information to about sensitive cases?'

Dr Michaels shrugged. 'I thought it would help him, allow him to deal with his trauma and realise he wasn't the only one that bad things happened to. And he was good at PR. I didn't suspect him. I didn't think he would purposely hurt Angela. I was wrong. I messed up.'

'I think we're all capable of doing that. When we're particularly close to a person, it's hard to judge them objectively,' Karen said, thinking back to the time she'd been betrayed by a colleague, a man she would have trusted with her life. She knew it was possible to be blindsided by betrayal.

'Thank you for being so understanding,' Dr Michaels said.

'But you should call him. Find out where he is.'

'I can't betray his trust.'

'You can. We can't let him drift around Lincoln, potentially endangering this investigation. I want him to go to the station where I can make sure he stays out of trouble.'

Dr Michaels hesitated for a moment before pulling his mobile from the inside pocket of his jacket. 'Okay, I'll try.'

Karen pulled over to the curb.

'What are you doing?' he asked. 'I can talk while you drive.'

'Not for long you can't. There's no signal once you get up there.' Karen pointed ahead to a field with a bare-branched oak tree beside the hedgerow. 'I'll wait.'

Dr Michaels hesitated and then got out of the car to call Zane. Karen watched him in the rear-view mirror. They had a complicated relationship – one influenced by guilt on Dr Michaels's side. Could he have left the car because he was only pretending to call Zane? Did he feel obliged to protect the young man he'd once thought was his son? Maybe she could ask to see the call log on his phone.

She frowned. Being a police officer made you suspicious of everyone. He'd confided in her, told her the truth about Zane's backstory, so maybe she should trust him.

Dr Michaels was probably too close to Zane to see it, but it was obvious to Karen that Zane was desperate for approval. All the stupid mistakes he'd made were because he wanted to please

Dr Michaels. He wanted the man who he'd once believed was his father to be proud of him.

Karen had seen kids like Zane fall into a life of crime after difficult childhoods, especially with the absence of a strong parental role model. Despite being furious at Zane, she felt sorry for him too.

As Dr Michaels talked, or pretended to talk, to Zane, Karen scrolled through the pictures on her phone. She came to the picture of the article on saving the wildlife sanctuary. She'd already looked at the article's picture of Tamara and Rachel standing by the sign at the sanctuary's entrance. But this time two things stood out.

The women were each holding one of those creepy, misshapen, whittled owls. And for the first time, she saw the name after the copyright symbol at the bottom of the picture.

How had she missed that?

She dialled Rick's number. It rang and rang. He must have left to check out the other property already. Finally the call was answered by a voice she recognised.

'Farzana, it's Karen. Could you do me a favour? I want all the details you can dig up on Nicholas Finney.'

'All right. I'll do it now.'

'He's a photographer. Freelance, but he's worked with a couple of the local papers. I'll send you over one of the articles he had a photograph in. I need an address, and family history too.'

'When do you need it?'

'As soon as possible.'

'I'll get right on it.'

'Thanks a million.'

Karen hung up and hooted the car horn. She wanted Dr Michaels to locate Zane, not have an hour-long heart-to-heart.

Dr Michaels hurried back to the car.

'Well?' Karen queried as he opened the door.

'He didn't pick up.'

'Then why were you out there so long?'

'I kept trying.'

Karen sighed and passed him her phone. 'Look at that.'

'A photograph of Tamara and Rachel. They seem happy enough here. No date on the article.'

'No, but see what they're holding? Those creepy owls.'

'Why are you so interested in the owls?'

She felt his gaze on her. Without turning to face him, she said, 'Don't look at me like that.'

'Like what?'

'Like you're trying to work out if I have an unhealthy obsession with owls.'

'Well, you mentioned them.'

'Look at the picture. Both girls are holding those weird owls. And now look at the name under the picture.'

Dr Michaels squinted at the print, before zooming in on the picture. 'Oh!'

'Exactly,' Karen said, satisfied. 'Bit of coincidence, isn't it? He covers your UK tour, *and* he's met both Tamara and Rachel. I've asked DC Shah to get some background and an address. We can pay him a visit after we check out this property.'

Dr Michaels nodded his agreement as Karen pulled on to a single-lane track. The car jumped and jolted as they went along the rutted mud road. At least, thanks to the cold weather, the track wasn't as muddy as it could be. Though there were still potholes and icy puddles in the mud.

The car's tyres sloshed through the freezing-cold water. Karen slowed the car to a crawl as they approached the building.

Dr Michaels leaned forward and peered through the windscreen. 'That can't be it, can it? It looks abandoned.'

The building was in a sorry state. The render was coming away from the brickwork. There were tiles missing on the roof and ivy growing around the chimney.

Karen caught her breath. On one side of the house, scaffolding had been put up.

'Do you see that?' Karen said, pointing out the metal poles.

'I do.'

Karen brought the car to a stop a few feet down the track and stared at the building. She checked her mobile phone. No signal, as she'd expected.

'Right,' Dr Michaels said, his voice brisk and louder than usual. Karen wondered if he too sensed that this property could be the site of Rachel's murder. 'Let's take a look, shall we?'

Slowly Karen got out of the car, her eyes fixed on the scaffolding section. It looked like it had been there a long time. There was no sign of other repair work going on and the poles had started to rust.

As Dr Michaels walked forward, Karen put her arm out to stop him, and she spoke quickly and quietly. 'Let's take this slowly. I'm going to walk around the perimeter before knocking, okay?'

Dr Michaels nodded. Karen thought about asking him to stay in the car, but she had to admit having someone else with her did ease the nerves just a little bit.

A rush of air blew by, making the leaves rustle across the ground. The beech tree on the other side of the track groaned and creaked as it moved in the wind.

There was the hoot of an owl in the distance, but other than that, and the sound of the wind, it was eerily quiet.

Karen and Dr Michaels circled around the back. There was a light on upstairs. Someone was home.

They were near the back door in the overgrown garden when they both heard a sound at the same time. They looked up sharply. Someone was sobbing.

Dr Michaels pointed to the house. 'Did you hear that?' he whispered.

Karen nodded. She checked her phone, and again there was no signal.

She leaned forward so she could whisper in Dr Michaels's ear. 'I need you to get back in the car and drive down the track until you get a phone signal. Then I need you to call DI Morgan. If you can't get through to Morgan, call the station. Ask for backup. I'm going in.'

Dr Michaels checked his mobile. 'I don't have a signal on my cell either. But you can't go in on your own. I can't let you do that.'

'I'm in charge here,' Karen said. 'We don't have time for a debate. Get back in the car and keep driving until you get a signal on your phone.'

'You can't go in *alone*. You should wait for backup.'

And that *was* the sensible thing to do, but the sound had got to Karen. Someone was in there crying. Maybe hurt, in danger. If she waited for backup, it might be too late.

'I'm going in,' she said. 'Get back to the car now.'

His gaze clashed with Karen's, and for a moment she thought he might argue, but then he saw sense, nodded once, and crept back around the side of the house.

Karen used the torch setting on her phone and looked around for something she could defend herself with. She saw one of the old, unused scaffolding parts on the floor. It was big, heavy and would take some effort to swing, but it was better than going in with nothing. She slipped on the nitrile gloves she had in her pocket and picked up the weighty pole.

She could knock, announce her presence as police protocol demanded, but everything about the scene told her to be cautious, to stay on guard and to work out what she was dealing with before she alerted the residents.

The back door was open. She pushed it and winced when it squealed on its hinges. She stepped into a kitchen. There was no light on, but the moonlight meant she could just about make out the edges of various utensils and a sink beside the window. There was a kettle, an oven and a stovetop.

The house looked abandoned from the outside, but inside there were definitely signs somebody had been living here. She stepped further into the kitchen and then the sound came again, louder now. Definitely human. A person in pain, distraught.

Karen moved forward, drawn to the sound. But she stopped when something crunched beneath her feet. She pointed her phone and angled the light on to the floor.

Wood shavings.

She shone the light over the kitchen worktops. On one, there was a selection of deformed, whittled wooden animals – not owls, but a lopsided hedgehog, one stunted fox, and others so deformed she couldn't tell what they were.

Karen shivered. Beside the creatures was the small, sharp knife that had presumably been used to whittle away the wood. Karen picked up the knife and slipped it into her pocket.

Then the sound came again, louder now. Definitely coming from inside the house.

She stepped out of the kitchen into the hallway and took a moment to get her bearings. It was darker here, and she needed to use the torch. She hoped that Dr Michaels didn't have to travel far to get a signal.

She moved towards the staircase, holding her breath as the wooden floorboards creaked beneath her weight.

The sobs were louder upstairs, and she crept towards them. The weight of the scaffolding pole was already making her arm ache with the effort of carrying it.

A soft, yellow glow came from behind a half-closed door. She crossed the hall, her breathing louder than she wanted.

Her skin prickled. Was she being watched?

She turned quickly, but there was no one there. Just darkness.

She held her breath as she pushed the door open. In the middle of the room there was a figure tied to a chair, head slumped forward, body wracked with sobs.

He looked up. It was *Zane*.

CHAPTER FORTY-ONE

Zane's arms were tied behind his back with green string, which was also looped around the chair spindles, and he had a gag in his mouth.

He looked at Karen, pleading, his eyes wild, his cheeks streaked with tears. He grunted and groaned, trying to speak.

She couldn't understand him through the gag. She dropped the scaffolding pole, and it clanged to the floor as she moved forward to pull the gag free from his mouth.

'He's crazy,' Zane yelled.

'Who is?' Karen asked.

Zane fell silent. His mouth gaped as he stared at a spot over her shoulder.

Karen whirled around and saw a huge, shadowed figure striding towards them. She made a grab for the metal pole but wasn't quick enough.

He put a heavy, muddy boot on to the pole and smiled.

'I see we have a visitor,' he said. 'Hello, DS Hart.'

'Hello, Nicholas,' she said. 'I didn't realise this was your house.' She spoke calmly, surprising herself. Her voice was steady, as though finding Zane tied up in one of the upstairs bedrooms was a totally normal experience.

'Yeah. Needs a bit of work,' he said, 'but it's home for now.'

'Do you own it?' Karen asked, wondering how on earth they had missed that connection.

His smile widened. 'I'm just borrowing it.'

'Do the owners know?'

He laughed. 'Doubt it.'

'What's going on, Nicholas?' Karen asked. 'What's happened?'

'It's his fault,' Nicholas said, nodding to Zane. 'Double-crossed me. I was supposed to get a scoop. It would have made my career and shown everyone what I could really do.'

'What was the scoop?' Karen asked.

'Tamara's return. Her amazing escape from her abductor. I would get the exclusive, then the story would be syndicated. Everyone would know my name, and Tamara would do more interviews and get enough money to save the sanctuary,' he said. 'But now it's all gone wrong.' He glared at Zane.

'Well, why don't I untie Zane?' Karen suggested.

'No,' he screamed. 'You mustn't do that.'

'But, Nicholas, you've got to understand you can't keep someone prisoner here. Why don't I untie Zane and we can all go back to the station and have a chat?'

'No. No, I'm not doing that.'

'Okay, why don't we go downstairs, make a cup of tea. We can talk this through. It's never as bad as it seems,' Karen said.

Nicholas clutched his face. 'It's all gone wrong. I never meant for any of it to happen this way.'

'Of course you didn't. I understand,' Karen said. 'Things just got away from you.'

'Yes, that's it exactly. I never wanted any of this to happen. All I wanted was a really good story. Just one. Just once I wanted them to all take me seriously.'

'Well, they will now.'

'No, they won't. They'll say I'm a nutter, a killer.'

And they'd be right, Karen thought. His eyes were wild, his skin sweaty. He looked nothing like the shy, inoffensive photographer she'd seen at the station or on the street. She took a deep breath, trying to keep calm.

A moth repeatedly collided with the bare lightbulb above them in a hopeless dance.

'Why don't you tell me what happened?' she asked, keeping eye contact. She needed him to trust her.

'He killed her,' Zane screeched. 'He killed Rachel and he probably would have killed Tamara as well.'

'No, that's not true! Don't listen to him. I wouldn't have killed Tamara. You don't understand. It wasn't supposed to be like this.'

'What happened, Nicholas?' Karen asked. 'You can tell me. I'll listen to your side.'

He took a deep, stuttering breath. 'I met Tamara and her sister, Rachel. They have a wildlife sanctuary, and I was doing a story on it for them. They wanted publicity. They wanted to get some donations.' He paused to wipe away a tear. 'They were nice. I talked to Tamara, and I promised I would help. She invited me to her house for a coffee to talk about it some more, and then, well, I saw all her books. She was really interested in true crime and that sort of thing, just like I am. And we talked for ages. She really took me seriously. She understood, you know. And so we came up with a plan.' He had a strange half-smile on his face. 'I took Tamara. It was planned. All fake. We were going to write about it, and she was going to come back alive and then it was going to be a big story, and it would have been in all the newspapers, and on the TV, and everything. We were even going to write a book about it and . . .' he said, reaching out to Karen. 'You've got to understand. I didn't mean to hurt her. We came up with the idea together, and she was going to stay here for two nights, and then she was going to escape. But then it all went wrong.'

'What went wrong? Rachel?'

He nodded. 'Yes. She saw the owl I had whittled for Tamara on the mantelpiece, and she knew I'd been to the house. She found me at work, and she said some horrible things.' He trailed off.

'What did she say?'

'I told her it was all make-believe, to save the sanctuary. She said she'd give me two hours to release Tamara, or she would go to the police.' He rubbed his eyes with the back of his hand. 'So I got the van again, and I abducted her too. I knew she'd be checking on the sanctuary. She always does it at the same time. I didn't mean to hurt her. I really didn't. I brought her back here. I was going to let her out, so she could spend the night here with Tamara. Then they could both sell their story. They'd both be famous and rich, and everything would still work out.'

The words dried up. He stared out of the window.

'But that didn't happen, did it, Nicholas? Rachel was never released.'

His face crumpled. 'She was so horrible. She said I was an evil pervert, and it would never work because as soon as I let her go, she was going straight to the police. She laughed at me, so . . .' His face was flushed, and he was breathing hard. 'So I picked up one of the scaffolding poles.'

'You killed her?'

'I didn't mean to. I just wanted her to stop. Why did she have to ruin our plan?' he said, wrapping his arms around his waist, breathing heavily.

'What happened to Tamara?'

'She heard me and Rachel shouting. I told her it was a woman from work, but I don't think she believed me.'

'What did you do with Rachel's body?' Karen asked.

Nicholas was quiet for a long time, sucking in lungfuls of air. He was starting to panic.

318

'It's all right now, Nicholas,' Karen said. 'You can tell me.'

He gave Karen a strange look that made her mouth go dry. 'Yes, I can tell you. I put her in the van and drove her to the field over the back, then I returned the van to Branston Chickens.'

'Why that van?'

Nicholas shrugged. 'It was easy to get the keys. Greavsie is my half-brother. But you have to believe me. I didn't mean for any of this to happen. It's like they say, you set things in motion and then you have to keep going. But I didn't want to.'

'What do you mean, Nicholas?'

'Well, I can't stop now. I'll get caught if I don't get rid of all the people who know.'

'You can't.' Karen took a step back.

'I'm sorry. I'll pray for you.'

I don't want your prayers. I want you in a cell, Karen thought, her mind spinning through her next steps. She'd attending a de-escalation seminar a few months ago. Fat lot of good that was. She couldn't remember a word of it, and now she was staring into the eyes of a madman.

'Other officers are on their way,' she blurted out. 'They know what's happened. The best you can hope for now is to come clean to everyone and go quietly.'

He shook his head. 'No. I couldn't live in prison. I wouldn't cope. I'm sorry,' he said. He took his foot off the scaffolding pole and picked it up.

'Don't do this, Nicholas. Rachel was an accident, but anything more will be cold-blooded murder. You'll be behind bars for the rest of your life.'

He hesitated, but then lifted the pole above his head as though it was as light as a feather, and let out a grunt as he aimed at Zane's head as though it were a baseball.

Karen reacted on instinct, pulling out the small whittling knife and plunging it into Nicholas's shoulder.

He screamed with outrage, whirling around to turn on Karen. As she backed out towards the stairs, every cell in her body was telling her to run, but if she did, Zane would be defenceless, tied up in the chair. He'd be battered to death.

Nicholas lumbered towards her, blood blooming through his shirt. He lifted the scaffolding pole to swing at her, but it caught on the light fitting, smashing it, sending shards of glass flying through the air.

Splinters of glass cut Karen's skin and landed in her hair.

She had to get him off balance. With a man that size and that strong, it was her only hope. He was angry, reacting blindly. She could do this. It was just a matter of choosing the right moment to attack.

There was a shout from downstairs: 'Karen!'

Dr Michaels had returned.

Nicholas turned to look towards the voice, bewildered, and Karen took a chance.

She darted forward while he was distracted and kicked Nicholas hard in the back of the knee. He screamed in pain, and lost his balance.

For an agonising second, he teetered at the top of the stairs. Karen pushed herself back against the wall, as far from him as she could, in case he regained his balance and took another swing at her.

He roared with rage as he grasped the banister, righting himself and lifted the pole again. Karen prepared to duck, but as he moved his hand to grip the pole with both hands, he wobbled, then staggered back.

He missed the first step, and the second, then tumbled down the stairs.

There was a sickening crunch as he reached the bottom. After that, he didn't move.

Karen raced back to the room to untie Zane. 'We're okay,' she shouted out for Dr Michaels's benefit. 'Nicholas killed Rachel.'

'Anything I can do?'

'Make sure he doesn't get back up,' she called back.

'What's happened? Oh no, what's happened? You've got to get me out of here. I can't take it,' Zane sobbed.

After she'd untied him, Karen tugged him by the arm. 'Come on, move,' she said.

She tried to pull him along behind her, moving quickly down the stairs, but halfway down, he froze and refused to budge.

'I can't, I can't, I can't.'

'We have to. We have to step over him to get outside. There's only one way out,' Karen said.

'I *can't*.'

'Listen,' Karen said. 'Sirens. They're on their way.'

Zane sank down to sit on the stairs, shaking and refusing to move.

Karen gingerly went down the stairs to check on Nicholas. Dr Michaels was trying to feel for a pulse without any luck. 'He's gone, I think. I can't feel anything. You try.'

Nicholas's eyes were open, staring upwards. Karen tentatively reached forward and pressed her fingers to the side of his neck. There was no pulse, and the angle of his neck suggested it had broken as he'd landed.

There were shouts of 'POLICE!' The front door burst open and soon the place was swarming with officers. Only then did Karen release her hold on the small, sharp knife.

CHAPTER FORTY-TWO

'I see you and Dr Michaels picked the right property,' Morgan commented as he walked into the hall.

Karen looked up. 'Lucky us.'

'Are you okay?' he asked, 'Was anyone else injured?'

'We're both all right. It's just me and Zane here. Though I didn't search the house. Pretty sure Nicholas Finney is dead though.'

'I've got quite sore wrists actually. The stuff he used to tie me up really chafed my skin.' Zane rubbed the red lines on his forearms.

Morgan snapped on a pair of latex gloves, and as Karen had done just a moment ago, checked Nicholas for signs of life. 'I think you're right. What happened?'

'He was trying to kill us,' Zane said.

'He used a scaffolding pole to take swings at us,' Karen said. 'It set him off balance. We had a struggle at the top of the stairs, and he fell.'

'Right,' Morgan said, straightening up. 'Sounds like a lot of paperwork.' He held out his hand and Karen took it to steady herself as she stepped over Nicholas Finney's body.

'Let's take this outside and let the SOCOs get started,' Morgan said.

'You've got a lot of explaining to do, Zane,' Dr Michaels said as the four of them exited the house.

It was cold outside, but the fresh air felt good. Karen was thankful to get out of the house in one piece. She inhaled a breath so deep it stung her lungs and made her cough.

'Care to explain what you were doing here?' Morgan looked at Zane.

'I'm too distraught to talk about it,' Zane muttered.

'Zane had been working with Nicholas Finney. They were aiming to get a story out. Nicholas thought it would be his big career break. Zane told Nicholas he could get Tamara to talk to him. But with Tamara unconscious in a hospital bed . . .' She turned to Zane. 'Is that when Nicholas lost his temper with you? When you didn't deliver on your promise?'

'He went crazy, babbling on about everyone betraying him. I told him Tamara was out of it, but I took a photo we could use. He thought I was lying, that Tamara had told me he killed Rachel. I had no idea he was behind the abductions until he said that. I tried to run, but he wouldn't let me leave. Said he had to kill me!'

'Wait,' Morgan said. 'What photo?'

'Yes, what photo?' Karen and Dr Michaels said in unison.

Zane's mouth formed an o-shape. He sheepishly said, 'Oh, didn't you know about that?'

'What photo, Zane?' Dr Michaels asked again, his tone low and furious.

Zane chewed on his lower lip before replying. 'I took a photo of Tamara for the article.'

'You took a photo of her unconscious in a hospital bed?' Karen asked, incredulous. 'That's why you were there, sneaking around, impersonating a police officer, wasn't it?'

He grimaced and nodded.

'That's disgusting!' Dr Michaels said the words through gritted teeth.

As Dr Michaels continued to tear strips out of Zane verbally, Morgan touched Karen's elbow and drew her away from them.

'We didn't get it all right,' Morgan said. 'But were we right about Tamara being involved?'

'Yes, it turns out that it was all a ruse that turned nasty pretty fast. Nicholas and Tamara planned her abduction together. According to him, anyway. We still need to get Tamara's side of the story. Apparently, he wanted to make a name for himself as a journalist, and she needed money for the wildlife sanctuary, so they didn't have to sell it. They were going to act out Tamara's abduction. Then stage her miraculous escape and sell her story. Nicholas was a bit spooked when he realised Dr Michaels was involved. He thought the game was up. I think that's why he was keen to work with Zane.'

'So Tamara was in on the whole thing? What about Rachel's murder?'

'That wasn't part of the plan. It seems Rachel put two and two together when she saw the whittled owl on the mantelpiece after Tamara went missing. She demanded Nicholas let her sister go. Then he decided the best way to deal with the situation was to abduct her too.'

'Why on earth didn't Rachel come to us with the information?' Morgan asked.

'I suppose she was trying to protect her sister. She didn't want to get her in trouble for faking her own abduction.'

Morgan peeled off his gloves and rubbed a weary hand over his face. 'Where did he kill Rachel?'

'Here somewhere. I'm not sure, but I think probably outside. He said Rachel tried to attack him when he let her out of the van.'

'So . . . on the property somewhere?' His gaze swept around the garden.

Crime scene technicians were setting up large floodlights to illuminate the area.

'Yes, I think so.'

'And Tamara? She really didn't know what Nicholas had done to her sister?'

'Nicholas said she heard the disturbance, but he told her he'd had an argument with a colleague, and I don't think Tamara believed him. I think when she realised what he'd done, she panicked. She must have found the opportunity to escape and made a run for it.'

'Straight into the path of an oncoming car,' Morgan said. 'Some people don't have much luck.'

'I suppose we should talk to Aiden,' Karen said.

Morgan nodded. 'Yes, he'll need to know. And he's no longer a suspect? He didn't know about this?'

'Not according to Nicholas. He was hiding something for sure, but I think it was his relationship with Rachel. He didn't want us to find out about that.'

'And he really was sleeping up in the loft after Tamara found out about the affair.' Morgan shook his head. 'Bizarre.'

'It's been a really strange case from start to finish,' Karen said. 'So now we have to wait for Tamara to get through her operation, and get her account.'

Morgan was called away by one of the SOCOs, and Dr Michaels approached Karen.

'I'm so glad you're okay,' Dr Michaels said. 'I had to go almost half a mile before I got a signal.'

'Thanks for getting help so quickly.'

As the area around the property started to fill up with officers and the forensics team, Karen and Dr Michaels turned to walk back down to the track. Now the large crime scene lights had been switched on, their surroundings were lit up. There was obvious blood spatter on a pile of leftover scaffolding poles, and beside them, a patch of muddy earth that was darker than its surroundings. It was likely where Rachel's murder had occurred. Karen had missed that in the dark coming in.

She shoved her hands in her pockets, shivering hard.

'It's freezing tonight,' she said.

'Yes, it's bitter. Are you hurt? You're shaking.'

'Luckily, no. It's just the cold. I managed to duck out of the way when he came towards me brandishing that scaffolding pipe.' She peeled off her latex gloves. 'It's not an experience I want to repeat in a hurry.'

'Well, it's over now.' He smiled, and his assessing gaze seemed warmer than usual. 'I'm really sorry about Zane. He says you saved him.'

'We can't let him off, though,' Karen said. 'He'll need to be processed the same as anyone else, and likely charged.'

'I understand,' he said with a sigh.

Behind them a phone rang. It was Morgan's.

He answered it. 'DI Morgan.' He mouthed at Karen, 'It's DCI Churchill,' and then took a few steps away.

Karen had been wondering where the DCI had got to. He'd been visiting one of the other properties in the area with Morgan.

A forensics officer approached, and Karen told her she'd stabbed Nicholas with the whittling knife she'd found in the kitchen and left it on the stairs beside his body. After swabs were taken and they'd been processed, Karen and Dr Michaels were asked to step outside the cordon, which they did, so as not to contaminate further evidence.

Morgan joined them at the perimeter of the property, his face grim. 'Bad news. That was Churchill.'

'Where is he? I thought he was teaming up with you to look at one of the other properties.'

'He was. But he's driving back to the station now. He heard from the hospital. We're not going to be able to talk to Tamara.'

'She didn't make it through the operation?'

Morgan shook his head. 'A massive blood clot formed in her lungs.'

Karen exhaled and stared up at the starry night sky. 'What a waste of life.'

◆ ◆ ◆

The following day, Sophie was up to her neck in paperwork, but she kept getting up and looking along the external corridor to make sure Dr Michaels hadn't left. She didn't want to miss the chance to say goodbye.

As soon as she heard the slight squeak of his office door opening, she was on her feet and scrambling towards him.

'Dr Michaels. Are you leaving now?'

'Yes, we're booked on a flight this evening.'

'So, that's the end of the book tour?'

'For now, yes. My publishing company has been very understanding. We need to get back to the States.'

'How is Zane doing?'

'Pretty good considering, but we've got some issues to work through. He's lucky he's allowed to leave the country.'

'Yes, I heard you'd pulled some strings,' Sophie said.

'Old colleagues of mine reached out at high levels. Of course, Zane will make himself available to answer questions at any time,' Dr Michaels said. 'Actually, I'm glad I saw you. I wanted to have a chat.'

'Oh, really. What about?' Sophie asked. 'I've nearly finished your new book. It's very good. One of your best.'

'Oh, right. It wasn't about the book, but I have to say, Sophie, I was incredibly impressed by the way you work. I feel privileged to have played a part in this team during the investigation – and, well, I want you to know that if you ever fancy a career change, perhaps a trip over to our side of the pond, I'd be happy to give you a job.'

'Work for you?' Sophie's eyes were wide. 'You mean actually *work* for *you*.'

Dr Michaels chuckled. 'Yes. I'm in the market for a new assistant, and I think you could do the job brilliantly.'

'That's so flattering. But I'm not really a PR expert.'

'You don't need to be. I want you to help me with my criminal work in the US. You're a talented investigator.'

Sophie was momentarily speechless. He was offering her everything she wanted from a career. 'I don't know what to say.'

'Well, you don't need to give me an answer now, but think about it, okay? You've got my email, right?'

'Yes, I have,' Sophie said.

'Okay then. Take care. I'll see you around.'

Sophie watched him leave. That was incredible. Rick would never believe it. She grinned to herself as she walked back to her desk.

How thrilling. Dr Michaels actually wanted to work with her. Amazing. She sat down at her desk and then turned her head to look into Morgan's office, where she saw him and Karen, heads bowed over the desk, and she wondered what it would be like to live and work in the US, chasing down killers and learning from Dr Michaels.

CHAPTER FORTY-THREE

There was a rap on the door of Morgan's office. Churchill stuck his head in. 'Karen, have you got a minute?'

She looked up from the paperwork she'd been going through with Morgan. 'Yes. Now?'

'Yes, my office,' he said. 'It's time to go through your personal assessment.'

Karen tried to hide her dismay. Morgan shot her a sympathetic look as she left the office and followed Churchill. She felt like she was walking to meet her fate at the gallows.

'It's been a particularly difficult case,' Karen said. 'I'm not sure it's the best one to use for my assessment. Maybe you should do it on the next investigation.'

'No need. I've already done it,' Churchill said, marching ahead of Karen up the stairs.

Great, Karen thought glumly. She'd had a relaxing evening last night with Mike. She hadn't told him any details about the confrontation with Nicholas. He'd only worry. She'd managed to push work out of her head for a few hours and unwind with an Indian takeaway and a bottle of red wine. But now there was paperwork to deal with, loose ends to tie up.

'I've spoken to Aiden,' Karen said, 'and he's agreed not to place any formal complaints. I think he's rather keen that the fact Tamara was behind her own abduction doesn't come out.'

Churchill nodded. 'Understandable, I suppose. What's going to happen to that wildlife sanctuary? Do you know?'

'It's still a bit up in the air at the moment,' Karen said. 'I'm not sure it's top of Aiden's priorities. It's a shame, but it looks like it will have to close.'

Churchill pushed open the door and let Karen enter. 'Take a seat, DS Hart.'

So now he was going back to calling her by her rank and last name. It was no longer the friendly *Karen*. That wasn't a good start.

Karen sat down as Churchill settled behind his desk.

'How do you think you've done?' he asked.

Great, he couldn't just get to the point, could he? That would be too easy. He was going to make her squirm and feel as uncomfortable as possible before giving her the result.

'I think I did pretty well, considering everything that was going on,' she said.

She thought back to when she'd been questioning Tony Hickman at his house about the missing van. Yes, she'd had a wobble when she realised the little girl had the same name as her own daughter, but she'd got past it, and she'd carried on doing her job.

'Are you happy with where you are now?' Churchill asked.

It seemed an odd question. After everything they'd just been through, her top emotion was relief. Relief that it was over, relief they didn't have a madman stalking the streets, trying to grab more innocent women. But happy? She hadn't really given the idea that much attention, but she supposed when she thought about it, she was. She had Mike and Sandy to go home to now. Home was no longer the echoey, empty space where in every corner she would remember Josh and Tilly with sadness.

She remembered them, of course, but most of the time they were happy memories. They still tugged and squeezed at her heart, but she wouldn't be without them.

But Churchill wasn't talking about that. He was talking careerwise. Was she happy with her job? Was she satisfied?

'I am,' she said. 'I think we've got a good team, and we work well together, especially during this latest case, which has been particularly challenging.'

Churchill nodded thoughtfully. 'Yes, it was a difficult one.' He looked up. 'I noticed when you were interviewing Tony Hickman, his daughter . . .'

Karen tensed.

'Sorry,' Churchill said. 'I don't want to bring things up if they're going to upset you.'

Karen paused for a few seconds, gathering her emotions. 'He mentioned his daughter was called Tilly. That was my daughter's name. It caught me off guard, but I carried on.'

'You did,' Churchill said. 'You did very well.'

Karen's eyebrows lifted.

'You don't have to look at me like that. I'm not a complete monster,' he said. 'I was very impressed. I have been very impressed by the team, but particularly by your work,' he said. 'And I would be happy to recommend you for detective inspector if you feel up to taking the exams soon.'

Karen was speechless. She really hadn't seen this coming. 'Oh, right. Well, I hadn't actually thought about it.'

'No? It seems a logical next step,' Churchill suggested.

'I suppose after . . .' She swallowed and took a breath. 'After losing Josh and Tilly, I was derailed for a bit.'

'That's understandable. But think it over and let me know,' he said, tapping his pen on the pad in front of him.

After leaving Churchill's office, Karen walked downstairs in a daze. There certainly had been some twists and turns with this case, but Churchill's assessment was the most surprising event of all.

She walked through the office, heading for her desk.

'Are you all right?' Arnie Hodgson asked, looking up from his desk and slurping from a mug of tea.

'I think so,' Karen said.

'How did the assessment go?' he asked with an exaggerated grimace.

'It went well,' Karen said. 'Really well.'

Arnie chuckled. 'See, I told you that you'd get the hang of working for him eventually. You just needed to learn how to handle him.'

Karen wasn't entirely sure she had developed a knack for handling Churchill yet. But, by the looks of things, he was here to stay.

Arnie slurped his tea noisily again. 'Sorry,' he said. 'Did you want one?'

'You know what, Arnie,' Karen said, 'I think I'll go to the canteen and get one. Maybe even get a sausage sandwich to go with it.'

'Well, if you're offering,' Arnie said, getting to his feet quickly.

Karen was about to tell Arnie that she hadn't actually offered to get him a sandwich, but decided she could probably stretch to it today. She walked past Rick and Sophie at their desks, heads down, working through a myriad of forms.

'Can I get you anything from the canteen?' Karen offered.

Rick shook his head and Sophie said, 'No, but I just have to tell you all something first because I'm bursting.'

'All right. What do you have to tell us?' Karen asked.

'Dr Michaels offered me a job.'

There was silence.

Karen felt a pang of something – sadness? But it was immediately followed by a rush of warmth for the slightly naive at times,

332

but very hardworking, Sophie. She had been offered her dream job, but Karen would miss her. 'Congratulations. That's huge news.'

'You're going to America?' Rick asked, looking at Sophie as though she'd just told him she was planning to shapeshift into a unicorn.

'No,' Sophie said quickly. 'I'm not actually going to go, but he offered me the job. I mean, that's amazing, isn't it?'

Karen smiled. 'It is. Really amazing.'

'It was an honour to be asked to work with Dr Michaels, but I've thought about it and I don't want to leave Lincoln. This is home. I've got a career I love . . . and the people I work with are pretty nice too.' She grinned. 'I'm not about to leave that behind. Not even for Dr Michaels.'

'You big softie,' Rick said, but he was grinning too.

'Actually,' Sophie said, standing and stretching, 'I think I'll come with you to the canteen. A bacon sandwich is just what I need to give me energy to get through the rest of these forms.'

Rick got up too. 'Yeah, good idea. I could do with a break.'

They popped their head into Morgan's office on the way through, but he wasn't there.

'He's gone to have his assessment,' Arnie said knowledgeably.

'Have you already had yours?' Karen asked him.

'Not yet, but it's the same every year – reliable, B-plus for effort, but could try harder, and I always promise to try harder, so we both know where we stand.' He chuckled.

Later, they were sitting around a large table, polishing off their sausage and bacon sandwiches, when Morgan came into the canteen. 'I wondered where you'd all got to,' he said.

'How did you get on?' Karen asked.

'Pretty well,' he said, looking happy, or at least as happy as Morgan ever did. 'Churchill's not that bad after all, is he?'

'I told you,' Arnie said, 'you just needed to learn how to handle him.'

'He's asked for you next.'

'Perfect timing,' Arnie said, and then shoved the remainder of his sandwich in his mouth. He got up, wiped his mouth with his napkin and walked away with a cocky swagger. He balled up the napkin and threw it over his shoulder into the bin.

Morgan pulled out a chair. 'This afternoon I'm off to Branston Chickens, to talk to Greaves and find out why he didn't mention his half-brother.'

Karen shrugged. 'Frustrating, but I suspect he'll just say he had no idea Nicholas was involved. I'll come with you if you don't mind. I'd like to speak to him again to see if he has any insight into his brother. Farzana gave me all the family details. They share the same mother, but two different fathers, hence the different last name.'

'Talking of frustrations, did you see the latest story by Cindy Connor?'

Karen put down the second half of her sandwich, no longer hungry. 'Yes – sensationalist load of rubbish.'

Cindy Connor apparently had no qualms about dining out on her photographer's notoriety. She'd written an article that managed to be a hit piece on the police, Dr Michaels and her old colleague, all at the same time. She'd even managed to imply her life had been in danger during the investigation, which wasn't true.

'I agree. She's a pretty wretched human being.'

Strong words coming from Morgan.

He eyed her plate. 'Are you not going to finish that?'

She laughed and pushed the plate towards him. 'You're almost as bad as Arnie.'

When Arnie returned from his assessment, Karen was at her desk.

Karen looked up from her computer. 'How did it go?'

'I don't want to talk about it,' Arnie said with a huff and slumped into his chair.

'Not well then,' Rick said under his breath.

'I don't see why, after all this time, he's changed. It's like having the rug pulled from under my feet,' Arnie, who clearly did want to talk about it after all, said.

'No B-plus this time?' Karen asked.

'No, he gave me a B-minus!' Arnie folded his arms. 'A B-minus!'

'Those grades aren't used, though,' Sophie said, trying to ease his disappointment. 'It's really a few tick-boxes and a written summary of your progress and your agreed areas of improvement. Churchill likes the grading for his personal use, I think.'

'It's stupid,' Arnie said petulantly. 'Like being back at school.'

'I'm sure it will be better next time.'

Arnie looked at Sophie. 'What grade did you get?'

'A-minus.'

Arnie shook his head indignantly and turned to Rick. 'You?'

Rick got up to collect some papers from the printer. 'Same.'

He turned to Karen. 'Don't tell me. You got an A-minus too?'

Karen nodded. 'Yes, as did Morgan, I think.'

'Unbelievable!' Arnie huffed.

With a stack of paper in his hands, Rick walked behind Arnie, heading back to his desk. 'Don't worry about it,' he said casually. 'You just need to learn how to handle him.'

He winked at Karen, who ducked her head behind her computer monitor so Arnie couldn't see her trying to stifle a smile.

'Humph,' Arnie grunted and began typing furiously, taking out his frustration on the keyboard.

◆ ◆ ◆

For what was hopefully their final visit to Branston Chickens, Morgan parked close to the office so they wouldn't have to walk across so much mud. All the same, by the time Karen reached the door, her boots were already covered in the sticky sludge.

Greavsie waved them in. He was hunched over and looked even shorter than he usually did.

'I still can't believe it,' he said as he pushed open the door to his office. 'Nicholas. My baby brother responsible for something like that.' He shook his head as he sat behind the desk.

Karen and Morgan sat too, and Karen spotted a cat's tail poking out from underneath the desk. 'You really had no idea it was him who'd taken the van?' she asked.

'Well,' he said, then hesitated. 'If I'm being totally honest, the thought had occurred to me. He'd visited me, you see, and he hardly ever did that. Didn't like the smell, he said.' Greavsie breathed in deeply. 'Nothing wrong with the smell of chickens.'

'So why didn't you tell me?'

He shifted in his chair. 'I wasn't sure. I didn't even consider it until after the van was returned, and even then I had no evidence. And he *was* my brother.'

The cat leapt into Greavsie's lap and curled up as he began stroking its fur.

'If he didn't visit much, I take it you weren't close?' Morgan asked.

'We were close enough as lads. I'd look after him while Mum was at work. And I was proud of him when he went off to university. First in our family to do that.' Greavsie smiled. 'But as time went on, he grew a bit big for his boots.'

'How do you mean?' Morgan asked.

'He wouldn't visit Mum, even when she got ill. Said he didn't have time. He was always working on the next big thing. Insisted he'd be famous one day. Daft thing was, Mum believed it. Thought the sun shone out of his backside. It broke her heart when he didn't visit her at the end.' Greavsie sniffed and then rummaged in a drawer before pulling out a photograph.

'That's us,' he said. 'I was fourteen, Nicholas was eight.'

Karen leaned forward. The brothers made an odd-looking pair. Even at eight years old, Nicholas was almost as tall as his brother. They were paddling in the sea, both boys in red shorts and white T-shirts.

'Skegness,' Greavsie said. 'We had a grand time.'

'When did he visit you?' Karen asked.

'A week ago.'

'And before that?'

Greavsie let out a sigh. 'Now you're asking. Must have been at least two years before that. Wanted a loan. All hoity-toity about the smell of this place, but funnily enough, the money was good enough for him.' His face crumpled. 'I miss him. I wish I'd talked to him more. Who knows, maybe I could have made him see sense.' He looked at Karen with glassy eyes. 'I heard he didn't mean to kill her, that it was an accident. Is that true?'

Morgan replied, 'That's what Nicholas said, but we're still gathering evidence.'

'That makes sense,' Greavsie said. 'It's the only thing that does really. When he was about ten, I remember he caught a butterfly. Over the moon, he was, but he got a bit too heavy-handed with it and crushed the little thing. Didn't know his own strength – that was the trouble. But he was a gentle giant really.'

Karen watched Greavsie as he opened up. A reply was on the tip of her tongue. She wanted to say that crushing an insect was in no way same as battering a young woman to death. Nicholas had been angry and picked up the metal pole intending to hurt Rachel. That was unforgiveable no matter how his brother tried to excuse his behaviour.

The cat began purring. Greavsie smiled down at it. 'You know she must have riled him up, provoked him in some way. He would never have done it otherwise.'

'Rachel was the victim,' Karen said. 'She was a teacher. A good one. She made a difference. It doesn't matter what she said to Nicholas. She didn't deserve to die.'

'No,' Greavsie said. 'Of course not. I didn't mean . . . I'm just trying to make sense of it.'

Morgan said, 'Did you know where Nicholas was living?'

'In that abandoned house, you mean? No, last I heard he was living in a flat in the city centre.'

'Do you have the address?'

Greavsie scrolled through his mobile. 'Yes, I think so.' He looked up and met Karen's gaze as he passed the phone over the desk. The address was on the screen. 'I'm sorry for what he did to her. I'm sorry the other sister died too.'

'Her name was Tamara,' Karen said, thinking she was sorry too. Their plan had been naive – stupid, even. The best possible outcome would have resulted in wasting police time and resources. By a cruel twist, their plotting had resulted in the loss of three lives.

After a few more questions, Morgan nodded. 'All right, I think we're done here.'

Karen stood up. She was looking forward to getting this case off her desk, but there was one more thing she had to do.

Molly McCarthy stood on the sofa and looked out of the window. She had unwrapped a shiny new bike on her birthday and wanted to play with it in the garden, but Mummy said it was dark and she couldn't play with it anymore until morning, and no, don't be ridiculous, Molly couldn't play with it in the house.

'Molly, what are you doing up there. You're supposed to sit on the sofa. Not stand.' Her mother walked over and looked out of the window. 'What is it? Did you see something?'

Molly looked up at her mother and shook her head. She hadn't seen the bad man again. Daddy said the police had probably caught him by now, but Molly still liked to check outside just to make sure it was safe.

'Oh, who's that?'

Molly turned to look back out of the window. A car was parked outside. 'It's the police lady.'

'So it is. I wonder what she wants.'

Molly slid down from the sofa as her mother went to open the door. She sneaked closer so she could hear what they were saying.

'That's very kind of you,' her mother was saying. 'I'm sure she'll love it.'

Molly gave the police lady a wide smile as she came into the living room.

'Hello, Molly. I've brought you a gift to say thank you for helping us.' The lady held out a teddy bear dressed in a police uniform.

Molly grasped the bear and tried to take off its hat, but it was stuck on.

'What do you say, Molly?' her mother reminded her.

'Thank you,' Molly said, inspecting the bear and undoing the buttons on its jacket.

'You're very welcome, Molly. How have you been?' She looked at Molly, but her mother replied.

'I was a bit worried, but she's been fine. No bad dreams or anything.'

'That's good to hear,' the nice police lady said. 'So, Molly, do you think you might be a police officer when you grow up?'

'I can't,' Molly said. 'I'm going to be an astronaut.'

That made both grown-ups laugh. Molly didn't know why. She hadn't told a joke.

'I could be a police officer after I'm an astronaut if you need my help.'

'That sounds like a good plan, Molly.'

Molly played with her new teddy for a few minutes while they chatted. Then the police lady knelt down beside Molly.

'I'm going now, Molly, but I wanted to thank you again for being such a brave girl and telling me what you saw.'

'Did you catch the bad man?'

'We did.'

'Is he in prison?'

'Yes.'

'Good.'

The police lady was smiling at Molly, but she looked sad. Molly dropped the teddy and put her arms around the lady's neck. Whenever she felt sad, her mummy and daddy gave her a hug, and she felt better. But when the lady stood up, she looked like she might cry.

Molly frowned. Hugs were supposed to make you feel happy. Grown-ups were weird, she thought, and turned her attention back to her teddy bear.

ACKNOWLEDGEMENTS

The fabulous editors, Leodora Darlington, Hannah Bond and Jack Butler, who have worked on the Karen Hart series deserve a massive thank you. It's been a pleasure to work with such a talented group of people at Amazon Publishing.

Special thanks must also go to the talented Russel McLean for his help and invaluable attention to detail over the series.

To my family, a special thank you – and as always, thanks to Chris for his belief in me.

And finally, most importantly, thank you to the readers who have read and recommended my books. Your kind words and encouragement mean the world to me.

ABOUT THE AUTHOR

 Born in Kent, D. S. Butler grew up as an avid reader with a love for crime fiction and mysteries. She has worked as a scientific officer in a hospital pathology laboratory and as a research scientist. After obtaining a PhD in biochemistry, she worked at the University of Oxford for four years before moving to the Middle East. While living in Bahrain, she wrote her first novel and hasn't stopped writing since. She now lives in Lincolnshire with her husband.